Frances Anne Bor... in Scarborough, ... shops, as secretary to a headmaster in a private preparatory school and in the social services. She is married and has two grown-up daughters. She has been writing since she was a child, and has previously had articles and short stories published. Her five earlier novels, *A Different Tune*, *Catching Larks*, *Darling Lady*, *Return of the Swallow* and *Dance Without Music*, are all available from Headline.

Changing
Step

Frances Anne Bond

From one circle member to another! All the Best. Happy reading

Anne Bond
xxx.

HEADLINE

First published in 1996 by
HEADLINE BOOK PUBLISHING

First published in paperback in 1996 by
HEADLINE BOOK PUBLISHING

10 9 8 7 6 5 4 3 2 1

ISBN 0 7472 5114 2

Typeset by Avon Dataset Ltd, Bidford-on-Avon, Warks

Printed and bound in Great Britain by
Cox & Wyman Ltd, Reading, Berks

HEADLINE BOOK PUBLISHING
A division of Hodder Headline PLC
338 Euston Road
London NW1 3BH

I am blessed with good friends so this book is dedicated to them. They know who they are.

Love comes from blindness,
friendship comes from knowledge.
(Comte de Bussey-Rabutin 1618–1693)

Chapter One

It was not until Pat Miller stepped forward to present the bouquet that Marigold Goddard realised the enormity of her own folly. She stared at the flowers, then at Pat's face and thought, I must explain. This is wrong. It's a mistake. I didn't mean it. I must have been temporarily insane, or ill. Yes, I remember now. I was ill. She shut her eyes, remembering.

Three months ago, when Mr Heywood had entered the office, dismal-faced and clutching the sheet of paper, she had been sitting at her desk with her head in her hands. She remembered that her head cold had made her feel fuzzy and the sound of the sleet rattling against the windowpanes had depressed her. Her throat hurt, her eyes felt gritty and she was indulging in a gigantic wave of self pity.

Her first telephone call of the morning had been disastrous. After half an hour of difficult conversation trying to convince her client that the staff of the Inspector of Taxes were not bloodsuckers, he had called her a rude name and rung off. Her second telephone encounter had been even more frustrating. The secretary had refused to put her through.

'Mr Carlson's busy. He's with an important client,' she had said.

Marigold had slammed down the receiver without another word. She was on Carlson's side, for God's sake. For two months

1

she had tried to persuade him to submit his books for inspection but he had ignored her advice. Well, enough was enough. I wonder whether his important client will visit him in jail, she thought sourly.

When Mr Heywood had stopped by her desk, she had scowled at him.

Coughing apologetically, he had handed her the sheet of paper. 'Bad news, I'm afraid. Heard whispers, of course, but I'd never have anticipated . . .' His voice dipped. 'Read it through carefully, Mari, and then let the others see it. But try and discourage idle chitchat; never helps in a situation like this one.'

Shaking his head, he had hurried from the room.

Marigold, her dark eyebrows drawing together, studied what she now saw was a memorandum from Head Office. Judging from Heywood's remarks, the news was not good. Her assumption was right.

With an admirable economy of words the memorandum stated that because of the state of the economy, cutbacks in their department were called for. Unless someone opted for voluntary retirement, one or two compulsory redundancies would be implemented.

Marigold digested the news and then raised her head and looked at her fellow workers, some of whom were her friends.

It would be Pat, she thought. Pat had only eleven months' service and possibly John Reed would go, too. Last in, first out – that was the rule, but the rule was unfair. Pat was good at her job and she was a widow with a child to support. And young John was so heartbreakingly eager to prove his worth. Despite his good university grades he had spent eighteen months on the dole before landing this, his first job. What would getting the sack do to him?

Marigold's headache worsened and she looked long and hard at Herbert Marsh. What a pity he had long service. His pomposity and narrow-minded attitudes irritated the hell out of everyone. And yet, she sighed, Herbert lived with his invalid mother and, by all accounts, looked after her magnificently. He, too, needed his job. Everyone in the room needed their job.

Everyone except *you.*

She almost smiled. So there really was a small, still voice of conscience.

She shut her eyes and faced the truth. She didn't have to work. Ian, her husband, earned plenty of money. His post at the university was safe. They didn't even have mortgage repayments to meet. A legacy from a distant relative of Ian paid that off. And Karen, their only child, was grown up now, living away from home and financially independent. But . . . Marigold clenched her fist . . . there were other reasons for holding on to a job.

'You look grim.' John Reed paused by her desk on his way to the photocopier. 'Would a cup of coffee help? I could nip down to the canteen?'

'Would you?' She hid her tight-fisted hands beneath her desk and managed a smile. 'But tea, please, not coffee.'

She was trying to cut down on caffeine. She'd read in a glossy magazine that too much coffee caused palpitations and shortness of breath. She watched John leave the room and then reread the memorandum.

The message was stark and unchanged. Someone in the team had to go. She slipped the offending piece of paper into her desk drawer. She wanted time to think. She would tell the others the news after lunch.

John returned with the tea and, shyly, offered two aspirins. 'Maybe these will help. I asked the receptionist in the front office if she had anything for headaches.'

She nodded her thanks, accepted the pills, swallowed them and then sipped her tea.

John began his photocopying and she tried to concentrate on

her work but the rhythmic clunk of the photocopier and her own thoughts distracted her.

She was fond of Pat and she liked John but really, they were not her responsibility. They were just people she worked with.

She remembered one day last month, a day when she had been feeling low. Pat had invited her over to tea. They had eaten in the pocket-handkerchief garden at the back of Pat's house. Miraculously, the weather had been good. Pat's son was tall and dark, unlike his rounded, fair-haired mother. He must have inherited his father's physical characteristics.

Pat's husband had been thirty-nine years old and on his way home when a lorry driver fell asleep in his cab: in the crash that followed both men died. His son had been shy of her at first, but she had soon got him talking. He told her that he hoped to go to university in two years' time.

Marigold shifted in her seat. Young John had shown her his new jacket last week. He had bought it because he was going to visit his girlfriend's family for the first time. He had asked her if she thought it was all right. She had told him he looked very smart.

She took another sip of tea and wondered why she got on so well with young lads and adolescent males. Perhaps if Karen had been a boy their relationship might have been warmer but, she shrugged, Karen had always been a 'Daddy's' girl.

Her thoughts went back to the memo. If Pat had to leave she would be given good references. She'd get another job, eventually. Marigold frowned, thinking of the present state of the job market.

And John would be OK. Wasn't a little hardship good for young people? Didn't it strengthen their characters?

She burped discreetly. The pills felt as though they'd stuck halfway down her gullet. Still, it was nice of John to get them for her.

4

What if she did offer to pack in her job? She fiddled with a pencil on her desk. What would happen? Her superiors on the top floor of the building might not accept her resignation; she was a senior officer and they might not want to lose her.

She tossed aside the pencil. Who was she kidding? Of course they'd accept her resignation; it would solve a difficult situation. Ten years ago it might have been different but not now; nowadays the staff, old or new, were statistics, numbers on a computer at Head Office.

John looked across at her and mouthed: 'All right?'

Marigold nodded her head, slowly, mechanically. I'm like one of those spindly nodding ducks that were the rage years ago, she thought. Karen had given her one for a mother's day present, oh, ages ago. She knew she had kept the damn thing on her desk for at least seven or eight years.

Quite suddenly, she knew what she was going to do. She would resign. But not out of kindness. Oh, no. Not to save the jobs of Pat and John. She would resign because she realised she had spent too many years of her life in this very room, poring over pages of statistics and columns of figures.

She didn't regret those years, not really. She'd enjoyed her work. She gave a rueful grin. She was one of those strange people who loved the purity, the wonderful order of mathematics, but the memo in her desk had jolted her out of her safe little niche and made her realise it was time for her to move on.

I've been a coward, she marvelled. Just because life's turned out to be disappointing, I've clung to this place. I'm at ease here. There's no pressure with figures. You're either right or wrong, and if you do make a mistake then you can quickly correct it.

She remembered again the ridiculous dipping duck and she snatched the memo out of the drawer and stood up, pushing back her chair so vigorously that the castors squealed out in protest. Everyone looked up.

'I'm going to see Mr Heywood,' she announced to the room in general. 'Cover my calls, will you?'

And that was why today was her last day at work.

Marigold looked at the group of people crowded behind Pat and managed to smile. She transferred the polystyrene cup filled with white wine from her right hand into her left and took a step forward to accept her bouquet.

'How lovely. Thank you.'

Mr Heywood produced a large white envelope. 'A small leaving present from your friends, Mari. We know you have a large garden so we thought you might like a voucher to spend at one of the garden centres. That way, you can choose the plants and shrubs you most enjoy.' He lowered his voice in the manner of a vicar conducting a marriage service.

'We hope many happy, leisurely days await you. It's a lovely time of year to leave the world of work behind and follow more leisurely pursuits.'

His head bobbed. The dipping duck again. Marigold stared at him, fascinated.

'I imagine you and your family have planned all kinds of pleasurable outings this summer?'

Marigold nodded and stuck out her hand for the envelope. She added it to her bouquet before raising the polystyrene cup to her lips. Ugh! The wine was warm and much too sweet. It slid down her throat and lapped her already churning stomach with such effect she thought she was going to throw up there and then.

Oh no! She mustn't be sick. She would disgrace herself and Pat, in whom she had confided in weak moments, might assume her sickness was activated by old Heywood's remarks about her family.

She blinked hard, met Pat's gaze. When her friend's left eye descended in a slow wink, she felt better. Recklessly, she held out her now empty cup. 'Fill it up, Mr Heywood. After all, we're celebrating.'

Pat drove her home. Marigold was not drunk but driving in York at the end of May, or at any time, demanded one hundred per cent concentration and by the end of the party Marigold's concentration was wayward.

It was nice to be relieved of responsibility. Sprawling inelegantly in the passenger seat next to the driver, she stared out of the window, concentrating on the cherry blossom fluttering down from the trees lining the road.

'It's like pink snow. Look, Pat.'

Pat sneaked a quick glance and then returned her gaze to the road ahead. York had never been intended for cars. The bridges, the bars and the narrow curving streets belonged to more leisurely times.

It was as well she remained observant. A couple of minutes later, a lemming-like tourist stepped out into the road in order to photograph the medieval church of St Michael and All Angels, and Pat swore beneath her breath as she stepped on the brake.

'Bloody tourists.'

'Umm . . .' The jolt did not disturb Marigold's reverie. As they continued on their way, she said, 'There was a church on this site before the Conquest. Did you know that?'

'No.' Pat glanced at her friend. 'I'm surprised you do.'

'Oh, Ian told me. On one of the few occasions he felt like talking. He'd been with his cronies drinking port and must have got a fair bit down him because, when he got home, he suddenly started talking about churches. I was astonished because, as you know, he's a scientist through and through.' Marigold yawned.

'What's more, I've remembered most of what he said. Bit of a miracle, really.' She held up her hand and ticked off each item on her fingers.

'St Cuthbert's mentioned in the Domesday Book. St Michael-le-Belfry is a wholly Tudor church and All Saints' has a horrible doorknocker.' She pulled herself up in her seat. 'It has, too. I went to see for myself. Its a beast of some kind swallowing a human being.'

Pat grimaced. 'Hardly saintly.'

'Ah, but the medieval churches were concerned with sinners as well as saints and the doorknocker served a good purpose. If someone was being chased by the authorities and managed to grab the knocker before they grabbed him, then he was given sanctuary.'

'Really.' Pat waited at the traffic lights and then turned right. 'Why did you go to see it?'

There was no reply. Marigold had gone to sleep.

Fifteen minutes later, Pat woke her. 'You're home, Mari.'

Marigold sat up and rubbed her eyes. 'God, I was flat out. Must have drank more than I realised.' She smiled at Pat and then reached for the doorhandle. 'Thanks, Pat. I'll be seeing you.'

'Just a minute.' Her friend caught hold of her arm. 'Ian won't be home yet, will he?'

'Oh, no. Not for at least another two hours.'

'So you don't have to rush indoors?'

'No, except Paddy will have heard the car. He'll be at the door waiting for his walk.'

'He can wait a couple of minutes! I want to talk to you.'

'What about?' Marigold subsided into her seat.

There was a short silence.

'Go on then.'

Pat said, 'We've never really talked this through, have we?'

'Talked what through?'

'Your leaving work.'

'What is there to talk about?'

'Heaps of things. Oh, Mari.' Pat shook her head. 'You did it for me, didn't you? You stopped me getting the sack.'

Marigold shrugged. 'I didn't resign to save your job, Pat.'

'I don't believe you. You'd never have left for any other reason. You enjoy your work too much.'

Marigold turned to face her. 'I'll admit the thought of you having to leave upset me. You need your job, Pat. I don't, but—' She held up her hand, anticipating Pat's interruption. 'That's not why I gave in my notice.'

'Then why?'

Marigold gazed out of the car window.

The grass verges outside her house had been newly mowed. She could smell the sweetness of the cut grass. A fair-haired little boy was wobbling along the nearside pavement on an ancient red-painted tricycle. She didn't recognise him. He must be a visiting grandchild of one of the more elderly couples in the Avenue. She smiled at him.

'I've been feeling restless lately,' she told Pat. 'I'm sick of my life as it is now but as for changing it . . .' She stared down at her hands. 'When Heywood brought in that memo, it seemed like fate giving me a nudge.' She looked across at her friend. 'I've worked for the tax department for twenty years, Pat. Somehow, I knew that if I didn't go now, I'd still be there in another twenty years. So, for once, I came to a decision and in doing so, I was able to help out my friends.'

'You've certainly done that.' Pat's brow was still furrowed. 'But what about your family? How did Ian take the news?'

Marigold's shrug was eloquent. 'You know how he is. I'm not sure that he's actually taken in the fact that I've resigned. So long as nothing affects his routine he'll be quite happy.'

'But what if something does happen to upset his routine? I mean, you're not going to settle for being a housewife, are you? You'll find another job?'

Seeing Pat's worried expression, Marigold laughed and sat up straight. 'I don't know what I'm going to do. I might get another job. I might not. I'm forty-four years old and for the first time in ages I've made a decision. I've forced a significant change in my life.'

She thought for a moment. 'I think I might enjoy being a housewife. On the other hand, I might do something positively outrageous, like have an affair.'

'Oh, Marigold. Be careful. I know you and Ian . . .'

'I'm only joking.' Marigold turned to collect her bouquet and her handbag from the rear seat of the car. 'What I *am* going to do is take Paddy for a walk. I'm later than usual and the poor dog must have his legs crossed.'

She got out and bent to say her goodbyes. 'You'll keep in touch, Pat? Ring me from time to time and tell me all the gossip?'

'Of course.' Pat looked at her affectionately. 'I'll do more than that. I'll give you a ring in about ten days, after you've settled down, and then we'll go out for a meal or something.'

'I'd like that.'

Marigold closed the car door, waved and then walked quickly towards her home. Her heart gave a tiny lurch as she heard her friend drive away. She would miss seeing Pat every day.

Her serious expression lightened when a deep-throated woof sounded a moment before she opened the door. Inside the hallway, a large black labrador dog greeted her, his heavy tail beating a tattoo of welcome. She patted him.

'Hello, old boy.'

In a fever of excitement Paddy wreathed himself around her and slurped wet kisses on the back of her hand as she caressed his broad head.

'Yes, yes. I'm glad to see you, too, but mind my flowers.'

She flung her handbag on to the hall chest before walking through to the well-appointed kitchen which was at the back of the house.

She deposited the bouquet in the sink, rinsed her hands and then went to look in the fridge-freezer which was well stocked as usual. Every month she went to a large supermarket on the outskirts of York and did a mammoth shop. Surveying the neatly packed shelves, she thought that perhaps she wouldn't do that any more. With more time to spare she could stroll along to see what the smaller, local shops had to offer. The thought pleased her.

She took out various items of food from the freezer, checked the contents of the vegetable rack and then ran upstairs to change into her flat walking shoes. She and her husband slept at the back of the house because it was quieter and also overlooked the large garden. She took the shoes from the wardrobe and then glanced out of the window.

The garden looked at its best in late Spring. The rockery, in the shade of the house, was bright with delicate creamy white lilies of the valley, grape hyacinths and miniature Dutch hyacinths, and around the lawn the lupins were beginning to show amongst the bright tulip heads. Down at the bottom of the garden, beneath the chestnut tree, ruffled-headed narcissi were ousting the fading daffodils.

Remembering the gift of the garden-centre token, Marigold sighed with pleasure. Old Heywood had got that right. She wondered if Ian could be persuaded to accompany her when she went to spend the voucher? He had so little time but surely he could spare an hour to help her choose new plants.

A woof from downstairs reminded her that Paddy was waiting. She ran downstairs and grabbed his lead.

'Come on, then.'

She stepped out until they reached the outskirts of the development and then she slowed down to allow Paddy to nose his way from tree to tree. The early evening sun touched her face with gentle fingers and the light breeze ruffled her hair and she was suddenly conscious of a feeling of wellbeing. She had made the right decision. Heavens, she laughed out loud, she had *made* a decision, that had to be worth something.

This problem with her marriage wasn't insoluble. They'd been married a long time. Marriages did go stale, but couples got over it. And with more time to spare, she could start building bridges. In fact, she glanced at her watch, she could start right now. She whistled for Paddy.

Back home she began work on an extra special meal. She mixed a cocktail of prawns and pink grapefruit and added chopped chives to freshly prepared mayonnaise. Ian liked fish, so the main course would be grilled lemon sole served with minted new potatoes, baby carrots and courgettes.

Marigold loved to bake cakes but her cooking was only moderate and her usual presentation was slapdash. She knew this irritated Ian but usually, after a full day at work, she was too tired to bother with niceties. But tonight was the beginning of her new way of life and so she placed her best tablecloth on the dining table and brought out the candles.

Finally, she fed Paddy, washed up the dirty bowls and pans and left the kitchen intending to have a bath. The door to the sitting room was open and as she passed by she noticed the answerphone was blinking. She had put it on before taking Paddy out and had forgotten to cancel it out.

She went in and pressed the play button. The tones came on and then Ian's voice. 'Won't be home until late, probably around eleven thirty. Another bloody meeting, would you believe? Don't wait up and don't bother to leave me any food. I'll grab a sandwich.'

She stared down at the hateful blinking red light.

'Another bloody meeting.' Who was he kidding? Ian *loved* his bloody meetings. He never missed one. And what about her? Not one word, nothing to show he even remembered today was her last day at work. He'd forgotten – about her work and about her. Well, sod him!

She rushed back into the kitchen, grabbed the food she had so lovingly prepared and binned the lot.

'I hope his bloody sandwich gives him indigestion,' she shouted aloud.

Ears down, Paddy retreated into his basket. Wistfully, he gazed at the pedal bin.

Fuelled by anger, Marigold swept through the house, locking doors and securing windows and then, still simmering, she went for a bath.

'So much for building bridges. I don't know why he bothers to come home at all. Not to see me, that's for sure. Is there something wrong with me?'

She glared at her reflection in the bathroom mirror. Her face was pink with temper and the heat from the bath, but her skin was smooth and relatively unlined. Her short, brown hair was curling around her ears and lay tangled on her wide forehead. She touched it, remembering Ian's reply when she had told him her name.

'Marigold, eh? It's different, but it suits you. It's right for you, goes with your colouring.'

And he had smiled into her brown eyes and touched her hair and she had loved him then, when she was only fifteen.

She couldn't see her own reflection any more because her eyes had filled with tears, so she got out of the bath, dried herself and went to bed.

Chapter Two

At the sound of breaking crockery, Sheila Scott was awake and out of bed. Once upon a time she had been a sleepyhead in the mornings but not now. The past three years had altered that. She rushed downstairs and was in the kitchen before Jack, her young son, had time to pick up the broken pieces from the tiled kitchen floor.

'What the . . .'

Sheila stared down at the kneeling figure of her ten-year-old, instantly registering the pieces of broken china in his hands and the mess of spilt milk and soggy cornflakes on the floor. Colour flooded her cheeks.

'You daft bugger.'

She bore down upon his thin figure and slapped him hard across his face.

'I *told* you to be careful. Do you know how much real china costs? If I can even match the pattern. Oh God, you've done for us now.'

Jack, his figure tense, kept his eyes fixed on the pieces of crockery. He muttered, 'It wasn't me. I didn't do it.'

'Oh, no?' She raised her hand again. 'Then who else? Billy, I suppose.'

'Yes,' he said. Now Jack looked up at her, his voice thick with resentment and his eyes bright with unshed tears. 'Yes, it *was* Billy. It was him.'

'Don't you dare try to blame your brother. Billy's too little to get his own breakfast. He can't reach the cupboards.'

'He did though.' Jack rose from his knees and, crossing the kitchen, placed the broken pieces of the china bowl on to the breakfast bar. He nodded. 'Look.'

Sheila looked. On the opposite side of the large kitchen was a run of wall cupboards and beneath them were more cupboards topped by a pale blue working surface. Close by was a gleaming white fridge-freezer. A high kitchen stool had been dragged to the area near the fridge-freezer and on the work surface stood a bottle of milk and a box of breakfast cereal. Above, the door of one of the wall cupboards stood open.

'He must have come down and decided to get his own breakfast. When I came in he was carrying the bowl over to the breakfast bar.' Jack sighed. 'I guess I startled him. He dropped the bowl and when it broke, he ran outside. He knew there'd be trouble.'

Worry sharpened Sheila's voice. 'Outside? Where outside?'

'He's not round the front. He's playing in the back garden, on his trike.'

'You'd better go and get him. It's Sunday morning, people are home, they notice things.' She made a gesture of impatience. 'Go on. Don't stand gawping at me.' Her thin face looked strained as Jack hurried out into the garden.

She went back upstairs and dressed hurriedly. Returning to the kitchen intending to clean up the mess on the floor, she paused in the doorway. Her two children, standing side by side, were waiting for her.

Billy's rounded, three-year-old face held an expression of fright mixed with defiance. 'Not my fault, Mum. Jack sneaked in and scared me.'

Sheila's face softened. 'It was no one's fault, Billy. Don't worry. It was an accident.'

16

She glanced at Jack's face and realised he looked much older than his years. I should apologise to him, she thought, but she didn't. Instead, she took a cloth and cleaned up the mess on the floor. Jack was old enough to understand her anxiety, he knew the risks they were running and he knew she was relying on him to behave like an adult. With his dad away in London, he had to be the man of the house.

'Man of the house.' Sheila's lips thinned into a sardonic smile. What a joke.

She finished wiping the floor and stood up. 'Do you want anything to eat?'

They both shook their head.

'Then you'd better get rid of the rest of the milk, Jack. Wash the bottle out and put it in my shopping bag. Put the cornflakes in there too, and whatever bread's left in the bread bin.

'Billy, go and look under all the beds and make sure you haven't left any of your toys, and don't move *anything*, do you hear?'

The little boy nodded, his face solemn.

Sheila put the broken pieces of crockery into a supermarket plastic bag and fastened the top. She gave the bag to Jack. 'Put that in with your stuff.'

The two boys left the kitchen and Sheila went over and studied the contents of the wall cupboard. She rearranged the contents and closed the door. With a bit of luck the missing cereal bowl would go unmissed for some time. There was only Mr and Mrs Cambridge living in the house and there were still five dishes left.

If the old dears did notice, then she'd pretend she had broken the dish on the first day she'd come in to clean and forgotten about it. She'd offer to replace it, of course.

Dismissing that particular problem from her mind, Sheila washed and dried the bread bin and then rechecked the pedal bin. Kitchens were so difficult, there were so many things to watch out for. She went upstairs to take the boys' sleeping bags from the beds, wondering if her good idea had been so good after all.

She checked the rest of the house. Immaculate. Good. It should be, she'd worked like a slave last night.

By twelve thirty, they were ready to go. Sheila, her anxiety mounting every time she glanced at the clock, took one last walk through the ground floor. She peeked into the downstairs cloakroom again, checking the washbasin was clean and glancing down into the toilet bowl. She frowned when she saw a shred of cream coloured toilet paper clinging to the side of the pan. Billy, probably. He couldn't help it. He was too little to understand. She flushed the scrap of paper away and came out, shouting for the boys to take their stuff out on to the porch.

She picked up the large suitcase she had brought down into the hall and staggered a little under the weight. She was only a little 'un. She permitted herself a small, tight smile. Mike used to tease her, telling her to fatten up a bit. 'A chap likes a nice armful to cuddle.'

Not much chance of that, given their present circumstances.

She carried the suitcase outside, checked they had everything with them and then locked the front door of the house. She posted the key through the letterbox.

'That's it, then.'

They walked towards the garden gate.

'Can you manage all that?'

Jack nodded, his face sombre.

Sheila knew he had caught her feeling of anxiety and now wore it like a cloak upon his bony shoulders. She turned away from him and looked at Billy. Although he had a sizeable parcel in the wicker basket attached to his bike and also carried a child-sized backpack on his back, her younger son had a wide grin on his face. Billy thought that what they had done had been a great adventure.

Surprising herself, Sheila found she too was smiling. Billy's cheerful nature always made her feel better.

'Come on.' She picked up the case and her shopping bag. Jack shouldered the rest of the baggage and Billy mounted his bike.

He asked, 'Are we going home?'

Sheila's smile vanished.

At around ten o'clock on Sunday morning, Marigold decided to let go the remnants of her anger. She was still annoyed about the waste of a good meal on Friday evening but there was no point in maintaining her silent treatment towards Ian because he simply did not realise she was not speaking to him.

He had returned home late on Friday, so late she had been fast asleep when he came upstairs. On Saturday he had left the house early, not saying where he was going but apparently in good humour and unaware of her non communication, and in the afternoon he had watched sport on TV. During the evening his head had been buried in a book.

Sunday morning had followed the usual routine. He got up about forty-five minutes after Marigold, showered, dressed and came in the kitchen for his breakfast. He muttered 'good morning', poured himself a cup of coffee and disappeared behind the pages of the Sunday newspapers.

Marigold, smarting at her husband's thoughtlessness, turned from the cooker and almost tripped over the recumbent body of the dog. In the kitchen, Paddy always stayed close to her. She pushed him out of the way with her foot, wishing she could treat Ian in the same way, then crossed to the table and slapped down his breakfast.

He lowered his newspaper, surveyed the plateful of grilled bacon and scrambled eggs with appreciation, murmured one word, 'lovely', and returned to the news headlines.

Deprived of the opportunity of a healthy row, Marigold snatched up her own cup of coffee and returned to stand by the sink. She found out that drinking coffee through gritted teeth was difficult.

Ian spoke once more before leaving the room. He promised Paddy a walk later.

Paddy, blinking long lashes, replied with a doggy grin and Marigold, cut to the quick by his betrayal, snapped her fingers at him. Paddy glanced her way and then, being a dog possessed of a deep perception of human behaviour, flew his ears at half-mast and came to press against her leg.

Feeling better, Marigold ran hot water on to the dishes in the sink. She watched the bubbles form and remembered an article she had read in a magazine, something about a custody battle between a divorcing couple over a family pet. She thought, If the worst comes to the worst, then I'll insist on having Paddy and Ian can have Karen.

Thoughts of her daughter drove her into a spell of domesticity and dusting and hoovering; she hoped she was disturbing her husband who was now closeted in his study. But slowly, her downbeat mood lightened. The sunshine was pouring through the windows of the house and she decided the day was just too beautiful to spoil by harbouring ill-feelings.

Feeling happier, and also virtuous – the house was tidier than it had been for ages – Marigold made herself a coffee and went out into the front garden.

She glanced around, admiring the fresh green of the lawn and then sat down in a garden chair, bending her head over the mug she carried and inhaling the delightful aroma of freshly brewed coffee. She drank a little and then looked up at the sky. Only two tiny clouds drifted above her. She studied them. They looked exactly like the fairytale clouds featured in story books for tiny children, much too pretty to be real.

Her wedding day had been a fairytale come true. At eighteen, in her long, white dress she had been Cinderella marrying her Prince. Ian had made a good Prince, being well bred, fair haired, with serious good looks and an appealing air of otherworldliness about him.

But he had been worldly enough on their wedding night. Marigold had been amazed because during their courtship he had held back somewhat. He had wanted her to be a virgin on her wedding day and so she was, although it had been a close thing as they had indulged in some heavy necking.

But maybe he had been right because their honeymoon was altogether special. On their wedding night, the novelty of being in bed together was a turn-on and to be kissed and touched in intimate places without guilt or shame had been thrilling.

But the second night was even better.

This time, Ian did much more adventurous things and by the time he finished Marigold had experienced her first orgasm. It was terrific and afterwards she had clung to her new husband and cried with happiness.

At the time, she had never wondered where Ian had learned his sexual expertise but now, twenty-six years later, she did.

He must have had an affair with an older woman, she thought, placing her coffee mug on the gravelled path near her garden chair. Perhaps he was seduced by the wife of one of the lecturers at Durham University? She felt instinctively that he had not had an affair with one of his female classmates. He had, she remembered, been less than attracted to them.

'Weird and wonderful, Mari. Not like you at all.' He had hugged her to him, a proprietary movement. 'Straggly hair, white faces, droopy clothes and ears disfigured by collections of cheap earrings. They smoke "pot", too. You're much prettier and more wholesome.'

Pressed against his chest, the seventeen-year-old Marigold had felt a momentary discontent. 'Wholesome' sounded like brown bread and she thought that given the chance, she too might have enjoyed being a little outrageous. She rather fancied wearing weird clothes and 'hanging loose'.

She never mentioned her feelings because she knew there was no way she could go to university and, if she wanted to hang on to Ian, she had to be the kind of girl he admired. Well, she'd got him, hadn't she?

Remembering the early, happy years of their marriage, Marigold grabbed her mug and gulped down the remainder of the coffee. Why, she wondered, had Ian grown away from her? And when had it started? She shook her head. She couldn't pinpoint one specific time or occasion.

They'd been married a long time and, in common with most middle-aged couples, had settled into a comfortable undemanding regime but she had thought they still loved each other. For the last couple of years, though, she hadn't been so sure. In fact, sometimes she wondered if her husband actually *liked* her.

'Enjoying the sun?'

She jumped. 'Oh, you startled me. Yes, I am.'

Ian had come round the side of the house and was standing, watching her.

'You've got the lawn looking good.' He glanced around. 'I'll put the roller on it later.' He shifted his feet. 'Think I'll take Paddy for a run now.'

'Oh, don't go rushing off. Sit down and relax for a moment.' With her foot, Marigold pushed the second garden chair towards him.

'Well.' He hesitated, then sat down.

Ian's movements were always economical and even in a garden chair he sat tidily. Marigold studied his profile. Over the years he had changed little. His wide brow was still virtually unlined and there were few grey hairs in his blond, brushed-back hair.

She asked, 'Do you remember the first time you took me out on a proper date, Ian?' When he hesitated, she continued. 'We went to a posh restaurant. At least, I thought it was posh.'

He nodded. 'Yes, that's right. It was your seventeenth birthday.'

'No, it was ages before that. I was fifteen.'

He turned a shocked face towards her.

'Rubbish. I was almost through university when we started going out together.'

'Ah, yes. When we became a couple. But you took me out before then. It was just after you and your parents moved to the big house at the end of our street.'

He stared at her and then nodded. 'You're right. I'd forgotten.'

'I haven't. I remember I was totally overcome by the occasion. You borrowed your dad's car and you were so handsome and so grown-up. I think I fell in love with you straight away.'

He wasn't listening. He pondered. 'Are you sure you were only fifteen?'

'Oh, yes. I felt older, though, because you didn't patronise me at all. You talked about all kinds of things.'

'I hope that's all I did.' He ran his hand over his hair.

She nodded. 'You were a perfect gentleman. Afterwards, when I was back home again, I wondered why you'd bothered with me at all.'

He stared down at the gravel path.

'I remember now. I was miserable. I hadn't wanted to move to a new town. I was nervous at the thought of going to

23

university and I didn't know anyone. Then, one morning, you walked past our garden wheeling your bike and you grinned at me and I thought how pretty you were. I was hellishly shy then, scared to death of girls but I felt OK with you.'

He looked up. 'You acted older than your age. You were very confident.'

'I wasn't really. I just pretended.' Marigold smiled. 'Anyway, I went to a secondary modern school, remember. You had to grow up fast there.'

Ian put his hands together, fingertips touching. It was a gesture Marigold disliked.

'I hope you're not implying there's anything wrong with single sex boarding schools?' He frowned. 'Anyway, what, in particular, prompted this trip down memory lane?'

'No reason. I've been doing some thinking, that's all, remembering the past, thinking about the future.' Marigold shrugged. 'Perhaps because, after all these years, I've finished with work, said goodbye to the Inspector of Taxes and am wondering what to do.'

A look of comprehension dawned on Ian's face. 'Of course. I knew there was something. You've left work. Sorry, I forgot. We got some weird results from the lab experiment on Friday and it slipped my mind about your leaving work.' He rubbed his nose. 'You sound depressed. Most people I know would be delighted at the prospect of unlimited leisure.'

Marigold frowned. 'Would they? I don't imagine you would like it.'

There was a short, uncomfortable silence.

Then Ian, his face blank, inquired, 'What does that remark mean?'

She lowered her head. 'Nothing.'

'Then why make it?'

'Because I'm angry.' Marigold's head came up again and

the face she turned towards Ian was bitter. 'I'm angry with you.'

'Me?' His look was innocent, totally uncomprehending. 'What have *I* done?'

'It's what you haven't done! You forgot Friday was my last day at work and you didn't come home and I'd cooked a special meal for us.'

'Good God, is that the reason you're in a rotten mood?' A note of sarcasm crept into his voice. 'Sorry about the meal but I didn't know, did I? Neither did you consult me about your decision to give up work.' He shrugged his shoulders. 'I could have told you it wasn't a wise move. Still, it's your life. You can do what you want. But if you're having second thoughts don't take it out on me.'

'I'm not.' Marigold shrank back in her chair. 'And I'm not having second thoughts, but—' She hesitated. 'It's a big change for me, Ian. If we could have discussed the implications for us both, I think I would feel happier about things. I know you're busy, but if only you'd make a little more time . . .'

'Yes, I am busy.' Ian stood up. 'I hold down a demanding job and I work hard, for my family.' His arm swept round, embracing the house and garden. 'Do you realise how lucky you are, Mari? Do you think a lifestyle like this comes easy?'

'I know it doesn't. But, Ian, I never particularly wanted such a high standard of living. I would be happier living in a smaller house and seeing more of you. Don't you realise how far apart we've grown? Why, some days we hardly exchange more than a couple of sentences.' She paused. 'And if, by family, you mean Karen, she couldn't care less about the house. She has her flat in London and her own life now.'

'Yes, she has.' A nerve began to jump at the corner of Ian's mouth. He stared down at his wife. 'And I wish to God you were more like her.'

He ran his fingers through his hair. 'Can't you find a hobby or something? You ought to listen to yourself, droning on about togetherness. God, you sound like a silly teenager.' He paused for breath. 'If you want the truth, I'll tell you how I feel: I was dismayed when you said you were leaving work. I mean, what are you going to do with yourself?'

He waited for her to speak and when she did not, he shook his head. 'Please don't expect me to dance attendance on you. I work long hours under stressful conditions. When I get home I need peace and quiet, not demands from a bored wife.' He turned his back on her and went back into the house.

Marigold pressed her hand to her chest. The pain was back. 'Too much damned coffee,' she whispered.

Deep breaths and a determined effort not to break down in tears enabled Marigold to get on with her day. There were plenty of people worse off than her and, as everyone knew, work was a good cure for depression. Besides, they had guests coming for dinner. Accordingly, she went into the kitchen and checked her menu for the meal.

Then she went into the front garden and studied the flower border. She would, she decided, pick some of the blooms and make a centrepiece for the dining table. Susan Cambridge, she knew, loved flowers.

Marigold was picking sweet-scented narcissi when she spotted the strange little group of people walking along the pavement on her side of the avenue. Or rather, two were walking. The little boy she had noticed on Friday was leading the way on his bike.

She straightened up as he drew level with her and waved her hand at him.

'Hi.'

His head turned in her direction. He grinned at her but did

26

not reply. Instead, he bent lower over his bike's handlebars and pedalled away.

Still smiling, Marigold looked at the woman and older boy who followed. They did not smile back. Instead, they quickened their steps and, staring straight ahead of them, marched past her as though she did not exist. Marigold felt chilled. How unfriendly could you be? She shrugged her shoulders and turned back to her garden but the little group interested her so she turned and looked after them again. They were certainly loaded up. Had they been visiting someone? Why had they no transport? The nearest bus stop to town was some distance away.

Briefly, she considered going after them and offering them a lift. It would be no trouble to her as the car was already parked by the kerb. But as soon as the idea suggested itself to her she dismissed it.

The mother – she presumed it was the boys' mother – didn't look as though she would appreciate a gesture of goodwill, but what if she accepted? If Ian looked through the window and saw the three of them climbing into her car he would be absolutely livid. He was always telling her she was too easy and friendly with perfect strangers.

Anyway, they were almost at the end of the avenue. Marigold, still watching them, had another worrying thought. Where had they come from? She knew all her neighbours, at least by sight, and she had never seen these people before.

She pulled at her lower lip, thoughtfully. The woman and her children were not the kind of people who lived in the avenue and it was strange they didn't have transport. And why hadn't they ordered a taxi to cope with all their bags and packages. Just supposing . . . Marigold frowned. Her imagination was running riot.

If there were female burglars, they would hardly take their children with them on raids. Despite her distress over the scene with Ian, Marigold's mouth quirked upwards in a smile. Particularly a child on his bike. Shaking her head at her own foolishness, she turned and carried her flowers into the house.

Chapter Three

Richard Cambridge put down his napkin and smiled at Marigold. 'The pork was delicious, Mari, particularly with the orange sauce. Only trouble is, I've eaten too much. The thought alarms me, but what if I have no room left for dessert?'

She smiled back at him. 'You'll manage, Richard. It's caramel cream and peaches in brandy for afters, all very light.'

'Really? Well, in that case I'll try a small helping of both of them.'

Amid the ripple of laughter, Marigold pushed back her chair and went into the kitchen. She listened to the murmur of voices from the dining room as she set out the dishes on a tray. If only all their dinner parties were so pleasant. But Susan and Richard Cambridge were neighbours and friends to both of them, whereas usually their dinner guests were Ian's colleagues at the university.

Marigold had tried to like Ian's friends but she had failed. *She* knew it, but evidently no one else did because the same guests kept coming back. Every few weeks Ian would give her notice that he had asked someone to dine with them. Sometimes it was a single male colleague of his; but usually it was a couple. They were educated, polite people who arrived on time and brought with them a bottle of good wine or a box of chocolates. Marigold would smile, usher them in and ask them to make themselves comfortable. They would sit down and begin a conversation. But, inevitably, as the evening progressed, Marigold would feel ignored, pushed out in some way.

Of course, as hostess, she was forced to keep popping into the kitchen, to ensure the meal was progressing satisfactorily, and in due course, to serve the food, but her sense of alienation was due to more than missed conversation.

Ian's friends were, without exception, connected with the university and their conversation mirrored the fact. Within five minutes of arriving at the house, someone would mention something to do with work and they were away. A proposed procedural change would evoke a discussion as to whether or not *their* department would be affected. Would it mean more work, or less? Would their status be lessened or enhanced?

Another time, a visiting professor from Europe or America became the chief topic of conversation. Then the talk became envious – how much money could be earned abroad and the marvellous facilities available there. After a bottle or two of wine, Marigold noticed how often the table talk became malicious. At their last party, Ian and his guests had spent over an hour chatting about the latest power struggle between two heads of department and the dirty tricks involved.

Knowing nothing of any of these subjects, Marigold would listen to them without speaking and, eventually, stop listening. After one such party she plucked up courage and told Ian how she felt.

'Don't your friends realise how rude they are? I'm not here merely to cook and serve the food. I always thought people with university degrees had good minds and enjoyed a wide range of interests. Why don't they discuss the latest films or plays, or even the state of the country, for God's sake?'

Her complaint was shrugged off. 'You know our dinner parties are for a reason. They're useful to me. I get to know what people are thinking. Anyway, shouldn't a wife take an interest in her husband's career?'

'I do, but I'm getting sick of just sitting there. You wouldn't like it if I talked about my work all the time.'

Ian had looked at her with a glint in his eye. 'If you're feeling out of your depth, why don't you invite some of your friends around for a change. I'm quite happy for you to do that.'

She didn't answer him. Ian knew that her friends did not give dinner parties nor attend them. Her friends, most of them people she worked with, socialised by going to the pub for a few drinks and then on to a Chinese or Indian restaurant. They would view with horror the thought of a dinner party.

Sometimes, Marigold felt adrift between two different worlds. The first world was the one in which she had grown up and the second was the world she had entered after marrying Ian.

Marigold's background was solid working class, with all its strengths and weaknesses. As a girl, she had absorbed her parents' philosophy: you kept your head down, worked hard and knew your place in society. But meeting Ian, falling in love with him and marrying him had changed and confused her.

She still understood, and admired, the strength of working-class ethics but she also saw the failings: the suspicion of other classes of society and the stubborn desire not to change.

During the first two years of her marriage, she had questioned her parents' attitude to life more and more but had tried to keep her confusion to herself. She loved her parents too much to upset them and she knew her marriage to Ian had rattled them. They thought their only daughter had made a mismatch and would live to regret her decision. She was determined to prove them wrong.

They *were* wrong. Being Mrs Ian Goddard was fun. Marigold began to enjoy herself and she delighted in learning something new every day.

At the start of her married life she enjoyed entertaining. In those days, guests had dropped in unexpectedly. They sat on huge floor cushions, consumed beer or wine and dined on crusty bread, cheese, nuts and crisps. Everyone argued – about feminism, politics, the existence of God – and gossiped about who was sleeping with who.

Listening and watching, Marigold blossomed like the flower after which she had been named. Soon, she was joining in the conversation and finding, to her own astonishment, that she could be witty. She also learned how to cook. Instead of chips, she cooked pasta; she started to put herbs in her stews and switched from cheap Spanish wine to German and then to French and, for about two years, life was wonderful.

But then things began to change. Students turned into grown-up people and friends began to drift away. They moved to other towns, got jobs in banking or industry. Some couples split up, others married. Marigold and Ian stayed in the same town but moved from their rented flat into their first house. It was a tiny up-and-down terrace but it had swathes of cloth draped at the windows instead of ordinary curtains and bowls of dried flowers everywhere and Marigold loved it.

Babies began to be born to the few couples remaining in the area and, to her great satisfaction, Marigold became pregnant as well. Once a week the pregnant women met up and exchanged anecdotes about pregnancy, childbirth and motherhood. Looking like pouter pigeons in their voluminous smocks they sat around, drank tea, ate biscuits and vied with each other in showing off their latest acquisition for the coming baby or for their home.

On arrival, they would hug, exchange symptoms and then settle down to view the new purchases and Marigold realised that, if one friend had recently bought a new coffee set or mirror, the next week someone had bought a bigger, better version. And, of course, there were the presents from relatives.

'You can buy cheaper but John's mother told me to get the top-of-the-range. "Only the best for my first grandchild," she said.'

Or, on another occasion, 'Daddy's paid for this, and this, and this. He can't wait to see his first grandson. Goodness knows what he will do if I have a girl?'

A look of mock horror of the face of one mother-to-be. 'It's from Selfridge's, the most wonderful christening shawl. Horribly expensive, of course.'

Marigold grew quieter as she listened. She liked her companions but she felt different from them. As she admired another present – an electric train set – she found herself hoping the couple in question would have a girl and she knew that she was becoming alienated from them.

Ian's parents no longer lived near them and they were certainly different from her friends' parents. Mr and Mrs Goddard senior were a self-contained couple and not, Marigold thought, particularly family orientated. Rarely did they write or phone their son and when Marigold had told them they were to become grandparents their reaction had been polite but curiously muted.

But Marigold's parents had been delighted with the news. Marigold remembered the smile that had spread over her mother's face. But once the good news had been digested, there had been a brisk, no-nonsense hug and the words, 'I'll start knitting right away, Mari. Some nice little coats in white and maybe a couple in lemon, then they'll do for boy or girl. And your dad'll want to open a savings account for the kiddy, to help him or her get a bit of a start in life. I hope you and Ian will agree to that?'

'There's no need, Mum.'

'Maybe not, but he'll want to do it all the same. It takes a lot of money to bring up a child nowadays.'

Tears had pricked at the back of Marigold's eyes, knowing how hard her father had worked all his life and how small had been his reward.

She had thought of these things when she listened to her friends and she came to the conclusion that, yes, they were attractive, intelligent and good company, but they hadn't a clue about real life.

The girls, noticing her increasing silences, asked, 'Anything the matter, Mari?'

She had stirred herself. 'No. It's nothing.'

Only thoughts, but thoughts had a way of driving a barrier between herself and other people.

And that's when it had started, the feeling of being slightly out of step with so many people.

She had learned to live with the feeling. She smiled and said nothing when Ian and his friends ranted against idle workers and scroungers living off benefits, and when her father raged against the government for giving grants to students and wasting money on the arts, she did the same. She often envied them – they were so different and yet so clear in their beliefs. She was so muddled, it was better not to try and articulate her own views. And so, over the years, saying nothing became a habit.

So, when Karen was born, and Ian, a besotted father, began to spoil her outrageously, she had said nothing.

Another burst of laughter from the dining room aroused Marigold from her reverie. She picked up the tray and hurried back to her guests.

Susan Cambridge was speaking about their Italian holiday.

'The Piedmontese region's marvellous, Ian. I can't think why we've never tried that region before now. It's so picturesque. We visited Canelli and Alba, and we went round Stupinigi which is one of the Royal House of Savoy's grandest palaces. The weather was superb and so was the food.'

Ian nodded. 'Yes, I've heard the food and the wine in that region's good.'

'It is, and now is the perfect time to visit.' Struck by a sudden idea, Susan paused, staring at her host. 'Why don't you go, you and Mari? You'd love it.'

Marigold was passing Richard his portion of peaches in brandy. She stopped, turned her head towards Ian and said. 'What a wonderful idea. We *could* go, Ian. It's the right time of year for you to take a holiday.'

'Impossible.' Ian's voice was curt. He jumped up and busied himself by setting out the coffee cups.

'Oh, but . . .'

Aware of the hurt look on Marigold's face, Susan spoke up. 'Why not think about it before deciding. A break would do you good. Surely you could spare a few days?'

'Actually, I couldn't.' Ian, keeping his head down, moved the position of a coffee spoon. 'I've work to do in the lab and masses of admin stuff to sort out. Just because Mari can now lead a life of leisure, doesn't mean I can.'

In the silence following his words, Susan's sniff was audible.

Then Richard, not usually a subtle man, saved a potentially awkward situation by saying, 'It was a good holiday, Susan, but I don't think the food was that great.' He looked across the table at Ian. 'They served loads of salamis and ravioli and I know some people like sauces and things but I prefer my meat served up plain.' He nodded towards Marigold. 'That's why I enjoyed the pork so much.'

His wife glared at him. 'That's typical of you, Richard. You never complained about the food when we were there.' She sniffed again. 'What about the meal we had at Castle Grinzane?' She removed her gaze from her husband and stared across at Ian, obviously determined to make him change his mind about the holiday.

'Tartufi, white truffles, ravioli stuffed with all kinds of wild mushrooms, game in season and then a magnificent chocolate dessert and zabaglione. Doesn't that tempt you? Are you positive you can't take a few days off?'

'Positive.' Ian's smile was strained. He glanced at Marigold. 'Speaking of zabaglione, are you ever going to pass those dishes round?'

Marigold jumped. 'Oh, yes. Sorry.'

She served everyone and they began to eat. Ian talked to Richard about the forthcoming cricket season and Susan took a spoonful of cream caramel and watched the two men, a thoughtful expression on her face.

When they had finished the meal, Marigold went into the kitchen to make more coffee and Susan followed her.

'Can I help?'

'No need.'

'Then I'll sit here and watch you.'

Susan perched herself on a kitchen stool. 'I enjoy sensible conversation but once Richard mentioned Botham . . .' She shivered theatrically.

Marigold smiled and tipped coffee beans into an electric grinder. 'Ah, but what *is* sensible conversation? People have widely differing views.'

'My dear, what do you think? What do all women enjoy talking about?'

Marigold's expression became guarded. 'I don't know.'

'Of course you do.' Susan settled herself more comfortably. 'Relationships, of course.'

Marigold turned her head away. 'Perhaps. I'm quite happy to listen to you talk about your marriage, Susan.' She flicked a switch and the noise from the coffee grinder growled in the quiet room.

'Ouch.' Susan flinched. She thought and then nodded her head. 'I deserved that. I'm developing into a nosy old bat, aren't I?'

'I wouldn't say that.'

Susan interrupted. 'I would. As I get older I appear to be losing the art of being tactful but—' She glanced at Marigold's profile. 'In mitigation, I'm being nosy because I like you. I know you're an only child and that your parents are dead. I, too, was an only child and as Richard and I have no children . . .' She hesitated. 'What I'm trying to say is, if you need a friend, I hope you'll remember I make a good listener.'

Marigold did not reply immediately. She picked up the coffee jug and ran hot water into it to warm it and then she turned towards Susan. The older woman was seated primly on the stool. Her feet were neatly side by side on the wooden footrest and her plump hands were tidily folded in her lap. The expression on her face made her look like an elderly, guilty schoolgirl.

Marigold put down the jug and, crossing over to her, patted her hands.

'I'm sorry, too. Perhaps I was rude but right now, I'm feeling vulnerable.' Seeing a frown appear on Susan's face, she added hastily, 'There's nothing terribly wrong, just lots of little things. But, still, I worry.'

She looked away and said conversationally, 'Sometimes, I fear our marriage is slowly disintegrating. We don't row, we don't talk enough for that. Ian's so distant. When he does notice me, he's usually disapproving. I don't know why. I've tried to talk to him about it but he won't admit anything's wrong. And if I press the point, raise my voice, he tells me I'm becoming an hysterical woman.'

'You're the least hysterical woman I know.' Susan's voice was soothing but her brow was wrinkled. 'Tell me, why did you give up your work? Did you think it would help solve your marital problems?'

'I just decided my whole life needed a shake-up.' Marigold bit her lip. 'But now I'm beginning to regret my decision.'

'What did Ian say about your leaving work?'

'Very little, but he's not too happy about it.' Marigold's shoulders rose and fell in a hopeless shrug. 'He said I must find something to do with myself because he can't spare time to be with me.'

Susan's lips pursed. 'He *is* very busy.'

Marigold realised Susan was studying her face. She turned away from her and went to make the coffee. Striving to add a lighter tone to their conversation, she said, 'I suppose things will sort themselves out. Every couple has ups and downs. It's not as if either of us is involved with another person.'

'Ian works from home sometimes, doesn't he? He's used to having the house to himself.'

Marigold nodded and Susan continued, 'Maybe he's worried about that. He thinks you'll invade his working space.'

'Good God!' Unusually, Marigold's temper flared up. 'There's so much space around him it's a wonder we can see each other. Anyway, what does he think I'm going to do? Hoover while he is marking papers, play loud music when he's conducting a tutorial? He knows me better than that.'

'Of course.' Susan soothed her. 'But his work is very important to him.'

'That's his trouble. All he thinks about is work.' Marigold's flash of anger departed as swiftly as it had arrived. She rubbed her forehead and added, 'It's as if I don't exist any more.'

'Then you must remind him.' Susan shook her head. 'You're an attractive woman, Mari. Stop feeling sorry for yourself and remind him of that.'

Marigold scowled. 'I won't play the bimbo, Susan, if that's what you mean. I'm not going to try and seduce my own husband.'

'Why not? Don't you fancy him any more?'

'Why, yes. But . . .'

'I'm not suggesting anything distasteful, Mari. All I'm saying is why don't you jog his memory a little, remind him of how you *used* to pass the time before he became so fixated on his work. Try a bit of glamour. If it works, who knows, you might manage an Italian holiday after all.'

'Oh, no. I don't think that's the answer.' Marigold stopped speaking when Susan yawned mightily.

'Sorry, Mari. I'm afraid our two a.m. start is catching up with me.'

'Oh my goodness.' Marigold hurriedly poured out two cups of coffee and handed one to Susan. 'I'd forgotten all about your travelling. Look, we'll take this through to the men, and after they've had a drink, you and Richard must get off home.'

Susan climbed down from the stool. 'We were so delighted when we found your invitation on the mat. I would have hated having to start cooking when we got in.'

'That's what I thought.'

The two women moved toward the doorway.

'Was everything all right at home? I did try and keep an eye on the house while you were away but because I was working, it was a bit difficult.'

Susan smiled. 'Everything was fine, and thanks to my cleaning lady we came back to an immaculate house. She's such a good worker, and a nice, polite little woman. Before we left I gave her my house key and asked her to do a bit of spring-cleaning. My dear, the place has never been so spotless. I must remember to give her a decent tip the next time she comes to me.'

'She sounds a treasure. Did you get her through an agency?'

'No. A friend's recommendation. Much the best way.'

* * *

'Went well, don't you think?'

Marigold, brushing her hair before the dressing-table mirror, watched the reflection of her husband as he came back from the bathroom and walked across the room towards the bed. He was wearing his pyjama bottoms. Without replying, he sat down on the side of the bed and bent forward to remove his slippers.

'Richard's all right, but that wife of his . . .' He dropped one slipper and then the other on to the dark green carpet.

Marigold's brush strokes slowed. 'Why? What's wrong with Susan?'

'Too damned bossy.' Ian pulled a face. 'Didn't you tell me she's involved in several charities? I can just imagine her chairing meetings.'

He yawned. 'She was determined to get us to go to Italy. Just because *she* enjoyed herself doesn't mean we would.'

Marigold put her hairbrush down. 'We enjoyed it the last time we went.'

'That was ages ago. I wouldn't want to go back to Tuscany. Half the villas there are owned by English people now.'

'Susan wasn't talking about Tuscany. From her conversation, I gathered that the Piedmont region is relatively unspoilt.'

'Maybe.' Ian yawned again. 'Are you going to be long?'

She stared at him through the mirror. 'Can't we manage a short holiday, Ian?'

He scowled. 'Oh, for God's sake, don't start that again.'

'I know you're busy, but there used to be more to life than work.' Marigold twisted round on her stool and faced him. 'Just take a moment to think about our last trip to Italy.' Her voice sank to a whisper. 'Remember standing beneath the clock tower in Venice, waiting for the figures of the Three Magi to appear? Remember the day we got lost? We ended up spending the night in that tiny little hotel high in the mountains. We enjoyed being in each other's company then.'

He stared at her. 'What brought this on?'

She shrugged. 'Listening to Susan's account of their holiday, I suppose.'

There was a moment's silence and then he cleared his throat, and asked, 'Is that a new nightgown? I don't remember seeing it before.'

She put her hand up to her throat and the colour deepened in her cheeks. 'I treated myself last Christmas, but this is the first time I've worn it. Do you like it?'

His eyes narrowed. 'It suits you.'

It did. She knew it. The nightdress was silk and a pale peachy colour which enhanced her creamy skin tones. She watched Ian's face, saw his gaze move down from her face and knew he was looking at the swell of her breasts which were clearly outlined by the garment's low-cut neckline. She felt her body glow with embarrassment. Her usual night attire was cotton pyjamas.

She felt awkward and rather silly, but when Ian looked back at her face and she saw the change in his expression, the heat of her embarrassment changed into something else. She held out her hand to him.

'Ian?'

He took a step towards her.

The telephone shrilled.

The sigh caught in her throat. 'Please, Ian. Leave it.'

He turned his head.

'Please. Just ignore it.'

'It could be the Bursar. I won't be a moment.'

'Ian . . .'

He had already left the room.

Five minutes later he was back, bounding into the bedroom, his face alight with pleasure.

'It was Karen. She's coming home next weekend. There's

been a delay, something to do with a magazine shoot. Anyway, she'll be able to stay for three or four days. Isn't that fantastic?'

Grinning, he strode over to the bed and jumped in. He turned round, plumped up his pillows and then picked up his book from the bedside table and opened it.

Marigold stood up, went to the doorway and switched off the centre light and then she walked to the bed and climbed in next to him. She slid down beneath the covers.

He glanced down at her. 'Not reading tonight?'

'No. I'm tired.' She closed her eyes and turned her face away.

'I won't be long.' He turned over a page of the book.

Chapter Four

The morning was dull and rainy but in the afternoon of the day Karen was expected, as if on cue, the sun came out. Marigold had been glancing out of the windows every half hour or so. When she saw an expensive-looking car slow down and then stop outside her home she first checked that the driver was indeed her daughter and then she rushed downstairs and out of the house. Her own enthusiasm surprised and pleased her.

She had awaited Karen's visit with apprehension because, although she was the mother, Karen had always been Ian's child. From the moment Ian had gazed into the newborn eyes of his daughter he had been besotted by her, and by the time the child was a year old, she had known it. By her second birthday, the pattern had been set – Karen the goddess, Ian the worshipper and Marigold the maid-of-work. Many years later, when Karen had moved out of the family home, Ian had been distraught and Marigold secretly delighted, but today, now that Karen was actually here, she couldn't wait to see her.

'Hi, Mum.'

When Marigold reached the car, Karen was already standing on the pavement, bent over and rummaging around in the back seat. She grabbed hold of a black leather vanity case then turned to look at her mother. 'How's things?'

Marigold took a moment to respond. As always, when face

to face with her daughter, she realised *why* Karen was a top model. There were hundreds of young and beautiful girls around, but only a few had the charisma that Karen possessed. That's why numerous photographs of her appeared in glossy magazines and newspapers. Whether she was portraying a sultry siren in black leather or posing serene and ladylike in a society ballgown, it was obvious the camera loved her. And now, away from the camera, dressed in a plain white shirt, jeans and boots, she still looked fabulous.

Marigold clasped her hands together. 'I'm fine. I don't need to ask how you are. You look terrific.' Her gaze went to the car. 'How long have you had this'?'

'Two months. Do you like it?'

'It's . . . impressive. But so was the other one you had. Why change so soon?'

'You have to move with the times, Mum.' Karen raised her eyebrows. 'It's to do with image.'

'Really.' Marigold studied the car again.

'It's a new version of the SLK roadster.' Karen rested her hand on the car for a moment, a proprietary gesture, and then looked towards the house.

'What's keeping Dad? I want him to bring the rest of my stuff in.'

'He's at the university. Rang twenty minutes ago to see if you'd arrived. He'll be home shortly.'

Karen pouted. 'I hope so. I've heaps to tell him.' With the back of her hand she swept her waterfall of straight blonde hair back from her face.

'Why have you brought so much luggage? I thought you were only staying three days?'

'That's right, but I've brought a few glad rags with me.' A smile spread across Karen's face. 'You know what Dad's like. I expect he'll want to show me off a bit.' She gave an exaggerated shiver. 'And I've packed some big sweaters. Yorkshire always feels so cold.'

'It's not cold today. And you've only come from London.' A little of Marigold's glow of welcome had ebbed away.

'Yeah, maybe so, but I was in Spain last week.' Karen headed towards the house. 'I hope you've got the heating on.'

Marigold glanced back at the car before following her. 'Don't you think you should garage that. For safety's sake?'

'I want Dad to see it first. He'll be green with envy of course, but also puffed up with pride.' Karen opened the front door and went into the house. She flashed a smile at her mother, dispelling any suspicion of rancour. 'You should have seen the expressions on the faces of the guys I cut up on the motorway.'

In the hallway she put down her case and shivered, wrapping her arms around her body. 'God, it's like Siberia. Can we have the heating up, please?'

Lips compressed, Marigold nodded. She opened the door to the kitchen and a large, black whirlwind rushed out.

It raced to Karen and wreathed its body around her.

'Hiya, Paddy.' She scratched his ears and looking over him, said to Marigold, 'All right if I take a bath?' And then, pushing Paddy away, 'Ouch, mind my feet.'

'But wouldn't you like a coffee first? I thought we could have a little chat?'

'I'd rather have a bath. And we'll be talking later, won't we, when Dad gets in.' Karen was already halfway up the staircase. She looked back at Marigold and Paddy. 'That dog's getting much too fat. You should cut his rations.' She ran up the last few steps and disappeared from view.

Paddy whined and sat back on his haunches. Marigold saw his ears had drooped. She grimaced at him and said, 'You really shouldn't have such high expectations.'

* * *

Karen was still upstairs when the door banged, signifying that Ian had returned home. Marigold glanced at her watch. Just after five, two hours earlier than his usual time of seven p.m. She went into the sitting room and poured out two dry sherries. He came rushing in.

'Where is she? Surely she's arrived by now.'

'She's upstairs. Still in the bathroom, I think.'

'Oh.' He stood on the blue hearthrug, looking undecided. 'Has she been here long?'

She put a sherry glass in his unresisting hand. 'About an hour. All the hot water will be used up, I expect. You'll have to shower.'

He shrugged away such trivialities. 'How does she look?'

'Fabulous, as always.'

He smiled. 'Might take her along to the golf club tomorrow lunchtime. One or two of the newer members are dying to meet her.'

Marigold nodded and sipped at her sherry.

Ian looked at his watch. 'What time are we eating?'

'Around seven. Oh, did you get the wine?'

'Yes. Two bottles. By the way, did she manage to get her car in the garage? Some idiot's parked a flash-looking sports car right across our driveway. I've had to leave mine at the end of the road.'

'The "flash-looking" car, as you call it, is your daughter's latest acquisition.'

'What!' Ian whistled. 'It must have cost a fortune.' He glowered at Marigold. 'She never told me she was going to change her car. Did she tell you?'

'When does Karen tell me anything?' With only a suspicion of a bang, Marigold put down her sherry glass. 'By the way, she's left some luggage in the boot of the car. She wants you to bring it in for her. Car keys over there.' She gestured to a cabinet on the far side of the room.

'I'll go now.' Ian drained his sherry glass, put it down, picked up the keys and walked towards the door. 'I'll take them up to her bedroom.' He hesitated. 'Dare I put her car in the garage, do you think?'

When Marigold shrugged, he left the room. As soon as he had gone, she went to open one of the casement windows. The room felt unpleasantly warm.

Ian brought in the suitcases. She heard him manhandle them up the stairs and into Karen's bedroom. She heard a click as the bathroom door opened and then excited laughter and animated greetings. She waited to see if husband and daughter were coming downstairs but after a moment, she picked up the sherry glasses and carried them through to the kitchen. There, she washed and dried them. Returning through the hall, she heard Ian telling some tale or other and Karen laughing and joining in. It sounded as though they were in Karen's bedroom, so Marigold decided she might as well go back to the kitchen to prepare the evening meal.

Twenty minutes later, Ian joined her. His eyes were sparkling and his face was animated. Marigold wished she could have a similar effect on him.

'She's explained about the car. She was given an unexpected bonus and decided to splash out. I told her she was an idiot, that model will *eat* money, but she just laughed and told me she could afford it. She looks great, doesn't she?'

'Yes.' Marigold continued to chop the fresh flat-leaf parsley. She was preparing one of her favourite pasta dishes, one that Karen also enjoyed. Ian wasn't too keen on it but she knew he would not complain tonight.

She asked, 'Did you mention visiting the golf club?'

'Yes. She pulled a bit of a face but then she laughed and said OK. She knows I enjoy showing her off.'

'What time are you going?'

'Oh, about noon.'

'Right. I'll come with you.'

'You?' Ian's mouth fell open, then quickly closed. 'Well, yes, of course you can come. Only, I thought you didn't like visiting the golf club?'

'Usually I don't, but as Karen's here, we can make it a family occasion. She's my daughter too, you know.'

'Of course she is.' Ian turned his head, noticed the bottles of wine. 'I'll open these, shall I? Give them time to breathe.'

'Yes, please.'

Marigold put the chopping board to one side and, with a certain flourish, opened a kitchen cupboard and produced a packet of rigatoni and two large aubergines.

'Anything else you want doing?'

'No, thanks.'

As Ian left the kitchen, Marigold winked at Paddy who was sitting beneath the kitchen table, nose twitching at the aroma of chopped-up bacon rashers.

'Change of tactics, Paddy.' She picked up the plate containing the bacon and walked towards the fridge.

Paddy moaned softly.

She looked at him. 'Karen's right. You are getting fat.'

He thumped his tail.

'Ah, well.' She shook her head and fed him a small piece of bacon. 'We can't all be perfect.'

Over dinner, Karen told her parents the events of the last few months. As she was not the kind of daughter who telephoned home once a week, they listened avidly. She spoke mostly about her career, her trips abroad, the people she met. Ian questioned her eagerly about the celebrities she had encountered at charity shows or at parties. What were they really like? Were they witty, good company? Or were they bores? Listening, Marigold was amazed at his interest. She couldn't understand his sudden curiosity in the media world.

She enjoyed Karen's stories but she wished her daughter spoke more of her personal life. It would be nice to know whether or not Karen was truly happy with her hectic life or whether she was secretly hoping for a change of direction. Six years in modelling was a long time. Would she soon begin to think of finding a permanent partner and settling down? And so she listened intently as Karen chattered on.

Karen's last trip abroad had been to Andalusia. She and two other girls had been filmed in various locations wearing the clothes of an up-and-coming designer who had previously worked for Calvin Klein.

'He's good. Most male dress designers hate women, you know, try and make them look freaky, but Mac designs *pretty* clothes, very sexy and flirty.'

Karen grinned at her father's expression. 'It's true. Didn't you realise that? They try and make us look ridiculous and then laugh behind their hands when silly fat old biddies spend a fortune trying to look like us. Most of them prefer their boyfriends.'

She held out her glass for more wine and as Ian refilled it, she chattered on.

'The first day we were filming out in the sticks, at a place whose name I can't pronounce. We posed beside some grotty buildings with chickens running around our feet and a sweeping backcloth of mountains. The old men, the peasants, didn't know what to think of us. They were torn between desire and disgust. They were appalled at the amount of flesh we showed but they were itching to get their hands on us, you could see it in their eyes. They hung around all day, watching us.' She shivered.

'Fortunately, we moved on to The Alhambra and that was like the Arabian Nights, absolutely dripping with ostentatious luxury.'

She put down her wine glass and spread out her arms. 'Masses of marble and coloured glass everywhere, fountains, and the constant splash of running water. It was brilliant.'

Watching the different expressions rippling over Karen's expressive features, Marigold thought, it's no wonder men chase after her. Would one eventually catch her, or was Karen's self-esteem so complete she had no need of a constant companion?

'Speaking of running water,' Ian's voice held a note of heavy jocularity. 'Don't you dare run off all the hot water tomorrow. You know I hate showering.'

'Poor old thing.' Karen pushed her chair closer to her father's chair and threw her arm around his shoulders. 'Sorry. Will you forgive your little girl?'

Marigold frowned. 'You're hardly that, Karen.'

'Oh, but she is.' Ian shook his head. 'Karen will always be my little girl.'

Marigold looked at the pair of them. Ian's face wore a fatuous grin and Karen's face was flushed. Of course – she realised that the wine was affecting them. Two bottles of good red had disappeared and she had only drunk a glassful. She got up. 'Time for coffee, I think.'

They went to the golf club in Karen's new car. Ian was allowed to drive. Karen sat beside him, radiant in a floaty and flirtatious multi-coloured skirt made of georgette. Above the skirt she wore a black silk waistcoat, which was low-cut and hugged her figure. Somehow she managed to look both sexy and demure. On her feet were flat, black-suede pumps. Whenever Ian spoke to her she laughed and shook out her long, blonde hair and Marigold decided that today her daughter was re-creating the role of Cinderella. A wide-eyed waif, innocent of the effect her beauty had on the male onlookers.

It was lonely sitting in the back of the car. Marigold felt self conscious as they swept up the winding drive to the clubhouse. She felt as though she should be wearing long white gloves and bowing and moving her hand up and down, much as the Queen did when she was acknowledging her subjects through the glass of one of the state coaches. Poor old Queen, she didn't have much luck with her kids, and she had four of them.

She was jolted from her thoughts when the car came to a clumsy stop.

Ian got out, bustled around and then actually came round to open the door for her. Perhaps the opulent car had steered his thoughts along the same lines as hers? Trying to appear queenly, Mari stepped out.

It was ages since she'd visited the clubhouse. Some years ago, she had considering taking up golf – indeed, she had paid for lessons and enjoyed them – but when she found out about the club rules, she had stopped going. The male members of the golf club had finally allowed women members but they made sure they knew their place. Females were allowed to play between certain hours on Tuesday, Wednesday and Thursday but they couldn't play at all during the weekends. And the admittance rules at the clubhouse were equally strict. Women could only use the main bar and dining room when accompanied by male partners and on Sundays, they were not allowed in at all.

'Frightened they'll miss out on their roast beef and Yorkshire pud?' Marigold had asked Ian.

He had looked uncomfortable. 'Don't be sarcastic. It's not my fault – it's traditional.'

She had said no more because it wasn't his fault and she knew that lately, she was using the weapon of sarcasm far too often. The more Ian ignored her, the more hurt she experienced, the more sarcastic she became. A foolish game of tit for tat was developing in which there could be no winner.

Today was the first day she had been back to the clubhouse

in over a year. Some members, knowing her views, would not be pleased to see her. She took a deep breath and followed Ian and Karen into the clubhouse bar.

Heads turned and conversation hushed as they entered. Ian had taken hold of Karen's hand, leading her forward like a circus ringmaster presenting his top act. There was an appropriate response. Greetings from various groups seated at the tables, a murmur of appreciation and a little surge of bodies towards them.

Ian bridled with pleasure. He smiled and waved to certain individuals. 'Hello, Terry. Did you win today? Come and meet my daughter. Simon! I told you I'd bring her along to meet you, you old reprobate. Now watch your manners. Karen's used to meeting gentlemen, you know.' He put his arm around Karen's shoulders. 'How about some drinks, love?'

A small crowd formed. One or two people smiled at Marigold as they pushed past her but they didn't know her and she didn't know them. She stepped backwards and wondered at their eagerness to reach Ian and be introduced to Karen. She was lovely, of course. They had probably seen her photograph in magazines, but she was just a model. She wasn't Meryl Streep or Emma Thompson.

Someone jostled her and Marigold drew in her breath and thought, my poor girl, but peering through the knot of admirers, she saw that Karen was enjoying herself. Head thrown back, greeny-blue eyes wide open, she was playing it for all she was worth.

Marigold waved her hand, trying to attract Ian's attention, but he was too busy to notice his wife had been pushed to the back of the crowd, so she side-stepped someone's feet and went to sit on one of the stools at the bar. She called to the bartender and when he managed to drag his eyes away from Karen and came to serve her, she asked for a gin and tonic.

He brought her order and she picked up the glass and drank. 'Are you related to that vision over there?'

Marigold jumped at the question. She turned to put a face to the deep brown voice.

He was a middle-aged man sitting on his own at the very end of the bar. He sat badly, his shoulders hunched inside his well-cut, but well-worn cord jacket. His thick brown hair was turning grey. His face was wide, his features blunt and his eyes were dark blue. He was staring at her, a thoughtful look in those blue eyes.

All this she saw in a moment, and what she saw intrigued her. A man who worked outdoors, she decided, observing the light tan on his face. A forester, perhaps, or a farmer. A brown man, but not a golfer.

'You're staring,' he said. There was mild reproof as well as amusement in his voice.

'Sorry.' She blinked and then blushed. 'I don't know why I stared.' But still she studied him. 'You're not a golfer?'

He laughed. 'No. Does it matter?'

'Not at all. I'm not one, either. I did think of joining, but I decided against it.'

I'm babbling, she thought. She gave him a brief smile then glanced back at Ian and Karen. A few people had returned to their tables but her husband and her child were still surrounded by people. Marigold felt a moment's sadness when she realised neither of them had missed her.

She turned back to her drink and tried to remember the brown man's question. Oh, yes. She looked back at him.

'The vision, as you call her, is my daughter. She's a well-known model. She lives in London. She's home for the weekend and my husband likes to show her off. Quite understandable, don't you think?'

'Oh, yes. But why are you sitting here, on your own?'

Marigold shrugged. 'I don't like a lot of fuss.'

'Well, in that case, if you've finished your drink, why don't we go outside for a stroll?'

'Oh, I can't do that. They'll miss me and . . .' She blushed again. She had been going to say that she didn't know him, but it sounded so Victorian.

He stood up, walked over to her and caught hold of her elbow, lightly, so she didn't feel threatened. 'Oh, come on. I'm bored, you're bored, and I promise I won't drag you off to the fifteenth hole and molest you. If you like, I'll show you what I've been working on.' He laughed at the expression on her face. 'You're right. I'm no golfer. I came here this morning to help my friend. He's the groundsman here. We've been laying new turf on the greens.'

Almost before she realised, Marigold found herself walking with him towards the French windows that led out into the terrace gardens.

'Then you're a gardener?'

'Sorry, but no.' He shook his head. 'I was just returning a favour today. My real work is restoring old furniture. I have a shop in The Shambles.' They stepped outside and both stopped to breathe in the fresh air. A breeze ruffled Marigold's hair and she put up her hand and then let it fall. What did it matter if she looked untidy? And yet somehow it did and again she realised how much she was aware of the man standing next to her.

'There's where I was working.' He pointed, then turned and looked down at her. 'That's better?'

'What is?'

'You. You've relaxed.'

She was surprised and also touched by this stranger's perception. 'I feel more relaxed. Coming here today was rather an ordeal for me.'

'Why is that?'

54

'On my last visit, I left under a cloud. Apparently I was overheard telling someone that the committee was a gang of old fogies.'

He smiled. 'Is that all?'

'Believe me, it's enough.' She smiled back at him.

'So what made you return?'

'Ian, my husband, is still a member and although he hasn't the time to play often, he did want to bring Karen, so—' She shrugged her shoulders. 'I thought I'd come too.'

'I can understand his motives. She's a beautiful girl. He must be proud of her.'

'Yes. He loves her very much.' Marigold watched a magpie strut cheekily through a sand bunker.

'He's a lucky man to have such an attractive wife and daughter.'

'Oh, please . . .' She turned her head towards him, an impatient movement. 'You can hardly compare us.'

'I wasn't doing that. Your daughter is, as I have already said, beautiful, but speaking as a mature male, *you* would be the one I would ask out to lunch – if you were unattached, of course.'

Her eyes widened in surprise. 'What did you . . . ?'

The door behind them creaked as it opened and both of them turned round. Karen appeared and looked at her mother inquiringly.

'So there you are. We wondered where you had gone to. We've decided to run over to The Green Dragon for lunch, instead of staying here. There's a gang of about eight going. Dad asked me to find you. We'll have to get our skates on.'

'Yes, all right. I'm coming.' Conscious of her flushed cheeks, Marigold smiled apologetically.

She looked at the man. 'Sorry, have to go.'

He nodded. There was an amused look on his face.

But still she lingered, reluctant to leave. 'Good luck with the furniture business.'

'Thanks.'

'Perhaps you'd like to come with us?' Karen's eyes were huge with curiosity. She glanced from her mother to the stranger.

'No, I'm afraid I can't today. But I hope you enjoy your meal.'

He turned to allow the two women to go back into the bar.

'Mum, who was that? Have you been holding out on Dad?'

'Don't be silly.' Glancing back, Marigold saw the stranger had not followed them back into the room. 'He was just a passing acquaintance, Karen.' Marigold smiled what she hoped was an enigmatic smile and basked in the rays of Karen's shocked curiosity.

As she walked towards Ian and the people with him, she saw herself and Karen in one of the bar's mirrors. Karen looked fantastic, but studying her own figure, dressed in her best tan-coloured trousers and with her teal silk jacket belted around her still-slim waist, she thought, Yes, and I look pretty good, too.

Chapter Five

There was a commotion on the third floor of the hotel. Sheila, who was climbing the stairs as the lift was out of action again, paused and tried to identify the source of the disturbance. The sound of a man's angry voice and then the sobbing of a woman came from the room to the right of Sheila, in the corner of the landing next to the communal bathroom and toilet. Sheila frowned; hadn't a new couple recently moved into that room, a young couple with Irish accents?

She shrugged, climbed a couple more stairs but stopped again when she heard the next noise, a dull squashy thud, the sound of a fist hitting flesh. The sobbing choked off, leaving an ominous silence.

Sheila's eyes darkened. She hesitated, then shrugged her shoulders again and continued on her way up to the sixth floor.

On the fourth floor she passed the kitchen, which was supposedly for the use of the residents but was rarely used. The kitchen door was wide open and a strong smell of curry wafted out. Sheila wondered if the Indian woman living next to her had finally braved the insanitary conditions and cooked a meal. If she had, she was a brave woman.

Sheila permitted herself a wry smile. She and her next-door neighbour, Mrs Aliraj, were not friends – residents in bed and breakfast accommodation didn't make friends, they kept to themselves – but the recently arrived Indian woman looked pleasant enough and she was quiet.

With a bit of luck, she'd cleaned the kitchen before making her meal.

At the butcher's she had paid out nine pounds for a large steak. *Nine pounds!* Sheila closed her eyes. She must have been mad. And yet, when she thought of the prime steak nestling moist and juicy at the bottom of her shopping bag, she felt wonderful, because tonight she would be cooking for her husband. After seven weeks on the road, Mike would be back with the family. And if Mrs Aliraj hadn't already cleaned the kitchen, then she'd do it cheerfully because tonight her family would be complete again.

The dog-eared postcard had arrived by first post. *Should arrive about six p.m.,* Mike had scribbled. He wrote that a friendly lorry driver was giving him a lift. He sent his love to her and the boys and then, right at the bottom of the card, he had scrawled, *Cross your fingers – may have some good news.*

A job! Oh, God, let it be a job, she'd prayed. Mike's a good husband and a good father and he's been out of work for so long. Please let him have found a job.

Sheila wasn't sure whether she believed in God, but in the present circumstances, a prayer was worth a try. If He was up there, surely he'd be more gracious than the DHSS.

She was on the sixth floor now. She went up to her own door and tapped out the signal she had taught to Jack. She had a key in her purse but, when she was out and the boys were in, she liked them to keep the door bolted. After a moment, she heard the rattle of the chain being removed and the sound of the bolt being drawn. The door opened and she stepped inside.

'There's been a hell of a racket, Mum. We heard a woman screaming. Did you see anything when you were coming upstairs?'

She frowned. She didn't like Jack using the word 'hell' but it was more acceptable than some of the words mouthed by other children in the hotel. But more than his choice of words, she didn't like the way he looked.

Jack's rangy figure was taut as a tightrope walker's wire and his eyes were wide and gleaming with excitement. Sheila noticed, as she had before, that any disturbance, any kind of trouble excited her elder son. The knowledge troubled her, but there was nothing she could do about it. Jack was growing up fast and the way they were being forced to live, the environment they were locked into was wrong for him.

'Go on, Mum. Tell us.' He couldn't wait to hear her reply. 'You must have seen something. It sounded like someone was getting killed.'

Before answering him, she glanced over to where Billy lay, flat on his stomach on the carpet, gazing up at the television. On screen, a prehistoric monster swept another one off a tall cliff with one swing of its tail.

Billy laughed, then looked across at her. 'Hi, Mum.'

'Hello, Billy.'

Silently, she prayed the same prayer. Please God, let Mike have found a job. Then she turned towards Jack and said, 'I didn't see anything.' She put her shopping bag on the floor. 'Put the kettle on, will you?'

His figure sagged. 'You must have. Didn't you even see an ambulance coming?'

'Stop wishing misfortune on people,' she snapped. 'Do something useful. Make me a cup of tea.'

He set his jaw and looked at her coldly. 'Now what have I done? I only wondered . . .'

'Don't wonder.' Narrow-eyed she watched him as he gave an impatient shrug and then slouched towards the tiny kitchen area in the corner of the room.

He took the kettle off the gas ring and shook it. 'It's nearly empty.'

'Is it? Well, you'd better go and fill it.'

He lowered his head quickly, but not before she saw the rebellion in his eyes. He brushed past her, went out of the room and banged the door behind him.

Sheila's figure relaxed. She sat down, kicked off her shoes and thought about her elder boy. She was hard on him but it was a hardness dictated by love and their circumstances. She had to keep control. There were juvenile offenders in the courts every day. Her son was not going to be one of them.

She dismissed her worries over Jack and conjured up happier thoughts. It was a facility she had honed and developed during the last four years. She looked at her surroundings, wondering how she could brighten the place up a bit for Mike's return.

If she could rearrange the furniture? No, it was impossible. There was no space anywhere. The double bed took up one third of the room and the table, chairs, chest of drawers and TV crowded the rest. Still, she shrugged, Mike had no illusions. He knew what the place was like.

She looked back at Billy, still on his stomach, his legs waving in the air, his attention glued to the TV screen. God, she thought, how I love him. He never gave her a scrap of worry, his nature was so sunny. Her lips twisted into a rueful smile. The so-called 'experts' in the women's magazines, the ones who wrote that babies in the womb experienced the stress of their mother, didn't know what they were talking about, but she did.

Two weeks after she realised she was going to have a baby, Mike had walked into the house and told her, his face white with shock, that the firm he was working for had gone bust. At first, she hadn't believed him.

Not Waltons. They *couldn't* be closing. They were an old-established firm. They must have plenty of orders on their books. Six months ago they had taken on extra staff. How could they be closing?

Mike had dropped into his favourite chair and put his head in his hands.

'They only took on the extra staff to finish a rush job. Then a regular contractor let them down and a new customer who had promised them big business went bankrupt.'

He shrugged. 'If only I'd known earlier.' He raised his head and looked at her. 'Christ, why did I rush to borrow money to improve the house?'

Sheila was silent. She began to realise the catastrophe that had overtaken them. She stared round the handsome kitchen, the kitchen that was her pride and joy, and thought of the new shower unit and the double glazing.

'We'll manage,' she said rapidly. 'I've still got my job.' For a few months at least.

She rubbed her forehead with the heel of her hand. 'We'll work something out with the building society. After all, we've put a lot of value on this place.' Her face brightened. 'I saw something in the papers; doesn't the DHSS help pay the mortgage interest if you're unemployed? Anyway, you'll get another job, Mike.'

Sheila sighed and studied the back of Billy's head, his mop of blond hair which last week had been fashionably cut into a wedge. He had been a big baby. In the sixth month of her pregnancy she had been huge. She had also been perpetually tired, worn out with worry about Mike's state of mind and about the future. She had tried to save their home.

She had written letters – Mike was no good at that – to their insurance company, to housing trusts and mostly, to their building society.

At first, the man she saw at the building society was sympathetic.

'Of course we understand your difficulties, Mrs Scott. We'll see what we can do.'

But when the DHSS refused to pay interest on the second mortgage – money borrowed for house improvements didn't count – then his smiles faded.

'You certainly took out a substantial loan. Not a wise thing to do nowadays. One should always budget for unexpected emergencies.'

And Mike had just sat there, in front of the large, mahogany desk, with a guilty look on his face, not saying a word. The only noise in the office had been his knuckles cracking as he twisted his hands together, tighter and tighter.

Perhaps unwisely, she had counterattacked.

'We were both working, with safe jobs, we thought. As to the amount of money we borrowed, you agreed it! And you're the bloody experts. You have responsibilities, too.'

The thin-faced man in the pin-striped suit had looked over his glasses at her. 'We've allowed you reduced payments, Mrs Scott, but we can't allow your debt to get out of hand. Also –' he steepled his hands '– when the original mortgage was negotiated, *your* earning capacity was taken into account. From our records –' he consulted the papers on his desk '– it is clear you stated you would remain in full-time employment. There would be no more children.'

That had shut her up. She had sat back in her chair, unable and unwilling to explain to this man the circumstances of Billy's conception. When she and Mike had signed the mortgage forms, the doctors had told them there would be no more children.

But then, miraculously, she had found the doctors had been wrong and she *was* pregnant again and even though her doctor had pulled a long face and warned that pregnancy would be difficult and the birth even more so, nothing had dented their joy.

62

But the doctors had been right about a difficult pregnancy and she had been forced to give up work almost immediately. Six weeks after that, Waltons had shut down for good. Such a small firm couldn't pay much in the way of redundancy, certainly not enough to satisfy the building society, and so they had lost their home.

Living as they did now, Sheila often cursed the impulse that made them blithely rip out the fixtures of their little home and try and turn the place into a palace. Lord, what fools they had been. She stirred in her chair. But they would never regret having Billy. They wouldn't swap Billy for Buckingham Palace.

Another thought struck her. Her younger son had been sleeping with her for over a week. The man living in the room to the left of them had screamed his head off one Saturday night, probably on a bad trip after using weird dope, and Billy had been terrified. Well, he'd have to move back in with Jack. He wouldn't like it, and neither would Jack, but there was no alternative. Jack's bedroom, a curtained-off cubbyhole adjoining the main room, contained a three-quarter bed and a wardrobe. When both boys slept in the bed, Jack occupied the top half and Billy slept at the bottom.

They'd moan, but they'd have to put up with it. She loved her children more than life itself, but the next few days belonged to her and Mike. Sheila closed her eyes and wrapped her arms around herself. Oh, how she'd missed him. Now she knew he was on his way home, she ached for him, his touch, the smell of him.

Jack barged into the room with the filled kettle. She opened her eyes and saw him giving her a curious look. She turned her head away, conscious of the blush on her cheeks. As he took down matches from a high shelf, where Billy couldn't reach, and lit the gas ring, she knelt down and rummaged beneath the bed, partly to give herself time to gain her composure but also to search for something. Ah, there it was. Her fingers touched the outline of a large cardboard box. She pulled it out into the light. She opened the top and pushing tissue paper aside, lifted out a stack of china dinner plates.

Jack had made the tea. He took out the teabag and brought the mug to his mother.

'Dinner plates. We're not using them, are we? I thought we were having a pizza tonight?'

She grinned up at him and the sheer pleasure showing on her face caused his surly look to disintegrate. He almost smiled back at her.

'Oh, no, Jack. No pizza tonight. I've good news. Your dad's coming home. He'll be back this evening so we're celebrating.' She paused. 'Tonight, Jack, we're eating steak, and we're eating it off proper china plates.'

'That was grand, pet.'

It was half past nine that evening and Mike was sitting in the one easy chair cuddling Sheila who was perched on his knee. Both boys were in bed.

'Yes, it was.' Happy and flushed with success for the meal had been lovely despite the lousy cooker, Sheila sighed and snuggled even closer to her husband. She had undone the top buttons of his shirt and now she lazily trailed her fingertips across his bare chest.

'It's so good to be back with you all.' Mike gave a contented sigh and rested his head against the cushioned back of the chair. 'This place isn't much, I know, but if you'd seen some of the flop houses I've slept in . . .' He rubbed his nose. 'And that meal! How you managed a meal like that in that foul kitchen . . .'

She twisted round to face him. 'It wasn't so foul when I began cooking, Mike. I scrubbed and disinfected the working surfaces before I started and I washed the floor. I couldn't do much with the cooker but I put foil over . . .'

Smilingly, he tugged at her hair. 'Calm down. I'm not worrying. I know your high standards.'

'You don't have to have high standards to avoid that kitchen.' Sheila flopped back against his chest. 'That's why I normally buy in food for us to eat. I know the boys shouldn't have junk food all the time, but there's no alternative. No one uses that kitchen, not even the nuts and the hard cases.'

'What hard cases?' Mike had been stroking her hair but now he stopped. He stared down at her, trying to read her face. 'When I left it was just families with children staying here. Has that changed? What kind of people are staying here now?'

'Not too bad.' Sheila mentally crossed her fingers. 'There's a few couples and about five or six single chaps but they don't bother anyone. Everyone keeps themself to themself. It's sort of an unwritten law. Whatever happens, even if it happens next door to you, you don't get involved.'

She sighed. 'It's sad, really. There's a woman on the floor below, moved in three weeks ago, who has two kids around Billy's age. I see them coming in and going out with their mum but that's all. We've never spoken. I keep thinking how nice it would be if Billy could play with them sometimes.'

'Why don't you suggest it, then? Apart from the kids being company for each other, you and she could help each other out. Maybe babysit from time to time so you could get away from this dump for a couple of hours.'

'Oh, no.' Sheila shook her head, thinking that although Mike had spent some time in the hotel, he really had no idea what it was like to live in bed and breakfast accommodation. 'It doesn't work like that, Mike. Everyone here has problems, lots of them. They dare not make friends because they want no involvement in anyone else's troubles, so they come in, hurry to their own room and stay there, usually with the door locked.'

'Ah, well, maybe that's wise. There's so much coming and going.' Mike shifted into a more comfortable position. 'I didn't want to say anything until the lads went to bed, Sheila, but I'm hoping we'll be out of here soon. On Monday, I'll find out whether or not I've landed a job. A proper job, full-time working.'

Sheila sat up straight. 'Oh, Mike, that's wonderful. I've been dying to ask about your message on the postcard, but I just couldn't. I hardly dare hope . . .' She clasped her hands together. 'Tell me everything.'

He smiled, but his first words held caution. 'It's not certain. The firm had loads of applications but three of us were short-listed. I met the other two guys. They were a bit younger than me and pretty smart but I've more experience than them.'

He told Sheila all about his interview and ended, 'I think I made a good impression.'

'And they're going to contact you here, on Monday?'

'Yes. They said they needed a permanent address for me so I gave them this one. I was bloody worried, I can tell you. I hadn't the train fare to come home but then this lorry driver offered me a lift.'

'So the job was the only thing that brought you home?' Sheila pretended to be angry but the smile on her face gave her away.

Mike gave her a smacking kiss. 'I'd have been back every weekend if I could have afforded the fare.'

'I know.' She kissed him back and then said, slyly, 'I think the boys will be asleep by now, don't you?'

'God, I hope so.'

'I'll check.' She slid from his knee and went and peeped round the curtain dividing the boys' sleeping area from the main room.

When she nodded, Mike got up, went to her and slid his arms around her waist. She turned to face him and they kissed. When he released her they were both breathing quickly.

He smiled down at her. 'Are they both still heavy sleepers?'

'Yes.' She laughed.

'Good.' He caught hold of her hand and led her towards the bed.

Sunday morning, they all slept late. When they awoke, Jack was dispatched down to the ground floor lobby to collect their breakfasts. He came back with four carrier bags. Relocking the door behind him, Jack kicked off his shoes and bounced back on to his parents' bed. He distributed the plastic bags.

Mike looked inside his bag. He saw two bread buns, a foil-wrapped, square-shaped pat of butter and two plastic packs, one containing jam and one marmalade.

'Bloody hell.' He tipped the contents of the bag on to the bed.

Sheila, who was now out of the bed and lighting the gas ring, asked, 'What's the matter?'

'This is.' Her husband's face was outraged. 'I'd forgotten, you know. I'd forgotten all this crap.'

Sheila's forehead creased and she sent him a warning look that he ignored.

'Tell me, Sheila. How much money does the council pay out to keep us in places like this?'

Her frown deepened. 'How do I know? Some people, the newspapers for instance, say hundreds of thousands of pounds.'

Mike groaned in anguish. 'Christ! Why couldn't they have used that money to build more council houses? No one should live like this, Sheila, especially with little kids.'

Tight-lipped, Sheila handed him a mug of tea. 'Don't you think I know? But this is not the time to talk about it.' She gave a little nod towards the boys and then asked, 'What shall we do today?'

Mike lowered his head and after a pause, Sheila asked her

sons, 'What would you two like to do?'

After various suggestions, impossible because they didn't have a car, it was decided they would take a trip on a river boat.

'And then, if you're good, I'll take you to McDonald's,' said Mike.

They enjoyed their boat trip but it didn't last long and when they had disembarked, Jack asked, 'Can we do something else?'

'Like what?' Mike's voice was cautious.

Sheila looked at him, guessing rightly that funds were low.

'Let's go to the Jorvik Centre. Most of the kids at school have been. They say it's great. You sit in little cars and go back through the past to Viking York. Phil West said there's proper sounds, like battles being fought and dogs fighting. There's even horrible smells, like rotting food and the place they used as a toilet.'

Mike pulled a face, Billy grinned and Sheila laughed, but then she looked thoughtful. She had often passed the site of the Viking excavation and once or twice she had stood on the wooden viewing platform and watched as layer after layer of York's past had been uncovered. It would be nice to see the finished result.

'We could go and see, Mike. It's becoming a well-known attraction but it shouldn't be too expensive. After all, it is a museum.'

'OK. We'll take a look.'

They went to Coppergate and joined the queue of visitors waiting to be admitted to the Jorvik Centre.

'You wait here. I'll just nip down to the entrance.' Mike walked to the beginning of the queue then walked back again. 'We might have to wait for a while.' He hesitated. 'I think it would be better if you stayed here with your mum, Jack, and I'll take Billy off to the park. He'll get bored waiting and, anyway, we're not interested in silly old Vikings, are we, Billy?'

Billy's face crumpled and he began to wail. 'It's not fair. I want to see the Vikings, too.'

Mike grabbed his hand. 'Don't start.'

Sheila saw the thin white line around his mouth.

There was a pause during which Billy's wails grew louder.

'Oh, shut it, Billy. We'll *all* go to the park.'

Surprised, Sheila looked round at her first-born. Of course, *she* had realised Mike couldn't afford the admission fees but she hadn't expected Jack to be so perceptive.

'It's too busy today. We'd have to hang around for ages.' Jack was addressing his brother. 'And when we got in, it would be so crowded we wouldn't see anything. We can come again another day.'

Billy's wails diminished. He scrubbed his eyes with his fists. 'But I wanted to see the smells.'

He looked surprised when they all laughed, but he stopped crying.

'I'm hungry,' he said.

'Then we'll go to McDonald's first, and then go on to the park.' Mike looked at Sheila who nodded.

They set off, the two boys running ahead of their parents.

Sheila linked her arm through her husband's. 'Jack handled that well, didn't he?' She waited for Mike to speak and when he did not, she gave his arm a little shake. 'Don't look so grim.'

'Why not? I feel grim. First time I've seen my kids since God knows when and I can't afford to give them a treat.' He sighed.

'Oh, Mike. It's a treat just seeing you. Anyway,' she smiled at him. 'You are giving them a treat. They love going to McDonald's.' She shook her head. 'I wish I could say the same.'

Reluctantly, he grinned. 'Not a beefburger or cheeseburger fan, are you?'

She pulled a face.

He touched her hair with his free hand. 'Never mind, we'll have our treat later.'

That night, after lovemaking, she and Mike talked.

'I'm sorry you've had to cope single handed with the boys, Sheila. I know it's hard for you, living like this, but things will change for the better, I'm sure of it.'

'Hush.' She pressed her fingers against his lips.

Mike slid his arm around her. 'If I get this job we'll save up and get us a proper home. And . . . Jesus!' He sat up in bed. 'What is that?'

They listened to the chorus of shrieking voices and the thud of drums.

'Heavy Metal.' Sheila's reply was a mixture of laughter and tears. 'Heavy Metal, that's what it is. It's the guy who's moved in next door. He puts his records on when he's been to the pub.'

'But it's ear splitting.'

'I know. That's one of the reasons I have bags under my eyes.'

He gave her an unseeing look, then threw back the bedcovers and swung his legs down to the floor. 'I'm not putting up with this.'

'No, please.' Sheila grabbed hold of his arm. 'It's not every night. Maybe one or two nights a week.' Realising Mike was not listening to her, she hung on to his wrist. 'Remember what I said, Mike. I don't want to fall out with anyone.'

'But this is ridiculous. What about the kids?'

'Jack would sleep through an earthquake and Billy . . .'

As if on cue the curtain screening off the boys' bedroom twitched.

'Mum.' A small figure in striped pyjamas scooted over to stand by their bed. 'Mum, I'm scared.'

Sheila sighed and let go of her husband's wrist. 'Put the light on, love.'

Mike got out of bed to do so and Sheila held out her arms to

Billy. 'Come in for a cuddle, then.' She glanced over to Mike. 'Sorry about this.'

'Don't worry.' Mike's face had softened as he looked at her with Billy.

'And you won't go next door?'

'Not if you don't want me to.' He came back to bed.

An hour later the music stopped and ten minutes after that, Mike and Sheila were fast asleep. Billy had been asleep for some considerable time.

Next morning, Mike woke up with a crick in his neck. He tried to roll over and found that Billy was clamped to his back like a limpet. Despite his stiffness, he smiled as he got out of bed.

Without waking Sheila he dressed and let himself out of the room. He hurried down the stairs to see if there was any post for him.

There was no one around in the lobby but on the reception desk lay a long white envelope. Mike picked it up. It was addressed to him.

Chapter Six

On a sunny June morning, three weeks after Karen's visit, Marigold began the day in a purposeful mood. After Ian left the house, she washed up the breakfast things, tidied the house and then ran upstairs to put on her new leotard. It was exercise time.

The leotard was functional and dark blue in colour. Marigold studied her appearance in the long mirror fitted in the wardrobe door. She pulled in her stomach. Not too bad. Anyway, it wasn't as if she was going to a fitness centre. No one would see her.

She went downstairs and shut Paddy in the kitchen. Three days ago, when she attempted her yoga exercises for the first time, Paddy had pushed open the door leading to the sitting room, raced in and jumped all over her, delighted with this new game. She was struggling with 'the plough' at the time and so the pair of them landed in a tangled heap on the floor. Paddy was now banned.

Marigold sat cross-legged on the sitting room carpet and opened her book. She read through the list of advantages to be gained from practising yoga on a regular basis.

Removal of mental strain and tension.
Improvement of shape.
Regained agility and look of youth.
Cure of back problems.

Increased knowledge of your own sensuality. (Marigold grimaced.)

Ability to stay relaxed under pressure.

She closed the book and sighed. If only . . . Still, she must think positively.

First, relaxation.

She lay flat on her back and shut her eyes; she breathed slowly and deeply. A few seconds later, she shifted position. God, the floor felt hard. It shouldn't, the carpet had been terribly expensive.

She tried again. That was better, her arms and legs were beginning to feel heavy but it was hard to relax her facial muscles. She realised she was clenching her teeth.

She sighed and sat up. 'The Corpse', said the book, 'is a posture that allows every muscle in the face and body to relax. Tiredness, nervous tension and anxiety will disappear.'

She *would* do it. She flopped back on the carpet and tried to make her mind a blank but despite her efforts, rebel thoughts drifted in and out of her consciousness.

Some time today, she thought, I'll try ringing Karen. We've only spoken once since she went back to London. Despite her attempts at tranquillity, a tiny buzz of anticipation throbbed through her veins. Karen's visit home had gone more or less as Marigold had anticipated. Karen had spent most of her time with Ian, but there had actually been a few moments when the two women had communicated with each other – really communicated – and Marigold treasured the memory.

The first time had been when the three of them had driven over to Robin Hood's Bay for a visit. She and Karen had sat outside one of the pubs and while Ian was inside buying the drinks, Karen had mentioned a weekend they had stayed there, when she was five years old.

'I'm surprised you remember anything about it, Karen. It was a long time ago.'

'Oh, yes. I remember quite a few things.'

Karen reminisced about a boat trip, the cottage they had stayed in and the hours she and Marigold had spent looking for soft-backed crabs and shrimps in the rock pools. Then, suddenly, she had said, 'You were a pretty good mum, you know.'

Silenced by surprise, Marigold had remained quiet for a moment and then she had said, quietly, 'I tried to be.'

'Yes, you did.' Karen laughed. 'But I was too young to appreciate you.' She thought. 'I remember it was always Dad who did the exciting things when I was little. He fixed up surprise trips to the panto at Christmas, or to a children's show. He was always bringing presents home for me. I remember when he bought my first bicycle. I'm afraid I associate you with mainly unpleasant things, Mum. You were the one who made me go to the dentist or the doctor, stood over me when I did my homework and—' She paused. 'Washed my hair.'

'We both hated that.' Marigold's smile was grim. 'You were a little demon, screaming and scratching. You bit me once.'

'Did I? What a horrible child I was.' Karen paused. 'But I remember it was a horrible business. My hair got into such terrible tangles and snarls, despite all the brushing. It really hurt when you washed it. Why on earth did you never have it cut?'

'Your father wouldn't hear of it. He loved your long hair.'

'But you were my mother. You should have insisted.'

There was a short, uncomfortable silence and then Marigold said, mildly, 'Well, you're a grown woman now, and you still have long hair. Why didn't *you* have it cut?

'Ah, but it's part of my image now.' Karen changed the subject. 'I'd love to see the cottage we used to stay in but I don't suppose you remember which one it was.'

'Yes, I do. We'll go and see it after we've had our drinks.'

And then Ian had come out of the pub carrying a tray and their conversation had come to an end.

For the rest of Karen's visit, her father had completely monopolised her, despite the amount of work he said he had to get through, and Karen had played up to him as usual. But on the day she left, just before getting into the car, she had turned and given Marigold a swift hug.

'Thanks for having me, Mum.' She had brushed Marigold's cheek with her own. 'And now you've more time, try living a bit.'

A cheeky grin and she was gone.

Marigold thought she had pins and needles in her left foot. She sat up and rubbed the afflicted area.

That's what she *wanted* to do, live a little, but how did you set about it? Everyone she knew was settled in their old life, except . . . The image of the man she had talked to at the golf club popped into her mind. She wondered if he was settled.

She frowned and banished him from her mind. She must be constructive; mend fences, not break them. But she must find things to occupy her mind and body because this was the third time this week she had thought of the stranger. She went back to her yoga.

She'd have to shop today. There wasn't much in the freezer and Ian had rung to say he might be bringing a guest home for dinner. A colleague, he'd called him. Why did he always use the word 'colleague'? He never said he was bringing a friend. Marigold's eyes were closed. Her eyelashes quivered against her cheeks. Did Ian have any friends?

She decided to cook something quick and easy; something they could finish tomorrow if the 'colleague' didn't come. Oh dear, she was stiffening up again. Her hands had become fists. She unrolled her fingers.

Last time a colleague came, Ian hadn't even introduced him. He had taken the man into his study and then stuck his head around the kitchen door twenty minutes later and inquired why the meal was late.

Well – bollocks to him.

'Bollocks': what a lovely, vulgar word. Would she ever have the guts to say it to his face?

Marigold smoothed her face again. Relax. Think serene thoughts.

Hey, it was beginning to work. It was actually *working*. Marigold felt her jaw unlock and her forehead smooth out. She felt dreamy. She actually felt her mouth fall gently open. She was getting there.

'Missis.' There was a pounding on the French windows. 'Missis, are you all right?'

Like a released elastic band, Marigold's upper body bounced upright. She could hear her heart thumping.

An elderly man with gingery whiskers and a flat cap was peering through the French windows. There was an anxious expression on his face.

Marigold scrambled to her feet and moved so quickly towards him that her head swam. She fumbled with the window catch.

'Yes, yes. Of course I'm all right.'

He studied her face. 'You're awful pale. You're sure you're all right?'

'Yes. I've told you.'

Hearing the impatient note in her voice, the old man's face assumed an injured expression. 'You didn't look it, sprawled on the floor like that with your mouth wide open. I thought you'd had a heart attack.'

'I was doing yoga.' Marigold tried to be conciliatory. She

held out her hand. 'Want fresh water, do you?'

'That's right.' The old man handed over his bucket. He put his head on one side. 'You know, Mrs Goddard. You look a bit of all right in that swimsuit.'

As Marigold put the plastic bucket in the sink and turned on the water tap, she made a mental note to practise her yoga at a different time when it was the day that the window cleaner called.

About the same time that Mr Penny, the window cleaner, began to clean Marigold's windows, Karen Goddard was finishing a particularly rigorous workout at an exclusive fitness centre in the West End of London.

When the music tape stopped, she bent over, her hands on her knees, and took some deep breaths. Her personal coach, a handsome young man called Patrick, grinned at her and threw her a towel.

'You did well, Karen. You're in good shape.'

'I need to be, Patrick. Believe me, at this particular moment in time, I need to be in fantastic shape.'

He nodded, but he had been Karen's trainer for over a year so he knew better than to ask questions. He headed for the door. 'Book you in for the usual time on Friday?'

'Yes.' Karen slung the towel around her neck and headed off for the shower rooms. As usual, she had no time to spare.

She had needed willpower to get to the gym and exercise because the evening before she had been out on the town. Her escort had been an internationally famous hairdresser and he had taken her to a restaurant where all the beautiful people hung out. He had been an attentive host, the restaurant had been elegant and the food superb, but Karen's mood had been sombre.

For a few weeks, Karen had been nursing a secret, the best kind of secret, but now her dreams of becoming an absolutely top-line photographic model had been dashed. She felt devastated, and searching for something good about the whole experience, the only comfort she could dredge up was that she hadn't told anyone, particularly her parents. Particularly her father.

She blanched, just thinking about it. If Dad had found out, he would have broadcast the news around the whole of North Yorkshire within an hour. She could imagine him, ringing up everyone he knew and then saying casually, 'Just been chatting to Karen, my daughter. Yes, the model. Just told me – in confidence, of course – about an amazing deal she's pulled off. She's already done remarkably well, as you know. Definitely in the top ten as regards modelling in this country but now she's hitting the headlines abroad. She's been offered a top American contract. Yes, it's wonderful. After this I imagine the sky's the limit.'

It was nonsense, of course. She was doing all right. She was paid well and it was rare she was out of work, but she wasn't absolutely top line and she knew it. But given the chance, she could have been. And three weeks ago, she had thought her lucky break had arrived.

Claudia Steiner, the boss of her agency, had phoned to tell her there was a strong possibility she was about to be chosen as the cover model for a winter issue of American *Vogue* magazine.

Karen's mouth had opened and she had gaped like a fish. 'No, I don't believe it.'

'It's true. They asked for a portfolio on you a month ago. I sent one but didn't say anything to you because it was long odds. However, they rang me yesterday and said you were just what they were looking for.'

'*Yes!*' Karen came out of her daze. She punched the air in jubilation. Cover girl for American *Vogue*. It was marvellous. The breakthrough she'd been waiting for.

'Not a word.' Claudia warned. 'Don't tell anyone. I don't want the media involved at this stage. When I receive the signed contract, then we can go public.'

'Can't I just tell . . .'

'No one, Karen.' Claudia paused. 'You know enough about the fashion business to wait until the proper moment.'

Karen shrugged. 'OK.'

Thank God she had taken Claudia's advice.

Standing under the needle-fine jets of the shower, Karen sighed and mopped at her face with her hand.

For almost a month she had floated on a pink cloud of happy expectation. She was a future *Vogue* cover girl. She was going to be rich and famous at last.

And then Claudia had contacted her again, but this time her voice had been tired, heavy. 'I'm so sorry, my dear. There's no easy way to tell you this, but we've lost the *Vogue* contract. The cover earmarked for you has been given to someone else.'

'But you said it was foolproof. You said they were crazy about me.' Karen had clutched the phone with a hand that had turned freezing cold. 'Why, Claudia? What happened?'

'I asked for an explanation but all they would say is that their requirements had altered. Oh, Karen,' Claudia had sighed. 'There's nothing wrong with you, it's just bad luck. I've made inquiries and found out that they've picked up on a sensational new girl by the name of Candy Greenwell. She's just a kid. I don't know her background but apparently she's only been modelling for six or seven months.

'She was working for a small-time French designer and Ungaro's scout spotted her. He grabbed her and Ungaro used her in his latest show. The camera loved her. The press took masses of pictures, they hit the papers and now it's a nonstop roller-coaster ride for the kid. *Vogue* are taking a chance using a relatively inexperienced girl but that's how they're playing it nowadays.'

Her voice low, Karen asked, 'How old is she?'

'Seventeen.' Claudia's voice sharpened. 'Don't draw unnecessary conclusions, Karen. I wish now that I hadn't told you about the offer. I should have waited, but they were so enthusiastic and I couldn't bear to keep the good news from you. I should have known better. In the fashion business, nothing is fail-safe until the papers are signed. We've both been in the game long enough to know that.'

'It's all right. It's not your fault.'

'It's not yours, either. Remember, Karen, you're one of my top models. You're twenty-four years old and you're a classy lady who is very much in demand. You're equally good modelling clothes or working on photographic shoots, and that's rare.' Claudia hesitated. 'And you can easily pass for twenty when you're made up. I can get you any number of assignments.'

'But you can't get me on the cover of American *Vogue*.' Karen put the phone down.

And that's why, when the phone rang again and Karen was invited out to dinner, she had dressed up and gone out with a man she didn't even like. She had also eaten too much and got a little drunk. She was rude to a particularly obnoxious photographer who pestered her at the restaurant and finally arrived home at three o'clock in the morning.

At least she hadn't gone to bed with her escort – she hadn't been that drunk – and she had removed her make-up before falling into bed.

At nine a.m. she had groaned her way out of bed. In the bathroom, she stared at the shadows beneath her eyes, studied her tongue and thought about retiring but then she checked her answering machine.

At first, she couldn't concentrate on the high-pitched voice of Sally, her booker, who was talking about a possible new assignment. Karen pulled a face, cut off the message but a moment later rewound the tape and listened again because Sally was important.

Sally was the woman who looked after her at the agency. She kept Karen's 'book' which contained her portfolio of photographs and also details of Karen's height and weight. The book also held a record of Karen's modelling work and a record of her accomplishments. Sometimes a client wanted a model who could ride or swim. Sally could answer any question about Karen and she also smoothed over any difficulties when Karen was working.

This morning, Sally was excited when Karen rang her.

'A television ad, Karen, but a classy one. Plenty of financial backing. If the initial shoot goes down well with the public, then there could be a whole series of ads extending the story line. Why, you could become as famous as the Gold Blend coffee girl.'

Karen's depression began to lift.

'Do you know how many girls they're looking at?'

'Three, but you're a natural for the job, Karen. They said they were looking for an "English rose" type. Natural but stylish looks and someone with photographic experience.'

Karen wavered. 'What's the address, and the names of the interviewers?'

Sally told her.

Karen wrote it all down. She hadn't heard of the names but then, she had never worked in TV. Might be time to try it. What was the saying? When one door closes . . .

'I'll be there,' she said. 'Do I need clothes, accessories?'

'No. Everything's provided.'

'Right.'

Karen was able to go straight from the gym to the address she had been given. The place where she worked out was highly fashionable and totally equipped with everything a modern woman, or man, could need. They had more beauty aids than Karen kept at her flat. Anyway, she reckoned that if the television people were looking for an English-rose type they wouldn't expect heavy make-up.

Accordingly, she brushed her hair until it shone, used a lick of mascara on her long lashes, gloss on her lips and a light dusting of powder and she was ready.

The taxi dropped her off outside a modern block of glass-fronted offices in the heart of London. Karen looked up and was unimpressed. It was what went on inside the building that was important. The huge doors opened automatically as she walked towards the entrance but as she walked through them she saw the vigilant uniformed security guard watching her. She went up to a vast mahogany reception desk.

'May I help you?'

The receptionist was young and attractive. She could have been a model herself. She directed Karen up to the tenth floor where, in answer to her knock, a young man opened the door and took her through into a reception room.

Two girls were already there. One was about twenty. She had dark brown eyes, regular features and her chestnut-coloured hair was shiny and cut into a simple bob. Her skin was beautiful, a pale creamy colour. She had a dusting of freckles across her nose. She looked up at Karen and grinned.

'Hi. We've met before, haven't we?'

Karen nodded and smiled. 'Yes. About nine months ago, wasn't it? A Harvey Nichols shoot?'

The girl nodded. 'Bit different today.'

'Yes.'

Karen glanced towards the second model and then she looked

again. She knew at once that the kid was new to modelling. She looked vulnerable and nervous but despite that, Karen immediately saw she had great potential. Feeling a little wrench in her heart – what she wouldn't give to look like her – she spoke. 'I'm Karen. What's your name?'

The girl swallowed and then whispered, 'Sarah Fenton-Brown.'

An upper-class gal. Of course. Karen noted Sarah's long, long legs folded beneath her minuscule skirt, her unusual looks – she was handsome rather than beautiful – and her rangy, athletic body. She wondered which agency Sarah was with and why they had sent her here.

She wouldn't get this job or any other of a similar nature, but she was a natural for the catwalk. God, she could be a knockout! Handled right, she could become one of the greats.

Karen smiled and sat down resolving to remember Sarah's name. She'd mention her to Claudia.

People had the wrong idea about models. They thought they were overpaid, vain, lazy and catty, especially to each other.

They were wrong, although Karen didn't bother telling them. Models worked long hours, were incredibly self-disciplined and, on the whole, got on very well with each other. Of course, there were exceptions but they were few.

The door opened and the young man came back.

'Will you come through together, please. The photographer wants to see you in a group and then separately.'

They trooped after him into the adjoining room. Karen was five feet nine inches tall and Ellie, the girl she knew slightly, was about the same, but Sarah Fenton-Brown towered over them. She must have been six foot tall. Karen noticed how she looked down at the floor as she lined up with them and she wanted to nudge her, tell her to stand up straight and be proud.

The photographer nodded to the girls but did not speak. He

was busy setting up spotlights and cameras. Karen noticed the dozens of framed photographs hung on the walls and she looked at them with interest until the camera man muttered something to their escort and he waved them towards a sofa at the end of the room.

'We just have to wait for a few minutes. Benny will take shots of you together, as a group, and then on your own. Then he'll take some close-ups and then we'd like you to slip into the outfits behind that screen.' He waved his head.

'But in the meantime, if I can get some details about you . . .'

Karen stopped thinking about the framed photographs on the wall and about Sarah Fenton-Brown and started working.

Chapter Seven

The warm weather continued and so Marigold wore a newly bought, short-sleeved summer dress for her lunch date with Pat. The women had arranged to meet at the White Swan in Goodramgate at one o'clock but because Marigold felt the need for company she left home early. She enjoyed the drive in, but, aware of the traffic congestion in the narrow city streets, she left her car in a car park outside the walls and made her way into York via Micklegate Bar.

She walked briskly and with an upturn in spirits. She always enjoyed seeing Pat and it was good to be part of the hustle and bustle of a crowd again. As usual, York's pavements were thronged with people. Groups of tourists dawdled along, taking photographs, stopping to study guides to the city. They wandered about gazing upwards at the ancient buildings, reading the information plaques on the walls and wondering aloud at the strange names of the streets.

'Hey, Norma.' A large man, sharing the pavement with Marigold, waved his street map under the nose of his wife. He wore a stetson and a fringed leather jacket. Marigold smiled when she heard him say, 'What the hell do ya think Whip-ma-Whop-ma means?'

In between the strolling visitors dodged the inhabitants of York, housewives with their shopping bags and business men carrying briefcases, all impatient to be about their business.

Just ahead of Marigold, a tour bus pulled up and a swarm of chattering Spanish students in dark clothes with tote bags slung over their shoulders poured off the platform and dashed across the road. The traffic jolted to an impromptu halt.

A taxi pulled up close by Marigold. The window of the cab was open and she could hear the driver muttering curses but still she smiled. After the quietness of her house she was enjoying the noise and the movement of the crowded streets. She decided that, instead of visiting Mulberry Hall to buy some replacement china tableware as she had intended, she would wander at will. She would be a pretend tourist for an hour and a half.

Accordingly, she turned off the street into one of the many alleyways which form a network linking the main thoroughfares of the city. Snickelways, the locals called them. She wandered along, following her feet. It was quieter now although the hum of the traffic could be heard distantly.

She stopped, from time to time, to look through trays of tattered books set outside tiny bookshops. She browsed through stacks of ancient sepia postcards and held up to the light a cracked china cup or saucer which could be valuable but more likely was discarded rubbish. She smiled at like-minded people: a little boy buying a stack of old comics; an old gentleman, his clothes looking as dusty as the books he was examining.

Some of the snickelways were silent and empty, untroubled by the tourists. These were hidden in the heart of the city. They had no shops, however quaint. Instead they had doorways clothed with cobwebs, and above them rusting Victorian gaslights no longer shining on to delicately wrought fanlights. Marigold studied them. The doors appeared to belong to no properties. There were only long blank walls and dark corners inhabited by mangy cats who crouched low and glared through slitted eyes.

In these alleyways, Marigold walked quickly but softly — careful not to disturb the ghosts of the past.

Then, just when she thought she was lost, she was back near the centre of York. She came blinking into the sunshine of Coppergate, a cheerful landscaped square where buskers entertained the shoppers and the inevitable queue of people waited to enter the Jorvik Centre.

Not far away from her someone was playing a violin and playing it well. Marigold turned and saw a pale-faced girl of about seventeen. She was playing 'Greensleeves'. Marigold watched her and she saw how the crowds of people hurried by, ignoring her.

Partly because the atmosphere of the snickelways remained with her, Marigold was intrigued by the girl. Why, she thought, she could almost be a ghost herself. The girl wore a white blouse and a long, drab-coloured skirt. Her light blonde hair was unkempt and there was a remote expression on her pale face. She finished 'Greensleeves' and began to play 'Danny Boy'.

She was a busker, of course. Marigold could see the man's cap lying on the ground in front of her. It held a small collection of silver coins. She moved towards the girl and when she finished playing, she dropped three one-pound coins into the cap.

'You play beautifully.'

'Thank you.' The girl inclined her head.

Marigold hesitated and then she asked, 'Are you studying music at the University?'

Three pounds did not buy attention. With a graceful movement, which was in no way rude, the girl raised her bow, smiled at Marigold and began to play again.

Mozart, thought Marigold. She stepped back to listen. But the music made her feel emotional and so she blinked her eyes and walked quickly away.

'I'm overdosing on atmosphere,' she told herself. Time for a reminder of the modern world. And yet the memory of the girl stayed with her as she wandered round Marks and Spencer.

How wonderful it would be, she thought, to be that girl. How wonderful to be seventeen and possess a talent and be so composed and self-possessed. Why, that girl could do anything. She could finish her education and then join an orchestra and travel the world, or – if she wanted a different type of life – she could backpack to India and study mysticism. She looked that kind of girl. What confidence.

She sighed. How the world had changed.

When she was seventeen she was working nine hours a day in an ironmonger's shop and she had made up her mind she was in love with Ian. Oh dear! She blinked her eyes. She was being stupid, again.

The girl, despite her ethereal looks and her talent, would have the same problems as everyone else: lack of money, of course; the relatively modern menace of accessible drugs; and the age-old problem of falling in love too soon with the wrong young man. Was it the Bible that said: 'There is nothing new under the sun'?

Marigold shook her head, bought two pairs of M & S knickers and went to meet Pat.

They arrived at the White Swan at the same time. They exchanged an affectionate hug, examined the menu and ordered lunch, then bought two spritzers and headed for a table tucked away in a corner where they could talk.

Pat told Marigold what was happening at work: they were frantically busy with Mr Heywood chasing them and driving them all crazy. Pat said that Mari was well out of it. Then she looked a little disconcerted.

She plunged on. She said John Reed had become engaged

and that they had all chipped in for a collection to buy a wreath for Mrs Marsh, Herbert's mother.

Marigold raised her eyebrows. 'She's finally passed on, has she? How's Herbert coping?'

'I'm not sure.' The choke in Pat's voice made Marigold look at her suspiciously. Mrs Marsh had been old; too old to be the cause of so much emotion.

Pat saw Marigold's expression and the choke turned into a chortle. Marigold looked perplexed and Pat, calming down, explained.

'The thing is, she didn't die. She recovered. You see, someone at the hospital rang Herbert when he was at work. They told him to get there as quickly as possible because she wouldn't last much longer. He dashed off straight away and when he'd gone, we had a whip-round.' She shrugged her shoulders. 'Put like that, I suppose it sounds callous, but it made sense. You see, it happened on a Friday afternoon. Two members of staff were off on their holidays on Saturday, so we thought we'd better sort things out straight away. We collected enough money for a nice spray and we rang the florists to arrange things.'

She paused. 'Then Herbert turned up on Monday morning and told us she was much better.'

'Oh, no.'

'Oh, yes.' Pat began to laugh again. 'She's back at home now, right as rain.'

'So what did you do with the money?'

'We've stuck it in the safe in an envelope with Mr Heywood's name on it. I suppose it will come in useful sometime, but God knows when. The old girl will probably outlive her son. And, of course, we had to cancel the spray.'

Pat chattered on and watching her, Marigold thought how well she was looking.

They finished their drinks and Pat bought two more and then

asked Marigold how she was getting on.

'Not too bad but I've nothing exciting to tell you. Go on with your news. You must have something to tell me apart from work and it must be good news because I've never seen you looking so well. Is it Sam? Has he been offered a place at university?'

A delicate pink colour washed Pat's face. 'No, it's not Sam. It's me.' She picked up her glass, swirled the ice around, took a drink and put it down again.

'I feel a bit silly telling you, Mari. I would have said something last time we met but . . . it was too early.'

She hesitated and Marigold prompted her. 'Go on, then.'

'It was five, nearly six weeks ago.' Pat drew a deep breath. 'I had an unexpected visitor. It was a man called Chris Harker. He was Geoff's friend, oh, years ago. They met when they were both in the army.'

Marigold nodded. She knew Pat's husband had joined the army soon after leaving school but had left after a couple of years.

Pat continued her story. 'Geoff kept in touch with Chris for some years. I remember, Chris came to visit us once, just before we moved to York, when Sam was about two years old.'

She sounded nervous. Marigold noticed how she kept plaiting her fingers together.

'Then Chris went abroad to work and we lost contact with him. I got quite a surprise when he turned up on our doorstep last month.'

She smiled and Marigold thought, she likes him. She more than likes him.

'He returned to England six years ago. He wanted to contact us then but he didn't have an address. But, about six months ago, he met up with a chap who used to work with Geoff. This man told him about Geoff's car accident and also told him where Sam and I were living. Chris wasn't sure what to do. He had been Geoff's friend rather than mine. However, he's been promoted to a new job up here so he decided to call and see us.'

Pat looked happily across the table at Marigold.

'Sam answered the door and Chris said he knew straight away that he had come to the right address. He couldn't believe Sam's resemblance to his father. Of course, Sam was a toddler when he last saw him.'

'And what about Sam? Does he like Chris as much as you do?'

The pink in Pat's cheeks deepened to red. 'Who said I liked him?'

'Oh, Pat. It's obvious. You look ten years younger.' Marigold tried hard to keep the envy out of her voice. She was pleased for Pat, she really was. After so much heartbreak, she deserved a little happiness.

'He'd better be worthy of you,' she said, only half-joking.

'He is, Mari. He's different from Geoff in many ways and yet he has the same honesty, the same integrity. And he's good for me. He enjoys talking, he's full of energy. He's always suggesting we go somewhere.' Pat's face was finding it impossible to lose its smile. 'These last few years I've been getting lazy and dull-minded. I've fallen into a routine; work, shopping, home, TV and bed. Honestly, in six weeks Chris has made me *feel* ten years younger.'

'Has he told you anything about himself? Has he ever been married?'

'Yes. He married young, when he first went to America but it didn't work out. They divorced after three years. He's been honest with me, Mari. And he's not trying to rush me into anything. We're just enjoying each other's company at the moment.'

Marigold shifted in her seat. 'What does Sam think about all this?'

'He approves. He said it was time I got myself a life again.

He gets on well with Chris and he told me that he thought his dad would approve of the way things are going.'

'Oh, Pat.' Marigold swallowed the lump in her throat. 'I'm glad for you. Now, tell me more.'

Pat did. She talked all the way through the eating of her prawn salad and finally, when the coffee arrived, she was talked out. She sat back and shook her head.

'Poor Mari. I've completely monopolised the conversation. Now it's your turn. What have you been up to?'

Improvisation's a wonderful thing. Unwilling to drag Pat down from her peak of happiness, Marigold found herself turning her anxiety and her disappointments into humorous anecdotes. First, she told Pat about her two efforts to find part-time work.

'The book-keeping job wasn't even in an office. They expected me to sit at the back of a draughty warehouse. When I went for an interview for the second job the chap interviewing me appeared shocked. He misread my application. He thought I'd written down twenty-four years old, not forty-four. God, I crawled out of his office feeling I needed a Zimmer frame.'

She then spoke of her abortive effort to make a new friend.

'A new neighbour moved into the avenue recently. I thought she looked interesting. She didn't wear the usual country casuals and brogues which are compulsory in our area. So I smiled at her a couple of times and she smiled back and then she asked me round for coffee.'

Marigold pulled a face of mock horror. 'When I went round to visit I discovered she was a complete health freak. Now you know me, I'm not averse to the odd course of garlic capsules, but this woman told me she takes thirty pills every day. She told me about them all. I tried to bend the conversation in a different direction but she would have none of it. She was determined to get her message across.

'She swallows things called antioxidants to boost her immune system and –' Marigold screwed her face up, remembering. '– pro-dophilus – I forget what that's for and something called ginkgo to aid her memory. She also spends a fortune on having all those treatments Princess Di has.'

Marigold shuddered. 'After a full description of a colonic irrigation I couldn't stomach her sourdough bread and de-caff coffee so I muttered some excuse and left. Now I skulk around the streets trying to avoid her.'

'Oh dear.' Pat spluttered with laughter but then she looked serious. 'And what about at home. How are things between you and Ian?'

'About the same.' Marigold avoided looking at her friend. 'Nothing really changes.'

Pat sighed. 'Have you ever considered leaving him?'

'Every night, my dear.' Marigold forced a smile. 'Sometimes I think it's separation or the carving knife.'

'I'm being serious, Mari.'

'I know, but what grounds have I for leaving him? He doesn't mistreat me, he just ignores me. Plenty of men ignore their wives. And we've been married for twenty-six years, Pat, I don't know if I could manage on my own. I've been with him since I was eighteen, remember?'

'Well, it's up to you.' Pat sighed, glanced at her watch and pushed her chair back. 'Sorry, but I'll have to go.'

'Yes, of course.'

Outside the pub, the two women paused to say goodbye.

'I'll ring you soon, Mari. You must come and visit us one evening. Sam often asks about you and I do want you to meet Chris. I'm sure you'll like him.'

'Thanks. I'd like that.'

'I bet you want to check him out, don't you?'

'Well . . .'

'It's all right. I appreciate your concern. We *are* best friends.' Pat hesitated. 'I do like him, Mari, but it's early days yet. And whatever happens, nothing will spoil our friendship.'

'I know that.' Marigold fumbled with her bag. 'You'd better go. You'll be late for work.'

'Yes.' But Pat still lingered. She asked, 'Are you going to try for any more jobs?'

'I don't know. There's not so many around nowadays.'

'But you must do something, Mari. You'll be lost without . . .'

'For goodness' sake.' Growing tension made Marigold's voice sound breathless. 'You're not my keeper, Pat. And please don't feel sorry for me because your life's on the up. I don't need sympathy. At the moment I'm enjoying my leisure but when *I* think it's time to change my ways, then I will. Why, only a couple of days ago someone asked me to give her a hand. She's a business woman involved with various charities and she wants me to overhaul their book-keeping system. It might be quite interesting work.'

Pat lowered her head. 'I'm sorry, Mari. I should mind my own business.' She shrugged. 'Me and my big mouth.'

Marigold stared unseeingly at her and rubbed her left temple where a nerve pulsed, and then her face cleared. 'No, I overreacted. I should apologise to you.'

'Oh, let's leave it. We're both too thick-skinned to fall out over a few hasty words.' Pat grinned. 'Look, I'll really have to go. You will come and see us?'

'Yes, of course.'

'Bye, then.'

Another smile, a wave and Pat stepped into the crowd of people surging along the pavement and was quickly lost to view.

Marigold stared after her and then she set out to walk to the car park.

When she reached home she saw Ian's car in the drive. She

went into the house and called out, 'Hello.'

There was no answer but, from the study, she could hear the occasional bleep of his computer.

Paddy had come to greet her. She let him into the back garden and then she went to the telephone and dialled Susan Cambridge's number.

Chapter Eight

When Marigold was fifteen, before she met Ian, she had favoured the Juliette Greco look. Despite the disapproval of her parents, she wore black eyeliner, pale lipstick and haunted the local jumble sales looking for a black velvet suit which, of course, she never found. Instead, she purchased a man's velour dress jacket, a pair of flared black trousers and some worn-out ballet pumps and made do with them.

She took them home where, despite her protests, her mother insisted on washing everything, including the velour jacket, after which Marigold carried her booty into her bedroom and with needle and thread tried to create the outfit of her dreams. She was not totally happy with the result but a week later, scrabbling about in a box of bits and pieces at the local Salvation Army's Saturday sale, she found a long, white, feather boa and it was love at first sight.

Twenty-nine years later, memories of the jumble sales and her feather boa came flooding back as she pushed open the door and walked into the Overseas Development Charity shop. For a start, the shop bell was an old-fashioned one and, she breathed in deeply, the smell was the same. It was not an unpleasant odour, suggesting dampness rather than that the second-hand clothes in the shop were dirty or perspiration-stained. Marigold wondered if the shop had been empty for a long time, before the charity acquired the premises. She breathed in again and decided she could also smell gas.

She felt a flicker of alarm before noticing the Calor Gas heater next to the counter, which had obviously just been lit. Moving towards the counter she tried to decipher the more elusive elements of the smell of the shop. There was furniture polish and something else, a faint trace of some musky fragrance.

Someone's been heavy-handed with the air-freshener, she thought, but then she looked around and saw the packets of incense sticks displayed in a wicker basket on the shop counter. Of course. She smiled to herself. There had been no incense at the Sally Army's jumble sales: the captain and his lady would not have approved.

The shelves behind the counter held a collection of hand-carved wooden bowls and brightly coloured woven mats. There were spider plants in raffia hanging pots and a spin-round display stand featuring greeting cards with pictures of tigers and elephants on the front.

Marigold glanced down the shop where rows of clothes-rails stood to attention, bearing the weight of various assorted clothing. On one rail, where men's jackets had been pushed together in a clump, several items of clothing looked as though they were slowly sliding from the wire coat hangers and Marigold thought they looked exactly like tired squaddies, still in formation but wilting after a long, hard training run.

There was no sight of an assistant.

She coughed and said loudly, 'Hello.'

'Who's there?'

From a low angle, a head popped round the rail of men's jackets to look at her. The head had permed grey hair and a large round face. It was breathing heavily. After a long stare, the head moved slowly up to an adult's level and the body it was attached to stepped out from behind the clothes.

'How did you get in?'

Marigold cleared her throat. 'The door was open.'

'It never was.'

'Yes. I just turned the handle and walked in.'

Like the head, the woman's body was large and round. She stared at Marigold and frowned. 'I'm sure I dropped the latch.'

'No.' Marigold gave an apologetic cough and advanced a step towards her. 'I tried the door, it opened and I came in.'

The stout woman's frown deepened. 'We don't open until quarter past, you know.'

Marigold stopped. 'I didn't know. I assumed that nine o'clock . . .'

'We'd like to, but it's impossible, there's always so much to do.' The woman pointed to the cardboard box near her feet. 'You never know what you're going to find on the doorstep. They dump things on their way to work. Sometimes, I have to fight my way through to the door. Oh, yes.'

The woman's helmet of grey sausage curls wobbled vigorously as she nodded her head. 'Clothes, of course, which have to be sorted. Most of them you have to throw away. Stepladders, bundles of coat hangers, as if we don't have enough, lawn mowers, we get lots of old electrical stuff. Useless. We can't sell them.'

'Why not?'

The woman gave Marigold a pitying look. 'Safety regulations.'

'Oh.'

Marigold knew nothing about safety regulations but tried to look as though she did.

'This morning, there was this box. I managed to get it into the shop by myself but it's so heavy.'

'Where should it go?'

'In the storeroom at the back.' The woman sighed. 'What we could do with is a young lad for a few hours a week. One that's strong but has a bit of sense in his head, someone to unpack boxes and sort them out, but young people today, they're not interested in helping.'

'Oh, I don't know. Perhaps if you put an advert in the window...'

The woman wasn't listening. She scratched her nose. 'Mr Butley comes in from time to time but he's useless. He's old and I'm sure he's going ga-ga. He's supposed to sort stuff out but all he does is sit on a stool in the corner of the shop and read old comics.'

Marigold wondered how he dared. She took another step forward. 'The box, I'll help you lift it through to the back.'

Close up, she saw the box was large and packed to the brim with clothing. It must be heavy. She appreciated the elderly lady's difficulty.

But her offer of help was *not* appreciated.

'Oh, no. That wouldn't do. You're a customer.'

'Well, actually...'

The stout lady gave Marigold a keen look and dusted her hands together. 'You're *not* a customer?'

'No.'

'Then... I take it you're the accountant woman, Mrs Goddard.'

Marigold shifted her feet. 'Yes.'

'I didn't expect you so early.'

'Mrs Cambridge said any time.'

The woman sniffed. 'You've picked a bad day.'

'Oh, why is that?'

'We're short-staffed today.'

The two women stared at each other and then Marigold straightened her back and said firmly, 'There's no reason why I should interfere with your work. All I need are the books and

102

somewhere quiet to work. The storeroom you mentioned, that will do.'

'It's not that simple. I'll need to sort the books out and we need two members of staff in the shop at all times. But Edna Harkness isn't in today. She's got stomach trouble and Mrs Jessop's not due until ten o'clock.'

'Why do you need two assistants in the shop? Are you that busy?'

The stout lady stared at her pityingly. She said one word. 'Shoplifters.'

'What? In here?' Marigold couldn't keep the surprise out of her voice.

'Oh, yes. Nearly every day.' Her informant nodded her head, sagely. 'We may sell second-hand goods for charity but you'd be surprised how much stuff we get thieved. It's so bad the police send us information about who is knocking about in this area.'

'That's very sad.'

'It's a disgrace. Stealing from those most in need.' The stout lady sucked in her lips. 'We've had to get tough. We have the law on them now, just like they do at Fenwick's and Debenhams. Not that it does any good.'

She thrust out her hand. 'I'm Freda Thomas, by the way. I do most of the work here. I come in Mondays and Saturdays full time and I do half days on Tuesdays and Thursdays.'

Today was Thursday. Marigold smiled and held out her hand. 'How do you do. I'm . . .'

'Mrs Goddard. I know.' A hard, quick shake and Marigold's hand was discarded. 'Yes, Mrs Cambridge rang and told me about your visit. You're an accountant and you're going to sort out the way we do our books and keep account of the money. I gather the way we operate at the moment is not to Mrs Cambridge's liking.'

'Not at all. Mrs Cambridge is very pleased with your work, but she's asked me to check things over and see if I can streamline the system. You see, if everyone at the various shops used exactly the same method of bookkeeping, it would be more efficient.'

Mrs Thomas's expression remained unchanged and Marigold, who had dealt with dozens of difficult characters via the telephone, wondered why face-to-face encounters could be so difficult. She drew a deep breath and continued. 'Charity shops are becoming more and more popular with a whole range of people. I'm sure you've realised that. And it's not just the sale of clothes that's increased. People are buying pictures, ornaments, all kind of third-world crafts, and more money is being taken. So it's important that a viable system of accounting is set up, more particularly because the shops are staffed by part-time staff.'

'What's wrong with part-time staff?'

Marigold winced. 'Nothing,' she said heartily, 'nothing at all. You do a wonderful job. The whole system of shops selling goods for charity would fall apart if it wasn't for people like you, but if we can work out a few rules acceptable to everyone . . .'

'I'm sure everyone here follows the rules.'

'Yes, of course.' Marigold dropped the smile. Her voice sharpened. 'But my job is to visit every shop and check procedures and I'd like to get on and do that, Mrs Thomas.'

Her adversary adopted a pained expression. 'I'll get the books for you then.' She brushed past Marigold and went towards the door of the shop. She caught hold of the handle and pulled. The bell tinkled and the door opened.

'Well, I never.' Mrs Thomas sounded surprised.

I didn't walk through the glass, you old bitch. Marigold said the words, but in her head.

She did say, 'The books, Mrs Thomas.'

'I must get the petty cash into the till and check to see if Mrs Jones, that's Wednesday's lady, has left me any messages.'

Marigold, remembering her yoga exercises, relaxed her shoulders and took a deep breath. 'Very well. I'll have a look around.'

There were posters on the walls, explaining the plight of the rain forests and giving details of other man-made tragedies. The rails full of clothes took up most of the space in the shop but there were also boxes scattered around the floor containing small items, scarves and gloves, socks and underwear. There were racks of shoes and boots and tables holding old teapots, plates, saucers and bundles of spoons, forks and knives.

Two large bookcases overflowed with books. Marigold wandered over to them and peered at the titles, running her hands over the faded covers. She took one or two of them down, flicking through the pages, hoping to find a personal dedication or some long-lost hand-written message in faded ink, but she had no luck.

A tattered copy of *Jane Eyre* had fallen on the floor. She retrieved it, smiling. At thirteen, she had wept tears over Jane's torments at school and thrilled at her romance with Mr Rochester.

There were lots of old bookclub books on the shelves, novels written in the fifties and sixties by people she had never heard of. There was a copy of *The Moon's a Balloon*. How many copies had been printed? she wondered. Surely, a great number? No matter how many second-hand book shops she browsed in, there was always a copy of David Niven's book.

Marigold looked at the children's books. She had tried to get Karen interested in reading but she had failed. Except for teenage magazines, her daughter had remained impervious to the charms of the written word.

Marigold picked up a child's geography book which had been published in the forties. She looked through it and, with a shock, realised that today it was absolutely useless. The world had changed completely. The exciting foreign names her class had recited at school, the mysteries of The Dark Continent, had all vanished. Now, every night on the television, you saw instead the stark reality. Dust, heat and flies congregating around the mouths of huge-bellied babies caught in yet another war.

She replaced the geography book on the shelf and it fell over, sliding down to lie flat, like a paper corpse.

Her lurking companion, depression, had grabbed her by the throat again. Marigold took a deep breath and went over to look at the clothes. Here, she met with better luck. A couple of would-be customers had now entered the shop and were looking around. One of them, a young girl with short blonde hair was working her way through the rail that held blouses.

She worked quickly, wasting no time. Her long fingers, the nails tipped with blood-red nail polish, clicked the wire coat hangers along the metal rail like a robot worker in a car factory. Click, click, click.

Marigold asked, 'Looking for anything in particular?'

'Yeah.'

The girl raised her eyes from the clothes, glanced at her and then returned her attention back to the job in hand. Marigold took a step backwards, telling herself that she must stop talking to complete strangers. Was she so hungry for conversation?

Nevertheless, she hung around, wondering what kind of blouse the girl would choose.

'Hey.' With a whoop of delight, the girl pulled a clothes hanger from the dress rail. She slipped off the blouse and held it against her. 'Exactly what I want. How much is it?' She turned towards Marigold.

'Er, I'm not sure.'

'Give it here.' Mrs Thomas bustled over. She snatched the blouse from the girl and peered at the square of white paper pinned to the bottom of the garment. 'Sixty pence.'

'I'll give you fifty pence.'

'Cheeky young miss.' Mrs Thomas started to replace the blouse on the hanger.

'All right.' The girl dug into her jeans pocket.

Mrs Thomas took the one-pound coin and strode towards the till. Noting the white blouse had a deep v-neck and long ruffled sleeves, Marigold dared to inquire, 'Is it for a show?'

The girl raised her eyebrows.

'Sorry.' Marigold blushed. 'I see you dress in a very modern fashion. I couldn't image why you would want that blouse?'

Obviously gratified by Marigold's comment about her clothes, the girl answered her question. 'It's not my normal gear, but I'm going to a fancy-dress party on Saturday. My mum's found a white pleated skirt at the back of her wardrobe and some white court shoes. I thought, if I cut the sleeves out of that blouse I can put the things together and go as Marilyn Monroe.' She grinned at Marigold. 'You know, that photo where she stands on the hot air grating.'

'Oh, yes. I know the one you mean. I think the film was called *The Seven Year Itch*. What a good idea.'

They smiled at each other and Marigold felt happier. She hoped very much that the girl would enjoy her party. The ghost of a white feather boa floated at the back of her mind. She said, 'Have a good time.'

'Thanks.' The girl went to collect her blouse from Mrs Thomas and before she left the shop, she turned and waved at Marigold.

A thin little lady had entered the shop. She removed her coat, took it through to the back of the shop and was now talking to Mrs Thomas. After a couple of minutes, she came over to

Marigold and introduced herself. 'Hello, I'm Amy Jessop. Mrs Thomas said you wanted to see the books. If you'll come this way.'

She led Marigold through to the room at the back of the shop.

Left to her own devices, Marigold set to work. The books presented no problems, for a simple method of accounting had been followed. The various entries had been made in different handwriting but all were legible and the dates and amounts of money taken and banked were set out in a straightforward manner. As she checked and flicked over pages, scraps of paper which had been attached to ledger sheets by paperclips occasionally fluttered free but she managed to find their correct home.

The problem was Mrs Thomas who, at fifteen-minute intervals, came through to Marigold to see what she was doing. She tried to read Marigold's notes, she insisted on explaining the procedure followed in each account book, although Marigold protested it was not necessary, and she made a Shakespearian drama over opening the safe. After one hour, Marigold was heartily sick of her.

At twenty minutes to eleven, Mrs Jessop brought her a coffee.

Marigold thanked her and sat back in her chair to drink it. Through the partially opened door, she watched the activity in the shop.

Without surprise, she noted that Amy Jessop did most of the work. Mrs Thomas dusted the displays, watched the passing shoppers through the window of the shop and fussed with her hair in the mirror. However, whenever there were more than two customers in the shop, she sprang into action.

Marigold watched as Mrs Thomas selected her prospective thief and stalked her prey. As the man or woman strolled around the shop she followed close behind, her eyes boring like an X-ray into the unsuspecting skull of the customer.

Nevertheless, the shop was busy. Marigold was surprised at the variety of the customers. *Everyone* came in. Young people and old people, housewives with toddlers who escaped and infants who couldn't because they were strapped into pushchairs and who bawled with boredom. There were old gentlemen who raised their hats in a delightful old-fashioned way to the ladies they passed on their way towards the books, and schoolgirls who rummaged through the ladies' shoes and screamed with laughter at the old-fashioned styles. Mrs Thomas had a word with them.

Just as Marigold finished her coffee, a group of teenage bikers in leathers swarmed into the shop and pushed and shoved at each other as they congregated around a box of music tapes. Mrs Thomas, her mouth set like a trap, hovered over them like Marley's ghost.

Marigold was fascinated by this parade of humanity. It was a lot more exciting than shopping in the British Home Stores. It was with reluctance she returned to the books.

At five minutes to one, Mrs Thomas was back again.

'Yes, Mrs Thomas?'

'No problems, Mrs Goddard?'

'None at all.'

'I didn't think there would be.' Mrs Thomas smiled.

Marigold sat back in her chair. 'I've about finished the actual bookwork. I want to calculate the increase in takings over the last three months and after that I plan to jot down a few ideas for possible modifications to the printing of the sales sheet. Then I'll be finished here.'

Mrs Thomas's smile disappeared. 'Oh. You intend working on into the afternoon?'

'Well, yes. It doesn't seem sensible to stop now. Another hour and a half is all I need. Then I won't have to bother you again.'

Mrs Thomas rested her clasped hands on her stomach. 'It's not convenient.'

'Oh.' Marigold's eyebrows shot up. 'Why is that?'

'I've already explained. We're short-staffed today. I have a dental appointment this afternoon so I can't stay on. Mrs Gladstone won't be coming until two thirty and Mrs Jessop can't be here on her own. The shop will have to be shut until Mrs Gladstone arrives.'

Marigold tapped her pen on the desk. 'And what does Mrs Jessop say?'

'I haven't consulted her. I suppose she'll go and get a bite of lunch and then come back and put in her hours this afternoon.'

'But why shut the shop when there's no need? If I'm here, then there are two people on the premises.'

'You're not a member of the sales staff.'

'Oh, really.' Marigold clamped her lips together to avoid saying words that would cause offence. She breathed deeply and then said, in a sweet, reasonable tone of voice, 'Look, suppose I bring my work out into the shop? I can sit behind the counter and keep an eye on things. I can do my work and help Mrs Jessop out if things become hectic.'

Mrs Thomas narrowed her eyes. 'I don't know if Mrs Cambridge would approve.'

'Mrs Cambridge wants the shops to do well. Closing down this shop over the busy lunch-time period will hardly help boost sales.'

'Well.' Mrs Thomas looked undecided.

Marigold glanced at her watch. 'You'd better decide quickly, Mrs Thomas. You don't want to miss your appointment.'

Another moment's hesitation and then Mrs Thomas snatched her coat from the back of the door and picked up her handbag.

'Very well, but understand, Mrs Goddard, I expect you to take full responsibility until Mrs Gladstone takes over.'

'I will, Mrs Thomas.'

Marigold heard the door close and gave a sigh of relief. She picked up the ledger she was working on and her pocket calculator and went through into the shop. She sat on the stool behind the shop counter and looked across at Mrs Jessop.

'I'm afraid I pulled rank a little, Mrs Jessop. You don't mind the shop staying open, do you?'

'Not at all. In fact, I would prefer to go at my usual time.'

The breathless quality in the little woman's voice suggested she was stunned at Mrs Thomas's retreat.

Marigold grinned at her. 'Well, I shall continue with my work out here but please make full use of me if you get busy.'

Mrs Jessop nodded.

Marigold settled down to her figure work and Mrs Jessop tidied up a shelf containing curtaining. Fifteen minutes passed pleasantly enough. One or two people came in and then the shop became busy again. People came and went. Marigold took the money for three hardback books on alternative religions and various items of clothing.

Her greatest triumph came when Mrs Jessop was busy with another customer. A woman came in hoping to spot an unusual wedding present and Marigold felt a glow of satisfaction when she sold her a large beaten-copper bowl for a good price. Then it was quiet again and Marigold began her notes on possible improvements.

Mrs Jessop had just gone through into the back when the shop bell tinkled again. Marigold looked up. A slim young boy, about ten or eleven years old, had entered the shop. He was on his own. Marigold noted he was neatly dressed in school uniform. Without looking at her, he headed for the bookcases and began to browse among the books. She watched him for a moment and then went back to her work.

A few minutes passed.

Good. She was finished. Marigold pressed the 'clear' button on her calculator and sat back with a sigh of relief. With a bit of luck she would never have to see Mrs Thomas again as long as she lived.

She glanced round the shop, seeking the boy. He had moved away from the books. He was now standing in front of the rack of boots and shoes. His back was towards her so she couldn't see his face but there was something about him . . . his shock of dark hair and the rigid set of his shoulders made her think she had seen him before.

Suddenly, her eyes opened wide with disbelief.

With one rapid movement, the boy swung his school bag from his shoulder, opened the draw-string top and, snatching a pair of sports shoes from the rack, dropped them into the bag. He yanked the cord on the bag to close the top and edged sidewards towards a display of pottery next to the footwear.

What should she do? Mrs Thomas was right, people did thieve from charity shops – the boy had just done so. And she had to deal with him; Mrs Jessop wasn't in the shop and, anyway, she was the one in charge.

She bit her lip. He had turned round and was strolling back, heading towards the doorway. He was a cool customer, all right. He was probably used to stealing things. She'd have to grab him, make sure he didn't get away. She could see his face now, so innocent looking. He'd have to walk by her to get out of the shop. A moment's hope surfaced. He might come up to the counter and pay for the shoes. Then why had he put them in his bag?

Her mind raced feverishly. How were shoplifters apprehended? Didn't the store detectives let the suspects leave the store before nabbing them, to prove they had never intended paying for the goods? But she couldn't let this lad leave the store. He was young and fit. If he legged it, she'd never be able to catch him.

For one brief moment she thought, let him go. He'd pinched

a second-hand pair of shoes, no big deal. He was only a kid. But as soon as the thought crossed her mind, she dismissed it. She'd be letting herself down and she'd be letting him down. Get away with the small thefts and he'd move on to bigger ones. She set her face in forbidding expression. His hand was out, reaching for the door.

'Excuse me.'

He looked at her inquiringly. He had deep-set dark eyes and an old-young face. Again she was struck with the idea she had seen him before.

'Haven't you forgotten something?'

'No.'

She slipped of her stool and went round the counter to stand in front of him, blocking off his escape. Her knees felt trembly.

'I think you have.'

He frowned and made a sudden movement as if to pass her.

She reached out and grabbed his shoulder with her left hand. At the same time she put up her right hand and dropped the catch on the door. She was on her own now, with the thief. She didn't know whether to be pleased or worried. His shoulder felt bony beneath her grasp. She stared into his face and saw his bottom lip was trembling. She relaxed. He was only a boy, after all.

'You've got a pair of trainers in your bag. You stole them.'

'Don't know what you're talking about.'

From the corner of her eye, Marigold saw Mrs Jessop come back into the shop and halt at the scene before her. Keeping a firm grip on the boy, Marigold motioned her forward.

'Yes, you do. I saw you steal them. You're in deep trouble, young man.' She looked across at Mrs Jessop. 'You'd better ring the police.'

'Oh, no. Please don't ring the coppers. They'll tell my mum and she'll kill me. Please don't call the police. I'll pay for the shoes somehow. Honest I will.'

Marigold stared down into imploring dark eyes and said, slowly, 'Now I know where I saw you.'

Chapter Nine

'You walked past my home one Sunday when I was in the garden. Your mother – I presume it was your mother – has dark hair like you and your little brother's blond.'

He wasn't listening. As soon as she stopped speaking his voice jumped into the silence as jerky and discordant as a badly played piano.

'I've never ever pinched anything before. I didn't think. I promise I'll never do it again, not ever. Please, lady, don't call the police.'

Marigold could feel the shivers running through his body and despite herself, she felt a wave of sympathy for the lad. Her grasp on his shoulder loosened. Really, she thought, involving the police over the theft of a pair of second-hand training shoes does seem extreme.

She looked across at Mrs Jessop and asked, 'What do you think?'

Mrs Jessop cleared her throat before speaking in a surprisingly strong voice. 'I think cases like these are nothing but a nuisance to the police. A constable will have to come here to the shop. He'll need to write a report and no doubt there will be other paperwork involved and, at the end of the day, they'll let this young man off with a warning. That is –' She studied the boy's face '– if he's telling us the truth and it really is his first offence.'

'It is.' He nodded his head violently.

Marigold sighed. 'I agree with you. But he did steal and he shouldn't be allowed to get away with it.'

'No.' Mrs Jessop hesitated. 'How much are the shoes?'

The boy, his face brightening, handed her his schoolbag. 'If they're really cheap, maybe I can pay for them?'

'Let's see.' Mrs Jessop fished the shoes out of the bag, found the sales tag and read aloud, 'Two pounds fifty.'

'Haven't got that much.' The boy stared down at the floor. 'But I could pay you fifty pence a week. Would that do?'

Marigold's eyes met those of Mrs Jessop in mutual understanding. *They* might have agreed, but Mrs Thomas never would. She took her hand away from the lad's shoulder. Without words, she knew that their threat of police action had vanished, but what were she and Mrs Jessop expected to put in its place? The boy was a thief. Some recompense was demanded.

With a rush of anger she rounded on him. 'What possessed you to do such a stupid thing?'

He raised his left leg and pointed at his shoe. 'Got a big hole in it, see. I put in some cardboard and inked over it but one of the kids in the class spotted it. He told everyone. They thought it was a great joke.' He shrugged.

'But why didn't you tell your mother you needed new shoes? Surely she would have bought you some?'

His eyes narrowed into slits. 'She doesn't know. I don't want to tell her, not yet.'

Marigold rubbed her chin and looked at Mrs Jessop. 'This is beyond me.'

'Me, too. But we'll have to do something.' Mrs Jessop glanced at her watch. 'Mrs Gladstone will be here any minute.'

'Maybe she will sort it out?'

'Well, she might but . . .' Mrs Jessop coughed. 'She's very friendly with Mrs Thomas.'

'Oh.' Marigold bit her thumbnail. 'I know, I'll pay for the damned things.' She frowned down at the boy. 'You can keep them but you're going to have to earn them.'

She said to Mrs Jessop, 'Mrs Thomas told me this morning that it would be useful to have a young lad to help unpack and sort the goods that come in.' Then, turning back to the boy, she said, 'You look wiry and you seem reasonably intelligent. If you work for the ladies who run this shop, say for a couple of hours, then you'll have paid for the shoes. Do you understand me?'

He considered. 'You mean, I won't have to give you any money?'

'Not if you're a good help.'

'What would I have to do?'

Marigold looked around. 'See that big box over there? You can start by unpacking it. Take the clothes out, carry them through into the back room and sort them into piles according to whether they're men's clothing, or woman's or children. Put them tidily on the table. When you've done that, Mrs Jessop will have found something else for you to do.'

'And you won't tell anyone that I nicked the shoes?'

'Not if you behave yourself. Remember, this lady will be watching you all the time.'

Marigold leaned towards Mrs Jessop and whispered from the corner of her mouth, 'Do you agree?'

'I suppose so.' But Mrs Jessop sounded dubious. To the boy, she said, 'You don't go anywhere near the till, mind.'

He flushed scarlet. 'I won't. I wouldn't pinch money. That's different.'

'I think he means it.' Marigold lowered her voice. 'I believe we can trust him, Mrs Jessop. In any event, I take full responsibility for him. Tell Mrs Gladstone I've arranged for him to help you but don't, of course, mention how the arrangement came about. If she wants to ask me anything, she can contact me at home. My card's in the back of the large account book.'

The boy tugged at her sleeve. She glanced at him. 'What is it?'

'I can only stay for one hour, Missus.'

'What?' Marigold's lips drew into a thin line. 'You cheeky little devil. I said two hours' work.'

'Yeah, but . . .' He shuffled his feet. 'I can only stay one hour today because I have to pick up Billy from the toy library at a quarter past four.'

'What?'

'The toy library. Don't you know it? It's in the housing centre. It's a place where little kids go when there's no one to look after them. I have to be there when it closes at four fifteen and it'll take me twenty minutes to walk there.'

'Oh. Well, in that case . . .'

'I can come on Saturday, in the morning. I'll do the other hour then.' He gazed into her eyes and smiled disarmingly.

'Yes. I suppose that will do.' Marigold wondered about the mechanics of explaining his presence in the shop on Saturday but it was all getting too much for her. Mrs Jessop, she thought, would have to deal with it. Feeling guilty, she found her purse, took out two pounds fifty pence and handed the money over to Mrs Jessop.

'Er, can you mention he's coming back on Saturday?'

Looking somewhat grim, Mrs Jessop nodded, took the money and gave back to the boy his bag and the pair of shoes.

Just in time.

A woman wearing a blue dress and a red cardigan appeared at the other side of the glassed shop door. She tried the door handle and looked surprised when the door did not open.

'Mrs Gladstone,' muttered Mrs Jessop.

Marigold hurriedly pushed up the latch. 'Sorry. I think the hinges need a little oil. That's the second time it's stuck.' She stood back and allowed Mrs Gladstone to enter.

Mrs Jessop made the introductions, the boy was sent to get on with his work and Marigold went to collect her belongings from the back room. She said goodbye to Mrs Jessop and, as she walked passed the boy, she whispered to him, 'Don't let us down.'

He was on his knees. Head down, he was delving into the large cardboard box but, hearing Marigold's words, he looked up at her and smiled.

'I won't,' he said.

And somehow she believed him.

She took another step and then, remembering she needed to shop for food before she went home, she turned round. 'Look,' she said, surprising herself. 'I've a couple of errands to run. What if I come back here at four o'clock. I could run you over to where this toy library is held and then I could take you and your brother home?'

He scowled at her.

'You still want to tell my mum what's happened, don't you, even though I'm working for you? Well, you can't. My mum won't be in. She's working, so you won't be able to tell her.'

Marigold felt her face going red. 'I never even thought about your mother. I was just offering you a lift. You said it would take you time to go and collect your brother.'

He stared down into the box. 'We're not allowed to get into a car with anyone we don't know.'

'Why, you ungrateful . . .' Marigold bit back the rest of the words. She studied his sharp-angled profile and his pale cheek and then she nodded. 'You're quite right. I'm sorry.'

She hurried away from him, out of the shop. She did her shopping and went home.

The house was quiet and empty but showed signs of previous

activity. A tray holding a coffee pot and two used coffee mugs stood on the draining board, testifying that Ian had earlier in the day conducted a tutorial. Paddy's lead was missing from its peg which meant the two of them were taking a walk. Marigold put away her shopping and checked the answerphone. There were no messages.

A small, square, green-coloured card lay on the doormat. She picked it up. It informed her that the performing poet, Daniel Crewe, was appearing this very evening at The Square Tower, close by the village of Barmby Moor.

Tony Neaves, the popular folk singer, was the supporting act, singing original ballads and accompanying himself on the slide guitar. Eight p.m. until ten p.m. Tickets available at the door.

A reminiscent smile played around Marigold's lips as she laid the card on the hall table. A long time ago, just after their marriage, Ian had taken her to gigs similar to the one advertised.

Kicking off her shoes she went into the kitchen and switched on the kettle. She was pouring boiling water into a mug containing a teabag when she heard Paddy barking at the back door. She let him in. He snuffled around the floor looking for any sign or scent of food and then flopped down in his basket. Ian entered more sedately.

'Oh, you've finally come home. I thought you said you'd be back around two o'clock?'

'I was delayed.' Marigold glanced at him through half-lowered eyelashes. 'Like a cup of tea?'

'Yes, thank you.' Ian flung Paddy's lead over the back of a chair and sat down. He watched Marigold take another mug from the cupboard and place a teabag in it.

'Did I need that walk. I had a raging headache. Do you know, I honestly believe that today I endured the thickest pupil I have ever had the misfortune to teach. How a second-year university student of physics could be so totally clueless as to the theory of electromagnetism is beyond me.'

'Oh dear.' Marigold's sympathy lay entirely with the unfortunate student, but she made a soothing noise and handed Ian his mug of tea.

He drank, studied her face and then asked, completely unexpectedly, 'Well, how did you get on?'

Taken by surprise, Marigold's head came up like that of an unbroken colt. 'Oh, well . . . yes.' She stammered. 'It was OK.'

'You enjoyed the work, then?'

'I did.' She peered at him anxiously. Yes, he was looking at her. She had his undivided attention.

She hurried into speech, rushing her words. 'Very different from anything else I've done. It's quite amazing, Ian, the number of people who actually frequent charity shops. I mean, you half expect them to be all down-and-outs but they're not, although some of them are . . .' She gulped and veered away from that particular line of conversation.

'The woman in charge was a bit of a dragon. I think she felt I was criticising her work. I was glad when she went for lunch. The other lady there was much nicer. She . . .'

Ian sighed, a little wearily. 'You didn't allow the manageress to bully you, I hope. It's damned good of you to volunteer to do the work. God knows what passes as financial management in the running of charity shops. I wonder if Susan Cambridge realises how lucky she is.'

'Oh, she does. And the woman wasn't too bad, just rather eccentric. The books were quite well kept. However, I managed to think of a way to streamline the system somewhat and I actually helped a little in the shop. They were short-staffed today.'

She noticed Ian's fingers had begun to drum on the side of his mug and she knew she was talking too much and too fast, but somehow, she couldn't stop. 'So, when the manageress left for lunch, I went and sat by the till. I sold a large copper bowl for quite a lot of money. I felt quite proud of myself because . . .'

Her gush of words slowed as she saw Ian stand up but it was as if she couldn't control her mouth. 'Mrs Jessop said the bowl had been in the shop for almost a year. It was too dear for most people, you see.'

Ian stood his empty mug in the sink. 'I think I'll go and mow the lawn, it's looking a mess.'

He walked past her and out into the garden.

She stared out of the kitchen window. He was right, the lawn did look shaggy. She ran water into the sink and washed up the two mugs. It's been a good day, she told herself. She'd enjoyed being at the shop, she had done what Mrs Cambridge had asked for, she had got on well with Mrs Jessop and she had sorted out the trouble with the boy.

And Ian *had* enquired about her day.

Drying her hands on the tea towel, Marigold thought how young he had looked when he walked into the kitchen. The strong breeze had made the front of his hair stick up, just as it used to do when he was a student.

Marigold recalled how Ian used to be, and then she thought of the boy in the shop. How similar they were . . .

The boy's hair had stuck up too, but at the crown of his head. Both Ian and the boy possessed the same kind of bodies, strong and wiry with no extra flesh on them. Their faces gave away nothing of what they were thinking, and there was a definite edge of tension about them both. But what caused the tension?

Marigold considered Ian's parents. She didn't often think about them because they heard from them so infrequently. Mr and Mrs Goddard senior had retired to Cornwall fifteen years ago. Since then visits had been rare and even telephone contact had dwindled. Calls were exchanged on Ian's birthday, at Christmas and in cases of illness.

When Karen had been younger, Marigold had suggested, more than once, that they go and visit his parents. 'Surely they'd like to see more of their only grandchild? We could go down at Easter for a few days, or in the summer holidays. Perhaps they'd like to come and stay with us?'

But Ian had been singularly unenthusiastic and, it must be said, so had his parents.

Not a loving family then.

Marigold's brow creased.

The boy in the shop had been so afraid of his mother finding out about the theft of the shoes. Why was that? Was he frightened? And was there a father figure anywhere in the picture?

'Goodness,' she said aloud. 'Parents have a lot to answer for.'

When Paddy pawed at her skirt she pushed him away and felt irritated until she looked at the wall clock and realised it was past his meal time. She took a tin of dog meat from the cupboard and laughed when he picked up his bowl in his mouth and brought it to her.

'OK,' she said. 'I get the message.' She scratched behind his ears and thought, thank God dogs are less complicated than humans.

After their evening meal, Ian tried to phone Karen. He dialled her number but there was no reply. Ten minutes later, he tried again. After a few moments listening to the tone he slammed down the receiver.

'No answer. Where can she be? That's the third time this week I've tried to contact her.'

'Didn't you leave a message when you rang her before?'

'Yes, but she's never rung me back.'

Marigold shrugged. 'Perhaps she's away for a few days.'

'Then she should let us know. What if there was an emergency? We wouldn't have a clue where to get in touch with her.'

'But there isn't an emergency, is there?'

'No, but there might have been.'

'In that case, I suppose the agency would have her address.'

'That's right, Mari, have an answer. You always do.'

Marigold relapsed into silence. Her feelings were undented. Ian didn't mean to be unkind. He always became edgy when Karen didn't ring.

Ian threw himself into a chair, grabbed the *Radio Times* and ruffled through the pages. 'There's absolutely nothing on the box.'

'Really? Still, it's a beautiful evening, Ian. Why don't we go out for a drive?'

He stared out of the window and rubbed the side of his nose, considering. 'Where should we go?'

'It doesn't matter. Anywhere.'

He gave an exasperated sigh.

Wrong. Wrong! She knew it instantly.

Ian hated what he called wishy-washy conversation. He liked sentences that led somewhere. He liked his questions to be answered. She must come up with a suggestion immediately, otherwise he would withdraw from her – disappear into his study to work or switch on the television and watch, without seeing, whatever BBC 2 was screening.

The memory of the green card popped into her mind. 'Hang on a minute.' She rushed into the hall, grabbed the card, returned to the sitting room and handed it to Ian.

'We could give this a try. It would be a pleasant drive over there and if we leave now, we'll be in time for the start of the performance. Afterwards, we could stop at a village inn on the way home and have a drink.'

He read the information and then dangled the card in the air, holding it between his thumb and forefinger as though it was a dead mouse.

'A performing poet and a folk singer! Good grief, Mari. Are you telling me you want to go to this place?'

He sounded so mealy-mouthed she wanted to scream.

'Yes,' she said. 'I do. I'm fed up with watching TV every night and I'm sick of cooking dinners for your friends who come here, totally ignore me and talk only to you. How long is it since we went out for a meal or to the theatre?'

'I never realised you wanted to go out. You should have . . .'

She interrupted him. 'This place that's advertised, it may be perfectly dreadful, but I still want to go and if you won't take me—' She drew a breath. 'I'll go on my own.'

Sitting beside Ian as he negotiated the winding country roads, Marigold felt exultant. She wound down the car window a little so she could smell the scent of the may blossom. Ian glanced at her, opened his mouth – he didn't like draughts, and then closed it again. The expression on his face made him look slightly shell shocked.

She touched his suit sleeve affectionately. He'll be better now, she thought. I've made the breakthrough. I've made him notice me. Now our life will improve.

She said, 'We could call in at The Pale Horse on the way home?'

He nodded. 'If you like.'

The Pale Horse was a low, rambling building nestling in a valley. It was a lovely old pub with heaps of atmosphere. Marigold thought they could sit in the bar and sip a good brandy and, perhaps reminisce about the gigs they had attended years ago. And then, in mellow mood, they would drive home and she would slip into her beautiful nightgown and this time, there would be no late telephone call to distract them.

'I think we're nearly there,' said Ian.

They were in the area but they couldn't locate The Square Tower. They drove through the village twice and then round and round the surrounding lanes before they spotted it. When they did, Marigold said, 'Why, it's not like a tower at all.'

Ian's lip lifted in the ghost of a sneer. 'What did you expect, a Norman keep?'

'Yes, or at least something tall and made of stone.'

He shook his head and drove towards the motley collection of cars parked to the side of a low, squat wooden building set in the middle of a field. The gate to the field was open and an orange-coloured notice told them they had arrived at the right place.

Ian turned off the car engine and looked around. 'Still want to go?'

She pressed her lips together and nodded.

'All right. On your own head be it.' He opened the car door, stepped out, and immediately swore.

'What's the matter?'

'Stood in a bloody cowpat. Better watch your step.' He scraped his shoe on a nearby stone.

Marigold stood by the car and looked at the building. 'Resembles a stable block, doesn't it? Perhaps there *was* a Norman tower here once, years and years ago.'

'That's right, my dear.' A huge lady dressed in a colourful tent-like dress bore down on them. 'Two tickets, is it?'

Marigold nodded and searched in her handbag for her purse.

'There you are, my dear.'

The woman pressed the tickets into her hand. 'Better get a move on, they'll be starting in a minute.'

'Thank you.' Marigold glanced at Ian's face. His expression made her earlier, happier feeling fade away. Nevertheless, she set out for the building and Ian followed her.

Once inside, her spirits rose again. The hall was clean, the white-washed walls were covered with brightly coloured posters. Lamps with red shades lined the windowsills and stood in a row along the front of the small stage. At the back of the hall, a collection of old-fashioned farm implements was displayed and there was a model of a carthorse forged in copper and standing about four feet high, near the leather ploughing harnesses and bale bags.

'It's quite nice.' She caught hold of Ian's arm.

He muttered something she didn't quite catch but she heard his next words.

'We don't have to sit on those, surely?' He nodded towards the large square cushions scattered around the floor in front of the stage.

'No. There are seats.'

But looking around her, Marigold saw that the rows of benches and the wooden chairs at the back of the room were fully occupied and listening to the buzz of conversation she realised the place was full.

Ian took hold of Marigold's left elbow. 'I'm not sitting there,' he hissed. 'Let's get out of this place.'

'Oh, but . . .' She wondered whether now was the time to remind him that twenty-four years ago, they had purchased similar cushions for their flat.

A young man with a beard and a ponytail came to her rescue. He came up behind them, tapped Ian on the shoulder and offered them his seats. 'You can have them, Dad. Me and my girlfriend can sit on the floor.' He grinned. 'We're students. We're used to it.'

Marigold saw Ian's form stiffen at the young man's form of address, so she smiled and thanked him. She gave Ian a little push. 'The seats are over there, to the right.'

'Mari, I don't know what's got into you tonight.'

'Hush, it's starting.' She hustled him along to the empty seats.

Someone closed the doors. The place was packed and people were standing at the back. Glancing round, Marigold saw the audience was predominantly young with a smattering of older people.

A wave of applause swept the room as a heavily built man dressed in boots, jeans and an open-checked shirt strode through the crowd and jumped on the stage.

'Hey, thanks for the welcome. It's good to visit you again.'

The poet, Marigold presumed, spotted a man he obviously knew for he grinned and waved at him. 'Pete, how's that daughter of yours?'

'She's fine, Danny. Out of hospital now.'

'That's good news.' The poet rocked back on his heels and surveyed his audience. He looked across at the people sitting on the chairs and he grinned. 'I see we have some newcomers this evening.'

He raised his right hand. 'Welcome.'

Marigold felt Ian shift uncomfortably in his seat but she was too busy studying the man's face. There was something about his smile and the shape of his face that reminded her of someone.

The poet settled to his task. He gave his audience a thumbnail sketch of his interests in poetry and then started to recite his work.

He was a restless man, striding up and down the stage as he declaimed his work. And yet, declaimed was not the right word, because for many of his poems he used a quiet voice.

His audience was a good one, utterly silent when he spoke of the death of love and the despair of the lonely, but laughing aloud at his comic tales of sexual lust and human stupidity. Some of his poems he read from a book but most he knew by heart. Reciting those, he became an actor, flinging out his arms, changing his facial expressions, or standing motionless, his wide shoulders bowed to signify sorrow.

At first, Marigold found it difficult to concentrate; the poet's physical presence was so powerful and she was conscious of her surroundings and of the waves of hostility emitting from Ian. But after ten minutes she relaxed and concentrated on the words and when the session came to a close she clapped as loudly as everyone else.

During the short interval, neither she nor Ian spoke. Ian sat with his eyes closed and she eavesdropped on other people's conversation. The audience appeared to be highly knowledgeable in the field of modern poetry. They seemed a friendly lot. One or two people smiled at her and she smiled back but with a hint of reserve.

What if someone asked her which modern poet she admired? She could hardly admit she had read none. Until this minute her favourite poet had been John Keats.

Daniel Crewe returned to the stage and this time, Marigold listened even more intently to his poems. It was true they bore little relationship to the classical poetry she had read at school but she thought she recognised a definite form and structure. Not all of his work appealed to her but others . . . Unconsciously, she leaned forward in her chair.

His poems spoke of childhood, which brought back to her bitter-sweet memories; some were about the havoc that love could leave in its wake; but it was his last poems that moved her most. They were about individuals: the lonely old man patiently waiting for attention in the DHSS offices; and the throw-away children living rough in the streets.

His words made tears prick the back of her eyes and brought back to her mind the boy who had stolen the shoes. She had the strangest feeling that she had been meant to hear the poems, that there was some reason why she had been drawn to come to hear Daniel Crewe's work.

Perhaps she was not the only one to have a lump in her throat when the poet's words finally ceased. There was a moment of absolute silence and then rapturous applause. Marigold clapped until her hands were sore.

When the poet finally left the stage another man took his place. He was tall and thin and wore spectacles. He was carrying a guitar.

Marigold blinked. Of course, he must be Tony Neaves, the folk singer.

In a gruff voice he sang a song about a dog grieving his dead master and he was quite dreadful. Marigold dared not look at Ian. There was a general shifting and moving of feet from the audience. Two songs later, while he was tuning his guitar, Ian nudged her urgently in the ribs.

'Let's get out of here.'

She nodded.

They left as quietly as possible. Outside, it was still light enough to see the rows of parked cars. Ian trotted gingerly over the grass towards theirs.

'Thank Heavens that's over. That damned chair. My backside's numb.' He unlocked the car. 'Get in.'

Marigold climbed in without speaking. Ian also got in. He unearthed a duster and rubbed the windscreen.

He glanced at her. 'You're quiet. I suppose you're as stiff as I am.'

She shrugged. 'No. I feel fine.' She hesitated. 'I enjoyed it. I found it interesting.'

'Really? I thought it was a load of codswallop. Oh, the chap had a gift for words, but his sentiments were nothing but left-wing rubbish.'

'I thought he was talking about the human condition, about

love for your fellow creatures, or the lack of it.'

'Oh, Mari, you're so naive. You want to be careful. Don't allow yourself to be sucked in by the vague posturing of poets and layabouts. What do they do? Damn all. What do they know about the real world? Nothing.'

He waited, expecting a reply. When she simply closed her eyes and put her head back on the headrest, he muttered something under his breath and turned on the ignition key. The car gears grated as he drove from the field.

On the way home – they didn't stop at The Pale Horse – Marigold thought about the poems she had heard. She wondered if Daniel Crewe had published his work. Then she thought about the elusive likeness to someone she had met. If only she could remember . . . She didn't think about her silk nightdress at all.

It was when Ian turned into their avenue that she remembered. Yes, of course. Daniel Crewe looked remarkably like the man she had talked to at the golf club. The man who was a furniture restorer with a shop in the Shambles. The man who had said that, given the choice between her and Karen, he would like to take her out for dinner.

For the first time since getting into the car, she smiled.

Chapter Ten

He was talking in his sleep again. If only she could make out the words.

Sheila Scott eased back the curtain and looked into the cubbyhole where her sons slept. Billy was sound asleep, curled up like a little hedgehog at the bottom of the bed. Jack – she shook her head – Jack was also asleep but he was not resting peaceably. She tiptoed to stand beside him. He was sweating, his face was flushed and his hair damp. His head moved restlessly on his pillow and then he started muttering again.

She bent closer, watching his lips.

'No, no. I won't. You can't . . .' The rest of his words were unintelligible.

'Hush.' Sheila stroked his hair back from his forehead. 'Everything's all right, Jack. Sleep now.'

His body jerked violently and his eyes opened but it was plain he did not see her.

He snarled. 'Leave me alone.'

Sheila sucked in her breath. She sat on the side of the bed, took hold of his shoulders and shook him, none too gently.

'Jack. Wake up.'

'Uh. What is it?' He fended her off with his hands. 'Mum, what are you doing?'

'You were having a nightmare.'

'Was I?' He lay back against his pillows.

She glanced at Billy, thankful he was still asleep, and whispered, 'What is it, Jack? What's bothering you?'

'I don't know what you mean.'

'Yes, you do. You keep talking in your sleep and you're so restless.' She put her hand on his forehead. 'Do you feel ill?'

He shook his head. 'No. I'm a bit hot.'

'It's warm tonight.' She sat back wishing she had a thermometer. 'Do you feel sick? Have you any pains?'

'Aw, Mum. I'm fine.'

Her eyes narrowed. 'You're eating school dinners, I hope. You're not spending the money on rubbish?'

'No. Stop worrying. I'm fine. Can I go back to sleep now?' He thumped his pillow.

'In a minute.' She studied his face. 'Jack, if something was bothering you, you would tell me?'

He gave her a blank stare. 'There's nothing bothering me, Mum. Like you said, I must have had a nightmare.'

'And two nights ago, was that a nightmare, too?'

He looked away from her. Shrugged.

She stole another glance at Billy and then moved closer to her elder son.

'Is someone bullying you?'

'Naw.' He clenched his fists and expanded his puny chest. 'No one would dare bully me. I can look after myself.'

'I know you can, but if a gang picks on one person in particular . . .' She touched his hand. 'If something bad is going on, I want to know, Jack.'

'Nobody's picking on me, Mum. School's all right. The teachers watch out for us. Please, let me go back to sleep now. We've a maths test first thing in the morning.'

Sheila stood up. Her face reflected her anxiety. 'You can always come to me.'

134

'I know.' He yawned widely and slid down beneath the bedcovers. 'Night, Mum.'

Sheila went back to her own bed. Damn it, a double bed was too big for one person. She felt lonely. She took the spare pillow and cuddled it to her and wished Mike was at home. Jack could have talked to his father – man to man stuff – but he wouldn't confide in her. Something was wrong, she was sure.

A letter had come from Mike two days ago. He said he was about to leave Huddersfield. A man who drove for a carpet firm had offered him a lift to Manchester.

Don't know if it will be any better there, he had written. *But at least I'll get a scenic route through the Pennines.*

Next time he phoned she'd ask him to pack it in. He was doing no good trailing around the country looking for nonexistent jobs. Half the men in the country were without work. There was no need for him to feel so bad about it. And he was needed here. The boys needed him and so did she.

She yawned. At least the chap in the next room was quiet. She slept.

Next morning, Jack walked to school. He walked spring-heeled, as though he hadn't a care in the world, but he skirted round alleyways and he walked near groups of other school children. Once in school, he relaxed. He even puffed out his chest when he went in to take the maths exam. If there was one thing he was good at, it was maths. At break he kept moving, always part of a group, or hanging on to the fringes of one.

Lunch was rubbish. He queued for spam fritters and chips but they ran out before he reached the serving area. He had to settle for greyish-coloured mince with potatoes and peas. Pudding was an apple or a bowl full of milk pudding which the kids called 'frog-spawn'. Jack had both. He bought an apple and ate his next-door neighbour's milk pudding. It tasted OK so long as you didn't look at it while you were eating. Then he realised he needed to pee.

The boys' toilet block looked deserted. He hesitated, but a pee wouldn't take long. He went in and approached the nearest urinal stall. He entered, unzipped his pants and sighed with relief. Then he heard a noise behind him. Someone had followed him. He felt the hair prickle on the back of his neck. He was so frightened he even stopped peeing.

He heard the voice he had been expecting.

'Well now, if it isn't Jackie Scott?'

Jack didn't look round. He concentrated on his need to pass water. It was a small victory when he managed it. He pulled up the zip on his trousers with fingers that trembled, then turned his head.

'What do you want, Trevor?'

'Why, nothing. We're mates, aren't we? I can spend a bit of time with a mate.'

'We're not mates, Trev.' Jack tried to sound strong and brave but his voice wobbled.

'Sure we are.'

Trevor Stokesby smiled and looked down at Jack. He was almost fourteen years old and big for his age. A bullet-headed boy with wide shoulders and huge, thick-fingered hands.

'Sure we are. We knock around together, don't we?'

Jack rang his tongue over his lips. 'We did for a bit, but not any more.'

'Oh dear.' Trevor swung his heavy head from side to side. 'I don't like what I'm hearing, Jackie. Just you think back for a moment. You owe me, remember? You were glad of my company when Con Travis and his gang were mucking you around. Remember, that day he was making fun of your crappy shoes?'

'Yes, but . . .'

'Snotty little git. They're all snotty little gits.' Trevor scowled and doubled his hands into fists. 'Taking the piss out of you. What do they know about anything? Their mums and dads give them money for everything. But you and me are different, Jackie. We know how to look after ourselves.'

He stared at Jack. 'I know what it's like having people on my back. Just 'cos my old man's been inside a couple of times, I get the blame for everything that goes wrong.'

Jack raised his shoulders. 'Yeh, Trev, I know and I'm sorry. And it was good of you to help me out, but that doesn't mean we have to knock around together all the time. You don't own me.'

'Own you?' Trevor raised his sparse eyebrows. 'What you talking about?'

Jack swallowed. 'I've been meaning to tell you. I won't be able to help you out any more.'

Trev frowned. 'But why? Why spoil a good thing? We've been helping each other, Jackie.'

Jack studied his shoes. 'I can't, that's all.'

He stiffened as Trevor moved closer to him and grasped his arm.

'I thought you enjoyed helping me, Jackie. And you made a bit of money, didn't you? We all need money.'

'Yes, I know, but what I didn't know . . .' Jack's voice faltered.

'Know what? There's nowt *to* know.'

'There is.' Jack tried and failed to shrug off Trevor's grip. 'But we needn't talk about it, Trev. Just let it go. Just leave me alone.'

'But you're my mate.'

'No, I'm not.' Jack stood very still. 'You see, I know, Trevor. I know what's in those envelopes of yours.'

Trevor grinned. 'OK. So you know. What's the big deal?'

'You're pushing drugs. I'm not getting into stuff like that. When you asked me to help you, I thought you were passing betting slips, or something like that. Then last week, one of the kids opened his envelope in front of me and I saw the drugs.'

Trevor laughed out loud. He released his grip on Jack's shoulder and tapped him playfully on his cheek.

'Daft bugger. It's not proper drugs. Where would I get crack or cocaine, hard drugs like that? No, Jackie, there's no need for you to worry. You see—' He lowered his voice. 'Me big brother goes to clubs and raves and sometimes he picks up a few happy pills and he sells them at a profit. Nowt wrong with that. Hell, my mum gets more drugs down her than the bits and pieces we flog. Doctor gives 'em to her. Keeps her from blowing her top, poor old bitch. Those pills you took round for me, they're harmless. Honest.'

'Maybe, but I'm not taking any more round the school for you.' Jack forced himself to stare into Trevor's eyes. 'I mean it, Trev. I won't say a word to anyone about them, but I won't touch them again and—' He drew a deep breath. 'I think it would be best if we stopped hanging around together.'

Trev's eyes half closed. 'Why, you prissy little bugger,' he mumbled. His fist shot out and gathered up a bunched-up handful of Jack's shirt. He shook him so violently Jack's head snapped backwards and forwards. 'Is that the thanks I get for helping you out?'

'You don't need me, Trev.' Jack's voice held desperation. 'You can run the whole thing on your own. You'll make more money.'

'My bloody hands are tied.' Trevor gave Jack a push that sent him spinning against the wall. 'Effing coppers have a down on my family. They watch us all the time. But you're safe. They'll never tag you. And if you think you can walk away from me, you're wrong. Listen, I'll have some more stuff next week and you're going to help me move it.'

'No.' Jack shook his head. 'I won't.' His eyes blazed in his white face. 'I won't touch drugs, get that into your thick head.

And if you come after me then I *will* tell the police. I'll tell them everything.'

'You bastard.' Trevor's beefy face infused with blood. 'After all I've done for you.' He reached for Jack again, but the younger boy sidestepped him and attempted to flee. Trevor started after him but stopped when the outer door banged and three boys came round the row of toilet cells. They paused and stared.

Then one of the boys grinned. 'Hello, hello, what have we walked into lads; a biology lesson perhaps?'

His friends giggled.

Jack, his back pressed against the cold, tiled wall, stared at them. His chest was heaving and the blood sang in his head.

Trevor Stokesby glared at the newcomers then spat on the floor and shouldered his way through them. 'You're all bloody fags,' he shouted.

The boys' faces sobered. They glanced uneasily at each other.

Reaching the door, Trevor turned back and stared at Jack. He even managed a smile. 'You'd better do some serious thinking, Jackie.' He ran his tongue over his lips. 'You've a kid brother, haven't you? Better take good care of him.'

He kicked open the door and left.

Three days after Jack's encounter with Trevor Stokesby, Marigold drove from Harrogate back to York. She listened to taped music and, from time to time, glanced out of the car window at the passing scenery. Late June, she thought, was a lovely time of the year. The trees, in particular, were looking at their best. She hummed along with the music. She had enjoyed her day.

The women staffing the charity shop at Harrogate had welcomed her visit. They had explained how they managed their books and served her with excellent coffee. At one point she had taken a break from figure work and looked round the shop. Some of the women's clothes for sale had been excellent. Indeed, one dusky pink blouse had appealed to her so much she had bought it. Ian liked her in pink. She wondered if he would notice the blouse. Probably not, but if he did, and asked her where she had bought it, she would have to lie. If she told the truth, he would be shocked. His wife in second-hand clothing!

She smiled. At least they had talked more during the past few days. Strange, really, because she had been more ... she frowned, not argumentative exactly but certainly more forceful. She had challenged his opinions over certain things instead of sitting quietly and repressing her own views. He hadn't always liked what she had to say but at least he had taken more notice of her. Perhaps her acquiescence had been one of their problems but, she sighed, she had always hated arguments.

She was approaching York. Taking a chance she drove into the city hoping to find a parking space. Normally she left the car outside the walls but today she had a large, heavy box to deliver.

Her neighbour, Susan Cambridge, had been delighted when, over coffee one morning, Marigold had expressed her willingness to become more involved in helping with charity work.

'My dear, that's wonderful. Volunteers are always needed. Do you have anything specific in mind?'

'Not really. I'll complete the report on financial management of course, but I'll help out in any way I can. In fact, I'd welcome some hands-on experience, if possible. I enjoyed my spell behind the counter at the first shop I visited. You get some interesting characters as customers.'

'Interesting, but sometimes odd?' Susan's eyebrows rose.

Marigold laughed. 'I'm coming to realise I'm at home with odd people.'

Susan had taken Marigold at her word and mentioned her name as a volunteer to local charities. Today she had been given the task of delivering a box of donated toys collected in the Harrogate area to the York council's playgroup and toy library.

Driving along Marygate, Marigold wondered whether the little boy called Billy, the boy who had so charmed her, would be at the playgroup today. His brother had said he went there. She'd like to see him again; his blond mop of hair, his wide grin and careless confidence were hard to forget. And, of course, there was the contrast with his brother.

She wondered about the boys; did they have different fathers? She wondered whether the elder child had kept his promise and returned to work the extra hour at the charity shop. She had wanted to know so badly she had been tempted to call in and find out but the thought of Mrs Thomas dissuaded her. Well, perhaps today she might find out.

She managed to find a parking space reasonably close to the large grey stone building which contained, according to the printed list on the board outside, the playcentre with the toy library and other meeting rooms. She took the box from the boot of the car and struggled up the flight of steps leading to the house. She was sweating by the time she reached the entrance and glad she was wearing low-heeled shoes.

She went inside the building and was about to ask directions at the information desk when she realised there was no need, all she had to do was trace the source of the noise. She turned to her right and walked down the corridor facing her.

Halfway down the corridor was a green-painted door and attached to the door was a poster depicting animals at the zoo. This was it. Marigold manoeuvred the box so that she could rest her fingertips on the doorhandle. She twisted it to the right, the door opened and she went in.

The noise hit her. She blinked. About twenty children were

141

in the room, all wearing little slipover overalls, all under the age of five and all engaged in frantic activity. They were crawling through tunnels made of boxes, hanging from climbing frames and rolling around on the floor. A large, plastic playhouse stood in one corner of the room. The door was rolled up and inside, Marigold could see a table and four tiny chairs. Four little girls, completely oblivious of the noise going on around them, sat on the chairs. They poured pretend tea out of a red plastic teapot and crooked their little fingers as they sipped at their empty beakers.

Despite the noise and the nonstop activity it seemed the play session was drawing to a close. Three or four women had already arrived to pick up their children. One woman was dragging a freckled, protesting boy from the climbing frame and another was peeling a green cotton slipover from her daughter and trying to replace it with a red cardigan. The little girl was crying, huge tears pouring down her face.

Marigold looked round for help and a tall, calm-faced woman dressed in a blue overall came to her assistance.

'Can I help you?'

'Yes.' Marigold dumped the box on the floor and explained.

The woman's face lit up. 'Oh, good. We've been looking forward to some replacements. Toys don't last very long here, as you can imagine.'

Marigold nodded her head. 'Yes. The children do seem a little out of hand.'

The woman's smile faded. 'Boisterous is the word I would use.' She studied Marigold's face. 'A two- or three-year-old child, living in one room with his parents and possibly other siblings would feel the need to be boisterous for a couple of hours a week, don't you think?'

Marigold blushed. 'Sorry, I didn't think.'

'That's all right.' The woman bent over the box. 'Give me a

hand to carry it through to the kitchen.'

'Of course.'

The toys safely deposited, Marigold returned to the playroom. She looked around and spotted them at once.

The little one, Billy, was sitting on a chair and his brother, whose name was still unknown to Marigold, was bent over him fastening the buckles of his sandals.

Marigold studied them with an interest that surprised her. Billy, his round face flushed, was giggling and twisting around, making his brother's task difficult. In stark contrast, the older boy's face was pale and strained. He snapped irritably at his brother, telling him to stay still.

Keeping her expression carefully neutral, Marigold walked over and stood beside them. 'Hey,' she said lamely.

The dark-haired boy glanced up and then stared at her. She saw his eyes fill with sullen suspicion.

'What're you doing here? If you're checking up on me, I . . .'

'I'm not. Honestly.' She hurried over her words. 'I'm on an errand. I've brought some toys from Harrogate. I didn't know you'd be here.' In her anxiety to communicate, she found she was crouching down beside him. Her eyes were on a level with his.

'I just saw you and came over to say hello.'

'I don't believe you.' He rubbed his face with the back of his hand. 'Why are you doing this? God, I only pinched a pair of second-hand shoes.'

His growing agitation exploded against his brother. He gave a vicious yank to Billy's foot. 'Sit still, will you? If you don't, I'll thump you.'

Billy's fair eyebrows drew into a straight line. He sat quietly and watched as his shoes were fastened and then he smiled at Marigold.

She smiled back.

'It's nice here, isn't it?'

He nodded and put his thumb in his mouth.

She searched for more words but before she had time to think of any, Billy's brother grabbed his hand and jerked the youngster off his chair.

'Come on.'

Marigold bit her lip. She didn't want them to leave. She straightened up. 'I'm leaving, too. I'll walk out with you.'

The dark-haired boy glared at her.

In an uneasy silence they left the building and walked down the stone steps.

Marigold cleared her throat. 'Did you ever go back to the shop?' she asked. 'As we arranged?'

He didn't bother to reply. He walked quickly, holding Billy's hand tightly and constantly glancing from side to side. He wanted to be rid of her. She slowed her pace and watched his stiff back retreating from her.

The sunshine had fled and grey clouds were massing in the sky. As they reached the bottom of the steps, a few fat drops of rain plopped on the ground in front of them.

'Oh dear.' Marigold glanced upwards. 'I think we're in for a downpour.' She wondered whether she dare offer them a lift but after the last time . . . she decided against it.

He had stopped walking. She came level with him.

'Well, I'll say goodbye . . .'

She bit back the last word. Something was bothering him and it wasn't her presence.

He was staring at something or someone across the street and his face was totally bleached of colour.

She touched his sleeve. 'What's the matter?'

'Nothing.'

'Don't lie.' She tugged at his sleeve, making him turn a fraction in her direction. 'You're afraid of something.' She followed the direction of his gaze. 'Or someone.'

Directly across the road where they were standing was the site of an old churchyard. A stone wall ran around it and behind the wall copper beech trees leaned over, casting pockets of shade on the footpath. In one of the patches of shade, even darker now the weather was overcast, two men were standing. No, not two men.

Marigold narrowed her eyes. One of the figures was a man about twenty-four but his companion was a boy. The kind of boy that was featured regularly on local television reports on petty crime, joy-riding or affray. A boy about thirteen but with the body of a man and the brain of an eight year old.

She sighed. 'You're in trouble, aren't you?'

Without waiting for his reply she turned on her heel. 'Come with me. My car's only round the corner. I'll give you a lift to wherever you want to go.'

They ended up sitting round a table in a Pancake House.

Marigold sipped her black coffee and watched them eat. Billy was having a whale of a time. He had asked for chopped nuts, honey and chocolate sauce on his pancake and he now sported a brown moustache as he scraped his plate clean. His brother had managed only a third of his banana split but at least there was a tinge of colour in his cheeks.

When he glanced at her, she asked, 'What's your name?'

He heaved a sigh. 'Why should I tell you?'

'Because I've helped you out of a tight corner. Because, for some reason, I'm interested in you and your brother. Because I want to know.'

'I didn't ask for your help. I can manage.'

'Oh, for God's sake.' She snatched at her purse and stood up.

'All right. I'm sorry. I'll tell you.' He swallowed hard. Laid down his spoon. 'I'm Jack Scott and this is my brother, Billy.'

Marigold nodded. 'Good. I'm Marigold Goddard but you can call me Mari, if you like.'

She held out her hand to him and after a second's hesitation, he took it. They shook hands formally.

'Thanks for the lift and thanks for bringing us here.'

'You're welcome.' Marigold sat back in her chair. 'Now, are you going to tell me what's going on?'

He shook his head. 'I can't. Anyway, it's nothing to do with you, is it?'

'Fair enough.' Marigold hesitated. 'But you have parents, I presume. Surely you can talk to them.'

'I don't want to.' Jack kept his head low. 'Dad's away and Mum has enough on her plate. I don't want to worry her.'

'Maybe she's worried already. Being a mum, I bet she suspects something's wrong.' Marigold studied his face. 'She'd be the best person to tell, Jack.'

'How do you know? Who do you think you are, God?' Jack slapped his hands palm down on the table and glared at her. 'You don't know us. You don't know anything about us. Why are you sticking your nose into things? Just leave us alone. I'll fix it.'

'Can you?'

'Yes, I bloody can.' He pushed back his chair and stood up. 'Come on, Billy. We're leaving.'

'I haven't finished.' Billy began to sniffle.

The couple at the next table had stopped eating and were listening to the conversation. They stared at Jack.

Marigold ignored them. In a quiet voice, she asked again, 'Can you fix it, Jack?'

He sank back in his chair, put his head in his hands and burst into tears.

Billy stared at him, wide eyed.

'It's all right, Billy. He'll be all right.' Marigold fished in her pocket and brought out a fifty-pence piece. She gave it to Billy.

'Go to the counter and ask the lady for a Coke, or whatever you want.'

She watched the little boy go to the counter and then shuffled her chair until she was sitting next to Jack. She put her hand next to his, not quite touching him.

'I don't expect you to understand, Jack, I don't really understand myself, but I do genuinely want to help you if I can. Ever since that day you took the shoes I've felt . . .' She stopped, biting her lip. 'Look, why don't you go to the washroom and tidy up. Then come back here and we'll decide what to do. I won't push you for information. You can tell me nothing or as much as you want to tell me. And then I'll take you home.'

She consulted her watch. 'Your mum will be home just after five, you said. If you want to tell her what's been happening, that's good. If you like, I'll come in with you. If you don't want that, I'll drop you off at home. I'll drive away and you'll never see me again. Is that OK?'

He brushed his hand over his eyes and nodded.

Chapter Eleven

Marigold edged the car round a collection of wheelie bins and turned left. She glanced at Jack. 'Second turning on the right, you said?'

He nodded.

She followed his directions, reflecting that the area she was travelling through was becoming more depressing by the minute. And yet, at one time, it must have been so very different. These streets had been thronged with people of substance. The large, detached houses she was driving past had been occupied by doctors, dentists, wealthy tradesmen. Their wives and children had gone to church on Sunday and entertained their friends to tea. They would have left the work to the servants, of course. Skivvies would have scrubbed the steps leading up to the houses. They would have carried buckets of coal up to the third and fourth floors and kept the brass door knockers shining. Sixty, seventy years ago, the paintwork of the houses would have been fresh and bright, the windows would have shone in the sun and the large front gardens would have been colourful with bay trees, scented shrubs and masses of flowers.

Now she looked through the car window and saw windows filmed with dust, as dim and dull as eyes with cataracts. Strips of paint were peeling from windowsills and doors and the only colour in gardens were dirty shreds torn from unwanted free newspapers.

Marigold grimaced. Not that there were many gardens left. Most of them had been concreted over. Clapped out cars and bikes littered the forecourts.

'Here. Stop here.' Jack's voice sounded gruff.

She stopped and looked across at him.

'This is where we live,' he said. He made no move to leave the car. Strapped in the back seat, Billy bounced up and down like a rubber ball.

Marigold glanced at her watch. 'It's after five. Do you think your mother will be home?'

He shrugged.

She switched off the car engine. 'Do you want me to come in with you?'

He shook his head.

She was ashamed at her flicker of relief. 'Right, then.' She reached over and opened the car door for him.

He slouched in his seat and worried his thumbnail with his teeth. 'I can't tell her,' he muttered. 'She'll kill me.'

Marigold shook her head. 'No. She won't. She's your mother. She'll understand.'

He gave her a brief glance which cut through her happy optimism and she flinched. Who was she to give an opinion? She didn't know his mother, she didn't even know what Jack had done that was so bad.

She remembered his insistence that his mother mustn't find out about the theft of the trainers. Perhaps she hit him, perhaps she hit both of the boys. It happened. Marigold thought of all the lurid cases of child abuse highlighted on the TV and in the papers. Jack wasn't a baby, but he wasn't very old. And they couldn't sit in the car for ever.

'You have to go home, Jack.'

He nodded and began to shiver.

Oh God, he acted so tough but he was only ten years old. She reached a decision.

She got out, went round and released Billy from the back seat and helped him out. She locked the car. Billy ran straight up the steps leading to the house nearest to them. Jack stared at her.

'Is that where you live?'

He nodded.

'Have you got a flat?'

'Sort of.'

'Well, we'd better go there.'

He blinked. 'You mean . . .'

'I'll come in with you and if your Mum's at home, I'll talk to her. If I can help, I will.'

God knows what I'll find to say to her, she thought.

Sheila Scott had arrived home at half past four. It was almost ten minutes past five now and she was spitting mad. Jack collected Billy at four o'clock and he had strict instructions to bring him straight home. So where the hell were they?

She paced round the room and then opened the door leading to the hallway and listened for footsteps on the stairs. There was nothing. She slammed the door shut. A tiny edge of fear eroded her anger. Jack *knew* she came home at five, even if he'd been up to some mischief he would have made sure they were home before she got in.

She had been so delighted when Mrs Connolly had let her go early; now she wished she had worked late, even though it had been a hell of a day.

Her first call had been on Mrs Fry who lived at Haxby. Once a week she was supposed to do light cleaning work for the old lady but for the last four months she had done much more.

Mrs Fry was recovering from a stroke. Some days she managed and some days she didn't. She had family but they were all busy working.

Arriving at the house at eight thirty, Sheila had found the front door unlocked. She had rushed upstairs to the old lady's bedroom. Mrs Fry was snoring loudly. She wouldn't wake up. Sheila tried to arouse her then she searched in the telephone book in the hall and called the old lady's doctor. Waiting for his visit, she had investigated further.

Mrs Fry's bed was saturated with urine. Sheila wondered how long she had been lying there. She unearthed a clean bedspread from the laundry cupboard and tried to spread it beneath the old lady, then she went down to the kitchen. She gulped at the mess she found. She threw out all the rotten food, washed the stinking milk bottles and then she started to clean the place. When the doctor arrived, she let him in.

She told him what she had found and he hurried upstairs.

Sheila collected the dirty clothes strewn about the house and put them in the washing machine.

The doctor came downstairs. He had a long, comic-sad face. He had seen too many similar situations. He asked Sheila some questions and she answered the best she could.

'Do you have the phone numbers of the relatives? We'll have a record at the surgery but it's a question of time.'

She shrugged. 'Phone book's in the hall.'

'Thanks.'

As he made his calls she searched for things to pack in Mrs Fry's bag and at a quarter to ten the ambulance came.

Sheila was half an hour late for her next lady, Mrs Connolly.

'For goodness' sake, Sheila, come in and get your coat off. You know I want to springclean the bedrooms today.'

For the next five hours Sheila shifted beds, washed paintwork and scrubbed out cupboards. She had a break at twelve thirty when she and Mrs Connolly drank a cup of tea and ate a buttered teacake.

At four o'clock Mrs Connolly rubbed her face and sighed. 'I don't know about you, Sheila, but I'm exhausted. Let's call it a day, shall we?'

She paid Sheila her normal money and Sheila was grateful. Mrs Connolly was all right. She worked alongside you.

And now it was fifteen minutes past five. Sheila took her handbag, opened it and tipped the contents on to her bed. Yes, there was one left. She took the remaining cigarette out of the crumpled packet, put it between her lips and lit it. Ah! She sat down, closed her eyes and drew in a lungful of exquisite smoke. Oh God, that was so good. She blanked the thought of her husband from her mind. He'd be so mad at her. He'd stopped smoking ten years ago and he thought she'd stopped, too. Well, she had, almost. This was her first ciggie for . . . she cast her mind back . . . almost three weeks. And she'd carried that one cigarette in her bag all that time without weakening.

It was Jack's fault. Why didn't he do as he was told?

She took the cigarette from her mouth and pinched the glowing end between her fingers. She was replacing the tab end in the packet when she heard the key in the lock.

Without giving Jack time to come in, she rushed over to the door and flung it open. Jack was standing there, Billy at his side, and behind them stood a complete stranger.

Sheila blinked. 'Oh, God. You're in trouble, aren't you?' She reached out and pulled Jack into the room.

'Who are you?' She stared at the woman.

'I'm . . . well, I guess I'm a friend of Jack.'

Sheila's eyes narrowed. The woman's voice was hesitant, she looked nervous. She wasn't from the police, then. And, Sheila took a good look at her, she wasn't from the social services, either. Her clothes were much too expensive for the anorak brigade. Sheila had seen clothes like these in the wardrobes of the houses she cleaned.

She demanded, 'What do you mean? How can you be a friend of Jack's? I've never seen you before.'

'Jack has something to confess, Mrs Scott. No, please don't look worried. I don't think it's anything too dreadful but I know he's anxious so I offered to come up with him.'

'So he's told you something that he can't tell me?'

'Oh, no. I don't know what it is. If I can come in for a few minutes, I'll explain.'

'You can go to hell.' Sheila grabbed at Billy and started to close the door but the woman put out her hand, blocking her.

Sheila's eyes flashed fire. The bloody woman was nervous but determined. Well, so was she. Just because the visitor spoke nicely and wore expensive clothes, that didn't give her the right to push her way into their home. Holding tight to Billy who was wriggling around, Sheila spoke through her teeth. 'Go away. Leave us alone.'

She saw the woman step back, she heard Jack catch his breath but it was Billy who stalemated her victory. Breaking free from her, he shot outside and clutched at the stranger's skirt, then he smiled at his mother and said, 'She's nice, Mum. Let her in. I've promised to show her my new garage.'

The woman ruffled his hair but her gaze never left Sheila's face. 'Please, Mrs Scott. I'll only stay for a couple of minutes and then, when Jack's said his piece, I'll go.'

'Well—' Sheila glanced at her elder son. He looked so miserable, her resolve faltered. She shrugged her shoulders. 'Just for a few minutes.'

'Thank you.'

The woman walked through the door and looked round for somewhere to sit.

Sheila, seeing the shabbiness of the place through the

stranger's eyes, found herself hurrying over to the one easy chair in the room and removing the pile of ironing occupying it. 'You can sit here.'

The woman took the seat. She inclined her head in a gesture of thanks and a strand of her glossy hair fell forward upon her creamy-coloured cheek.

Suddenly aware that her own hair was scragged back in an unbecoming ponytail, that her face was shiny and her overall dirty, Sheila asked, 'What did you mean about being Jack's friend?'

'We've met from time to time.'

'Where? Are you a teacher at his school?'

'No.' The woman paused.

Billy had been busy dragging a toy garage from beneath Sheila's bed. Now he came running over waving a red car in his hand and attempted to climb on to the woman's lap.

'Stop it, Billy.' Sheila spoke absently and then she frowned. 'It seems you're his friend, too?'

'Not exactly.' The woman hoisted Billy on to her knee. 'That is,' she glanced over to where Jack was standing. 'I work at the toy library. That's where I met the boys. And today, I could see Jack didn't look well. I felt sure something was upsetting him.'

'And what is that?'

'I don't know, Mrs Scott. I asked him but he wouldn't tell me. However, we left the building together and something happened which made me realise that he must confide in a grown-up and the obvious person was you. But he said,' she hesitated, 'he didn't want to worry you.'

Sheila turned and stared at Jack.

'I knew it. I knew something was wrong. All that talking in your sleep. Why didn't you tell me when I asked if you were being bullied. Is that it? Is someone bullying you?'

He stared at her. 'Sort of.'

'Sort of. What kind of answer is that?'

He dropped his head. 'It's worse than just bullying, Mum. I think I'm in bad trouble.'

Sheila was silenced. What on earth had the lad been up to?

Billy was chattering away to the woman. His babble unnerved her. She went and took him from the stranger.

'You can have the telly on, Billy. There might be some cartoons.'

She switched on the TV, adjusted the volume to low and dumped Billy on the floor in front of it. The picture flicked on. No cartoons, unfortunately, but a programme about a zoo. Billy liked anything to do with animals. Sheila ruffled his hair and fished in her overall pocket.

'Look, I've a surprise for you.' She handed him a packet of jelly babies.

He took them but without enthusiasm.

'He won't be very hungry, Mrs Scott.'

The woman's voice was so cool, it infuriated Sheila.

'How do you know?'

The woman shifted uneasily. 'I took the boys for a snack before bringing them home. Jack said you didn't get in until after five. I hope you don't mind? It seemed a good idea. Jack was very tense and I thought . . .'

Sheila stiffened. 'You think a lot, don't you?'

'Sorry?'

'You come walking in here. I haven't a clue who you are. I don't even know your name.'

'Oh, I'm sorry. I'm Marigold Goddard.'

Marigold. What a bloody silly name. Sheila tried to keep her expression neutral. She asked, 'Have you children of your own, Mrs Goddard, or do you make a habit of borrowing other people's?'

She'd scored a hit. She saw the woman's eyes blink before she replied.

156

'I have a daughter. She's grown up now and lives in London.'

A grown-up daughter. She looked too bloody young. Sheila ground her teeth together.

'Well, Mrs Goddard, now I know that Jack has something to tell me I would like you to leave now. We'll manage our own affairs, thank you very much. And before you go—' She paused. 'Might I suggest you buy yourself a kitten or a puppy. You'll be kept too busy then to stick your nose into things that don't concern you.'

'No, Mum. Don't!' Jack's cry rang through the room; even Billy looked away from the television screen for a moment.

'Mrs Goddard's OK. Don't get mad at her. If she hadn't been around, Trevor Stokesby and his brother would have beaten me up for sure, and maybe Billy, too.'

'Beaten you up?' Sheila sat down on the edge of her bed. 'What are you talking about? You'd better tell me everything right now.'

He did. He stuttered and stammered when he got to the part about the pills, but he continued to the end and the two women listened to him.

When he finished, Sheila's hands were clenched tightly in her lap.

She said, 'Come here.'

He approached her apprehensively.

She pulled him down to sit next to her and then draped her arm about his shoulders. 'Oh, son, why didn't you tell me about all this?'

'Dad's not here.' He shrugged. 'What could you do? It's drugs, Mum. The police will nick me if they find out. But I swear to you that I won't touch them from now on.'

'You were coerced, Jack. The police would recognise that. They wouldn't hold you responsible.'

It was Marigold who spoke. Sheila and Jack stared at her and, for the first time, she saw the resemblance between them.

Their faces were blank, so she explained. 'You were forced into doing what you did. And you didn't know there were drugs in the envelopes.'

'But will the police believe him?'

Marigold answered Sheila's question. 'I think so. They know a villain when they see one and Jack doesn't fit the bill. But this boy Trevor might.'

'Did you say he's a Stokesby?' Sheila rubbed her forehead. 'I'm sure that family's been in court. It was in the local newspaper. His older brother's been fined for stealing.' She looked at Jack. 'Would he be the one that was waiting for you?'

He nodded.

'If only you'd told me.'

'Look, I think it's time I went.' Marigold stood up. 'Your mum knows everything now, Jack. And she'll know what to do about it.'

He dropped his head. 'Thanks, Mrs Goddard.'

Sheila bit her lip. She still resented this woman, Mrs Goddard or whatever she was called, but the truth was, she didn't know what to do and she suspected that Mrs Goddard did because she had a look about her. Sheila guessed Mrs Goddard would be the kind of woman who could do anything from filling in a tax return to changing the wheel of a car.

Sheila was frightened of official-looking forms, she couldn't even drive a car, and the thought of contacting the police filled her with horror. Nevertheless, for Jack, she would do it. She rose to her feet and said, quietly, 'I'll see you out.'

'Thanks.'

By the door, they stood awkwardly, both aware of the vast gap between them.

Sheila muttered, 'I'm sorry I was rude to you.'

'It doesn't matter. If I had been you, I would have been

resentful as well. But I wanted to help Jack.'

'I know. So,' Sheila sighed. 'You'd advise me to get in touch with the police?'

'I think you'll have to, otherwise this Trevor will continue to terrorise him.'

'But if they don't believe Jack, we're in worse trouble. And if they do, the rest of that family could come looking for him.'

'May I suggest something?' Marigold's voice was cautious. When Sheila nodded, she went on. 'Don't do anything tonight. I'll contact someone who may be able to give you advice. She's a friend of mine and she's involved in all kinds of things. She's a magistrate so she knows all about police procedure. I'll speak to her tonight and then contact you tomorrow. Will you be working?'

Sheila nodded. 'But only from eight until eleven thirty.'

'I'll try and get round about lunchtime. And because it's Saturday, Billy and Jack can stay indoors.'

Sheila bowed her head. 'It's good of you to bother.'

'Yes, I'm like that.' Marigold's sudden grin broke the tension. 'Kind but nosy.'

They both laughed.

Sheila opened the door. 'We'll see you tomorrow, then.'

'Yes.' Marigold peeked over Sheila's shoulder and waved goodbye to both the boys.

She paused. 'By the way. Your advice to me, about getting a pet . . .'

Sheila blushed. 'I'm sorry. I was so rude.'

'It's all right.' Marigold shrugged. 'I just thought I'd tell you. I already have one. A great, soft labrador called Paddy.'

Paddy practically knocked her off her feet when she entered the house. Ian followed closely behind the dog, an aggrieved expression on his face.

159

'You're very late.'

'Something cropped up. It's not that late, is it? I've plenty of time to cook the evening meal.'

'Thing is, I was delayed, too. I came in the back way, through the kitchen. Paddy had peed all over the floor, Mari, and I walked through it. Not a pleasant experience, as you can imagine.'

'Oh dear. It's this warm weather, I expect. I supposed he's emptied his water bowl.'

Ian frowned. 'I've washed the floor for you.'

Marigold's forehead creased. 'For both of us, Ian. We both tend to walk around in our stockinged feet, remember.'

He stared at her. 'You're in a funny mood.'

'Hilarious.' She looked round at her surroundings, the thick hall carpet, the glimpse of her attractive sitting room through the half-opened door, and she remembered the smell as she was climbing the stairs that led to the cramped fusty room, which was home to the Scott family.

She felt impatient with Ian's injured tone of voice. She turned on her heel.

'Where are you going now?'

'Have to make a phone call.' She went into the sitting room and picked up the receiver. She covered the mouthpiece with her right hand. 'Don't worry, I won't be a minute.' She dialled Susan Cambridge's number. Waiting for a reply, she smiled at her husband. 'What do you want for dinner?'

Chapter Twelve

Two o'clock on Saturday and once again Marigold was knocking on Sheila's door, but this time her greeting was more cordial.

'Come in, please.' Sheila stood to one side to allow Marigold to enter.

'I'd offer you a cup of tea but . . . ' She glanced towards the gas ring.

'No, I'm fine, thanks. I'm sorry I couldn't get here earlier. I knew you'd be anxious but I had to wait until Susan, the friend I told you about, got in touch with me.'

'And has she?' Sheila looked round for Jack who came to stand beside her. They both stared anxiously at Marigold. 'Can she help? What did she say?'

'Let's sit down and I'll tell you.'

Sheila and Jack went to sit on the side of the bed and Marigold walked further into the room and looked round for Billy.

He was playing in the curtained-off area where he and Jack slept. He had propped up the quilt with something, it was obviously supposed to be a cave, and he was crawling around pretending to be an animal, possibly a bear. He saw Marigold and gave her a wave before resuming his deep-throated growling.

She returned his wave, pleased that he was occupied, and

then she sat down and told Sheila and Jack her news.

'I contacted Susan as soon as I got home yesterday and she promised to find out what she could. She rang me an hour ago. Apparently she spoke to a police inspector she knows. He put her on to someone working within the drugs squad.

'She explained the situation – without mentioning any names, of course, and asked for his advice. He said the sensible thing to—' Marigold paused. 'The only thing to do, is for Jack to talk to a police officer.'

Jack's body jerked. 'But if I do, what will happen to me?'

Marigold put up her hand, stopping his outburst.

'No, listen. The police already know that drugs are traded at raves. They also know that local pushers are increasingly targeting school children. They know, but without hard evidence they're helpless. Susan told me that the second man she spoke to was very interested when she told him about the stuff being passed around on school premises. He said most of the drug pushers approach pupils on their way home.'

'If they know so much, why don't they make more arrests?'

Marigold looked at Sheila's frowning face.

'Before they charge anyone they have to make sure the charge will stick in court. Dealers are good at getting rid of the evidence. There's the same problem at raves. There is always an undercover police presence but detection rates are poor. The places are always packed, which doesn't help freedom of movement and there's a lot of fringe drugs going down. People smoking pot, for example. The police are expected to react to stuff like that but while they're doing it, the professional drug pushers find somewhere they can sell the hard drugs.'

Marigold paused for breath. 'Susan said this man was keen to have names. He gave her a special phone number. She's given it to me. If Jack's prepared to meet someone, you must ring up immediately, Sheila.'

'But what about Jack? Will he be charged?'

'Susan asked the same question. The man wouldn't commit himself to a definite promise but he said that if Jack's information leads to an arrest, then he'll probably be let off with a warning.'

Jack gripped his hands together. 'But it's not just the police. If the Stokesby family find I've split on Trevor and his brother they'll like as not kill me.'

Marigold leaned forward in her chair. 'That's the beauty of it, Jack. They won't find out. If you name them, the police will know who to look out for at the rave. As it happens, there's one tonight. It's being held at an old, closed-down engineering plant on the outskirts of York. The organisers are reputable. They've notified the police. If you give the policeman the name and description of Trevor's brother, they'll know who to look for and your name needn't appear in the charges.'

'Trev did mention there would be more stuff coming through soon.' Jack spoke slowly.

'You must do it, Jack.' Sheila rested her hand on his arm.

'But Trevor . . .'

'Trevor will think it's just bad luck if his brother's picked up. He won't bother you. He knows the best thing he can do is keep his head down.'

Jack continued to look undecided. 'But it seems so sneaky, telling the police.'

Sheila's sympathetic mood vanished. She said sharply, 'Don't be so stupid. Getting youngsters hooked on drugs is about the worse thing anyone can do. How can you feel sorry for them?' She scowled. 'Billy will start school next year. How would you feel if a big kid got him started on drugs?'

Jack studied the back of his hands and then sighed. 'All right. I'll talk to the police.'

Sheila looked across at Marigold. 'Where's that number?'

'Here.' Marigold took a slip of paper from her handbag and

handed it to her. 'Ask for Mr Sinclair. He's waiting for your call. He said he'd come and see you, if you want, or you and Jack can meet him at the police station.'

'We'll go there.' Sheila grimaced. 'If he sees where we live, he'll probably decide we're criminals too. Anyway, I don't want a policeman knocking on my door.'

'I doubt whether he'll be in uniform, Sheila.'

'Can't risk it.' Sheila clenched the paper in her hand. 'Right, I'd better get myself to the phone box and ring him.'

Marigold watched her put on her jacket and check that she had her purse.

'Shall I stay here with the boys?'

'Would you?' Sheila looked towards Jack. 'Are you coming with me?'

He shook his head.

She sniffed. 'Please yourself.'

His face was white and completely expressionless. Marigold realised he was scared stiff.

She said, 'He's all right here although . . .' She hesitated. 'I expect Mr Sinclair will want to see you as soon as possible. If you like, I'll drive you to the station and then I'll entertain Billy until you're through there.'

Sheila looked doubtful. She asked, 'Can you spare the time?'

'Oh, yes.'

'Well, so long as you're sure it's all right.'

'It is.' Marigold shrugged. 'Now I've got involved in all this, I want to know how it turns out.'

Marigold watched Sheila march Jack into the police station and her heart ached for him as she saw him manfully straighten his shoulders as they disappeared from view. She turned round to look at his brother who was strapped into the back seat of her car.

'Now, young man, what am I going to do with you?'

He didn't reply. He was absorbed in breathing on the car window and drawing funny faces on the steamed-up surface. She realised he had no qualms about being left alone with her and the thought pleased her.

Watching his stubby little forefinger trace an upturned smile on a circle of a face, she wondered at her feeling of involvement with the boys. It couldn't last, of course. She was nothing to Sheila Scott and her family and as soon as this business was settled she must stop seeing them. In the meantime, how to occupy a three-year-old boy for an hour?

Billy had finished his finger drawing by putting a clown's hat on top of the round head. Admiring the picture gave Marigold an idea. She started the car.

Billy asked, 'Are we going somewhere nice?'

'I think so.'

When Karen had been seven years old her favourite place in York had been the Museum of Automata in Tower Street. The unique collection of ingenious machines, which ranged from ancient times to modern technology, had kept her amused and entertained for hours. Marigold remembered that her all-time favourite had been called 'The Miser'.

It was a hand-cranked exhibit, one of the machines that had kept countless day trippers entertained on seaside piers so many years ago. Open-mouthed, Karen had turned the handle, bent down and watched the story unfold.

A shabby room, an old grey-beard seated by his table counting out piles of money. On the upper landing, squeaks and groans as doors opened and closed, allowing phantoms and spirits to drift down the stairs. The old man was too intent upon his wealth to notice the skeleton dancing behind him or the pictures falling off the wall.

Karen had laughed out aloud at the pictures and the flowers

in the vase on the table which suddenly faded and turned into dry twigs. But when the scene darkened and the ghosts and skeletons gathered round the miser, she had shivered, and when the lights went out she actually screamed, though whether the cause was terror or delight, Marigold never knew. All she knew was that Karen demanded to visit the museum at every possible opportunity. It was only when Ian had told her she was too big for such stupidity that she had stopped asking to go there.

Marigold was gratified when she saw Billy's reaction to the mechanical clowns, musicians and acrobats but true enchantment came for him when he saw the modern-day robots which had been added to the collection. He would have happily stayed with them until closing time and Marigold had to promise a return visit before she could drag him away and return to collect Sheila and Jack as promised.

Fortunately, she arrived at the police station just as they were coming out of the main entrance. She peeped the horn, they looked round, then walked towards the car. Marigold thought they looked shattered. She sighed and opened the car door.

'Hop in. We'll go somewhere quiet and have a snack.'

Sheila roused herself. 'Oh, but . . .'

'No arguments.'

She took them to a modest cafe in one of York's backstreets. She knew more attractive places in which to eat but on a Saturday afternoon they were bound to be busy. She went up to the counter and ordered tea and toasted teacakes for herself and Sheila and more appropriate fare for the two boys.

When she returned to the table she heard Billy chattering away about robots. Jack was silent. She looked at him but refrained from comment until the food arrived. When sausage and chips were placed before Billy he concentrated on eating and Marigold had a chance to ask how things went.

'What was Sinclair like?'

'Tough.' Sheila's smile wobbled. 'He asked us to sit down then told Jack to tell him everything he knew. He said he would know if he lied and he would have done, too. Jack told him what he told you and me. When he finished speaking we all sat in silence for about five minutes. I could have screamed. Then he said that he would do his best to keep Jack out of it.'

'Thank God.' Marigold let loose a gusty sigh of relief.

'Yes, he's been lucky.' Sheila shot a glance at her elder son. 'But then he tore strips off him, reduced him to tears.'

In his chair, Jack stirred in protest but he remained silent.

'Sinclair said he'd been criminally stupid and he warned him to be very careful in the future. "I've got your name," he said.'

'I told him I didn't know what was in the envelopes.' Jack's voice was strained and Marigold, glancing at him, realised he was again close to tears.

'I didn't know Trevor's brother was into drugs.'

He was only ten years old. She felt a familiar rush of sympathy but his mother was made of sterner stuff.

'You were damned lucky today. If they'd charged you it would have been a black mark against you all your life and it would have blown your chances of ever getting a decent job. Mind you,' she sighed. 'Who *can* get a job nowadays?'

'Cheer up, Sheila.' Marigold refilled their teacups. 'Things haven't worked out too badly.'

'Thanks to you.' Sheila's eyes moistened. 'I can't think why you're bothering with all this.' She picked up her buttered teacake and bit into it. She glanced across at Marigold and said, thickly, 'You're spending all this time with us, are you sure it's all right?'

'Of course it is. Why shouldn't I?'

Sheila swallowed. 'Well, it's Saturday. I expect your husband's at home. Doesn't he mind you gadding about on your own?'

Marigold stirred her tea. 'Ian's away. He's on a field trip this weekend.'

'Field trip?' Sheila looked mystified.

'Yes, it's half work and half pleasure.' Marigold replaced the teaspoon in the saucer. 'Anyway, weekends are not that important. Ian often works from home so I see him during the week.'

'You lucky thing.' Sheila reached across and wiped Billy's mouth with a tissue. 'I haven't seen Mike for ages. What does your husband do for a living?'

'He teaches physics at the university.'

Sheila's eyes opened wide. 'Goodness. You mean he's a professor?'

'Yes.'

'Well.' Sheila pondered. 'I always thought professors were old men but you're young.'

Marigold managed a smile. 'I'm forty-four and Ian's forty-eight.'

'He must be clever.' Sheila wet her forefinger and picked up the crumbs on her plate. 'I'm don't even know what physics are.'

Marigold laughed. 'To tell the truth, I'm not sure either.' There's lots of different kinds, you see. There's laser physics, surface physics, nuclear physics . . .'

'Like what they made the atom bomb with?'

Both women looked across at Jack.

'That's right, Jack, although that was ages ago. They've moved on since then.' Marigold's smile was grim. 'Thank goodness Ian isn't involved with that particular science. He lectures on laser physics and he's involved in experiments at the Rutherford-Appleton Laboratory with people from London and Belfast.'

'Lasers! That's neat.'

'I wouldn't know.' Marigold shrugged her shoulders. 'It's above my head, I'm afraid.'

'I'm not surprised.' Sheila reached for her jacket. 'Jack, take Billy to the toilet and makes sure he goes. Then we must be off. We mustn't take up any more of Mrs Goddard's time.'

Jack did as he was asked. The two woman watched the boys walk across the room towards the door marked 'Men'.

Marigold said, 'I'm surprised Jack made the connection between physics and the atom bomb.'

'I'm not. Jack's only middling at most subjects at school but he's always top at science and maths. If he has any money to spare he always buys magazines about space travel and suchlike.'

'He's a good kid.' Marigold smiled. 'I'm so glad he got off with a warning.'

'So am I. It would have killed his dad if he had landed in court.'

'Does your husband know what's happened?' Marigold caught her breath and apologised. 'I'm sorry, it's nothing to do with me.'

'I don't mind you knowing. No, I haven't said anything to him. He's in the Manchester area trying to find work and he's got enough to cope with without worrying about Jack. Of course, if Jack had been charged, he would have had to know.'

Marigold looked down, moved the position of her plate. 'I hope he has some luck soon.'

'I'm not counting on it.' Sheila sighed. But we've got to find somewhere else to live. A little flat would be fine, but the owners usually want a deposit. That's why I've taken on more cleaning work. I don't like leaving Billy so much, making Jack take on the responsibility after school, but it's the only way.' She glanced towards the door leading to the toilets. 'They're taking their time. I bet it's Billy, playing around with the hand-drying machine.'

Marigold laughed. 'He's a character, isn't he?'

Sheila nodded and then said, quite unexpectedly, 'Why do you work at the toy library?'

'The toy library?' Marigold's face turned red. 'I only work there part time.'

'But if your husband's a professor – well I don't suppose you need to work. Is it because you like kids?'

'Yes.' Marigold pointed. 'Look, the boys are coming back.'

'Good. It's time we were off.'

Sheila stood up. 'Come on, kids.'

Jack turned towards the door but Billy disappeared under the cafe table.

'Don't want to go home.'

'Don't you start.' Sheila bent down and grabbed for him but he eluded her.

Marigold picked up her bag. 'Yes,' she said loudly. 'I must go too. Paddy, my dog, will need walking.'

'I wish we had a dog.' It was Jack who spoke. Hearing his brother's voice, Billy's head popped out from beneath the table.

'Can we, Mum? Can we have a dog?'

'No. It wouldn't be fair. It's bad enough for us . . .' She met Marigold's eyes and stopped. 'Come out from under that table, Billy.'

Marigold chewed her lips. 'Look, please don't take this the wrong way, but you must have realised I enjoy the boys' company. Would it be possible for me to see them again? You said yourself you were busy working. I have lots of spare time. I take my dog, Paddy, for a long walk most days.

'With your permission, I would gladly pick up Jack and Billy after Jack leaves school, say, one day a week. Paddy would enjoy having the boys to play with. He's very friendly. And the weather's so lovely at the moment.'

Sheila was nonplussed. 'But why should you want to see them?' She looked at Marigold and her back stiffened. 'You don't have to feel sorry for us, you know. We don't need help. We get along fine.'

'It's not that. You'd be doing *me* a favour.' Marigold fidgeted with the clasp of her handbag. 'The truth is, Sheila, I often feel lonely.'

Sheila frowned. 'So do I, but my man's away from home. You've a husband and a daughter. If you're fed up, you ought to visit your own child, or drag your husband away from his phy . . .' She stumbled over the word. 'Psychology.'

'It's physics.' Marigold's smile was forced. 'Ian, my husband, would be no good at psychology.'

'Go on, Mum. Say yes.' Jack tugged at Sheila's elbow. 'I'd like to help her walk her dog.'

'Yes, yes, yes,' chanted Billy, his body emerging from beneath the table.

'Well,' Sheila wavered. 'All right then, but only once a week.'

'Great.' Three faces were wreathed with smiles. Billy ran in front of Marigold towards the door but Sheila caught hold of Jack's arm as he moved to follow them.

'Just a minute.'

He turned and stared at her. 'What?'

'Don't get too stuck on this woman, Jack.'

'Why not? She helped us.'

'Yes, and I'm grateful, but there's something not quite right. Why should she bother so much about you and Billy?'

He shook his head. 'She's all right, Mum.'

'I hope so. But don't you get too involved with her fine ways and her posh car. She likes you now but she could dump you next week. People with money are like that. I know, I work for them.'

'I'm not too bothered about her posh car. I want to see her dog and . . .' He flushed and was silent.

'And what?'

'Nothing.'

'Come on.'

He rubbed his nose. 'She said her daughter was a model. Some of the guys at school have been collecting pictures of models. I thought Mrs Goddard might have some photos I could borrow.'

Sheila's brow creased. She looked serious but inside she was laughing. It was a good feeling.

'What sort of pictures are they, Jack?'

'Different kinds.'

'Have the girls got clothes on?'

A pause, and then. 'Yes, almost all of them. But they're wearing bikinis, stuff like that.' He pointed to the door. 'Look, they're waiting for us.'

'All right.' She took her hand away from his arm.

'I think you're going to be disappointed, Jack. I can't see a daughter of Mrs Goddard's posing in the nude.'

Chapter Thirteen

The power went off around eleven p.m. Ten minutes earlier, Karen Goddard had got out of her bath, wrapped herself in a white towelling robe, poured out a dry martini and flopped out in front of the TV.

'What the . . .'

She sat in the darkness and watched as the picture on the television shrank into a tiny dot of light in the middle of the screen and then vanished. Then she sat and watched the nothingness. At first, she was merely annoyed. Channel Four was running a series of old films staring such screen idols as Doris Day, Joan Crawford, Henry Fonda and Gregory Peck. Karen had been looking forward to a nostalgic wallow in yesteryears but now what was she to do? She didn't feel like sleeping, not yet.

She got up and prowled around the room. Was it just her building? She groped her way to the window and pulled back the curtains. No, it was a proper power cut, the whole of the neighbourhood was blacked out. And yet, because it was early July, the night wasn't completely black, it was a strange dark grey colour and high in the sky she could catch glimpses of the slip of the moon as it swam between dense passing clouds.

From her sixth-floor flat, Karen peered downwards. All she could see below were occasional twin searchlights from cars moving cautiously along the main road which was close to where she lived. She let the curtains drop back into place and turned her back on the window. She stood for a moment, becoming aware of the absolute silence.

No sound from the freezer, the fridge or the air conditioning, and the lift wouldn't be working. She felt like the sole survivor of some catastrophe. The man who occupied the only other flat on this floor of the building had flown to Saudi four days ago. He had given her a key and asked her to water his plants. She felt the palms of her hands beginning to sweat.

Hey, this was ridiculous. What had she got to be scared of?

She went back to her favourite chair and sat down, curling her legs up beneath her and tucking the bottom of her robe around her feet because they were beginning to feel cold. She'd just sit a little while. With a bit of luck the power would return within a few minutes.

She rested her head against the back of the chair. If she'd been at home, there would have been frantic activity by now. Dad would be stumbling around looking for candles and probably fretting about losing something important on his computer screen. Paddy would be under everyone's feet and Mum – Karen smiled a little – ever-capable Mum would have already produced a torch and most probably would be in the kitchen making tea for everyone.

Karen sighed. She'd like a cup of tea but she couldn't have one. The flat was all electric.

Mum hadn't visited her new flat yet but she had been less than impressed by Karen's description. 'Six floors up and all electric! It wouldn't do for me. I'd miss my garden and I'd never be able to cook a decent meal with an electric oven.'

But she could have. Mum was a kind of modern-day version of Doris Day who, in fifties films always looked delicious, smiled all the time and solved everyone's problems for them.

And she always ended up marrying the hero and living happily ever after. Of course, it was all make believe. In real life, if present-day magazine articles were to be believed, Doris Day had had several marriages and they were all unhappy.

Karen rubbed her cold toes and thought about her parents. For a long time she had considered their marriage nigh on perfect. In her early teens she had been a tiny bit jealous of her mother, but not really because even then she knew that she came first in her father's affections. God. What a selfish little bitch she had been.

But then, was it her fault she had taken after her father?

She stopped fiddling with her toes and stared into the darkness.

Awareness of the emptiness of her parents' relationship had dawned upon her slowly, over the last eighteen months. Perhaps that meant, she grimaced, she was growing up at last. In her teens she had been too self-obsessed to think about anyone else and leaving home at eighteen hadn't helped.

Captivated by her new life in London she had practically forgotten her parents for months at a time. Only occasionally did she remember to return their telephone calls and when she did, inevitably it was her father who hogged the line. But that was fine because he was the one eager to hear about her successes and she was only too happy to tell him. He was proud of her, he said. He loved her – and she believed him.

But eighteen months ago, things had changed. She had broken up with the man she thought was the love of her life. She was unhappy and when she rang home to chat, some of her unhappiness had seeped through. Her mother had spotted it. Her usually brisk voice had softened and there had been pauses in their conversation which, Karen now realised, had been invitations to unburden herself.

But no, all she had wanted was her father. He would

understand. He would listen to her, comfort her and tell her she'd be better off without Carl. Her father would bolster up her self-esteem.

But he didn't want to know. He distanced himself from her unhappiness.

'Stop fretting, Karen. Remember, you're a lovely girl, successful in your career. You can have anyone you want.'

But she wanted Carl.

Still she had mopped her eyes and talked more cheerfully about her next modelling job because that's what he wanted to hear and she wanted him to be proud of her. But why did she have to be a success to deserve his love? Was it because she was not only his daughter, but also his mirror image – in behaviour and looks?

Karen sat upright in her chair. The silence was so intense she could hear the pulse beating in her throat.

If that was true, and everyone who knew them commented on their likeness to each other, then his love wasn't so much love for her, it was self-love. And when he told his friends of her successes and showed her off to them it wasn't her he was praising, it was himself. Look, he was saying, look at my creation. And she had played along with him. And Mum had known, all these years.

Christ, why was she thinking so much?

She jumped up and turned to her right, meaning to go to the table which housed her telephone.

The darkness was depressing her. She'd phone a friend, they could crack a few jokes about the power cut. They could indulge in girl-talk. Anything to drive away serious thinking.

Ouch! Her little toe caught against one of the castors on her Victorian button-back chair. It hurt. She groaned and bent over, tears starting in the corners of her eyes. Her own fault. If she'd bought the usual traditional armchairs for the flat it wouldn't have happened but she had to show off, didn't she? She had to pretend she was cultured and knew about books, art and antiques.

She fell backwards into the chair and cautiously wiggled her toe. If it was broken it would affect her work, although remembering some of the shoes she'd worn on the catwalk lately, it was a wonder all her toes hadn't been broken.

Her mum would advise her to put ice on her toe. She'd do it in a minute, when it didn't hurt so much. Karen breathed in short gasps, telling herself it was the pain from her injured toe, not thoughts of her mother that were bringing tears to her eyes. She'd been a pig to her mother when she was growing up and even full grown, she had shut her out of her life. I'm not getting married, she thought. It wouldn't work. I'm too selfish, I'm like Dad. I'll stay a career girl.

But then, as the pain lessened, she thought of the hours she spent hanging around, waiting for camera men as they moved lights and adjusted backdrops, and standing motionless as a statue as costumes were pinned and stitched on to her. She thought of the endless photographic shoots with the air machine blowing her hair and the make-up artists rushing forward to touch up her eyebrows, paint out a blemish on her skin, emphasise the hollows in her cheeks. And the finished result? It wasn't her. She wasn't the girl on the cover of the magazine.

She sighed and said aloud, 'Then who am I?'

She'd acquired a city veneer, but that's all it was, a veneer. She often felt a stranger among her peers. When she first came to London she had ironed out her Yorkshire accent and cultivated a southern way of speaking but she needn't have bothered because now regional accents were 'in'. The girl last week, the one she had done a show with, had been so cockney she hadn't understood what she was saying half the time.

But she'd played along with her, just as she played along with the other people she mixed with. At the Berkeley Dress Show she had nodded and looked intelligent while the county set had chattered about horseflesh and polo. And last week, escorted to the theatre by a young man with a plummy accent who fancied himself as a journalist, she had listened silently as he had poured scorn on the lower-class daily newspapers.

'Total bum-paper, darling. And those page three girls, all backsides and tits. No artistic merit whatsoever.'

Maybe not, but at least the girls' bottoms and breasts were for real. Karen's breasts were often padded, sometimes flattened and regularly held up with sticky tape. And her hit photograph of last year, the one in which her breasts, bottom and carefully rouged bikini line had been tastefully filtered through pink gauze as she sprawled across a bed, was still porn with a sugar coating. She blushed even now just thinking about it.

Suddenly, the light flooded back. The freezer hummed and the blip reappeared on the TV. The little round dot widened into a courtroom scene.

Karen, feeling disorientated, stood up and went and took a yogurt from the fridge. She settled down again to watch as Joan Crawford, resplendent in huge shoulder pads and high heels, stamped into view looking for revenge.

Karen shoved her musings into cold storage and sat back to enjoy the film, but as she removed a smear of yogurt from the corner of her mouth with her little finger, she thought, Now that woman knew exactly who she was.

Next morning, Claudia Steiner phoned.

'Karen. I want to see you. Shall we do lunch?'

'Of course.' Even if she'd had a previous engagement, Karen would have cancelled it. When your boss offered you lunch, it had to be important.

178

'What time and where?'

'How about one o'clock at Le Gavroche in Brook Street? They do wonderful things with duck there.'

Karen laughed. 'Fine. I'll see you there.'

She dressed with special care, selecting wide-legged linen trousers, a lime-green short pinched-in jacket and rope-soled moccasins. Claudia insisted her girls be well groomed, particularly when they were in her company. When Karen followed the waiter over to the table and saw Claudia smile approvingly she relaxed and sat down.

'I've ordered the wine,' Claudia said. 'Just a light Orvieto. Is that all right?'

Karen nodded. Both she and Claudia knew that a glass apiece would be sufficient. Models had to watch their deportment and their figures and, anyway, they were here to talk business.

The duck, carved at the table and served with mild horseradish sauce and chutney, was delicious. Both women refused a dessert and opted for coffee. When that had been served, Claudia told Karen her news.

'You've got the TV job.'

'Honestly?'

'Yes. They rang at ten this morning.'

'That's great. Time's passed and I thought . . .' Karen stopped talking and reflected on the good news. 'It is definite, Claudia?'

Her boss lit a cigarette. 'I wouldn't do that to you twice, Karen.'

'No.' Karen flushed.

'The delay was nothing to do with choice of model. There's been some wrangling between the accountants and the ad men.' Claudia rolled her eyes. 'When isn't there, nowadays? But they've reached agreement and now they're raring to go.'

'When do they want to start filming, and where?'

'In ten days' time. They've hired a place in the country,

179

stately home from what I can gather.' Claudia opened her capacious handbag and took out a large white envelope. She handed it to Karen. 'Full schedule, story line, layout et cetera, all in here. They want to see you next Tuesday or Wednesday, to run through things.'

Karen held the envelope without opening it. 'What kind of money are we talking about? I remember Sally told me before the interview that only one advert was scheduled but there may be more, even a whole series. Does my contract . . .'

Claudia pushed back her chair and stood up. 'We're both going to do very well out of this, Karen. Come back with me to the agency and I'll go through the figures. I think you'll be well satisfied.' She paused. 'Oh, there is one condition you might not be happy about.'

'*You've what!*'

'Had my hair cut.'

'But why?'

'It was necessary, Dad. In the advertisement, I'm supposed to be an ultra-modern business woman.'

'Don't business women have long hair?'

'Not often. They're busy dashing around making deals and, as I know to my cost, washing and drying long hair takes time.'

'You could have pinned it up, worn it in a coil or something.'

Marigold tapped Ian's arm. 'Let *me* talk to her.'

'In a minute.' Ian transferred the phone to his other ear. 'I think you'll regret it, Karen. After all, your image has always been partially based on your beautiful hair.'

'Maybe it's time I changed my image.'

Seeing his frown, Marigold again jogged his arm. 'Ian!'

He pushed the phone at her. 'Yes, you talk to her. She seems in a very funny mood to me.' He stalked off to his study.

Marigold cradled the phone to her cheek. 'How are you, love?'

'I'm fine. Have you been there all the time? Did you catch what I was saying?'

'You've landed a good job, something to do with television?'

'It could be special, Mum. They're investing a lot of money in the scheme. They are hoping to produce a whole series of ads with an on-going story line.'

'It sounds terrific, Karen. I'm so pleased for you.'

'Dad's not particularly enthusiastic.'

'I know. What's all this about your hair?'

Karen explained. 'I've had it cut, into a short bob. I was a bit apprehensive because, as Dad said, my long hair has been a bit of a talking point over the last five years but now that the deed has been done, I'm delighted. I look like a woman now, not a girl, and the TV people are pleased with the new image.'

'That's all right then.'

'Yes.'

'Where are you phoning from?'

'Stannington Manor, the place we're going to use for the filming. That's why I'm ringing you, to give you the telephone number. I'll be staying in the hotel in the village but you know what hellish hours we work when we're filming so you might as well have the phone number for this place too. Do you want to write it down?'

'Yes.' Marigold picked up a pencil. 'Go ahead.'

Number safely noted, she asked, 'What's it like?'

'The house, you mean? Oh, it's gorgeous, Mum, a perfect gem of an old country manor house; the main staircase's Elizabethan.' Karen laughed. 'I do hope I get to sweep down those stairs during one of the takes. And the gardens are gorgeous, too. All the shrubs, flowers and bushes have been chosen for their perfumes as well as for colour and there's even a maze.'

'Good Lord.' Marigold's voice held a trace of irony. 'It

sounds like fairyland. Will you ever recover, I wonder?'

There was a short silence. Then Karen asked cautiously, 'How are things?'

'Fine.'

'Have you decided what to do with yourself? I mean, have you thought about getting another job or are you keeping busy at home?'

Marigold hesitated. 'Actually, I've done some work for Susan Cambridge. It's to do with her charity schemes but . . .'

Karen groaned aloud. 'Oh, Mum.'

'No, it's interesting, Karen. I move around from place to place and I meet people.'

'What does Dad say about it?'

'He doesn't seem to mind. It doesn't affect our home life, you see.'

'I see.' Karen looked across the room, at the sunlight falling through the window and pooling on the polished oak floor.

'When I've finished this job, Mum, why don't you come up to London and stay with me for a couple of days? We can take in a show and do some shopping.'

'Will you have the time?'

'Of course I will.'

'It would be rather nice. I haven't visited London for ages.'

'We'll do it then. I'm not certain how long this job will take, but it shouldn't be too long. I'll let you know.'

'That would be lovely, Karen. I'll look forward to it. In the meantime, enjoy your work.'

'I'll try, although filming is pretty hectic and we work long days. Still, I'll catch up on my sleep during the nights. Nothing much to do hereabouts. What about you? Have you any treats planned?'

'Actually, I have. This evening I'm dining with my friend from work. Pat, do you remember her?'

'Yes, I think so. She's the widow with a son, isn't she?'

'Yes.'

'Is Dad going, too?'

'No, just me. Your father's never met Pat.'

'Well, enjoy yourselves, although it might be difficult with no men present.'

'Actually, I'm going to meet her new boyfriend.'

'Chris, this is Mari, a very good friend of mine. Mari, this is Chris.' Pat, looking flushed and attractive in a new dress, sounded nervous as she made the introductions.

Marigold shook hands with Chris and accepted a glass of sherry. She looked round for Sam, Pat's son.

Pat anticipated her question. 'I'm afraid Sam's out with his new girlfriend. He send his regards to you though.'

Marigold raised her eyebrows. 'Sam has a girlfriend? He *must* be growing up.'

Pat smiled. 'He has. He's almost as tall as Chris.'

He had grown then, for Chris was six foot tall and handsome in a rugged, middle-aged way. Marigold felt a sudden pang of envy as she saw the couple exchange a loving glance. She went and sat down.

Pat said, 'I'll leave you two to get acquainted. I have to put the finishing touches to the meal.' In the doorway, she looked back at them. 'I've a cream sauce to make and you know I always have great difficulty in getting rid of the lumps.'

'That's rubbish.' Marigold smiled and looked at Chris. 'She's a good cook.'

'I know.' He gave Pat an affectionate wave as she disappeared into the kitchen and then he sat down in a chair facing Marigold.

'I'm pleased to meet you at last, Mari. I know what good friends you and Pat are, and how much she values your opinions.'

He paused, twisting the stem of his sherry glass between thumb and forefinger. Then he looked at Marigold and said, 'I love Pat and I want to marry her and to further my plans I'm going to be as charming to you as I possibly can this evening. Of course—' He threw back his sherry with a gulp. 'I hope we can become genuine friends, but that would be a bonus. I love that woman and I'm determined to have her. I thought it only fair to tell you.'

For a long moment Marigold studied his face then she nodded, raised her glass to him and said, 'Fair enough.'

Over dinner, an excellent meal, the conversation was easy and without strain. Marigold learned more about Chris and she liked what she saw and heard. There was a definite close relationship between him and Pat and the thought of the couple marrying became more and more apt.

Delicately, Marigold inquired about Sam's feelings.

'Oh, I think he's relieved.' Pat, on her third glass of wine, was becoming expansive. 'You see, Sam was forced to become the "man of the house" too early in life. He sees that Chris and I are happy together and he's not a bit jealous. I think he's looking forward to a future unencumbered by a solitary, clinging parent.'

Marigold shook her head. 'You were never that, Pat.'

Her friend's face went pink and she reached across and patted Marigold's hand.

Chris defused a potentially emotional moment. 'You have a daughter, Mari? I gather she's quite famous?'

'Not famous, but yes, Karen's a successful model. She rang today.' Marigold spoke briefly about Karen's new modelling assignment.

'So, we might be seeing her on TV? You and your husband must be proud of her.'

'Yes, we are.'

Amidst mellow lighting, good food and pleasant conversation, the evening slipped away. When the time came to go home, Marigold was reluctant to leave, but she had previously ordered a taxi for eleven thirty and it was almost that now. Pat accompanied her upstairs to collect her coat.

'What do you think of him, Mari?'

'I like him very much but it's what you think that matters.' Marigold smiled into Pat's anxious eyes.

'You really like him?'

'I do.' Mari hugged her friend. 'I think you make a lovely couple. I've thoroughly enjoyed my evening but now I must be off. The taxi will be arriving any moment.'

Pat's smile disappeared. 'Isn't Ian coming for you? I would have invited him too, you know, but I thought . . .'

'You thought right. You've never met Ian and it wouldn't have worked so well.'

'I hope he wasn't upset.'

'Not at all. Ian doesn't get upset about things like that.' Marigold's lips gave a rueful twist. 'I don't suppose he's missed me at all.'

At the top of the stairs, Pat put her arm around Marigold's waist. 'I'm so happy, Mari. I wish you could find the same happiness.'

'I'm fine. Don't waste your time worrying about me.'

'But I do. You deserve better than what you've got.'

'I've been married for twenty-six years. I have a grown-up daughter, a lovely home, no money worries and a husband who, although not exactly attentive anymore, provides for me, doesn't sleep around and lets me do more or less what I want. That's not so bad, Pat.'

'I still think . . .'

There was the sound of a horn. The taxi had arrived.

'I must go.'

Glad of the excuse, Marigold hurried downstairs. She said

goodbye to Chris, who had come to the door to see her out, smiled and waved at Pat and promised to phone soon. Then she was out of the house, down the path and into the cab.

But going home, sitting in the back of the taxi and seeing the splattering of stars lighting the sky above, she felt a yearning inside her and she knew that, for all her brave words, she would give up all she had for a man who would look at her in the same way that Chris looked at Pat.

Chapter Fourteen

Marigold decided to go into York to do her shopping. Tomorrow, she was looking after the boys. Jack's school was closed because of a teachers' training day so she was helping Sheila out. Marigold thought that, weather permitting, she would take them for a picnic. She wondered what food to buy. Children, particularly boys, had enjoyed sausages, pickled onions, fizzy pop and crisps at Karen's parties but, she sighed a little, that had been years ago and times had changed. She decided to buy the pickled onions and the sausages but also purchase a ready-cooked chicken and bread rolls. If the boys didn't eat them she could have a chicken salad tomorrow evening. She wouldn't be cooking tomorrow because Ian was staying at the university. He had an important meeting with the head of his department.

Marigold thought for a moment and then decided. If she was going into the city she would also buy Ian some new clothes. He would need to look smart for his trip abroad and, who knows, perhaps this trip would lead to many more. Remembering the expression on her husband's face when he had opened the all-important anxiously expected letter a week ago, she smiled. Never, she thought, had she seen him look so delighted.

He had read the letter, read it again and then thrust it towards her.

'Look, Mari. See how much they've given me.'

She had taken the letter, read it and blinked. She already knew that Ian's paper on protein-crystal structures, published seven months previously, had caused something of a stir within scientific circles. She knew that her husband had been informed he had been awarded a research grant by the Commission of the European Communities to help continue his work, but the figure mentioned in the letter was way beyond expectations.

She handed back the letter. 'How wonderful.'

'Yes. Yes, it is.' He read the letter again, still disbelieving, then he grinned. 'This will make such a difference, Mari. I must speak to the head of department as soon as possible. I'll have to cut back on the teaching,' he shrugged. 'No regrets there. I'll be able to upgrade the lab equipment and once the news gets around there'll be more chance for me to collaborate with scientists abroad. The size of the grant will not go unnoticed. This is good news for me *and* the university.'

Marigold found she had a little tightness around her chest. She was delighted for Ian, of course she was, but she shared little enough of his life as it was. Would the grant mean she would be squeezed out altogether?

But she made herself relax and thrust the thought away from her. How could she be so mean-spirited when Ian was so thrilled? He had worked so hard for so many years. He *was* a brilliant scientist and, at last, the world was beginning to acknowledge him.

Then, just two days ago, the letter had arrived from Norway. Could Dr Ian Goddard attend a symposium to be held at the University of Tromsø? One of the speakers had been taken ill and had to withdraw. It was short notice but if Dr Goddard could attend and present his recent paper on protein-crystal structures they would be pleased and honoured to receive him. The head of their physics department was looking forward to being his host for the four-day event.

'Shall I accept?'

The fact that Ian had asked for her opinion had startled Marigold. She had looked across the room at him. He was standing by his desk, the letter from Norway dangling from his fingers, and seeing the self-doubt in his face had awakened in her a feeling of tenderness for him. A feeling that had been absent too long.

'Of course you must go. It's a wonderful opportunity for you to promote yourself and your work.' She thought for a moment. 'What about here?'

'Work, you mean?' He shrugged. 'The term's finished, only a few students remain and there's a couple of senior supervisors around if they need help. Summer students are coming in, of course, but they don't affect me.'

'So, there's no problem?'

'No. In fact, I think the general opinion would be that I *should* go.'

'Then you must ring and say yes. When would you have to leave?'

Ian consulted his letter. 'Saturday.'

'So soon? We'll have to get busy.'

And that was why she was shopping for new clothes for him.

As she had made an early start, Marigold had finished her shopping by a quarter to eleven. Rather than go straight home, she called into the coffee shop at the Theatre Royal and treated herself to a coffee and a Danish pastry. There was no one there she recognised so she stayed for only a short time. She had never enjoyed eating and drinking in public when she was on her own.

As she left the coffee shop she spotted a poster near the exit which advertised an evening of prose and poetry. Spotting the name Daniel Crewe she stopped and read the details. The venue was at the York Arts Centre, easy enough to get to, but it was for tonight.

Marigold frowned. She would like to have gone but she knew Ian would not and in view of his impending departure she thought it would be wrong to go without him. As it was, she was spending most of tomorrow looking after Jack and Billy, although that wouldn't affect Ian in any way as he intended spending the whole day in the laboratory. Ah, well. There would be other poetry recitals.

She returned home, let Paddy out into the back garden and unpacked her shopping. By the time Ian walked through the back door into the kitchen at three thirty, she was taking a tray of freshly baked scones from the oven.

Ian raised his head and sniffed. 'Something smells nice.'

'Yes.' Marigold held the tray in one oven-gloved hand and with the other gingerly flicked the scones on to the wire cooling tray, then she blew on her fingers.

'Would you like one?'

'Now, do you mean?'

'Yes. The coffee's perking.'

'But they're straight out of the oven. Won't we get indigestion?'

'Lovely with best butter.' Marigold smiled at him and, after a moment's pause, he smiled back.

'Go on then.'

The invitation to lecture in Norway has changed him, thought Marigold, that and the news of his grant. He seemed less unapproachable. Over the last fifteen years, Ian had become more and more absorbed in his work and Marigold had often thought that the academic life he followed had caused him to become rather pedantic and detached from the real world; but now he was different. His expression was almost lively and when he looked at her, he was really *seeing* her.

As if reading her mind, he dropped his gaze. 'You pour the coffee and I'll get the butter.'

His body brushed against hers as he moved towards the refrigerator and now it was her turn to look away. How long had it been since they made love? Too long. She took down the coffee mugs from their hooks with hands that shook a little. She poured the coffee and they drank, ate and talked.

'No trouble about the trip to Norway. I knew it would be all right. After all, even the students get the chance to study abroad through the EC Erasmus exchange schemes so why shouldn't I travel a little?'

'No reason at all.' Marigold reached over to give his hand a little squeeze. 'And if you're well received at Tromsø, you'll probably receive a lot more invitations to lecture abroad. After all, your work was done here at York. Your sudden prestige will include the university.'

Ian laughed. 'Thank you for your loyalty, Mari, but presenting a paper at another university is no big deal. Several people I know have travelled to America and Russia to speak about their work.'

'Well, now it's your turn.' Marigold put down her coffee mug. 'I've been shopping today. I've bought you a sweater, a couple of shirts and another tie. I hope you like what I've chosen. I've laid them out on the bed for your approval.'

'Thanks.' For once, he made a move towards her. He reached for her hand. 'You're a good wife.'

She stared down at their intertwined fingers. 'I try to be.'

He squeezed her hand then released it. He stood up. 'Why don't we go upstairs and look at the shirts together?' He touched her cheek.

Her eyes opened wide. She stared at him and then murmured, 'Oh, yes.'

The shirts were fine, he said, although he barely glanced at them. He moved them on to a chair and then pulled Marigold down on the bed with him. They kissed each other, gently at first, and then with growing passion. As Ian began to unbutton her blouse, Marigold began to tremble. She'd been alone so long, so long. When Ian eased away from her to remove his own clothes, her hands fluttered around him, touching his neck, his hair, his mouth. She couldn't bear not to feel him against her.

At last, they were both naked and Marigold pressed her whole body against his, slipping her arms around his neck and closing her eyes. She felt she could have stayed like that forever because at last, their bodies were in tune with every movement. At the touch of his fingers upon her skin the hard, hurting mass of her loneliness started to melt away, and in its place was the reawakening of love.

As his fingertips flickered over her breasts she moaned and pressed herself even closer to him but he pushed her back against the pillows and moved slightly away from her. She opened her eyes and caught a glimpse of his face, pale and tense, before he bent his head and began nuzzling at her nipples. A pang of desire shot through her body and she gasped but then she stiffened because his gentle mouthings had suddenly become uncomfortable as his teeth nipped her.

'Ian, please. You're hurting . . .'

Her eyes snapped wide open in disbelief. His hands were between her legs now and he was forcing them apart. His body came down hard on top of her.

She gasped. 'Not yet. Not just yet.'

He didn't hear. He was forcing his way into her. It hurt. She stiffened and made a small sound of dissent but he was unaware of anything but his own need. A minute later, he groaned as he came and then he slumped and lay inert and heavy upon her body. Then he muttered something and rolled away from her.

She curled up in a tight ball at her side of the bed and Ian lay, limp and sated, by her side. Then he stirred.

'Lovely,' he said.

She wanted to hit him. She wanted to scream. She couldn't believe what had just happened. She had thought their coming together would be a positive act to reaffirm the validity of their marriage and reawaken their love but instead he had used her like a whore.

A proper whore would have been happy with such a short encounter whereas she was taut as a wire, full of a need he had been too selfish to satisfy. At that moment, she hated him. She gasped and moved and felt the stickiness on her thighs and thought she might be sick.

She rolled away from him, got off the bed, went into the bathroom and showered. She rubbed herself dry until her skin tingled. The water had been warm but when she finished she was still shivering. She took clean clothes from the airing cupboard and put them on. Then she went back into the bedroom.

Ian had dressed. He was bending over looking at the dressing-table mirror as he brushed his hair. He met her eyes through the mirror and turned towards her, smiling.

'All right?'

She stared at him, her face white. 'Not really.'

His smile faded. 'Why? What's the matter?'

She shook her head. 'If you don't know . . .'

He blinked. 'My fault, I suppose. I was too quick for you. Is that what you mean?'

'You might say that.'

He looked sulky. 'Is there any wonder? A man can only stand so much, Mari. For ages now, living in this house with you has been like living in a monastery. Oh, you're a good cook and housekeeper, but a man needs more than that.'

She gasped and wrapped her arms around herself as her shivering intensified. 'I didn't realise you felt that way.'

'Well, it's not an easy subject to talk about, is it?' Oblivious to her distress, Ian continued voicing his own line of thought. 'I know women don't feel the need so often and I know I sometimes get distracted by work but that doesn't mean I like living a life devoid of sex.'

'And what about love?' Mari's voice was so low, he hesitated, uncertain of her words. And so she repeated them, louder this time. 'What about love, Ian? What about companionship? Do such things figure in your life at all? Don't you know I've been desperate for you to make love to me for months but you're always so distant. Today is the first time for ages that we've actually communicated with each other.' She saw his face begin to close up and she hurried on. 'I need encouragement too. Most of the time you act as though I'm invisible.'

He threw up his hands in exasperation. 'God, don't start on that track again. We've been married a long time, Mari. Surely we don't have to bill and coo at each other before we have sex?'

She leaned against the wall to steady herself. 'No, but I expect something from you. I'm a woman, not a piece of furniture. I have feelings, too. Perhaps you'll think about that while you're away in Norway because—' She took a deep breath. 'Things can't go on like this.'

He made an impatient movement with his head and stared out of the window.

She turned and walked out of the room. Her legs felt like jelly but she managed the stairs and then, without really thinking, she went out into the back garden. She walked down to stand beneath the old chestnut tree where she began, very quietly, to cry.

So that was it. After a long, painful illness, their marriage had finally expired. She acknowledged the fact. She leaned her back against the trunk of the tree and shut her eyes. Her tears still forced their way out from behind her eyelashes. She felt tired and lonely, as she had so many times before, but now a new feeling was added. Shame.

She remembered the faces of her parents at her wedding. They had been nervous of Ian's relatives but they had been so proud of her, so happy for her. Thank God they were no longer around to see her failure. They wouldn't be proud now. When a marriage failed, both partners were responsible, both were accountable. Marigold scrubbed savagely at her face. If only she could stop crying. She had to stop crying and start thinking.

What now? Divorce?

Common enough, nowadays, but to her parents and to their generation, divorce had been unthinkable. You made your bed and upon it you lay, regardless of how uncomfortable it was. But perhaps less had been demanded of a marriage in their days.

She shook her head. Hidden in the greenery above her head, a bird cheeped loudly, making her start. She looked round her as if seeing the garden for the first time. She studied the flowers in the borders, the flowers she had first grown as seeds; she admired the velvety green lawn. She glanced towards the house. A divorce would lead to quarrels about property and items of furniture. Was she strong enough for that? Ian had always been the provider. She might have to leave this house that she loved. She might end up in a pokey flat, living on her own.

She touched her mouth with nervous fingers. She had never lived on her own. She had moved from being a daughter living with her parents to being Ian's wife.

And Karen – how would Karen react to her parents splitting up? At least she was a grown-up, thank God. She was living her own life, but she'd still be upset. And she had always been close to her father. What if she took Ian's side and expelled her mother from her life?

Marigold shivered. The tee-shirt she wore was thin. She ought to go back to the house. She squared her shoulders. She *would* go back to the house. She'd challenge Ian, tell him she could not go on living like this. He wouldn't want to hear but she would force him to listen. And if he refused to face their problems, then there must be a separation or a divorce. She would not – could not – go on living a half life. She took a deep breath and walked back towards her home.

Ian wasn't in the house. A note on the kitchen table said he had gone to work in the lab and he'd be home late. He advised her not to wait up for him. He had scrawled a postscript. *I really do like the shirts.*

Marigold screwed up the paper and threw it into the bin. She felt an hysterical laugh bubbling up inside her. While she had been in the garden, agonising over their marriage, Ian considered they had indulged in a tiff, nothing important.

Her laughter died before birth. Should she follow his example? Return to the status quo?

When they were courting, Ian had taught her a few Latin phrases. She remembered how impressed she had been at his cleverness. She had memorised them but now the only one she could remember was *Statu quo ante bellum* – In the state in which things were before the war.

Paddy had crept up to Marigold and now he pressed his head against her leg. She started and then laid her hand upon his neck. Good, faithful Paddy, he knew things were all wrong.

She stroked him and came to her decision. No, she wouldn't go back to the status quo but neither would she be packing her bags, not just yet. She'd invested a lot of time and effort in her marriage and now she was going to protect her investment. She wouldn't do anything in a rush. And she'd keep busy while she was studying her options.

She took a deep breath. Keeping busy was important. She'd

have a full day tomorrow, looking after Jack and Billy, but as for this evening . . . She held up her head. This evening she was not going to sit at home and feel sorry for herself. Oh, no. This evening she was going out, to listen to some poetry.

Chapter Fifteen

Later, Marigold found she had no memory of whole sections of the night of the poetry reading. She did recall that the weather changed, becoming dank and miserable, and that, driving to the Arts Centre, she had continually activated the windscreen wipers to clear the mist obscuring her view.

She remembered that, on arriving at the venue, there were few people around but as she went to purchase her ticket, a sizeable crowd appeared as if from nowhere and formed a queue behind her. She had glanced round and felt pleasure that the name of Daniel Crewe commanded a reasonable-sized audience. Once again, the majority of the people queuing up behind her was young but there were also some middle-aged people like herself.

Inside the hall, of which later she could remember little as to colour scheme or decor, she looked round for somewhere to sit, and it was then she spotted a man she *did* remember later.

She noticed him first because he was sitting in the middle of a row of chairs and was surrounded by emptiness. And then she realised why. He, too, was middle aged – that word again – and he was a tramp. He was dressed in a miscellany of tattered clothing, he was bearded, and his black hair flowed thick and long down his back. He sat quietly in his seat and cradled to his chest a crumpled black bin liner which, Marigold assumed, held his worldly possessions.

She had never seen him in the streets of York and his presence here, at a poetry reading, disconcerted her. She stopped and stared.

A woman following her up the aisle also stopped and whispered, 'Disgraceful, isn't it? They should never have allowed him in.'

Marigold swung round towards her, noted the expression on her face, her narrowed eyes and sucked-in lips.

She said, 'Well . . . I don't know. If he's paid for a ticket . . .'

The woman's whisper had been loud. From the corner of her eye, Marigold saw the tramp had turned his head and was looking at them. She bit her lip, feeling uncomfortable and then she looked back at him.

His beard covered the outline of his mouth and chin but she saw that his forehead was broad and unlined and his eyes large and light grey in colour. Their eyes locked for a moment and then the tramp half smiled and dropped his gaze.

The woman walked away, tut-tutting, but Marigold stayed where she was. She continued to look at the tramp but he stared down at his bin-liner bag and rocked gently backwards and forwards.

Then Marigold, motivated by some strange act of perversity which she didn't understand, found herself walking along the empty row towards him. About fifteen seats in she caught the smell of him and stopped. Oh, God, she was an idiot; there was no way she could sit next to him. Flushing to the roots of her hair she edged backwards and finally sat down about eight seats away from him. She looked down as she unbuttoned her jacket and blessed the fact that the weather had turned colder.

It was time to start the evening. The last late stragglers settled in their seats, the lights dimmed and Daniel Crewe strode on to the stage. Forgetting the tramp, Marigold joined in the applause.

A few of his poems she recalled from her visit to see him at The Square Tower but many were new to her. As before, she succumbed to his magic, forgetting all about Ian and her marital problems. There was something about the poet that affected her deeply. The energy emitting from his physical presence invigorated her and the words he spoke, the essence of the meaning of his poetry, opened up her understanding and made her aware of her ignorance of so much of life. The realisation humbled her but made her feel hopeful because, as she listened to him, she began to realise what middle age actually was; the middle of your life. And, OK, she was middle-aged, frustrated and unhappy but, God willing, she had half of her life left in which to put things right. She had only to be brave enough.

The poet fell silent and gave a slight bow. Marigold took a deep breath and joined in the applause. There was a short interval. Marigold didn't remember much about it. She knew she had stayed in her seat while others stampeded for the exits, seeking coffee, drinks or the toilets. A couple seated somewhere behind her were discussing where they could buy a copy of the poet's latest book. Marigold didn't look round but she looked towards the tramp. He, too, had stayed in his seat. His head was bent and was looking down at the floor. She wondered what he was thinking.

After the interval a newcomer came on stage. Marigold consulted her programme. The second poet was a woman, stout in build with a round, cheerful-looking face. She made a good contrast to Daniel Crewe for her poetry was light-hearted and made the audience chuckle. She received generous applause when she finished her stint.

There was a five-minute interval before Daniel Crewe came back but this time, the lights remained dimmed. Marigold settled herself in her seat but she was distracted when someone came hurrying up the aisle, paused by her row of seats then walked along and plumped down in the seat next to her. Half frowning, she turned to glance at the late arrival but as she did so he leaned forward, ignoring her, and waved his hand to attract the tramp's attention.

'Hey, Tommy. How are you, man?'

The tramp looked across, smiled and raised his hand in acknowledgement of the greeting. 'I'm fine, Adam. How's yourself?'

'The same.' The man sat back in his seat and Marigold was able to see his face. She froze. It was the man from the golf club.

Simultaneously, he recognised her and his eyebrows shot up in surprise. Recovering from her shock, Marigold thought it was quite funny because it was obvious the astonishment on his face was mirrored on her own.

He asked, 'I *am* right. We did meet in the bar at the golf club and went outside and talked for a short time?'

'We did.'

'Well.' He thought for a moment. 'I must say I'm surprised to see you here.'

'Why is that?' She glanced towards the stage as Daniel Crewe walked on. She studied him and then looked back at the man by her side. Yes, there was a definite resemblance.

He replied, 'I wouldn't have put you down as a lover of poetry.'

She smiled. 'I could say the same thing about you but then, how should a poetry enthusiast look?'

He rubbed his chin. 'Sorry, it was rather a fatuous remark but you see . . .'

'Shush.' The disembodied voice from behind them sounded annoyed.

They exchanged amused glances and fell silent.

Marigold enjoyed the second half of the programme but

found she was unable to recapture the intense communication with the poems she had experienced earlier. She knew why. She was too aware of the man sitting next to her. He was quiet now, concentrating on the words, and so she was able to steal glances at his profile, unobserved.

His features were strong, particularly his chin, and she guessed he could be stubborn. She wondered why he interested her so much. Over the years men had tried to flirt with her but she had always felt totally indifferent to them. With him it was different though. She remembered how she had walked round The Shambles trying to locate his shop after their first meeting and how disappointed she had been not to find it, and she warned herself to be careful.

And so, when the performance ended, she rose to her feet immediately and looked down at her neighbour, hoping he would take her hint that she was in a hurry to leave.

Still in his seat, he stared up at her and frowned. 'You're not dashing off for dinner again, are you? Once is quite enough.'

Delighted he remembered so clearly their first meeting, Marigold smiled.

'I'm not going for a meal, but there's bound to be a rush to get out of the car park and I thought . . .'

'If there's a rush, it makes sense to wait a little.'

She hesitated, remembering Ian would be home late. And thinking of Ian brought back to her the fiasco of their lovemaking that afternoon and her face stiffened. She said, 'Yes, I suppose it does make sense,' and sat down again.

Further down the row, the tramp was preparing to depart. He stood up, nodded his head towards them and then shuffled away, his bin bag still clasped firmly to his chest.

Marigold asked, 'Do you know him?'

'Not really. We've spoken a few times.'

'But you know his name.'

'I know everyone calls him Tommy. Whether that's his real name . . . He's quite a mystery man.' He studied her face. 'Why the interest?'

She sighed. 'I'm just curious, that's all. Why would a man like that pay to come and listen to a poet?'

'Why shouldn't he?' He raised his hand and ruffled his hair, his eyes intent on her face. 'You asked how a poetry lover should look,' he smiled. 'Perhaps they should look like Tommy.'

She frowned. 'I don't know what . . .'

He interrupted her. 'Tommy's discarded most of the things people hold dear in life. He has no family, no home, no money. Perhaps he's trying to fill the space with something else.'

While Marigold was considering his words he stood up and, bending towards her, lightly placed his hand beneath her elbow. 'Come on then.'

She allowed him to help her to her feet. 'Come where?'

'We're going out to supper.'

She stiffened. 'Oh, no. I don't think so.'

'Why not? You're all right, aren't you?'

She looked at him in surprise. 'Of course.'

'I'm glad. You looked strange a moment ago, quite fierce.'

She blushed. 'I'm fine.'

'Good, then you'll have supper with us?'

'Us?'

'Yes, I'm meeting my brother and his wife.'

'Oh, I couldn't. I don't want to intrude.'

'You won't intrude. You'll fit in well. My brother likes people who likes people.'

She shook her head, bewildered. 'I don't understand half you say.'

'It's simple. You sat on the same row as Tommy. You were the only person who did that. Of course,' he laughed, softly. 'It could be that you have a rotten sense of smell, but still, you made a point.' Seeing she still looked puzzled, he took her hand and began to walk to the end of the row. 'You won't intrude. You'll be welcomed, and after all, you're a fan.'

She stopped dead. 'You mean, Daniel Crewe is your brother?'

'Yes. Come on. We'll go backstage and I'll introduce you to him.'

She pulled her hand away from his grasp. 'Just a minute. There's something you've forgotten.'

'What's that?'

'You can't introduce me until you know my name, and I know yours.'

He hit his forehead with the heel of his hand. 'God, you're right. What an idiot I am.' He smiled at her. 'It's just that, somehow, I feel as though I've known you a long time.'

She started to say something, stopped and held out her right hand. 'I'm Marigold Goddard.'

He shook her hand and, keeping hold of it, asked, 'Marigold?'

'My mother's favourite flower.' She was acutely aware of the warmth of his clasp. 'Mostly, people call me Mari.'

'Then I shall stick to Marigold because it's the perfect name for you.' He gave her fingers a quick squeeze and then released them. 'And I'm Adam Jonathan Crewe, younger brother of Daniel.' His smile reappeared. 'My mother wasn't a gardener. She preferred reading, particularly passages from the Old Testament.'

Seeing the two men together, their relationship became obvious. Daniel Crewe's eyes were also dark blue and he shared the same lively expression as his brother. He was about an inch taller than Adam and he carried a little too much weight. His manner verged on the exuberant and Marigold felt slightly nervous of him but she was charmed to see the obvious affection which existed between the two brothers.

In the dressing room, Daniel had greeted Adam with a bearhug which swung him off his feet, then he had turned towards Marigold with a look of expectant inquiry in his eyes.

'Hello. We haven't seen you before, have we? I'm delighted to meet you. I told Adam it was high time he got himself a girlfriend. He spends too much time on his own. You look intelligent as well as being attractive. I'm sure you'll be good for him.'

Without giving her an opportunity to speak he swung round towards his brother. 'Vast improvement on your last date, if I may say so.'

Marigold blushed and Adam frowned.

'No, you may not. Marigold is not my girlfriend. We hardly know each other but she's a fan of yours and so I offered to introduce her to you.' His voice was cold. 'I was hoping you'd welcome her kindly but you've excelled yourself this time, Dan. Two seconds flat and you've managed to embarrass both of us.'

Daniel Crewe threw back his head and scowled. 'Now what I have done?' He turned towards a slim, slightly built woman with fair hair who was packing clothes into a travel bag and demanded, 'I didn't say anything too alarming, did I, Helen? It was just a friendly inquiry.'

The woman left off packing and came towards them. She stood on tiptoe to kiss Adam on his cheek, smiled at Marigold and then linked arms with Daniel.

'He doesn't mean to be rude,' she said to Marigold. 'After a show, Danny's always on a bit of a high. He blurts things out without thinking.'

Marigold shook her head. 'It doesn't matter.'

'Yes, it does.' Adam was still annoyed. 'I should have warned you, Marigold. My brother has a genius for putting his foot into it verbally, which is remarkable when you think his poetry is described as being a model of meaning and resonance.'

'Oh, but it is.' Marigold forgot her embarrassment and took a step forward. 'I've only been to see you twice, Mr Crewe, but your poetry has had a great effect on me. I don't know how to explain it but I feel it's changed me in some way. I find I'm looking at things from a totally different perspective somehow. I've put in an order for your books and . . .'

She suddenly heard her own rush of words and fell silent, blushing yet again. I sound like a stupid adolescent, she thought, yet I mean what I say, I mean every word.

Daniel Crewe had slipped his arm around his wife's shoulder and was looking at her. 'Thank you,' he said. And this time his voice was quiet. 'I can see you're sincere and that makes me feel proud and also humble.' He studied her face. 'And please, don't feel embarrassed. If more people communicated what they really feel, the world would be enriched.'

There was a moment of silence and then Daniel stirred and said, only half-jokingly, 'Adam, if this lady isn't your girlfriend may I suggest she becomes so as soon as possible.' He pulled a face and went on. 'Girlfriend, what a dreadful word. Why don't we use the word sweetheart anymore, or even mistress – mistress of my heart.'

He threw back his head and declaimed.

' "Had we but world enough, and time,
This coyness, Lady, were no crime." '

He looked at Marigold. 'Don't suppose you've read Andrew Marvell?'

She nodded. 'Yes. I have. When I was fifteen I had a very romantic phase and I read Keats, Donne and Lovelace and cried over them all.' She smiled. 'Marvell was a little more cynical, wasn't he? Those are the beginning lines of *To his Coy Mistress*.'

Daniel threw up his hands. 'That's right.' He grinned at Adam. 'You've met a true woman, Adam. She's lovely and she has a good mind, too.'

The expression on Adam's face showed that he was still tense. He gave a shrug of apology to Marigold. 'I'm sorry. I should have warned you that Danny's impossible directly after a performance. He'll be better when he simmers down.'

Marigold ignored him. She was fascinated by the poet. She asked, 'You mean you approve of sixteenth and seventeenth century poetry? Your own work is so modern in form and content, I would have thought you had nothing in common with the poetry of the past.'

'Not at all. People like Marvell wrote about their time and I write about mine, but they were scholars and perfectionists. They had discipline. A lot of so-called modern poetry is mere doggerel.' Daniel shrugged. 'Still, enough about them. Adam says he hasn't known you for long. Obviously, he hasn't had time to tell you that I have two lives. I'm a poet, yes, but I also need to live so I'm a tutor in English Literature at a boys' school near Stockton-on-Tees. A single man may starve in an attic but I have a wife—' He landed a smacking kiss on Helen's cheek. 'And a twelve year old son to support so I need a reliable form of income.'

'That's right.' Helen gave him a little push. 'And your wife is hungry, so please stop talking so much because I want to go out and eat.' She glanced at Adam. 'I hope you and Marigold will join us.'

'Well.' Adam scratched his chin. 'That was my idea when we came round to see you but it depends whether Marigold still wants . . .'

'Oh, yes,' she said. 'I do.'

She arrived home at a quarter to twelve. She garaged her car and then let herself into the house. The security lights were on but it was obvious she was the first one home. It didn't surprise her. Once Ian was in the lab, he often stayed there until the early hours of the morning.

She let Paddy out and then made herself a coffee – it was absolutely fatal to drink caffeine at this time of night but then, she wouldn't be able to sleep, even without coffee. She sat herself down, elbows on the kitchen table, hands clasped round the coffee mug and took small sips of the boiling-hot liquid and allowed kaleidoscopic pictures of the evening to form, dissolve and re-form in her mind's eye.

They had eaten spaghetti and drank red wine and mineral water at an unpretentious Italian restaurant close by the Arts Centre. The men had drank most of the wine as Marigold knew she had to drive home and Helen confided in her that any kind of wine always gave her a crashing headache.

'Besides,' she had said, smiling at Marigold, 'Adam was right when he said Daniel went over the top after giving a poetry recital, so I have to keep a level head for both of us.' She had looked at her husband fondly. 'He's actually a very sensitive man and putting his innermost feelings on show takes it out of him, hence the reaction. I hope he didn't offend you, Marigold?'

'No, of course he didn't. I'm just delighted I was able to meet him.' Marigold looked across the table at the two brothers. 'They're close, aren't they?'

'Oh, yes. We're staying overnight with Adam. My sister's looking after Nicky for us.'

'It must be nice having a brother or sister.'

'Haven't you any siblings?'

'No.' Marigold shrugged. 'But I've a daughter and a couple of good friends. Karen lives in London. I'm thinking of visiting her soon.'

'You're a widow?'

'Oh, no. I'm married.' Marigold realised she had, without even noticing, omitted any mention of Ian, and Helen must have recognised her embarrassment because she simply touched her hand and changed the topic of conversation.

In the garden, Paddy barked loudly. Her mental snapshot of the conversation in the restaurant vanished as Marigold put down her mug and went to let him in. When she opened the back door the dog rushed past her into the house but Marigold lingered a moment and then stepped outside.

The security light at the back showed up the garden table and chairs and the flowers and shrubs near the house, but everything looked a little peculiar, drained of colour and substance. And beyond the security light lay the darkness. Marigold shivered. It was as if the rest of the garden, the lawn and the chestnut tree, had disappeared. She took a step forward and searched for a familiar object. Ah, she breathed a sigh of relief. She could just make out the dim outline of the tree against the night sky. It was all right. She hadn't dropped off the edge of the world.

But it wasn't all right. The dim outline of the tree brought back memories of the tears she had shed beneath it after the so-called act of love with Ian. Marigold pressed her hand to her chest. Going out this evening to listen to Daniel Crewe had been good for her but it was only a temporary escape. She was back home now and still uncertain as to what to do next. She sighed and went back into the house.

As she undressed for bed, she recalled the expression on the tramp's face as he had looked across and smiled at her. After the evening's rain the ground would be cold and damp. Where would the tramp sleep tonight? She remembered Adam's comment about her choosing to sit on the same row as – she wrinkled her forehead – Tommy, that was his name. Adam had approved of her action.

Her face grew warm as she remembered the way he had held

on to her hand when they had finally introduced themselves. Adam Crewe. Adam. Was he as straightforward as he seemed to be? It was true that his face, his very attractive face, mirrored his feelings – she thought of his sudden anger at his brother's first words to her – but was he genuine or did he cultivate such openness in order to charm people, particularly women? She was sure he had known plenty of women. He was so attractive it was inevitable, but neither Daniel nor Helen had intimated he had a partner.

After years of living with a man who masked his feelings completely, Marigold knew she was attracted and intrigued by Adam but she also knew that she had to be wary. It would be all too easy for her to be swept off her feet. She sighed. She had enough complications in her life so why should she add to them?

But as she turned off the light and settled in bed she knew they would meet again. And if she got her fingers burned, then so be it. She had lived a half life for too long.

Chapter Sixteen

The boys were ready and waiting when Marigold called for them at eleven thirty.

Billy asked, 'Where's your dog? You've brought your dog, haven't you?'

'Oh, yes.' Marigold looked at Jack's long grey trousers and polished shoes. She saw Billy's crisp white shirt and light-blue shorts. 'He's in the car.' She turned to their mother.

'They look very smart, Sheila, but . . .' She coughed nervously. 'Perhaps they should wear something more casual. I was thinking of taking them for a picnic, you see, and as it rained last night, they might end up getting a bit mucky.'

Sheila withdrew behind a noncommittal expression. 'I wish you'd told me what you'd planned. I like my children to look smart when they go out but I suppose they'd better put something else on if they're going for a picnic.'

Marigold inclined her head. 'Yes, it think it would be wise.'

'Right.' Sheila grabbed hold of Billy and said to Jack, 'Get into your jeans and a tee-shirt, son. And you'd better see if you can find your wellingtons.'

She swept Billy away into the curtained alcove and Marigold was left wondering who was doing the favour here.

However, when Sheila reappeared again, she had relaxed. In a pleasant voice she said, 'It's so good of you to do this.'

'Not at all. I've been looking forward to today.'

Marigold was speaking the truth. She had been asleep when Ian came home and breakfast this morning had been a strain. Ian had behaved in a hearty, let's-pretend-nothing-has-happened manner which had jarred upon her. She had responded to his forced joviality with monosyllables but when he had looked hurt, she had felt guilty. When he had slammed out of the house at nine o'clock she had felt a wave of relief. She had prepared the picnic thanking heaven it was good weather and looking forward to a few uncomplicated hours with the Scott boys.

Billy looked more himself dressed in a pair of denim overalls worn over a lurid lemon tee-shirt. He hopped from one foot to the other. 'Can we go now?'

'Yes, as soon as Jack's ready.'

Jack came out carrying a plastic bag and dived beneath the double bed, coming out clutching two pairs of wellingtons. He added them to the sweaters in the bag and pronounced himself ready. A brief 'goodbye' to their mother and the boys headed out of the door and down the stairs.

Marigold lingered a moment. 'Jack seems OK now?'

'Yes, he is. The boy that was bullying, him – well, he was away from school for a few days after the police pulled in his brother – and since he came back, he's avoided our Jack.'

'Thank God for that.'

'Yes.' Sheila nodded. 'You know, I never did tell Mike about it. I don't know whether I did right or not. I mean, Mike is Jack's dad and he deserves to know what happened, but what's the point? He wasn't here. He couldn't do anything.'

'Do you resent that, Sheila – Mike missing all the trouble?'

'I do a bit. I know he has a rough time travelling round looking for work. I know he's doing it for us, but I sometimes wonder if he does it for himself, too. It's no fun for him when he's home, stuck in this blasted B and B with nothing to do all

214

day, but it would help me out. As it is, I have to make all the decisions regarding the boys and it's difficult, fitting in my jobs with playschool for Billy and ordinary school for Jack. Anyway—' Sheila managed a small smile. 'That reminds me, I must be on my way. I finish today at three p.m. Is that all right for you?'

'Yes, I said I'd keep them occupied until about four.'

'I hope they'll be no trouble.'

Marigold laughed. 'I'll manage.'

Downstairs, Billy and Jack were staring through the car window at Paddy who stared back at them, tongue lolling out and an amiable expression in his brown eyes.

'He's a big 'un,' said Jack.

'He'd be good at biting burglars,' said Billy.

Marigold laughed and unlocked the car doors. 'He's big but he's soft. The only way Paddy could hurt a burglar would be to lick him to death.'

Jack smiled but Billy looked at her suspiciously. 'How would he do that?'

Jack gave him a shove. 'She was joking, stupid.'

'Come on, get in.' Marigold took the plastic bag from Jack and bustled the boys into the car. Once they were strapped in and making the acquaintance of Paddy she drove away from the dismal street, threaded her way through the town traffic and headed out towards the country and towards The Knavesmire.

Originally, she had thought of a picnic somewhere by the river but the rain had changed her mind. The river banks would be boggy, the water running swiftly and Billy was so young – better to find somewhere safer. The Knavesmire racecourse seemed to be the answer. All around the actual racing area was a pleasant green park, ideal for kicking a ball about or picnicking beneath a shady tree.

Driving along, Marigold asked Jack if he had ever been to the racecourse and was pleased to learn that he had not. Even more gratifying, as they arrived, the sky began to lighten and the sun appeared.

Marigold left the food in the car but unpacked an elderly rounders set she had unearthed from the garage and a swing-ball game. She remembered how easily Karen had become bored at picnics. In the event, she needn't have bothered. All Jack and Billy wanted to do was to play around with Paddy. They ran around with him chasing after them. They threw stones for him and when he collapsed beneath a tree, tired by the activity, they lay down next to him, rubbing his ears, his chest and, in Billy's case, trying to catch his lazily wagging tail.

'You look hot. Would you like a drink?'

When they both nodded, Marigold unearthed cans of cola for them and put down a bowl of water for Paddy and then she began to set out the picnic.

'What did you say this place was called?' Jack rested his can upon the grass and wiped his hand across his mouth.

'It's called The Knavesmire.' Marigold pointed. 'That's where the horses race. People come and stand here to get a glimpse of the horses but most of them pay to go into the stands where they get a better view.'

'And they bet with the bookies.'

'That's right.'

'I think my dad must have come here once. I remember, he came home and said he'd won a lot of money. He and Mum were laughing and happy and we all went out for a meal in a posh restaurant.' Jack sighed. 'That's when we lived in a trailer.'

'A trailer?'

'Yeah. It was good. We'd travelled around in it, you know. And then it was on a park and there was a little white-painted fence around it. It was heaps better than the dump we're in now.'

Jack had stretched out on his back with his hands behind his head. He squinted up at the sun. 'We had a sofa that turned into a bed and another little bed and a kitchen and everything, but it was cold in winter and Billy kept on coughing all the time, so we had to sell it.'

'I see.'

'No, you don't.' Jack moved, put his arm across his face so she couldn't see him. 'You're nice, but you don't see, not really. You've got everything – a house and a car and a dog. We had a house once, when I was little. I can remember it. It had a garden and a shed and I had a pet rabbit. I had to give him away when we moved. Mum thinks I've forgotten about Patches, but I haven't. I haven't forgotten about anything.' He rolled over and buried his face in the grass.

Marigold looked across at Billy but he wasn't listening to their conversation. He was too busy trying to sit on Paddy's back. Blessing her pet's good nature, she looked back at Jack.

'Things will get better again, Jack. When your dad gets a job . . .'

'He won't get a job and things won't get better, they'll get worse.' With a movement that was almost violent, Jack scrambled into a sitting position, facing her. 'Why do grown-ups always bloody lie to kids? You shouldn't lie. You tell us off if we do it.' He glared at her. 'There are no jobs, not for my dad or for Billy and me when we grow up. We'll have to stay in that horrible place for ever. Dad hates it there. That's why he goes away so much and one day, maybe, he just won't come back and I'll have to look after Mum.' He scrubbed his hand over his eyes.

'Oh, Jack, that won't happen.' Marigold leaned forward, aching to touch him but afraid to do so. 'Your mum and dad love each other and they love you and Billy. They won't split up.'

He stared down at the grass, stubbornly refusing to meet her eyes.

Paddy, getting sick of Billy's attempts to sit on him, rose to his feet and walked away. Billy came over to Marigold.

'I'm hungry.'

Marigold sighed and ruffled his hair. 'Yes. Do you want to help me set out the food?'

She spread a cloth over a flat piece of grass. 'Will you get the crisps and fruit, Jack?' She began to unwrap the cooked chicken.

Moving slowly, Jack took items of food from her shopping bag.

Marigold searched for a subject interesting enough to distract his thoughts. 'Do you know why they call this place The Knavesmire?'

He raised his shoulders in a disinterested shrug.

'It's because in the fourteenth century this was a place of execution for thieves and murderers. Knave is an old-fashioned word for a wrongdoer and mire means a sort of a bog or a piece of marshy land.' Marigold gave a theatrical shiver, blessing the fact that Billy was too busy stuffing crisps into his mouth to listen to her.

'Just think, that tree over there,' she waved her hand, 'could have been one of the trees they hanged someone from.'

Jack glanced towards the tree she had indicated. He scowled. 'Naw, it's not old enough. At least—' He shielded his eyes with his hand and squinted at it. 'Do you really think so?'

She nodded, blessing the fact that even this generation of small boys were ghoulish enough to be fascinated by horror stories.

'Could be.' She handed him a paper plate containing chicken and salad.

'I suppose in those days the crowds came to see the hangings and not the horses.'

He managed a smile as he accepted the food. 'Thanks.' Then he laughed when Paddy came at a run and hurled himself at him.

218

Marigold relaxed and served herself.

She had thought the boys might become bored but the time went quickly. After eating, they again chased about with Paddy. They went looking for unusual stones and leaves and played a little swing-ball. By the time Marigold began collecting up their gear and storing it back in the car, all three of them were sun flushed and untidy.

'Oh dear, you're covered in mud, Jack.' Marigold frowned. 'Your shirt looks like a rag. Where did you find it all?'

He shrugged. 'Over there, by those trees,' he pointed. 'It was Paddy. He jumped at me and I was off balance.'

Marigold sighed. 'Your mum will be cross.'

He stared at her. 'She'd have been more cross if I'd kept my best clothes on.'

'That's true. I did wonder why you and Billy were so smartly . . .' Marigold broke off halfway through her sentence. She didn't want Jack to think she was criticising his mother, but he knew already what she was thinking.

He explained. 'Mum's not a fusspot but she's real keen on us looking good if we're taken out. She's worried that people look down on us for living where we do. She says we have to have extra-good standards.'

'Oh dear,' Marigold frowned, spotting for the first time the large green patches on the back of Billy's overalls. 'She's not going to be happy with me, is she, when I take you home looking like this?'

'No.' Jack narrowed his eyes and said, slyly, 'Maybe you could stop off at your place and clean us up a bit.'

'You mean, wash your clothes?'

'It's only my shirt and Billy's overalls. You see, Mum doesn't have anywhere to wash our clothes. She goes to the launderette twice a week.' Jack gave Marigold an innocent look. 'I bet you have a dryer as well as a washer.'

'I have.'
'Well then.' He smiled at her.

Back at her house, Billy and Jack sat partly dressed at her kitchen table and consumed milk shakes. Paddy lapped noisily at his water bowl and Marigold watched the boys' clothing flip round and round in her washing machine.

Jack sighed and wiped a white moustache from his upper lip. 'Nice here. Even better than I thought.' He looked round. 'Haven't you any pictures of your daughter?'

'Karen?' Marigold looked at Jack with surprise. 'Not here in the kitchen, but in other parts of the house. Why do you ask?'

He picked up his empty glass and carried it over to the sink. 'I wondered what she looked like. She's a model, you said?'

'Yes.' Marigold studied his shirtless back. He was a skinny, lanky boy but his bones were long – he would grow into a tall young man. She found herself saying, 'Would you like me to get a photograph, so you could see?'

'Naw.' But when he turned round she saw he was blushing.

She smiled and left the kitchen, returning a minute later with a large, framed photograph which she handed to him. 'There you are. That's Karen.'

He took the frame and held it carefully in his hands. 'Wow. She's beautiful.'

'Yes. I think so.'

The washing machine clicked off; she waited a moment and then opened the door and transferred their clothes to the dryer.

Jack took Karen's photograph back to the table and stood it where he could see it. He said, 'She's not like you, is she?'

Marigold's eyebrows arched. 'Thank you very much.' Then seeing the puzzled expression on his face, she added, 'Karen looks like her father.'

Jack sat back in his chair and sighed and then he said, in a clumsy but touching attempt to please her, '*You* look very nice, it's just that she's like a princess.'

'I know.' Marigold scratched her nose, which itched. 'When she works for the fashion houses she sometimes dresses in ballgowns and then she does look just like an old-fashioned princess.' She smiled at him. 'She's shooting a TV commercial at the moment, so you may get to see her on the television soon.'

'Honest?' Jack's face lit up. 'Will you tell me when to watch?'

'Yes, I will.'

'I don't like this.' Billy was tired. His lips formed a petulant pout and, with a wave of his hand, he sent the remains of his milk shake flying.

'Oh, Billy!'

Marigold dived for the glass but Paddy was there before her. As he leapt forward he tipped over his water bowl and Marigold's sandal slid in the stream of water spilling over the kitchen floor. She tottered for a moment and then fell, landing on her bottom. She gasped.

She was not hurt but she was shocked. So were the boys. They looked down at her in silence. She stared back, again scratching her nose. Then the door to the kitchen opened.

Ian stopped in the doorway and surveyed the scene before him.

The half-clothed boys, a guilty-looking dog and his wife stared back at him.

'Ian,' gasped Marigold.

His eyebrows rose. 'Marigold?'

'I thought you would be home late today?'

'The experiment was successful. We finished early.' Ian put his briefcase on the floor, then picked it up again when he saw the milk and water sloshing about. 'Do you mind telling me . . .'

'I can't. Not now.' Marigold had caught sight of the wall

clock. She struggled to her feet. 'I'm so late. I promised I'd have them back home about four o'clock and it's past that already.' She went over to the clothes dryer.

'But who are they?'

'It's complicated.' She scratched her nose. 'I'll tell you later. I promise.'

He scowled and threw up his hands in disgust. 'My God, and you're encouraging me to go away to Norway. How on earth will you manage without me?'

Marigold ground her teeth. 'Perfectly well, Ian.' She drew a deep breath. 'I know this is all confusing but it's a one-off situation as you will see when I've explained. And you know I generally manage very well.'

'You have up to now but the way you've been lately . . .' Ian retreated to the door. He fired a parting shot before disappearing. 'And for God's sake, leave your nose alone. It's already bright red and peeling. You'll have no skin at all if you keep scratching at it.'

On the way home the children were quiet. Marigold glanced in the car mirror and groaned. Ian had been right about her nose.

But Jack cheered her up a little when he climbed out of the car. He whispered, 'Never mind, your nose will go brown, you know.'

'You think so?'

'Oh, yes.' He nodded and then touched her hand. 'But you were wrong about your daughter.'

'How do you mean?

'She's not a bit like your husband.'

Chapter Seventeen

Looking gorgeous in a low-cut, misty-blue dress, Karen walked over to the marble balcony, threw back her head and gazed soulfully across the garden. For a few seconds there was absolute silence and then a voice called out, 'Cut.'

Immediately, the area was transformed into a mad whirlpool of full-scale activity. People clutching clipboards darted across the lawn, machines and human labourers moved wires and cables and the main camera man, who secretly lusted after Karen, sighed as he lost the focus of his close-up shot of her half-bared breasts.

Karen sighed, too.

'Can I have a break, Max?'

'No, my princess. You can't.' The first assistant to the director, a small plump man given to wearing canary-coloured sweaters, shook his head. 'We're ready for your next shot and, as you know, time is money.'

'Just five minutes so I can loosen my corset.' Karen rested her hand on her midriff. 'The bloody thing's squeezing the breath out of me. I feel faint.'

'Ah, that's good, that's authentic.' The first assistant rubbed his hands. 'Why do you think the ladies of yesteryear spent so much time lying on their beds?' He smiled a licentious smile. 'Apart from the obvious reason, of course.'

'I won't look good on film if I don't have a break,' she warned him. 'I'm beginning to feel sick.'

He sighed and came closer to her. He looked at her face. 'You're certainly pale.'

He shielded his eyes with his hand and squinted towards the entrance to the maze where another group of technicians waited, surrounded by a cluster of cameras. He noticed one large camera was still chugging along the camera track towards the new location and he frowned and then shrugged.

'OK.' He raised his voice. 'Take fifteen minutes, folks.'

There was a collective sigh of relaxation and beneath it, he murmured to Karen, 'Get yourself a drink of water or something. You do look out of it. And then ask Betty to touch up your make-up, put a bit of life back in your face. Pale's interesting but you're so white you resemble a potato. We can't have that.'

His gaze wandered towards a group of business suits watching the procedures, marketing men who held the purse strings, and he smiled and hurried towards them.

Fuming, Karen stared after him, then she picked up her skirts and walked towards to a parked caravan which, she knew, contained an assorted miscellany of props. Inside, surrounded by a lawn mower, parasols and a plastic bust of a garden nymph, she struggled to undo the back of her dress and let out her stays. Ah! She managed it.

She closed her eyes, bent over and drew in some deep breaths then she straightened again, picked up a fringed shawl which lay on the top of a wooden box, threw it over her shoulders to hide her unbuttoned dress and, leaving the caravan, went over to the refreshment tent to get a glass of ice-cold mineral water.

She sipped at the water and hitched up the shoulders of her dress – Betty, the wardrobe assistant, would have to rebutton her before the next scene – then made her way towards her own, personalised canvas chair. She sat down.

The chair had her name emblazoned on the back. When she had arrived at Stannington Manor to start filming, the first assistant director had presented her with it and she had felt proud. She had smiled and sat down and thought to herself: No one else can sit in this chair. It's mine because I am the star of this production. But more than that, it means I get the chance to act.

But after the first day of shooting she realised she had been naive. The fact that she was a well-known model meant nothing; neither did the gift of the personalised chair. It was a toy to keep a child happy. To the producer, the director and the backers she was just a good body and a stunning face. They didn't want her to act. All she had to do was to present an attractive picture.

Even the publicised cutting of her hair had been a gimmick to attract media attention. On her first day of shooting, standing in the Great Hall and wondering why she was wearing a costume dress, she had been given a wig to wear.

A thin man balancing a sheaf of papers had rushed up to her and thrust it into her hands. 'Betty will be along in a minute to see if it looks OK.'

She had stared down at the mass of curls and ringlets and stuttered, 'But I was told I was to promote the image of a modern woman?'

'You will, Miss Goddard, you will. But the writers have come up with a new twist and we're shooting that scene first.'

The man had shuffled his papers nervously. 'It's like this. You and Roddy quarrel and you clear off and then there's a dream sequence which suggests that you and he have met before, in a previous life. That meeting ended in tragedy but in the modern world you get to work out your destiny.' He sighed. 'Great idea.'

Karen turned scarlet and threw the wig on the floor. 'It's a crappy idea. It's ridiculous. This reincarnation thing – no one's mentioned it to me.'

'Does that matter, darling? You're getting well paid, aren't you?'

She bit her lip. 'I think I could have been told about this earlier.'

The man relented. 'This is your first TV job, isn't it?'

She nodded.

'Well,' he sighed. 'It's a crazy business, but see, what you have to remember is, it's all about money. When the backers came over to see this ancient pile, they realised the photographic possibilities were enormous. They'd paid out a fortune to hire the joint and they wanted to make sure they got their money's worth so they contacted the ad men and said they wanted more pizzazz.

'The advertising agency's creative team thought up this reincarnation idea. They reckoned a couple of scenes set in soft focus showing your character in a tasteful, low-cut dress, meeting Roddy in his polished boots and sideburns in the garden after a ball – music in the background, that sort of thing – would emphasise that the ad was expensively done and of gold-plated calibre.'

'But I was told I had to look ultramodern. And they insisted I cut my hair. Do you know how long it takes for hair to grow back?'

'Oh, for God's sake, woman.' He sighed and walked away from her, saying over his shoulder, 'You'll get over it.'

Well, she had got over it, and she'd got used to waiting around for hours and she'd got used to smiling lovingly into the eyes of the obnoxious Roddy but she was still smarting about that canary-clad Max likening her to a potato.

'Mind if I sit?'

'What?' Distracted from her thoughts, Karen looked up.

A tall, slim, smartly dressed young man was gesturing to the chair which stood next to hers.

Karen frowned. 'Well . . .'

'I don't want to intrude, but I spotted you sitting here on your own and I was hoping you'd give me your autograph?' He saw her eyebrows climb and added, hastily, 'For my sister. She's a great fan of yours. She cuts out all the fashion photographs of you in the magazines and puts them in a scrap book. She'd be absolutely thrilled to have your autograph. She wants to be a model when she's grown up.' Without waiting for a reply, he drew a notebook and pen from his breast pocket and offered them to Karen.

She scrawled her name across a page and asked, 'How old is your sister?'

'Eleven. Nearly twelve.'

He'd sat himself down next to her. Karen didn't want her space invaded. She hitched up her dress and scowled at him.

'Thank God for that. She's got a few years in which to change her mind then. Not many though.'

'Sorry?' He leaned towards her and took the notebook from her hand.

'Don't you read the papers? Child models are all the rage at the moment and I wouldn't wish their lives on anyone. They are manipulated by all and sundry and half of them are anorexic.'

He frowned. 'That's an unduly pessimistic picture of modelling, surely?'

She had a proper look at him. He was handsome in a cute sort of way. His thick dark hair flopped forward on to his forehead and there was a pronounced dimple in his chin.

Her scowl vanished. 'What's your sister's name?'

'Clare. Why?'

'Give me back your notebook.'

She took it from him and wrote the words, *With love to Clare* above her signature. 'There you are.'

'Thanks.' He slipped the book into the breast pocket of his jacket and smiled at her.

She smiled back. 'Sorry I was so grouchy. It's been a hard morning.'

'Yes. Filming's hard work.'

Karen realised she fancied him. She hadn't fancied a man for ages. She had led a celibate life for almost a year and although she had been surrounded by men since she arrived at Stannington Manor, none of them had attracted her.

The older ones had been too fat, or too old or too lecherous and the younger ones had looked better but had turned out to be twitchy, boring and totally without charm. Their one interest seemed to have been the cost of everything and their discussions had been based on how to cut back on expenditure.

The worse disappointment had been her co-star. At their first meeting, Karen's pulses had leapt but Roddy Champion had proved a great disappointment on closer acquaintance. He looked good but he had as much charisma as a flatfish. He showed no interest in her as a woman or a human being and between takes he droned on about his prized collection of Roman coins and how he managed to keep his weight constant. Karen had begun to wish her co-star had been gay; then, at least, they might have had a good gossip about everyone.

She sipped her water and took another sideways look at her companion. Where had this hunk sprung from? She was certain she hadn't seen him before. A thought struck her and she sat upright in her chair. Surely, he couldn't be the main producer? There had been rumours he was planning to drop in today and see how things were going.

No. She sneaked another peek. This man was too young, too pretty and too pleasant. The producer, if rumours were to be believed, was nearer fifty in age and believed that he was God.

'Er, are you part of the team? I don't believe I've seen you around.'

'No, I'm not involved in this project. But I am in the business.' He flashed his devastating smile again.

'I'm a production assistant. I've got a meeting with the producer when he arrives, to discuss the next job which I'm helping to set up.'

'Are you? I . . .' Karen jumped as a Tannoy blared out orders to return to the set. She jumped up.

'Shit. I'll have to fly.' She grabbed at the sliding bodice of her dress, bunching the material in her hand. 'I need the wardrobe mistress to make adjustments to this.'

'Do you? What a pity. I reckon it's perfect as it is.' His eyes played speculatively over Karen's half-revealed breasts.

She looked down, saw where he was looking, and felt a little thrill of anticipation. She asked, 'Are you going back to London this evening?'

'Well, I was but . . .'

'I'm staying at The Old Oak.' She laughed. 'Sounds like ye old village pub, doesn't it? Actually, it's a gem of a hotel. The food's marvellous and it even boasts a sauna.'

He stared into her eyes. 'What about the wine?'

She gave a little laugh and shrugged, which was dangerous. 'I don't know. I don't like drinking on my own.'

He looked thoughtful. 'I'll need to clear up several problems with the producer and if he's late arriving, there may not be time to deal with everything. Perhaps I ought to stay over. Do you think I'll find a bed at your hotel?'

She lowered her eyes demurely. 'I'm sure you will.'

She was a few minutes late on set and Max gave her a bollocking but then he calmed down and said she looked delicious.

'Betty's wonderful with make-up. She's totally transformed you.'

Karen nodded. She didn't bother to tell Max that Betty had merely laced up her corset and rebuttoned her dress. She hadn't needed any help from the wardrobe assistant to put colour in her cheeks. Someone else had done that.

On the evening of the day that Ian departed for Norway, Marigold dialled the telephone number of The Old Oak. She had wanted to call her daughter earlier in the day but she remembered what Karen had told her.

'Never call during working hours, Mum, except in an emergency, like death or an accident, and even then, think twice.' She had chuckled but Marigold knew she was serious. 'You see, if we're shooting a scene and I'm called away, then thousands of pounds go down the drain. Anyway, they wouldn't do that. They'd tell you to ring later.'

As Marigold's dilemma could not be called a major disaster, she had waited until after nine before ringing Karen.

'Miss Goddard? Just one moment.'

The desk clerk rang Karen's room, waited and then reported back to Marigold that Karen was not answering her phone and should she look for her.

Marigold drummed her fingers on the table. She didn't want to alarm Karen but she did want to settle something.

'Yes, please do that,' she replied.

A few minutes later, she heard Karen's voice. 'Hello.'

'It's me, love.'

'Mum. Is that you? What's the matter? Has something happened?'

'No, no. Everything's all right. But I did want a word with you.'

'God, Mum. Is that all? You want a chat! When the boy came

into the dining room calling out my name, my blood ran cold. I thought there'd been a car crash or something.'

'I'm sorry about that, but I haven't had much chance to contact you, have I? I'm not allowed to ring you during the day and it's been at least a week since you rang us.'

Karen muttered, 'Big deal.'

'What was that, Karen? I couldn't hear you.'

'Nothing, Mum.'

Marigold didn't pursue the matter. She clutched the phone tightly and launched into her prepared speech.

'You know you invited me up to London to stay with you for a few days? Well, now that your father's flown off to Norway...'

'Has he gone already?' Karen sounded surprised. 'I thought it was next month.'

'Oh, Karen, we told you all the details about his trip the last time we spoke.'

'Sorry, I forgot.'

Marigold gritted her teeth and ploughed on. 'He'll be away for the whole week so I thought it might be a good time for me to come and visit? I believe you said you'd be through filming on Monday evening and going back to London. I could catch a train on Tuesday morning and spend two or three days with you. We could shop for clothes – I could do with a new outfit.'

She waited for Karen's reaction. After a moment, she asked, 'Karen, are you there?'

'Yes.' Another small silence and then. 'Look, Mum, can I ring you back tomorrow. Actually—' A little laugh. 'I'm halfway through my dinner.'

'Oh, I'm sorry. I didn't know.'

'No, it's OK . . . but the thing is, I'm dining with someone.'

'Oh?' Conscious of the row of question marks behind the word, Marigold bit her lip. 'I'm sorry I disturbed you. Yes, of course. Ring me when you have time.

'I will . . . but Mum, as regards your visit . . .'

'Yes.'

'Can we leave it for a little while?'

Another short silence, this time on Marigold's part.

'You see, I might not get back to London on Monday. They may want me to re-shoot a couple of scenes. And I'm pretty tired, you know. Perhaps next month would be a better time.'

'Yes, of course. I didn't think. Well, look after yourself.'

'I will, Mum. Bye.'

Marigold put down the phone. That was it then. She stared down at the phone. 'Perhaps it's fate.'

Ever since Ian's departure, Marigold had been thinking about Adam Crewe. As she hoovered the sitting room she was remembering how his mouth creased when he smiled. As she energetically pummelled the quilt into fluffiness she was dwelling on the deep blue of his eyes, and when she opened a can of dog food for Paddy she almost cut her finger because she was dreaming of how Adam's hands had lingered on hers in the Arts Centre. But most of all, she remembered his detailed instructions as to how to find his shop and the way he was adamant that they would meet again.

Almost in panic, she had sought an escape route through Karen but her daughter had let her down.

Marigold looked at her wristwatch. Ian would be landing in Tromsø about now. She supposed someone from the university would meet him. He'd be so excited, eager for a tour round the physics laboratories and to chat with his Norwegian colleagues. He'd probably forgotten all about York already, and about her.

She shivered and thought she would get out of the house and walk in the garden. But as she slipped on a light jacket, the phone rang.

Perhaps it was Karen. She might have changed her mind. Marigold picked up the receiver.

'Is that you, Marigold?'

'Yes.'

'It's Adam Crewe.'

She already knew it. She recognised his voice.

'Can we talk?'

'Yes.' She half smiled. We're already behaving like lovers, she thought.

'I was wondering . . . You said you'd like to see round my place of work?'

'Yes, I would.'

'How about tomorrow?'

'But tomorrow's Sunday.'

'I know, but I'm working weekends at the moment. I've a lot of work on hand.'

'But, if I come, won't I keep you from your work?'

His voice deepened. 'That rather depends on you, Marigold.'

She drew a deep breath and then she said. 'What time?'

Chapter Eighteen

After parking the car, Marigold crossed the River Ouse by the nearest footbridge. She glanced at her watch. Oh hell! She was early, much too early. There was an hour to fill in before she presented herself at Adam's shop.

Normally, Marigold loved to wander around York, especially on a Sunday when the sun shone. The city had a different atmosphere on Sundays. Marigold wondered if it was caused by the sound of the church bells, which echoed through the centuries-old thoroughfares around the Minster, overlaying the chattering of visitors, who strolled more slowly than on a weekday, sight seeing and window shopping.

Sunday was the day Marigold felt her loneliness most keenly because it was a day for the family. Karen was away now and Ian, who had no religious convictions, treated it like any other day, working in the lab or catching up on paperwork in his office. And now, of course, he was in Norway.

Marigold usually visited York Minster first. If she was in luck, the choir would be practising for a service. She'd sit at the back of the church, close her eyes and listen to the voices, soaring like larks in a cornfield, higher and higher until their praise reached the top of the exquisite vaulted roof of the magnificent building.

Then, to bring herself back to earth, she would stroll through the streets, listening to and observing the family groups of tourists. The serious historians would consult maps and guidebooks, asking her for directions to specific places. The more light-hearted couples would sit on benches or on walls, their children swinging their legs and eating ice cream. Marigold envied them.

But today she was not people-watching. She had too much on her mind. At first she walked quickly, but then she slowed down. Why on earth was she hurrying? Adam did not expect her until after eleven.

She halted, looked around and realised she was close to All Saints' Church. She wrinkled her brow, trying to recollect a memory. Why was this particular church significant to her?

She remembered. The day she had left work, she had told Pat about the peculiar carving, the sanctuary door-knocker. Saints and sinners. Was she about to sin? Marigold felt a shiver run down her spine and she wished she hadn't walked this way. Then she flattened her lips into a thin line and told herself not to be stupid. She was attracted to Adam but that didn't mean she was going to fall into bed with him the moment she saw him. She might have day-dreamed a couple of times about doing such a thing but what would probably happen was that he would show her round his shop and then they'd go to a pub for a drink and a sandwich.

Nevertheless, she found herself walking towards the church and looking for the door. She stopped in front of it and stared at the doorknocker. There was no doubt the carving was a wonderful piece of craftsmanship but it was decidedly gruesome. She could understand how superstitious people in the past had credited it with magic powers. She almost wanted to touch it herself but she resisted the impulse.

Instead, she behaved childishly, pulling a face at the beast-like creature and hurrying away.

She walked fairly quickly until she came to The Shambles, where she slowed down to a stroll. From time to time, she stopped to admire a window display in one of the shops. Many of the goods on view were expensive luxury articles. There was a shop dealing only in teddy bears and another which sold huge ragdolls and golden doubloons.

She paused outside Culpeppers, the herbalists, a shop she loved and frequented, and she studied the books on display in Blackwells.

Since there was no traffic in The Shambles, the voices and laughter of the passers-by echoed in the narrow streets and floated upwards towards the sky. Marigold looked up at the thin strip of deep blue showing between the roofs of the closely clustered buildings and the tightness in her chest, which had developed when she was standing by the door at All Saints', dissolved.

She could hear the strains of a flute, obviously a busker was somewhere near by, and it brought back memories of the tramp, Tommy. She wondered how he was faring.

She looked at her watch. It was still early but she couldn't wait any longer. She took a scrap of paper out of her pocket and followed Adam's instructions on how to find his shop.

'It's tucked away, Marigold,' he had said.

He was right.

In Coffee Yard, formerly Langton's Lane, she turned a corner and there it was, the middle property of a group of three. The supporting houses were two-storeyed. One was an antiques and curio shop and the other, Marigold read from the board outside, was the property of a seed merchant. Adam's house, obviously the oldest of the three, was long and narrow and crowned with a roof of mellow red tiles. The front windows on the ground and third floor looked original – they were small-paned and gracious – but Marigold, looking upwards, saw that the second floor flaunted a large bay. It made the house look strange and rather humorous, like a tall thin man sporting a huge stomach.

The woodwork was well preserved, painted dove-grey and white and the front door, which was closed, was navy-blue in colour with a brass doorknocker.

Marigold peered through the ground-floor window. The glass had a certain bloom about it which told her it was very old but, she thought, it certainly didn't make for good viewing. She put her hand over her eyes, to cut out the sunlight, and tried again.

Ah, yes. Within the front room – the shop section, she presumed – a carved chest and a small chair stood on a blue carpet. They were attractive pieces of furniture but Marigold wondered how Adam managed to sell anything when he had so little space for display and when prospective buyers couldn't even see the goods properly.

She moved back to the doorway and rang the doorbell. A couple of minutes later, when nothing happened, she banged on the door. She heard footsteps on the stairs, the door opened and Adam looked out.

Marigold subdued a little lurch of her heart and said, severely, 'Your bell doesn't work.'

'I know, I keep meaning to get it fixed.' He stood to one side and opened the door wider. 'Please come in.'

She stepped into the entrance.

'This way.' He started up the stairs. 'I wasn't expecting you just yet. I've got to finish something I can't leave. If you don't mind waiting for ten minutes, I'll clean up and then show you round.'

She flushed. 'Yes, I know I'm early but . . .'

He opened a door at the top of the stairs. 'In here.'

Her first impression of the room was how large it was and the second was how cold, despite the warm weather. She shivered.

Adam, pulling a kitchen chair forward for her to sit in,

noticed the shiver. 'Sorry. I'll find something warm for you to put on.'

'No,' she protested. 'I'm fine.'

He ignored her. He crossed to a battered chest of drawers at the far side of the room, pulled open a drawer and, hunting around inside, produced a large, paint-spotted sweater that he threw towards her.

'Here, put this on. It's ancient but it's clean.'

She pulled it over her head; it smelt of beeswax and methylated spirits and pipe tobacco. She smiled at him. 'Thanks.'

'No problem.'

He picked up a pair of gloves, put them on and taking hold of a pad of coarse steel wood, dipped it into a bowl. Then he began slopping solvent on to the large sideboard that stood on newspaper in the middle of the room. He worked in silence for a moment and then glanced at her.

'Sorry about this. And sorry about the draught but the opened windows and the fan are necessary. This stuff throws off fumes. I'd hate you to collapse unconscious on the floor.'

'So would I.' She watched for a moment and then asked, 'Surely you didn't get that sideboard up those narrow stairs?'

He grinned. 'No. I've a special block and pulley contraption at the back of the house.'

'Oh.' She nodded and looked around, studying the workshop. The floor was lino-covered and the miscellany of furniture in the room was all in need of repair. A Victorian lady's chair with a collapsed leg lurched drunkenly in one corner. A mirror with a spotted surface leaned against one wall and faithfully reproduced the image of an elegant escritoire facing it. There were assorted chairs, including a rocking chair, and a chest of drawers which looked as though it had been attacked with a hammer.

Marigold studied these things and then she said, 'I've never thought of it before, but you're a furniture doctor, aren't you?'

He nodded. 'That's a nice way of putting it.'

'It must be a satisfying occupation.' She gestured towards the escritoire. 'That's beautiful. Eighteenth century, isn't it? It doesn't look damaged. What's the matter with it?'

'Yes, it is eighteenth century.' He looked at her with increased respect. 'A lovely piece of furniture and, fortunately, there's nothing too much amiss with it.' He paused in his work. 'You know, nowadays, people laugh at the Victorians for their habit of using little mats and fancy doilies, but it's a pity such things went out of fashion. At some time or another, the escritoire was defaced by an idiot who got into the habit of resting his mug of tea on it.' Adam raised his shoulders in a shrug. 'My customers bought the piece at a sale. When they contacted me I told them they could do the job themselves. It's quite an easy process, but they were too scared they'd spoil the piece so I got the job.'

He recommenced his work.

Marigold shifted in her seat. 'I looked in your shop window.'

'Oh, yes.'

'Yes.' She cleared her throat. 'The carved chest's attractive.'

'It's a nice piece.' He looked at her sidewards. 'Are you interested in buying it?'

Oh God, is that why he invited me here; to try and sell me something? Marigold blushed furiously. 'No.' She paused. 'I don't think I'll be buying anything for the house. You see, I don't think I'll be there for much longer.'

Horrified by her own words, she shrank back in her chair.

He glanced at her but did not speak. After another five minutes, he straightened up and tossed the pad of wire wool into the bowl. 'That will do for now.'

He stripped off his gloves, gave her a brief smile then went over to the sink in the corner of the room. He scrubbed his hands and dried them. He turned to her and said, 'What would you like to do?'

Marigold was totally nonplussed. Last night, after his late phone call, she had gone to bed and mentally prepared for this meeting, dreaming up several scenarios.

Adam would sweep her up in his arms the moment she entered his home and make passionate love to her. Or, he would welcome her gravely and with exquisite sensitivity. He would pour drinks for them and get her to tell him why she was so unhappy, and then he would comfort her with a kiss, which would lead to another kiss, and another. Or, he would tell her he had been driven crazy by her at their first meeting and he would ask her to leave Ian and run away with him.

Marigold had known, of course she had, that her dreams had been fantasies, but she had expected more than what was happening now. She wished desperately that she had not come. Adam's expression, when he looked at her, was merely friendly and as a result, she hadn't a clue what to say or how to behave.

She took a deep breath to calm her quivering nerves and said, 'Would you show me round the house?'

'Sure.' He opened the door and ushered her out on to the landing. 'The top floor is pretty basic. Two bedrooms, bathroom and toilet. You don't want to see them, do you?'

Speechless, she shook her head.

'This floor, as you can see, I use as my working area. There's a small room where I store things.' He opened a nearby door and shut it again before she had a chance to look inside. 'But downstairs is much more interesting. Come on, I'll show you.'

He clattered down the narrow staircase and Marigold followed him.

'The shop area's rather nice.' Adam produced a key from his trouser pocket and unlocked the door.

He waited for Marigold to enter the room. 'It was obviously someone's cherished front parlour. The wallpaper was on when I bought the place ten years ago. I liked it so I left it alone.' He paused. 'It's early Victorian, I think.'

'It's lovely.' Marigold admired the faded creamy-coloured wallpaper, which was delicately embossed with tiny sprays of orange and dark-blue flowers. 'But isn't the room too small for a shop?'

'Of course it is.' Adam grinned sheepishly. 'I knew it from the start.' He shook his head. 'But there was something about this house which got to me. Also, it was going cheap and I couldn't afford anywhere else.'

His face darkened. 'I bought the place nine months after my divorce, mostly because I wanted a bolt hole. I was very unhappy at the time. I wanted to lie low and lick my wounds. I had a nice house in County Durham but my wife got that. I moved to York to put some space between us.'

'Oh.' Marigold was taken aback, both by his honesty and by what he was saying, but then she realised she was being stupid again. Adam was an attractive, middle-aged man. He was alone now but it was obvious he must have had some kind of relationship in his past. Perhaps there had been many.

She glanced at him. 'I hope things settled down, and you're happier now.'

He brushed his hand over his face as though knocking away a fly. 'You get used to things. Maggie allows me to see my daughter once a month.'

He had a daughter! Marigold took a step backwards at yet another blow to her equilibrium. Seeking desperately for another topic of conversation, she said with forced cheerfulness, 'Well, despite the size of this room, you appear to have built up a successful business.'

'Yes, I've been lucky in that respect. Over the years I've

acquired a reputation for doing a good job of work. The restoration side of the business keeps me busy. Nowadays, I don't bother much with the selling side.'

'In fact—' He looked round the room. 'I've decided to sell.'

Ignoring her sound of protest, he went on. 'Three months ago I bought a cottage on the outskirts of York. There's land with it, which I need, and a good, big shed. It's perfect for me. But I know I'll have trouble selling this place.' He shook his head. 'With all those steps it won't appeal to a young couple with children or an elderly couple.'

'But the house is charming. Surely you'll find a buyer?'

'Thank you for the vote of confidence.' Adam grinned. 'But wait a moment, you haven't seen the best bit yet.'

He relocked the shop door and led the way towards the rear of the house. 'This room,' he said, 'is my particular favourite, although I don't know how you'd describe it in an estate agents' brochure.'

Marigold stepped into the room and gave a little gasp of pleasure. The scene before her was organised chaos, but what delightful chaos.

She saw immediately that it had been two, maybe three small rooms which had been knocked through and made into one. The first half of the room facing her was a mixture between a study and a sitting room. She saw and admired the collection of prints in matching black frames which decorated the plain cream walls. The floorcovering was some kind of unbleached hessian and a sofa and easy chair, both covered in old rose-strewn fabric printed on a loose-weave material, took up a considerable amount of space.

The rest was invaded by a vast number of books and magazines. They were everywhere, on the sofa and the chair, on the small, antique desk squashed in a windowed alcove and stacked on top of the portable TV set balanced on a spindly occasional table in one corner of the room.

'It's a bit of a mess.' Adam sounded sheepish but not particularly concerned.

She didn't answer him.

A Magi-coal gas fire had been installed in the Edwardian fireplace and above the high wooden mantel was a large collection of old unframed prints, haphazardly pinned to a large piece of drawing board. She went over to study them.

Amongst the mass of drawings, she recognised a yellowing print of William Shakespeare, some architectural drawings of a stately home which could have been Castle Howard and a sketch of someone she thought was Richard III. She studied some of the old, yellowing political cartoons and she smiled. She felt, rather than saw, Adam come and stand behind her. She pointed to one of the prints that had caught her eye and asked, 'Is it Richard III?'

'Yes.'

She turned round. He was standing very close to her. She rested her hand on his arm. 'You know, I always thought he got a very bad deal from the press of that time. Have you ever read . . . ?'

'*A Prisoner of Time*.' He finished her sentence for her. 'Yes, and I go along with Josephine Tey's verdict.'

They exchanged grins and Marigold began to feel the lovely warmth of compatability again. Nevertheless, remembering Adam's unemotional welcome when she arrived for her visit, she stepped away from him and returned to her examination of the room.

Through an archway, she could see into the kitchen area. Sunlight was streaming in; there must be a large window in there. She walked forward to see. Her first impression was of the masses of red and white china cramming the wall shelves, then she saw a mahogany cupboard which ran all the way down one side and presumably housed the fridge and washing machine.

'Your work?' She raised her eyebrows at Adam who had followed her and now lounged against the frame of the archway.

He nodded.

'Very nice.'

She looked at the small but adequate sink unit and ran her hand across the back of one of the four beech dining chairs surrounding the square-shaped kitchen table. At the end of the kitchen, French windows beckoned the eye to the green of the small garden beyond. She itched to get outside and see what delights awaited her there. She swung round to face Adam.

'It's lovely. You've done a wonderful job.'

He didn't move but she realised he was watching her expression carefully.

He said, 'I'm glad you approve.'

She shook her head. 'You must have worked so hard.'

'I did.' He straightened up. 'When I moved in there were huge holes in the roof of this particular part of the house. Pigeons were nesting in here. But I could see the possibilities and I welcomed the challenge. I needed something to engage my whole attention, you see.'

A certain tenseness crept into the atmosphere, which Marigold thought she must lighten. Accordingly, she said, 'May I see the garden?'

'Of course.' He came to stand by her side. 'But don't expect too much. I'm no gardener.' As he opened the door, he added, 'I guessed *you* were though, so I cut the grass.'

Marigold stepped through the French doors and again, she was speechless.

The garden was small and surrounded by a stone wall high enough to render it private. The flower borders looked neglected. There were weeds and patches of last year's dead foliage everywhere but there were also old-fashioned roses climbing in profusion over the stone wall, sending out the most heavenly perfume. A buddleia nodded and swayed gracefully, playing host to a squad of droning honey bees and beneath a shiny-leafed holly bush, Marigold spotted a clump of shy lilies of the valley. She also could smell, although she couldn't trace, the scent of honeysuckle.

'But Adam—' Her face alight with pleasure, she turned towards him. 'This is wonderful.'

He took a step towards her. 'So are you,' he muttered. And before she could draw breath he was kissing her.

For a split second, Marigold wondered if she was hallucinating. After all, this was so much part of her fantasy. But another second passed and another, and he was still kissing her. This is *real*, she thought, and then she began kissing him back.

Feeling her response to him, Adam groaned and pulled her closer to him. He kissed her cheeks, her closed eyes, the corners of her mouth and then her throat.

Her lips parted and he took possession of her mouth. His tongue teased the softness of her lips and the inside of her mouth until she thought her legs would give way under the sheer intensity of her emotions.

'Adam.'

'Hush,' he said. 'Hush.'

His fingers flickered over her throat and neck, hesitated at the opening of her dress.

Marigold lay back against the security of his arms. She dug her fingers into his shoulders and gave herself up to pure sensation.

Breathing heavily, Adam slid his hand inside her dress and cupped her left breast.

She gasped.

He eased his fingers inside her bra and began to touch, to caress. His movements were feather soft but she felt the impact

of them through the whole of her body. She arched her back and
her breath came in short gasps. 'Adam.' She murmured his name
again. 'Adam, oh please . . .'

His caress stopped. She opened her eyes.

He stared down at her, his face a picture of conflicting
emotions. 'I'm sorry. I thought you wanted me.'

'But I do.' The colour flamed in her face. 'That's why I . . .'
She broke off, embarrassed.

He stared at her and then, realising what she was trying to
say, he laughed out loud. 'God, Marigold, I'm a fool. I thought
you were asking me to stop, but you weren't, were you? Tell me
I'm right. I haven't deluded myself. You want me to make love
to you?'

She nodded.

He touched his lips to hers, very gently. 'I'd hoped for this,
ever since our first meeting, but it was a daydream. But now—'
He hugged her to him.

'Let's go upstairs?'

She stared into his eyes, a little smile twitching the corners
of her mouth.

'Must we?'

He wrinkled his brows, once more uncertain of her.

She gave a breathless laugh. She felt wonderful. She felt
powerful. She felt capable of anything and, just once in her life,
she wanted to be outrageous.

'All those stairs, Adam. And you said yourself that the
bedrooms are nothing special.'

As he began to understand, a quizzical look appeared on his
face. 'But, Marigold . . .'

'Whereas your garden –' She turned her head and looked
towards the climbing roses. '– your garden *is* special.'

'You really mean it? You want us to make love here?'

'Why not?' She brushed back her hair from her face, hoping

he would not let her down. 'The wall's pretty high. There's no one around. And it's Sunday, so the adjoining properties are empty.'

A smile slowly spread across his face. 'Marigold,' he said. 'You're priceless. Are you going to make a habit of surprising me?'

She dimpled. 'Perhaps.' Then her animated expression became sombre. 'But again, perhaps not. This happens to be an extra-special day.'

Adam put his hands on her shoulders and clutched her so hard it hurt.

'If you're trying to warn me, tell me this is a one-off occasion, then I don't believe you. We both know something special is happening between us.'

'Do we?' She saw the expression on his face, and so she touched his cheek and sighed. 'Yes, you're right. But everything's such a mess and . . .' Adam saw the shadow move across her face and he tried to dispel it.

'Yes, I know it is, but today we're not going into the whys and wherefores, are we?'

He waited for her to shake her head, which she did.

'Do I get another smile?'

She obliged.

'Then please wait for a couple of minutes.'

She came out of her mood of introspection. 'Why must I wait?'

'You'll see.'

'Don't keep me waiting long.' She was smiling properly now and the light was back in her eyes.

'Two minutes, and then I'll be back.' Adam explained. 'I'm going to get a rug. I cut this grass with shears and although I can't wait for us to fulfil our lust in the open air, I can't afford to get lumbago afterwards.'

She laughed out loud. 'Oh, Adam. How unromantic.'

'Is it?' He kissed her soundly and then turned towards the house. 'Never mind, I'll make it up to you when I get back.'

He hurried into the house.

For a few moments, Marigold was alone. She listened to the sound of a bird chirping away in the holly tree, she smelt the honeysuckle and she turned up her face towards the sun. Deliberately, she banished all thoughts of worry and guilt from her mind. After all, she reasoned, when a fantasy starts coming true, the only thing to do is go with it.

Chapter Nineteen

'I'm glad you've found time to come for coffee.' Susan Cambridge gave Marigold a kindly but inquisitive glance. 'I rang you earlier in the week. Twice, in fact, but you were out.'

'Yes.' Marigold accepted her cup of coffee with a smile. 'I've been busy.'

'Have you?' Susan plumped down in her chair. It was clear she was bursting with curiosity but she asked no questions. She held out a plate of biscuits for Marigold's inspection.

'No, I won't, thanks. I'm not hungry.'

Susan picked out a chocolate biscuit for herself. She smiled at Marigold. 'You're looking well, much better than the last time we saw each other. Whatever you're doing, it's suiting you.'

'It is indeed.' Marigold buried her face in her coffee cup to hide the telltale blush.

There was a pause and then Susan, accepting Marigold's decision to keep her own counsel, said, 'Oh, there's something I want to tell you. The committee members were impressed by your report and they have decided to follow through on your recommendations. They asked me to thank you for all your work.'

Marigold nodded. 'I was glad to help.'

'Yes, I know you were. But I think it's probable they may call on you again and if they do, then things must be put on a proper footing. The next time you must charge a fee for your work.'

Marigold shifted in her seat. 'I don't think I would feel comfortable, Susan, charging for helping people involved in charity work.'

'Nonsense. You had to train, didn't you? You must know that you are a wizard with figures and therefore you deserve to get paid for your work.'

'Well, we'll see.' Marigold's shoulders lifted in a small shrug. 'Actually, I seem to have lost my appetite for accountancy. I think I want to do something else, but what can I do? I have no training for anything else.'

Susan sat upright in her chair. 'How about me getting you on to a couple of committees? You know the business world, you're bright and we need to recruit younger people with a modern outlook on life. You could do a lot of good, Mari.'

'Oh, Susan. I'm flattered, I really am, but it's not what I want for myself. When I say I need a change, I mean a *real* change. I'm tired of sitting behind a desk making telephone calls. I want to get really involved in something. A proper job with hands-on experience.'

'My goodness, you are thinking of changing your life, aren't you?' Susan looked amused. 'What does Ian think of all this? Or doesn't he know yet? He's due back tomorrow, isn't he?'

'Yes. His plane arrives at Manchester mid-morning. I'll pick him up at York Station around two o'clock.'

'Well, you'll have plenty to talk about for once. You'll want to discuss your plans for a new career, and, I suppose, he'll be eager to tell you about his trip to Norway.'

'Oh, I doubt that.'

Marigold had spoken without thinking. She glanced at Susan Cambridge and she thought she saw her friend's eyes narrow slightly. She felt a momentary chill. Had the older woman heard something?

She hurried on. 'Ian will be full of what he's seen in the labs at Tromsø – he'll want to dash off and speak to his colleagues here about them.'

'Oh, surely not. He can't have spent the whole time lecturing or working. He must have travelled around a little and mixed with some interesting people.'

Yes, there was a definite edge to Susan's voice. Perhaps she had heard something, although Marigold couldn't imagine how. She and Adam had been extremely discreet – except for the first time, in the garden.

A smile insisted on curving Marigold's lips. She glanced at her watch and stood up.

'Sorry, but I must go. I don't know whether I mentioned it, but a friend of mine, someone I used to work with, is getting married in a few days' time and I promised to call and see her this afternoon. She wants me to help with the arrangements. And I must walk Paddy before I go to her place.'

'Yes, all right.' Susan put her hands on the side of her chair and levered herself upright. 'Pity you couldn't stay longer, but we can catch up on things in a day or two. And do remember, Mari, there's a place on the charity shops committee, if you change your mind.'

'I'll remember.'

Walking back to her own house, Marigold thought how glad she would be when everything was out in the open. There had been a moment, arriving at Susan's house, when the older woman had greeted her with a hug and she had been sorely tempted to blurt out her news. If only she could have said, 'I'm leaving Ian because I have been terribly unhappy for a long, long time. But now I've met someone who has reminded me what happiness is and I cannot go on with the life I'm leading.'

Susan, she knew, would not have approved of her sentiments.

Susan, like Marigold's own parents, would have talked about duty and conscience. And Marigold would have accepted her disapproval. What she couldn't accept was living a lie.

But she couldn't tell Susan, much as she wanted to. In all conscience, the first person to know must be Ian.

Marigold swallowed the lump in her throat. It would be hard. What a homecoming for Ian. But she couldn't delay, she just couldn't. She couldn't pretend the last week hadn't happened. She couldn't lie beside Ian in their bed and pretend to be the same person she had been before he left.

She realised, with a slight shock, that she was outside her home. She unlocked the door, went in, changed her shoes and then shouted to Paddy. He must have been asleep because it took him a couple of minutes to appear but when he saw her he came at a run. She slipped on his collar and lead and left the house again.

She walked down the avenue at such a pace, Paddy had a job keeping up with her. After he had wheezed a couple of times and pulled back on his lead, Marigold slowed down.

'Sorry, old boy. It's because my feet are trying to keep up with my thoughts.'

She caressed his smooth head and suddenly thought, What will happen to Paddy? Ian wouldn't want to part with him, although Paddy was really her dog. But if she left him behind he would surely pine for her. But would she be able to find somewhere to live that would be suitable for a dog of Paddy's size? She had savings, it was true, but she'd never be able to afford the kind of property she was living in now. How would Paddy feel, living in a flat with no garden? She bit her lip hard.

They had reached the end of the road. Marigold crossed over and went towards a twisting pathway which wandered off towards a patch of common ground. She pressed the release catch on Paddy's lead and watched as he shot off at a gallop, slowing only to lower his head and sniff optimistically after rabbit scents.

Marigold stood and watched him.

When Susan Cambridge learned the truth, would she remain a friend? She might, but it would be a different friendship. Pat would still be there for her, though; they had grown close during the years they had worked with each other. But Pat was getting married and Chris would be at the centre of her life from now on.

Marigold began to walk again, slowly, with her head down.

She must make new friends. She could do it. Daniel and Helen Crewe had liked her. But Daniel was Adam's brother.

Marigold sighed and ran her fingers through her hair. It needed cutting. She had never worn her hair long. Did Adam like women with long hair? There was such a lot she had to learn about Adam. She knew she loved him and she was pretty sure he loved her, but there were so many spaces in their lives that needed filling in. What would he think when she told him she was leaving Ian? He might think she was trying to trap him into some sort of commitment. She could tell him that she wasn't, but would he believe her?

Childishly, she rubbed her stinging eyes with her knuckles. She must have faith. It would all work out.

There'd be the legalities to attend to. Ian had his own solicitor. She would have to find one to act for her. God, she hoped she and Ian wouldn't start rowing over possessions. She didn't expect him to pay towards her support but they had been married for a long time. She'd put money, time and effort in creating their home. It was fair she should have some of the furniture. Would Ian, she wondered, keep the house on or would he sell it?

Paddy barked. He had put up a scent and was in the ditch

digging violently. She would have to clean him up when they got back home.

Home, she thought. Am I actually going to go through with this? Have I the energy? She felt so tired.

Then she remembered the hours spent with Adam and she knew she would. And it wasn't because, after years of repressing her natural instincts, Adam satisfied her sexually – although that was terribly important. It was because he made her feel needed again. He made her feel like a real person. He had taken the emptiness away. She had no choice, really.

Pat looked as rosy and shiny as a teenage bride. When she spoke, she sounded as though she was on the edge of a nervous breakdown. Marigold knew that in the last two weeks, she had contacted her parents, her brother who lived in France and her late husband's mother who lived in Wales. And tomorrow and the day after that they would all be arriving in York to attend her wedding.

Chris's remaining parent, his father, was due tomorrow night.

When Marigold walked into the room, Pat clutched her arm and wailed. 'Why did Chris want to get married, Mari? We're happy now, living together. What if his dad disapproves of me? Chris is his only child. He's the most important person in his life.' She paused, breathless with nerves. 'You've met my parents. Do you think they will take to Chris?'

'Of course they will. He's a nice guy.' Marigold patted her hand. 'Almost good enough for you.'

A smile twitched Pat's mouth. 'He's pretty gorgeous, isn't he?'

Marigold nodded.

'But I'm worried most about my mother-in-law. How will she really feel about me remarrying?' Pat's smile disappeared as she worried at her lip. 'Maybe I shouldn't have invited her?'

'You had to invite her, Pat. You've kept in touch with her all these years. She sees her grandson regularly. Think how hurt she would have been if you had left her out.'

'But she loved Geoff so much.'

'So did you.' Marigold gave her friend an affectionate squeeze. 'But the years pass and life has to go on. Geoff would have been so happy for you.'

Pat's smile flickered back into life. 'Yes, you're right.'

'And the fact that Chris has pushed you to get married is a compliment. It means he's quite sure that he wants to spend the rest of his life with you.'

'I already knew that.' Pat's smile became a grin. 'But indirectly, Mari, this wedding is because of Sam.'

'Sam. What has he to do with it?'

'Well, as you know, I rather enjoyed living in sin but Chris felt we ought to get married because of Sam. He said young people like to fool around themselves but draw the line at their parents doing it.'

Remembering her conversation with Chris at the dinner party, Marigold hid a smile. 'I don't think that's the only reason for this wedding, Pat.'

'Oh, I think it was. Sam was OK about Chris and me sleeping together, but he was delighted when we told him we were going to be married, so perhaps Chris was right.'

The thought of Karen flashed into Marigold's mind and distracted her attention from her friend's conversation. Karen was older and much more sophisticated than Sam; surely, when the first shock was over, she would be magnanimous about her mother having an affair.

' . . . so if you could help me out the day before the wedding. There'll be so many people, you see, and a couple of late arrivals and . . .'

'Sorry?' Marigold tuned back into the present.

Pat paused to draw breath. 'You can help me out with the catering?'

'Oh, yes. Of course. What shall I do?'

Pat gave her a curious look. 'You all right?'

'Of course I am. Why?'

'Well, you seem a bit absentminded, but it's more than that. You're different in some way.'

Marigold felt a blush beginning. 'In what way?'

'I don't know. Just different.' Pat put her head on one side. 'There's a sort of bloom about you.' Her eyes widened. 'I've got it. You have, haven't you?'

Marigold turned her head away. 'I don't know what you're talking about.'

'Yes you do, Marigold Goddard. You've got yourself a lover!' Pat pursed her lips. 'You threatened to do that the day you left work.'

'Nonsense.' Marigold blushed crimson. 'Just because you're fantastically happy, you're seeing everything through a rosy haze.'

'No, I'm not.' Pat's eyes had gone large and round. 'And I'm glad for you, Mari. Maybe I shouldn't say it, but I am. You deserve better than . . .'

Gently Marigold shook her head. 'Leave it, please. I don't want to talk now. Perhaps later.'

Pat nodded, placed two fingers over her mouth and then, after an eloquent glance, returned to the subject of catering.

'If you haven't time, Mari, then it doesn't matter, but you make such gorgeous cakes and scones. If you could let me have some, then they'll be there for people arriving early or late or for the unexpected visitor who might turn up. I mean, the wedding breakfast's all set up but it's the day before the wedding and . . .'

'Leave it to me. I'll do them tomorrow. Do you want anything in particular?'

'Your honey and sultana buns are delicious, and maybe some cheese straws. Oh, and maybe a date and walnut loaf.'

'I'll make two.' Marigold scribbled a list in her notebook. 'I'll bring them round in good time. Will it matter if I have two little lads with me? I've told you about Jack and Billy, haven't I? I have to look after them for a day this week. We won't stay. We'll just bring in the baking.'

'Bring them by all means. I'd like to meet them.'

'Good.' Marigold put her notebook away. 'Anything else I can do?'

'No, thank you.'

'I'm so looking forward to your wedding.'

'Well, it's only a register office do, but I must admit, so am I.' Pat lowered her voice. 'Ian is due back any time, isn't he?'

Marigold nodded.

'Well, under the circumstances, you might not want to bring him with you, but if you do . . .'

'I don't.'

Conscious of the baldness of her comment, Marigold hurried on, 'Ian and I have a lot of talking to get through, Pat. I think the last thing he'd want to do is go to a wedding.'

'I see.'

'No, you don't. I don't, either,' Marigold sighed. 'But I will, in the end.'

She looked at Pat and had a sudden change of heart. Pat was the one person she could trust.

'There is someone I'd like to bring with me, though. If you don't mind?'

'You mean . . . ?'

Marigold nodded. 'Yes. Adam's important to me and I would dearly love for you two to meet. Of course, if you'd rather I didn't, then I'll understand.'

'Please bring him, Mari. I should like to meet him.'

'You're quite sure?'

'Yes.' Pat thew her arms around Marigold. 'If you like him, then I know I will. Anyway, my matron of honour will need an escort.'

Ian's train arrived on time. Outside York station, Marigold, in a highly nervous state, was sitting in her car waiting for him. She tensed as she saw the first-out-of-the-train, busy-looking individuals hurry out into the sunshine.

She watched as a trio of business men dressed in pinstriped suits came by, laughing and joking with each other and she fumbled in the glove department for an antacid tablet as a serious-looking, blonde woman, carrying an attaché case, walked past the car.

Then she spotted Ian. He looked well but pale. She wondered whether the weather had been poor or, as was more likely, he had spent most of his visit indoors. Ashamed at her thoughts, she wound down the window and waved to attract his attention. He saw her and came towards the car.

She opened the door for him. 'Had a good flight?'

'Yes. Delayed for about fifteen minutes at the start, but that's all.'

He slung his case into the back of the car and got in next to her. 'Anything exciting happened here?'

She swallowed painfully. 'Not really.'

'Glad to hear it.' He smiled a little. 'No more small boys causing floods in the kitchen?'

Oh, God, Ian. Don't suddenly develop of sense of humour. I couldn't handle it.

She stepped on the gas as the car moved away from the kerb.

'Steady on, Mari. What's the matter with you?'

She mumbled an apology and concentrated on the road.

'What's the news on Karen? All right, is she?'

'She's fine.'

Ah, that was more like the Ian she knew.

'I phoned her just after you left for Norway. I suggested I go and visit her in London for a couple of days but she put me off.' Marigold glanced at Ian and added, almost brutally, 'I got the impression she has a new man in her life.'

He hunched his shoulders and didn't speak until they drew up in front of their home.

Paddy welcomed Ian with great enthusiasm and, seeing the brief but genuine smile that lit up her husband's face when the dog bounded up to him, Marigold felt another jab of painful confusion. Ian could receive and give affection – love even – to an animal but not to his wife. Was that her fault, or his?

Hardening her heart, she said, abruptly, 'Ian, during the past week I've been doing some serious thinking about the way we live our life and I've come to a decision. Tonight, we really must sit down and talk.'

He made an irritated gesture with his hands. 'For God's sake, I've just arrived home. I don't want a serious discussion, Mari. Tonight I want to take a long, leisurely bath – it's all showers in Norway. I want to sit down in front of a decent meal and have a rest and then I must check my correspondence. I'm expecting a letter—'

'Haven't you forgotten something?'

He looked suddenly uncertain, perplexed by a certain note in Marigold's voice.

'What is that?'

'Don't you want to kiss your wife on the cheek, or sit and chat for a moment?'

'Oh, I see.' Hesitantly, he moved towards her. 'Of course I do.'

She jerked her head away as he gingerly leaned forward to kiss her.

'Now what is it?'

'If you don't know, Ian, then I can't be bothered to tell you.'

'Oh Christ, I thought we could have had one evening peaceably together, Mari, after my absence. But you have to spoil it, don't you?'

'How can you call this being together?' Marigold turned on her heel and walked out of the room.

He stood still for a moment, rubbing his chin, and then he went to stand in the doorway of the kitchen. Marigold was putting a handkerchief back in her pocket but he didn't notice.

'Marigold?'

'What?'

'Did a letter come for me, from the Science and Engineering Research Council?'

She went to stand facing the sink, her back towards him.

'Yes, I think so. It's on your desk.'

'Oh, good. I'll just read that one letter and then I'll go for my bath. Is that all right?'

'Of course.'

Marigold heard him go upstairs. She put water in a bowl and began to wash the vegetables. He probably wouldn't notice the bed had been made up in the spare bedroom but even if he did, it would not faze him. He had been away for a week. There were his notes to compile to take to the university tomorrow. There was his post to read. Ian always dealt with the important things in life first.

She put the vegetables into a pan. Ah, well. Their talk could wait, until tomorrow.

Chapter Twenty

'Will you repeat that, please.'

Marigold clenched her teeth until her jaw hurt and then she asked, 'Why? Didn't you hear me the first time?'

She heard the aggression in her words and it appalled her. This wasn't the way she had planned it. She and Ian were civilised people. She had expected a civilised conversation. But then, could the breakup of a marriage ever be civilised? She stared at her husband, willing him to look at her but he did not. He stood up, crossed to the coffee pot and poured himself another coffee.

It was early morning, just after eight, and they were in the kitchen. Sunshine was struggling to get through the partly opened window blinds and Paddy snoozed in his basket. It was a morning exactly like thousands of mornings before but there would never be another one like this. Oh, they might continue to live in the same house for a little while. They might be together in the kitchen again, making toast, flicking through the newspapers, but it would never be the same. With her few words Marigold had shattered the pattern of their lives forever.

She stared at her husband's averted face and the remorse she felt bit into her like acid.

'Ian,' she pleaded. 'For God's sake, say something.'

He raised his head and stared at her as if she were a complete stranger.

Paddy sighed in his sleep.

The quiet was a black hole she had to fill. She dashed her hand over her eyes and said, jerkily, 'I'm sorry, Ian. I'm so sorry, but there's no other way. If only you'll think about it, you'll realise that it's too late for us. We've nothing in common any more. We've been drifting apart for a long time and now we're just two strangers, living in the same house.'

At last, he spoke. 'And that's your opinion?'

'Yes, it is. And if only you'd think, you would . . .'

He interrupted her. 'You want us to separate.'

She nodded.

'And then, divorce, presumably?'

'Yes.'

Carefully, he replaced his coffee cup in the saucer. 'Am I allowed an opportunity to state my views?'

'Why, of course you are.' Her forehead creased.

'Well, in my view, you're heading for a nervous breakdown.' Ignoring her exclamation, he continued to speak, his voice low, but firm. 'You've been acting strangely for some time. The way you suddenly threw up your job . . .'

She tried to say something but he shook his head and said, 'It's my turn, remember?'

She lowered her eyes.

'I think what you should do is make an appointment to see Dr Clarke. He'll give you a thorough checkup.'

Marigold clenched her hands into fists. 'I don't need a checkup, Ian. But I do need to get away from you, and your remarks just now have only confirmed to me that I am right to do so.' She drew a quivering breath. 'I'll be moving out of here as soon as I can find somewhere else to live. I'm sorry if my leaving causes you embarrassment, but I'm sure you'll think of something to tell your colleagues. After all, I've always been a slight embarrassment to you, haven't I?'

'And that's it?' He stared at her as if she was an alien from out of space.

'Yes.' She shrugged. 'I find I just can't live with you anymore.'

He stormed out then and Marigold stared into space for a few moments and wondered why she didn't cry. At last, she had told him. She should feel relieved, she thought, glad that the ordeal was over. She should feel sorrow at the death of their marriage but, in truth, she felt absolutely nothing.

She glanced at the clock and remembered she had promised Pat to bake cakes for her wedding guests. Moving like a clockwork soldier she washed her hands and began opening cupboard doors and taking out sugar, butter, flour, baking trays and two cartons of eggs.

Around noon, Marigold was climbing the stairs which led to Sheila Scott's room. She was breathing heavily. Today in particular, it was a long haul to reach the sixth floor.

On the fifth floor she paused for breath and she heard a baby crying. She listened, and for the first time that day, tears came to her eyes; for the crying wasn't the usual demanding cry of a normal baby, it was a sad wail from a scrap of humanity who had already learned that you did not always get what you wanted or deserved. Marigold gulped, wiped her nose on the back of her hand and tackled the next flight of stairs.

A sandy-haired, well-built man answered her knock.

'Yes?'

'Oh.' Marigold stepped backwards. 'I'm sorry, I was expecting . . .'

'Who is it, Mike?' Sheila Scott appeared behind the man.

'Oh, it's you, Mari. When it got to eleven thirty, I thought you weren't coming.'

'I know I'm late, but I didn't want to disappoint the boys.'

Marigold's words ended in a croak. Her eyes rapidly filling with tears, she stared at Sheila.

Sheila's face flickered. She reached out, grabbed Marigold's arm and pulled her into the room.

'Sit down for a minute, love.'

She turned to the sandy-haired man. 'This is the lady that Jack and Billy are always talking about, Mike.' She looked back towards Marigold. 'This is my husband, Mike.'

'Pleased to meet you.' Mike looked at Marigold and then at his wife.

Marigold gulped and said nothing.

'She'd arranged to take them out today but now that you've turned up, well, she needn't bother. You can take them instead.' Sheila nodded towards Mike and then bawled out, 'Come here, you two. Your dad's taking you out.'

Marigold, sitting motionless in the chair into which Sheila had pushed her, dared not look in Mike's direction. She stared at the floor. The two boys erupted from their curtained-off bedroom.

Billy ran over to Marigold and clasped his arms around her legs and Jack said, 'Marigold. We thought you weren't coming.'

For the life of her, she couldn't speak. She put her hand on Billy's blond hair.

Mike, a look of bemusement on his face, rebuked his elder son. 'You mustn't call the lady by her first name.'

'Why not? She said we could.' Jack swung round towards her. 'Didn't you?'

Marigold nodded. She even managed the ghost of a smile.

'Oh.' Mike ran a hand over his hair.

Sheila, having successfully prised Billy away from Marigold, fastened his shoes. 'There you are, all ready. Off you go with your dad. It'll be nice, three men out together.' She gave them a proud smile.

'Where shall I take them?'

'Oh, Mike, use your brain. Anywhere they want to go, of course. Have you got some bus money? Maybe you could get them a drink before you come home.' Sheila glanced round, looking for her bag. 'I can give you some money.'

Mike blushed beetroot red. 'I've got some. Come on, lads.' He sneaked a glance at Marigold. 'Nice meeting you. Expect I'll see you again.'

She nodded.

'You come with us.' Billy hopped on one foot in front of her. She cleared her voice and managed to say, 'Sorry.'

'But I wanted you to bring Paddy.'

Sheila grabbed him. 'Come on, Billy. Don't keep your dad waiting.' A mother hen, she ushered them out of the door. She shut it, leaned her back against it and said, 'What you need is a good, strong drink. Trouble is, we don't have any of the hard stuff.' She moved towards the cupboard holding the single gas ring. 'Will a cup of tea help?'

Marigold nodded.

Sheila picked up the kettle and shook it. 'Good, there's enough water.' She lit the gas ring with a match, popped the kettle on and searched around for two clean mugs and as she did these things, she chatted.

'I got such a surprise when Mike turned up. Pleasant one, of course. We never know when he's coming home. It depends on where he is at the time and whether he can cadge a lift. I was hoping he had good news for us. Well, you always hope, don't you? He hasn't though. I think he's getting sick of traipsing round the country. Maybe I can persuade him to stay at home.'

Marigold listened and felt her body relax. The kettle began to boil, the water made comforting plopping sounds. She cleared her throat and said, hesitantly, 'I'm sorry, Sheila.'

Sheila was poking the teabags with a spoon. She looked over at Marigold. 'Whatever for?'

'Well, your poor husband. What on earth will he think?'

'Oh, you don't have to worry about Mike. He's an easy-going chap. That's one reason I married him.' Sheila smiled and handed a mug of tea to Marigold. 'There's only a splash of milk. We're nearly out.'

'Thanks.' Marigold sipped at the almost-boiling liquid. It slipped down her dry throat and warmed her insides. 'It's lovely.'

Sheila nodded. 'Great stuff is a mug of hot, strong tea. That's why they give you some after birthing a baby. It's good for shock, you know.'

'I'm not exactly shocked.' Marigold swallowed another mouthful. 'At least, I don't think so.'

Sheila came and sat on the end of the bed, next to the chair. 'If you want to talk about it, I'll listen.'

Marigold sighed. 'Oh, no. Why should I burden you with my worries?'

Sheila pulled a face. 'My God, you stiff-upper-lip kind of people, you really get my goat. Don't you know the old saying, "A trouble shared is a trouble halved"?'

'Yes, I do. But why should you have to listen to my problems? You have enough of your own. Anyway, it's personal.'

'And mine aren't? Listen, you know about our money troubles and about Mike trying to find work and *you* told *me* about our Jack. If you hadn't, God knows what would have happened to him. And if you're worrying about me opening my mouth, well – you needn't. I know more secrets about people than some have had hot dinners.'

'I appreciate your offer, Sheila, but somehow, I can't.'

Sheila frowned. 'Well, it's up to you. I guess I'm not the kind of woman you'd want to confide in, am I? I mean, we don't have that much in common. You in that big house and me stuck here.'

'It's not that.' Marigold sat upright in her chair. 'It's just that I find it hard to talk about personal things.'

'It's your husband, isn't it?' Sheila nodded her head, sagely. 'Most women's troubles are connected with men, or kids.' She narrowed her eyes. 'Does he thump you?'

'Good Lord, no. Nothing like that.'

'Well, you needn't sound so shocked.' Sheila finished her tea with a gulp. 'It's not just lower-class women who get duffed up. There's a solicitor's wife I used to work for—' Sheila folded her lips. 'No, I mustn't talk about her. So what's wrong with you, then? Has he got himself another woman?'

'No, not that, either. Actually, it's me that . . .' Marigold's voice faded into silence. She glanced at Sheila and saw, with relief, that there was not a trace of condemnation on her sharp-angled face. 'It's me that's caused all the trouble.'

With a shuddering sigh she began to tell Sheila everything.

When she'd finished, she dared not look into Sheila's face so she studied the lurid pink roses wreathing around her mug. She heard a creak as Sheila got up from her seat on the bed.

'Fancy a fag?'

'What?' She looked up, startled.

Sheila tucked her hair behind her ears before rummaging in her handbag. She produced two crumpled cigarettes. She offered one to Marigold who shook her head.

'No, thanks. I don't smoke.'

'I bet you've never tried one, have you?'

'No, I never have.'

'I knew it.' Sheila struck a match and lit up. 'I reckon that's the cause of most of your problems, Mari. I can call you Mari, can't I?'

'I wish you would.' Marigold didn't mention that she had asked Sheila to use her first name on several occasions, but this was the first time she had.

'And you were only a kid when you got married, I bet.'

'I was eighteen.' Marigold shifted in her seat. 'What are you getting at?'

'You didn't sow your wild oats when you should have, so you're wanting to do it now, before you get old.'

Marigold felt her face stiffen. 'It's not like that.'

'Are you sure?'

'Yes, I am.' Haltingly, she tried to explain. 'You're lucky, Sheila. Your marriage is a happy one, isn't it?'

'Yes. Mike needs a bit of a push now and again, but we get on fine.'

'Well, my husband's not like Mike. He likes to live his own life and he's irritated if I even suggest we do something together. I've tried everything I can think of, Sheila, but things are getting worse rather than better and I've suddenly realised I've had enough.' She frowned. 'You think I should stay with Ian, don't you?'

'Good God, no.' Sheila blew a smoke ring. 'I've already had my own idea of your marriage and after what you've told me, I think you should get shot of him as quickly as possible. He sounds a pain in the arse.' She looked surprised when Marigold laughed.

'What's funny?'

'You are. Sorry.'

Sheila shrugged. 'Don't apologise. I'm glad if I've cheered you up. You looked like a month of wet Sundays when Mike opened the door.' She studied Marigold's face and she smiled herself.

'Why don't you try a fag?'

'I don't think so.'

'Go on, live dangerously. You can stub it out if you hate it.'

'Well . . .'

Sheila took out her second cigarette and, lighting it, handed it to Marigold. 'Here you are.' She took a puff of her own. 'I'll have to spray this place before Mike gets back. He'll go mad if he thinks I've been smoking. He thinks I've stopped completely. Well, I have, almost. I'm down to about five a week, but sometimes I need a drag.'

She inhaled deeply. 'It's all right for him. He's on the road, meeting people, seeing different places. I'm stuck in this place, scrubbing floors for people to earn money and looking after two kids.'

Reverting back to Marigold's problems and apparently unaware of Marigold's blinking eyes and reddening face, she went on, 'No, what I mean is, you're a good-looking woman, but you're not getting any younger. You've wasted too much time already on this professor chap. You want to get away from him and get together with this other man who's after you.'

Marigold coughed. 'I don't know if he's after me.' She stared thoughtfully at the threadbare carpet beneath her feet. 'It's such early days, Sheila. It's lovely being with him but I don't know what he wants and I don't really know what I want either.'

Sheila stubbed out her spent cigarette. 'You don't believe in a simple life, do you?'

Marigold shook her head and, once again, familiar guilt engulfed her. 'I shouldn't be telling you all this. You have so many worries of your own.' She looked around her. 'It must be so awful for you, living here with no proper home. You must think I'm an idiot, walking away from the life I have.' She grimaced. 'No money problems and a lovely house.'

'Well, the thought did occur to me but then I thought, I'd rather have Mike and the boys than a grand home. Mind you, we'll soon have one thing in common.' Sheila grinned. 'If you do leave your husband, you'll be looking for a home, too.'

'Yes.' Discreetly, Marigold turned away and stubbed out her cigarette.

She said, 'You know, I can't believe we're talking together like this.'

'That's partly my fault.' Sheila looked guilty. 'I've been a bit funny with you, I know.'

'Well, I can't say I've really noticed it, but why, Sheila?'

'It's the boys, see. I'm their mother and they're used to me but they think you're great. You give them treats all the time. I get a bit jealous.'

'Oh, surely not?'

'Yes, it's true.' Sheila nodded her head. 'It's Marigold this and Marigold that. They like you a lot. Mind you, they also like your house and your car and your dog. There's been times when you've had them out and they've come home and all they talk about are your wonderful things. I felt like strangling them.' Sheila looked down at the curl of smoke from her cigarette. 'Kids are mercenary little devils, aren't they?'

'Oh, Sheila.' Marigold felt a wave of compassion for her. 'I should have realised.'

'It's nothing. It's just . . . some days, I get low. I miss Mike not being around.'

'Well, in future, when you feel like that, you must let me know and I'll come round to see you or we'll meet up somewhere. You've been wonderful to me today, and I won't forget it.' Marigold looked at her watch. 'Oh, God. I'll have to fly. Another friend of mine is getting married tomorrow and I've done some baking for her. It's in the car. I promised I'd drop it round for her and I'm late.'

Sheila stared. 'Are you saying you did a load of baking after telling your husband you wanted a divorce?'

'Yes.'

Sheila burst out laughing. 'And then you came here because you'd promised the boys and it was only when they left you started crying?'

'Yes. I know it sounds strange, but I couldn't let Pat down and . . .' Marigold's voice died away. 'I sound a bit weird, don't I?'

'Mari Goddard, you're quite a surprise. When I met you, I'd pegged you as a spoilt woman with too much money. I thought you'd only taken up with Jack as a whim. Boy, was I wrong.' Sheila shook her head. 'You're a survivor, Mari, just like I am. You go ahead and leave your husband. Whatever happens, I reckon you'll cope.'

'Thanks for your vote of confidence.' Feeling an uplift of spirit, Marigold got up and, on impulse, hugged the smaller woman. 'Thanks again for listening to me.'

'That's all right.' Sheila looked a little uncomfortable at their close contact but she returned Marigold's hug before pulling away.

'I hope things work out for you.'

There was a noise outside. The two women exchanged glances.

'Did you hear that?' Sheila's eyes widened. 'Surely Mike's not back already. Oh, Lord. Where's that spray?'

When Mike came in he was disconcerted to find their visitor still there. In a gruff voice he told his sons to take off their shoes and as they did so, he asked Marigold, 'Feeling a bit better, are you?'

'Yes, I feel a lot better, thanks to your wife.'

She gave him a smile which made him look more closely at her. After Sheila had shown her out, he said to his wife. 'She a friend of yours?'

'Yes, she is now.'

'She's quite a looker, isn't she?'

'Yes.' She grinned at him. 'Out of your league, though.'

He flushed. 'I know that.'

He glanced around the room and sniffed the air.

'What's that smell?

'What smell?'

'I don't know. A flowery smell.'

'Oh, it's Mrs Goddard's perfume. She wears good stuff. It lingers.'

'Does it now?' He slid his arm around her waist. 'Find out what it's called. When I manage to find a job, I'll treat you to some.'

'Is that a promise?' She leaned away from him and laughed.

'It is.'

'Right. I'll remind you.' She put up her face and kissed him.

Chapter Twenty-One

Marigold was uncomfortable because she was too hot. For Pat's wedding, she had bought a double-breasted, cream-coloured jacket which, she thought, would look equally good worn with her straight black skirt or her wide-legged silk trousers. But on the day itself, she rejected the trousers as being too casual for a wedding and so she had worn the skirt. The trouble was, she hadn't anticipated the heat wave. True, it was August and the height of summer but although the weather had on the whole been mild, there had also been cold days and rough winds. Today, however, it was *hot*.

Standing in the register office and listening to the registrar, Marigold felt the beads of perspiration gathering on her upper lip. She sneaked a handkerchief from her pocket and dabbed discreetly at her face and then she studied the backs of the happy couple.

Chris stood straight and smart in a new grey suit. From time to time he turned his head and glanced down at his bride as if he couldn't believe his luck. Pat, with her usual sunny optimism, had gone wholeheartedly for a summery outfit and she looked perfect. Dressed in a floaty, bluey-green dress with a scoop neckline and short sleeves, she looked so young it seemed impossible that the tall young man giving her away was her son. Her hair shone with health and her face with happiness and the posy of anemones she carried in her white-gloved hands made her look the epitome of a happy bride.

Marigold suppressed a sigh and dabbed at her face again.

'You look flushed. Are you feeling all right?'

'Yes.' She smiled at the man standing next to her, and suddenly, it didn't matter that she was uncomfortable, or that her feet were complaining about the high-heeled court shoes she wore, because Adam was with her. He had agreed to escort her to Pat's wedding.

Marigold thought that was brave of him. He didn't know the setup: for all he knew the other people present might know Ian. But he had agreed to come. As it happened, few of the wedding guests knew of Marigold's situation. There had been only two difficult moments.

Pat's mother-in-law, standing close by and talking to Pat had said, in her distinctively loud voice, 'I thought your friend's husband had blond hair?'

Pat's reply had been an indistinguishable murmur. Marigold had no idea what she had said.

The second embarrassment had been when Mr Heywood, accompanied by his wife, had hurried to catch up with Marigold and Adam as they went into the register office. Her former boss had turned to Adam and said: 'Ah, at last we meet. I'm happy to make your acquaintance, Mr Goddard.'

Marigold had been struck dumb but Adam had shaken hands with Mr Heywood and then said, 'Actually, I'm just a friend. Mr Goddard was unable to attend.'

She had given him a grateful smile.

Now he whispered, 'You'll be able to sit down in a moment.'

Marigold looked to the front again.

Pat and Chris were making their vows.

Pushing away regrets and worry about her own marriage, Marigold listened intently.

Pat's voice was low but clear. Chris's responses had a hint of breathlessness about them.

Tears pricked Marigold's eyes and she used the handkerchief again.

The couple were pronounced man and wife and in an outburst of genuine pleasure and enthusiasm the gathering of friends and relatives cheered and clapped. The registrar, a cheerful-looking man, paused and smiled. He completed the formalities and then warned, 'Celebrate by all means but no confetti inside, please.'

Marigold put away her handkerchief, wiped the corner of her right eye with her finger and asked Adam, 'Has my mascara run?'

'No.' He studied her face and she saw that his expression was serious. He asked, 'Do all women cry at weddings?'

Did he expect an answer? Staring back at him, Marigold wondered if he was thinking of his own wedding day. She caught hold of his hand. 'I do. Come on.'

They were amongst the last to leave. Emerging from the building, they walked into the clouds of confetti being flung at the newly married couple. The tiny flecks of colour spun and wheeled in the air and peppered the intense blue of the sky above them like flocks of tiny birds. There were flashes from cameras and the sound of laughter. Marigold blinked.

A group of women shoppers was waiting outside on the pavement, smiling and waving at the happy couple. The women made clucking sounds of approval and their offspring stood beside them and gazed wide eyed at the scene. A policeman passing by touched his helmet and wished the newly married pair good luck.

Marigold pressed Adam's arm and then left him and rushed over to hug her friend.

'Oh, Pat. I'm so pleased for you. What a lovely day for your wedding. Now, promise me you'll be happy.'

Pat hugged her back. 'I will be, Mari. I promise.'

A beribboned car came round the corner and drew up, waiting to take Pat and Chris back home to welcome guests to their wedding breakfast. Pat whirled round and, in response to requests from the crowd, hurled her posy of flowers into the air. Automatically and without thinking, Marigold stepped back. A dark-haired girl caught the posy and blushed prettily.

Marigold went back to stand beside Adam. 'Thank you for coming with me, Adam. I can't thank you enough.'

He nodded. 'I'm glad I did. It was a good wedding.' He glanced at her face. 'You're very fond of Pat, aren't you?'

'She's my best friend.' She hesitated. 'Would you come back to their house with me, or would you rather call it a day?'

'I'll come for a little while.' Adam's gaze bore into her. 'But after that, we must go somewhere and talk, Marigold. Your husband's back home now, isn't he?' When she nodded, he sighed. 'I think there are decisions to be made.'

A wedding was no place for her to tell him of her decision to leave Ian. She nodded again, and promised, 'We won't stay long.'

The interior of Pat's little house felt like a warm beating heart. It was full of people enjoying themselves. A group of elderly people, having commandeered a bottle of whisky and a bottle of sherry, had congregated in the sitting room. They had got to know everyone and now they were starting to reminisce about the old days.

Adam was pushing his way through the throng to get some drinks as Marigold lingered by the open doorway and listened to the conversations going on around her, before walking down the hallway.

Sam, having done his serious duty at the register office, was now enjoying himself. He and his friends had brought down the compact disc player from his bedroom and contemporary music boomed through the house. The more confident young people were dancing in the hall, others sat on the stairs and knocked back red or white wine.

Marigold threaded her way through the throng and tapped Sam's arm. When he turned to face her, she congratulated him. 'You did well, Sam.'

He bent his head towards her. 'Sorry?'

She shouted. 'You did a good job at the wedding.'

'Thanks.' He grinned. 'I've got a speech to make later. Luckily, it's only a short one.'

'You'll be fine.' She nodded her head. 'Didn't your mum look lovely?'

'Yes. You could see she's happy.'

'Of course she is. She and Chris adore each other. And I know she's delighted you and he get on so well.'

Sam blushed, so Marigold changed the subject. 'What are you doing while they're away? Looking after the house?'

'No, didn't Mum tell you? I'm off backpacking tomorrow with two of my mates.'

'Sounds interesting. Where are you going?'

'We're starting off in Italy.' Sam raised his voice so Marigold could hear him over the din. 'Actually, I didn't know I was going until a week ago. My pals planned out the route last month. They asked me if I wanted to go then, but I didn't think I could afford it. They were getting student rail-travel cards but it was still quite a bit of money.' He paused. 'Then Chris found out about it and insisted on paying for me to go with them.' Sam gave Marigold an quick, embarrassed smile, and asked, 'Do you think that's OK, Mari?'

She frowned. 'In what way?' She studied his face. 'Do you mean, is it all right to let Chris pay for your holiday?'

Sam shuffled his feet. 'Yeah.'

'Of course it's all right. Why shouldn't it be?'

'Well, it's a bit like a pat on the head for being good, don't you think? Sort of, you've allowed me to court your mum, so I'll reward you.' Sam's face flushed dark red. 'I wouldn't want it to be like that.'

Marigold looked at him incredulously. 'Sam, I thought you had more sense. For goodness' sake, Chris *likes* you. He loves your mum and he's grateful to you for not causing problems. Can't you see, he's happy and he wants you to be happy, too. So, stop imagining things, grab the opportunity and go off and enjoy yourself.'

Sam shuffled his feet. 'I suppose you're right. It's just that I feel uncomfortable taking handouts. You know how it's been for Mum and me. There was never any money for treats.'

'Well, now there is.' Marigold spoke in a firm voice. 'Accept Chris's gift in the spirit in which it was offered and go and have a great time.'

He scratched his head before giving her a shy grin. 'Right, I will. And thanks, Mari.' He nodded. 'I hope things work out for you, as well.'

She smiled. 'I hope so, too.'

Adam touched her elbow. 'Here you are.' He handed her a glass of wine. 'Sorry I took so long. The dining room's absolutely packed out.' He glanced at Sam who blushed bright red.

Marigold thought he was probably worrying that Adam had heard his last remark. She hastened to introduce Sam to Adam and they shook hands.

Sam returned his gaze to Marigold. 'The food you brought round yesterday proved to be a godsend. Trouble is, there was none left for today. Mum says that without your home-made goodies, we would have been hard pushed to cope.'

Adam asked, 'What goodies were those?'

'Oh, Mari makes the most wonderful cakes and things.' Sam grinned, at ease again. 'I ate a whole date and walnut cake.'

Marigold laughed. 'No wonder they didn't last long.' She explained to Adam. 'I'm good at cakes, pastry, stuff like that. I'm not so good at cooking fancy dinners.'

'I'll remember that.' Adam nodded to Sam as he made his excuses and went to join his friends again. 'He's a nice lad. You seem to have quite a rapport with him.'

Marigold drank her wine. 'I've known him a long time.'

'And I've known you such a short time.' Adam twisted the stem of his wine glass.

'Yes.' Marigold felt a stab of apprehension. She added, 'It's the same for me.'

He nodded, without speaking.

'Hello, there.'

Marigold felt herself stiffen as Mr Heywood, his wife in tow, pushed through the crowd of dancers and came to stand beside them.

'How are you enjoying your retirement, Mari? Did you spend the gardening voucher? What did you get?'

Retirement! God, it made her sound like an old-age pensioner.

Marigold gritted her teeth and lied. 'Yes, I'm enjoying my leisure, thank you; and I bought a lovely selection of plants with the voucher.'

'Good.' Mr Heywood glanced at the silent Adam and then back at Marigold. 'I'm sorry not to meet your husband, Mari. I hope he's not indisposed?'

Her ex-boss, Marigold decided, had a nose like a ferret. She replied, 'Oh, no. Ian is not indisposed, he's just terribly busy.'

She began to move past him. 'Sorry, but I must find Pat.' With a nod of her head, she pressed through the throng of people

281

and left Mr and Mrs Heywood behind her. Adam followed closely in her wake.

'Sorry about that,' she hissed over her shoulder.

In the kitchen, she found Chris. She kissed him on his cheek. 'Congratulations, Chris.'

'Thank you, Mari.' Now slightly inebriated, Chris threw his arms around her and lifted her off her feet in a little whirl. 'Wasn't the service wonderful? And the weather, and everything?'

'Yes, it was.' She smiled, extracting herself from his embrace. 'You're a lucky man.'

'I know it.' He waved his arm. 'Have you met my father?'

'No, not yet. But, Chris . . .'

'Oh, but you must. He's about somewhere.' Chris gazed vaguely around him.

'I'd love to, but I'm afraid we're pushed for time. We must leave soon and I do want a word with Pat. Can you tell me where she is?'

'But you can't leave yet.'

'Sorry, we have to. I'll ring you when you get back from your honeymoon, shall I?'

'Yes, you must.'

Marigold asked again, 'Chris, where's Pat?'

'Oh, she went upstairs to freshen up.' Chris mopped his forehead. 'It's hot today, isn't it?'

'Yes.'

Marigold turned to Adam. 'I'll nip upstairs, have a word with Pat, and then we'll leave.'

He nodded.

Upstairs was cooler, the window shades had been drawn, and it was quieter, although the boom of the music could still be heard. Marigold walked along the landing and tapped on the door of Pat's bedroom.

Her friend called out, 'Who is it?'

'It's Mari.'

'Come in.'

Marigold entered the room, closed the door behind her and, for a moment, stood and stared at her friend. Then she smiled a big smile. 'Well, Mrs Harker. You've done it now.'

Pat, who was standing by the dressing table, a hair brush in her hand, laughed and put down the brush. 'Yes, I have, haven't I?'

She opened her arms and Marigold went to her and the two women hugged each other.

Smelling Anaïs Anaïs, Pat's favourite perfume, Marigold whispered, 'I wish you health and happiness, Pat. You deserve it.'

'Thank you.' Pat's eyes were brimming with tears. 'You know, just now, enjoying a few moments of quietness, I've been thinking about the past. You were such a good friend to me when I started work with you, Mari. You helped me over a bad patch. You know, when Geoff died, I thought I would never be happy again.'

'And you've been proved wrong.' Marigold drew back and smiled at her friend. 'And one thing I do know, from all you told me about him . . .' She paused. 'Geoff would have wanted you to have this happiness, Pat. I'm sure of it.'

'Yes, I think you're right.'

'And,' Marigold strove to turn her friend's thoughts away from sad memories. 'You looked gorgeous, Chris looked handsome and the wedding was wonderful.'

'Was it? I was so nervous, I don't remember much about the ceremony.'

'You looked very calm.' Marigold grinned. 'But I think Chris was nervous.'

'Yes, I know. His voice shook, didn't it, when he made the responses?' Pat's eyes were twinkling again. 'I'll be able to tease him about that.' She put her head on one side. 'And talking of men, I've had a peek at your friend, Mari. He's looks nice, but I haven't had a chance to talk to him yet. Don't you dare leave until I do.'

'That's why I've come to find you, Pat. I'd like to introduce him to you but we have to leave soon. Now that Ian's back, there's a good deal of sorting out to do.'

Pat's face assumed a serious expression. 'Yes, I've been wondering about that.'

'Oh dear!' Marigold ran her fingers through her hair. 'I don't *want* you to wonder. You're going on your honeymoon, Pat. You must think only of yourself and Chris. I forbid you to worry about me.'

'All right.' Pat sighed. 'I promise. But please, tell me a little. I've confided in you often enough.'

'All right.' Marigold took a long breath. 'I've already spoken to Ian. I've told him I'm leaving him.'

Pat's lips rounded into a soundless circle of astonishment. Then she asked, 'What did he say?'

'Very little.' Marigold's voice was bitter. 'He refuses to take me seriously. I'm ill, he says. He suggested I have a medical checkup.'

'Oh, God.' Pat put her hand up to her face. 'What will you do now?'

'I'm moving out of the house as soon as possible. I can't live with him any more. I'm going to look for somewhere to live. I know that Ian won't take me seriously until I move out.'

'You've not considered moving in with Adam?'

'God, no. We haven't even discussed the matter.' Marigold shook her head. 'We've a long way to go yet, Pat. I have no idea what Adam wants. I don't even know what I want yet. I think I love him, but whether he loves me . . .' Her voice trailed away. There was silence.

Pat looked thoughtful. 'Finding somewhere decent to live won't be easy. Have you seen anywhere?'

'No. Everything's happened so fast. But I'll find something.' Marigold forced a smile. 'There, I've told you the situation and I refuse to discuss it any further. This isn't on, you know. I have no business talking about separating from my husband today. Chris would never speak to me again if he knew what we've been discussing.' She turned towards the door. 'Will you come and meet Adam before we leave?'

'Of course I will.'

Pat started to follow Marigold and then she stopped and picked up a cream-coloured handbag from the bed.

'You know we're off on honeymoon in the morning?' Marigold nodded.

'We'll be away two weeks.' As she spoke, Pat was rummaging in the bag. 'By tomorrow night, the guests will be gone and the house will be empty. Ah, here they are.'

She pulled out a set of house keys and tossed them to Marigold. Surprised, Marigold managed to catch them.

'You can move in here until we get back.'

Marigold stared at her friend. 'Oh, but I couldn't. There's Sam and . . .'

'No, Sam's going away, too, with his friends. Didn't he tell you?'

'Oh, yes.' Marigold collected her wits. She stared down at the keys. 'But I can't move in here, Pat.'

'Why not?' Pat took a step forward. 'Honestly, Marigold, you'll be doing us a favour. With the amount of burglaries around, I would be happier with someone staying in the house, and it would give you more opportunity to look around, see if you can find anything permanent.'

Marigold started to say something and then she choked. She bit her lip and then managed to say, 'Oh, Pat. If you're sure.'

'Yes. It's settled, then.' Pat walked past Marigold and opened the door. 'Come on. I want to meet this chap of yours.'

'Well, did I pass muster?'

Adam's car was parked a little way up from the house. He put the key in the lock and then opened the door for Marigold.

'Yes, you did.' Marigold felt tired. She did not smile as she answered his question. She settled herself in the passenger seat and watched as Adam got in and started the engine.

She asked, 'Is that how you saw today, as a challenge? Did you think I wanted to parade you before my friends and gauge their reactions to you?'

He shrugged. 'Well, now that you mention it, I did wonder whether I would be asked to perform magic tricks.'

Shocked, she drew in her breath. 'That's a lousy thing to say!'

He pulled away from the kerb before replying. Then he said, 'You're right. I'm overreacting. I apologise.' He glanced at her. 'But think of it from my point of view. Right now, Marigold, I don't know where we're going or what I am supposed to think.'

He drove in silence for a few moments and then, when she didn't reply to him, he went on. 'I've been trying to make sense of it in my head.' He paused and then continued, 'I meet an attractive woman at the golf club. We talk together and both sense a mutual attraction.' He glanced at her again. 'Am I wrong?'

'No.' She stared straight in front of her. 'No, you're right.'

He resumed, speaking slowly and carefully, as he thought aloud. 'We meet again by accident, a fortuitous whim of fate. We get to know each other that little bit better. You send out certain signals which I interpret as encouragement. I invite you to come and look around my place, and you come.'

The road they were travelling was quiet. Adam's foot increased pressure on the accelerator pedal and the car surged forward. When Marigold made a small sound of dissent, he checked his speedometer and slowed down again. Then he suddenly swore under his breath, pulled the car over to the side of the road and stopped. He turned to face her.

'I'm not a particularly scrupulous person, Mari. I saw you at the golf club and I liked what I saw. I knew you were married but I surmised, rightly I think, that the marriage was not a happy one and so I thought – why not? But when I asked you round to my house and you came, I suffered a few qualms of conscience. I was pretty sure you were not in the business of regularly cheating on your husband, but I pretended that didn't matter. You see—' He smiled briefly. 'Fate – or sex – call it what you will, was in control round about then.'

He waited, expecting her to speak but when she did not, the muscle at the corner of his mouth clenched and he spoke more loudly. 'I don't make a habit of bedding married women. As a matter of fact, since the end of my marriage, my life has been, apart from a couple of brief episodes, remarkably chaste. You see—' He paused again. 'My ex-wife *did* make a habit of visiting other mens' houses.'

'Oh!' Marigold shifted in her seat. 'I'm sorry, Adam.'

He shrugged. 'It's all right. It's in the past.' He stared through the windscreen at the road ahead. 'So, I stopped thinking about your husband.' His voice thickened. 'And you came to see me and we made love and then . . .' He bent his head. 'Everything changed.'

'Did it?' Marigold sat upright. She could feel her heart hammering. 'Did it, Adam?'

He didn't reply. It was as if he was too busy formulating his own thoughts and feelings to listen to her.

When he did continue, he said, 'I realised I not only wanted you, I *cared* about you, and that put a totally different perspective on our relationship. But now, the fairytale's over, isn't it? Your husband's back, to the family home and your bed.'

He rubbed his hands over a face in a tired gesture. 'The thing is, I don't know how you feel, either. As I said earlier, we don't know each other at all, do we? And I can't help wondering if you're using me as a kind of escape route, to take your mind off your unhappy marriage. I wonder, do you genuinely care for me? Do you want us to keep on meeting? Because, if you do, I don't think I can continue with things as they are.' He sighed, gently. 'And that's why, when you asked me to go to this wedding with you, I wasn't sure of your motive.'

Marigold studied his profile and then asked, in a cool voice, 'Shall I tell you?'

He nodded. 'Yes, I think you should.'

Now it was Marigold's turn to concentrate on her words.

'I asked you to come to Pat's wedding with me on an impulse, I suppose.' She raised her shoulders in a shrug. 'Or maybe, I just needed a shoulder to cry on, and you were the person I thought of. You see, I care about you, too.' She tried to smile, but failed.

'For a long time now, Pat and I have always been there for each other. And then Chris arrived on the scene and she fell in love with him. I'm happy for her, I really am. I'm glad they've married, but I realise things will change. Oh, we'll stay good friends, I know that, but I can't help feeling a little bit jealous and a little bit sorry for myself. You see—' Marigold folded her hands in her lap and stared down at them. 'Last night, I told my husband I was leaving him. I told him I wanted a divorce.'

Adam started. 'You did what?' He stared at her. 'Is it because of me?'

She met his gaze, held him in a long look and then shook her head. 'No, it's not because of you, although I think the way you've made me feel has given me the courage to think about changing my life. You were right about our marriage; it's been rocky for ages and during the last few years, it's been intolerable. At least, it has been for me. Ian thinks we're doing fine. He thinks I'm out of my mind for even suggesting we separate.'

She gave a laugh that was more of a sob. 'That in itself, shows you how well we communicate.'

'I see.' Adam took hold of her hand.

'No, you don't.' She tried to smile at him. 'Your marriage ended a long time ago, Adam. How long did it take *you* to understand the reason why it failed?'

He sighed and said, ruefully, 'I think I've sorted things out now.'

'Well, then. You'll appreciate how much time I'm going to need to make sense out of this mess.'

He stroked her hand, gently. 'I'm not pressuring you in any way, Marigold. But, if you want to talk, I'll listen.'

'No. We've done enough talking for today.' She put her head back against the headrest. 'I wanted to tell you of my decision, even before Ian came home, but it wouldn't have been fair. Not to you, nor to Ian. I don't want to pressurise you, either. I'd like us to keep seeing each other but I'm not looking further than that.'

She stirred. 'I have to find somewhere to live. A flat, I suppose. Do you know, I've never lived on my own. I moved straight from my parents' home into marriage with Ian. I think I'd like to live alone. I want to get to know myself before I make any more big decisions.'

Adam leaned over and dropped a friendly kiss on her brow.

'OK. It's a deal.'

She smiled at him. 'Thanks. And thanks for coming to the wedding with me. You gave me the support I needed.'

'Think nothing of it.' He hesitated. 'What would you like to do now?'

'I needn't go home, thank God. I left a message for Ian,

saying I was staying with friends and would see him tomorrow.' She sighed. 'Tomorrow I have to try and make him realise that I'm serious about wanting a divorce.'

'Poor love.' He touched her cheek. 'Am I, by any chance, "the friends"?'

She smiled. 'If you'll have me?'

'Of course I will.' He started the car. 'We'll lock ourselves in, take the phone off the hook and talk all night, if that's what you want.'

'Oh, Adam.' She shook her head. 'I'm tired out with talking.'

'Is that so?' He glanced at her. 'Then, what would you suggest?'

She put her arms above her head and stretched. 'I've decided that the "new" me is going to speak her mind. So, what I'd like is for you to take me back to your place and undress me and then we'll make love.' She gave him a half laughing, half sheepish look. 'It may sound inappropriate, after what we've just been saying, but Adam, I've gone so long without experiencing genuine loving.'

He nodded, his expression serious. 'I think it sounds exactly right, my dear. Long, slow, gentle loving, will that suit you?'

'Hmmmm . . .' She relaxed back in her seat and closed her eyes.

Chapter Twenty-Two

Karen had to push hard to open the door because of the pile of mail lying behind it. Once inside the flat, she put down her case and gathered together the collection of envelopes, catalogues and two small parcels which lay scattered on the mat. She flicked through them with absolutely no sense of anticipation. In her world, personal communication had become as instant as coffee. Chatty, newsy letters had disappeared with the invention of the telephone and what she had here was dross.

Her assumption was correct. Her post consisted of offers for cheap car insurance, and assorted hypothetical questionnaires such as: did she want to win a holiday in Greece? Was she considering buying a new music system? It was just boring junk mail. Even the two packages were samples. A box of pills from a health shop and a lipstick of the most unbelievable bright pink from a firm calling itself *Make-up by Mail*. Karen threw the whole lot into a bin strategically placed near the door.

Entering her living room she saw, and ignored, the red blinking light on her answerphone. She opened a window, kicked off her shoes and went through into the bathroom where she turned on both bath taps. She decanted half a bottle of expensive foaming bath essence into the water and undressed and then, with a sigh of hedonistic pleasure, she lowered her body into the frothing, silky water. She lay back, closed her eyes and relived, most pleasurably, the last four days.

David Asher, the man who fortuitously possessed a young sister wanting to be a model, had turned out to be the sort of man that every maiden dreams of. Not that she was a maiden, of course – Karen indulged in a cat-like stretch – but he had made her feel like one. He was an incredibly skilful lover. Eyes still closed, she compiled a mental list of his assets. First of all, he was good-looking with a tall, well-proportioned body, not too heavy.

Karen's forehead creased. That was perfectly true, but it wasn't his looks that had got to her. She had dated plenty of good-looking men who had bored her rigid. She had also gone out with short, ugly men who had been witty and charming because she had enjoyed their company; but, she stirred restlessly, she had never ever become really involved with anyone – not since Carl.

But David – Karen opened her eyes, scooped up a handful of bath foam in her hands and blew it into the air – David was different. He was nigh on perfect. He was a sensitive lover, he had a sense of humour, he seemed to have plenty of money and, even more important to her, he had a wonderful, deep, cultured voice.

Karen had a thing about voices, which was why she was a fan of black and white movies. Ronald Colman was one of her favourites. She also loved James Mason's voice and watched his films, particularly the earlier ones, over and over again. David's voice, she decided, was a cross between the two. She grinned and slid lower into the bath water. She didn't need extensive foreplay to be ready for sex with David, all he had to do was whisper in her ear.

She stretched out her hand and grabbed the bath sponge which was floating serenely through peaks of foam bubbles like a liner cruising the Baltic Sea. Leisurely, she stroked her shoulders and breasts with the sponge and as she did so, she felt herself beginning to relax. She yawned, acknowledging that she was tired.

Working on the television commercial had been harder than she had imagined and then, on the last day of shooting, she had found David, or to be correct, he had found her, and tiredness had been the last thing on her mind. She had dined with him at the hotel and then taken him up to her bedroom and the four-poster bed and it had been passionate lovemaking ever since.

It was David's idea that she should go back with him to his flat. At first, she had refused and driving back to London they had engaged in a lighthearted argument.

She had said, 'I *must* go home, David. There may be important messages for me. My agent may have called about a new job or my parents might have phoned.' With a pang of guilt she remembered she had not returned her mother's phone call. 'Besides, I need fresh clothes to wear.'

David's wonderful eyes had clouded. Were all these people more important than him? And he was going to Paris at the weekend. They would be apart for two, maybe three days. Did she want that?

Then his eyes had began to twinkle. As for her clothes, they could send the whole lot to the cleaners and for a few wonderful hours, she could remain totally starkers.

And she had laughed and given in to his pleading.

This morning, she had waved as his plane flew overhead and now she was home again and already missing him. He had promised to ring her this evening.

Karen let go of the sponge and closed her eyes again. He'd be in Paris now. What would he be doing? She frowned and thought it was just as well she was spending a little time on her own. For one thing, she needed to sleep and she also needed time to think, because this thing with David had happened so swiftly, she was frightened she was getting out of her depth. Since her breakup with Carl, she had steadfastly remained in the shallow end of the pool as far as emotions were concerned. But David was getting to her. Take the morning after their first night together.

She had woken up with a start to feel someone touching and stroking her body. Opening her eyes she had found David's face smiling down at her. She had opened her mouth to speak but he rested his fingers lightly on her lips, indicating she should remain silent. She had nodded and the lovemaking that followed had been so wonderful and yet so gentle that, afterwards, she had burst into tears. She had cried and cried despite her efforts to stop and all the time she was thinking, What will he think of me? She prayed he would not spoil everything by saying something jokey.

He did not. He remained silent and put his arms around her, holding her in what was almost a brotherly way and then, when her tears finally ran out, he pressed her back on to the pillows, swung his legs out of bed and went for a shower. He had made no mention of that morning ever since.

He was definitely too good to be true. She'd have to watch herself. With a shiver, Karen realised the water was getting cold. She sat up, pulled out the plug and got out of the bath. She wrapped herself in her bathrobe and padded through to the living room. The red eye was still winking, reminding her that there were other people in the world.

She sighed, perched on a stool close by the telephone table and pressed the play button on the answerphone. When the machine switched off, Karen was frowning. She sighed again, rubbed her forehead and then rewound the tape and listened to the messages for the second time. The first two calls were unimportant, a call from her garage and another from a man she had been trying to avoid for weeks. She listened more intently to the last three.

The first of the three was from Claudia Steiner.

'Karen, where are you? I've been expecting you to call in. Just to let you know that the initial reaction to your film work's fine. The agency's pleased and so are the backers. We'll have to keep our fingers crossed about the possible series. Ring me as soon as you can. One of the fashion mags has contacted me about using you. They're putting on a grand fashion show in support of an Aids charity. See you.'

The next call was brief, unemotional and from Karen's mother.

'Karen, not to worry about anything but I really need to speak to you. Please ring me. If I'm not at home try me on the following number.'

Karen, frowning, scribbled down the telephone number.

The third call was from her father, but it sounded strangely unlike him.

'Karen, where are you, for God's sake? Please ring me immediately. Something dreadful's happened. You'll never believe . . .' A pause and then, 'I can't talk to you on this damn thing.'

Listening to the words for the second time, Karen's stomach lurched. She thought, Oh, no. Please no. Don't let anything bad happen. Not now, when I'm happy.

She ran her tongue over her suddenly dry lips as she dialled her parents' number. She listened as the ringing went on and on. She replaced the receiver. No one at home, there was nothing she could do. She didn't know whether to be pleased or sorry. She took a couple of sleeping pills and went to bed.

Waking at eight thirty the following morning, Karen deliberately refrained from phoning home. If something awful had happened she preferred not to know about it until she had got her head together. Besides, she was in London and her parents were in Yorkshire. Whatever had happened, whatever had shocked her father so much, she couldn't fly directly to his side. Not today.

So, she went shopping. Her extended absence from home meant the fridge and freezer needed filling. She brought her groceries home, unpacked them and put them away and then she went out again, to see Claudia.

Claudia chatted away for half an hour before realising Karen was not really listening to her. Karen excused herself by saying that she thought she was coming down with a cold. Then she turned down an offer to lunch and went home where she fidgeted around, plagued by two, equally important worries. Whatever had happened between her parents? Should she try ringing home or should she ring the telephone number her mother had left on the answerphone for her? But she didn't want to become involved in a long telephone conversation, in case David rang from Paris.

David was her second worry. Last night she had taken her sleeping pills and gone to bed, thereby missing David's call from Paris. What had he thought when his call had gone unanswered? But had he actually rang? Surely she would have heard the ringing of the phone, even in her sleep? What if he thought she had snubbed him? What if he never rang again?

When the phone trilled about five thirty, she snatched at it as though it was a drink of fresh spring water in the middle of a desert. Nervously, she asked, 'Who is it?'

'Karen?'

It was her father. Her breath expelled in a long sigh. 'Yes, Dad.'

She braced herself for his usual recriminations about her neglect.

He said, 'Has your mother been in touch with you?'

He sounded strange. She replied, carefully, 'No, that is, not personally. There was a message on my answerphone. She wants to speak to me but I haven't reached her yet. You see, I've been terribly busy.' She set up her defences. 'I've been shooting extra scenes and I've only just arrived . . .'

'She wants to speak to you? I bet she does.' Her father laughed. It was a painful sound.

Karen gripped the phone tighter in her hand. 'What's happened?'

'She's walked out on me, Karen. That's what's happened. She says she wants a divorce.'

Karen was struck dumb.

Her father waited for a moment and then asked, 'Did you hear me?'

'Yes, but I can't believe it. I mean, where's Mum now, if she's not at home? *Why* has she left you?'

'Karen, I can't tell. I honestly don't know. Has she talked to you at all?' Ian cleared his throat. 'It's so ridiculous. You know we had a perfectly good marriage. Has your mother gone mad?'

Karen was silent. She remembered the night the electricity went off in the flat and the thoughts she had had then. She said, carefully, 'There must have been some warning signs, Dad. Have the two of you been having rows? Was there some really bad disagreement over something?'

'Of course not.' Her father thought for a moment. 'In fact, we've been getting on quite well lately. She was a bit moody when she gave up her job – I still can't think why she did that – but she was pleased for me when the Euro grant came through, and when I received the invitation to visit Norway, she went out and bought me new clothes. That doesn't sound like a woman who hates her husband, does it?'

'Oh, Dad. I'm sure Mum doesn't hate you.'

297

'Then why did she walk out?'

When Karen remained silent, Ian continued to speak his thoughts aloud. 'I think she's suffering from a chemical imbalance of some kind or another. You read about such things in the papers.' He coughed uncomfortably. 'She's into her middle forties now. You're a woman, Karen. Do you think it could be something to do with her age?'

If it had been someone else's father, Karen might have smiled but now she felt like crying. She managed to say, 'No, Dad. I don't think it's anything to do with the menopause.'

'Then what's possessed her?'

'I don't know. Since I've been in London, we've never had much time to talk about serious things, except . . .' Karen chewed on her lip. 'She did have rather a lonely life.'

'That's rubbish! Your mother had an enviable life, Karen. A beautiful home, enough money, her own car. What more is there?'

For the first time since hearing the shocking news, Karen felt a pang of sympathy for her mother.

She coaxed, 'Come on, Dad. Think for a moment. Mum must have said something to you before she left. Try and remember.'

'She said—' Ian's voice went tight. 'I remember she said something about us being two strangers sharing a house. She said we had nothing in common any more, but that's ridiculous, Karen. Your mother and I have been married for years and years, of course we have things in common.' He paused. 'You, for instance.'

Karen dropped her head. She wanted to cry. She asked, 'What else?'

'Oh, I don't know. I can't remember. I was in shock. In the end, I couldn't bear it. I left the house, thinking that when she was on her own, she would calm down, see sense. But the next day, she started again. She said her mind was made up and she wouldn't change it. She said she was going to stay at a friend's house for a few days, so that I could think things through.'

Karen's throat was dry. She swallowed. 'And have you, Dad?'

'Have I what?'

'Thought about what Mum said. Thought about the state of your marriage?'

'Oh, for Christ's sake, don't you start on all that claptrap. What is there to think about? It's obvious. Your mother's developed some form of depression. She needs treatment.'

There was a long silence. He waited and then asked, 'Karen, you're still there, aren't you?'

'Yes, Dad.'

'Well, haven't you anything to say to me?'

'I don't know what to say.' Karen stared blankly at the wall, then she ventured, 'You've got to be realistic, Dad. Mum sounds very determined about this, as though she's been considering the move for a long time.' She coughed. 'Perhaps you ought to think about other reasons for her leaving.'

'Such as?'

Karen found she was coughing again, a nervous cough. She clutched the receiver tightly. 'Mum's an attractive woman. Perhaps she's formed another relationship with someone.'

She could feel the shock in her father's silence.

'Dad?'

No answer.

'Dad, I'm not saying she has, but there's always a possibility. You must admit, you don't spend much time at home and Mum's an attractive lady.'

'Your mother wouldn't do that to me.' Ian's voice was cold. 'Just as I wouldn't look at another woman. I can't believe you said that, Karen.'

'I'm sorry. I was just trying . . .' Karen's voice shook. 'I've had a shock too, Dad.'

'Yes, I know.' Her father's voice softened again. He said, 'Karen, please come home. I need your help.'

'I'd like to, but . . .' Her mind raced, considering and rejecting his suggestion. 'I can't come immediately, Dad. I've been out of London, as you know, and I've just got back. My boss at the agency wants to see me urgently and there's heaps of things I have to see to.'

She smiled ingratiatingly, even though he couldn't see her. 'Let me sort things out at this end and then I'll come home. And, in the meantime, I'll talk to Mum as soon as I can.' She decided not to divulge the telephone number her mother had left for her. She had listened to her father and now she wanted to hear her mother's side of the story.

'But Karen . . .'

'I'll call you tomorrow night, Dad. Around seven.' Karen put the phone back on the rest and stared into space. She said aloud, 'Who'd have believed it!'

There was a momentary flash of admiration for her mother but it was quickly obliterated by her anger. How dare her mother do this? How dare she throw such an almighty spanner into the smooth running of their lives? Didn't she realise she was totally disrupting not only her husband's life but that of her daughter? And just when she, Karen, was getting her life together. How could she be so selfish?

Karen felt the tears welling in her eyes. Determined not to cry, she collected her duvet from her bed and dumped it in her favourite chair. She collected a bottle of decent red wine from the wine rack in her kitchen, took a wine glass from a cupboard and a corkscrew from a drawer. She arranged the items upon a coffee table which she drew closer to the chair. Then she slotted a tape of *The Man in Gray* starring James Mason into the video recorder, pressed the play button and opened the wine. She turned down the sound, in case David rang her, poured out a full glass of wine and settled into her chair determined to erase from her mind the troublesome antics of her parents. They were old enough to know better.

Chapter Twenty-Three

It was strange staying in Pat's house. Marigold felt like a snake that had shed its skin and was getting accustomed to the new one. It was peculiar cooking meals for one, finding out where the pots and pans were kept and strolling to the corner shop each morning to buy fresh bread and milk. Marigold missed her pre-breakfast visit to her garden, the paperboy's grin as he handed her the morning paper and, most of all, Paddy. She missed him dreadfully but she tried to think positively about their separation. She told herself that she was missing him more than he was missing her, which was probably true, and she knew that Ian would look after him well.

She never considered going back to her former home to see Paddy. During her last discussion with Ian, or perhaps quarrel would be a better word, her husband had laid down no ground rules. He had not refused her access to the family home. Nevertheless, Marigold felt it was impossible for her to return there without his knowledge or consent. It was she who had rejected Ian and their marriage. To sneak into the house when her husband was absent would have made her feel like a burglar. So, for the moment, she concentrated on her new life.

Daily, in her mind she thanked Pat for giving her a bolt hole for a couple of weeks. Pat's washing machine came in handy, too, as Marigold had left home with one suitcase and had to make do the best she could. Later, she hoped, when she and Ian could meet amicably, she could collect the rest of her clothes and the question of deciding what belonged to whom could be dealt with in a civilised matter.

In the meantime, she was finding it hard to settle her thoughts on anything in particular. She kept Pat's house immaculate but that didn't take up much time because she was rarely in it.

She walked a great deal, sometimes wandering aimlessly and sometimes with purpose, going to view flats. She had visited several estate agencies to ask about the possibility of finding suitable accommodation to rent. She had decided upon a firm of solicitors and was now waiting for an appointment to meet one of the partners to discuss divorce proceedings. And, most evenings, she went round to Adam's home. But she always returned to Pat's house to sleep.

'Why don't you stay over?' Adam asked her.

She shook her head. 'Right now, I'm a restless sleeper and I don't want to disturb your nights. Anyway, I promised Pat I'd keep an eye on their place.'

'But I'd like to spend the night with you now and again.'

She smiled. 'Would you? We've already made love, my dear.'

He shook his head. 'I didn't mean that. I want to sleep next to you. I want to wake up in the morning and see you there.'

Her emotions vulnerable, Marigold felt sudden tears sting her eyes.

'I'll stay overnight soon, I promise. When I settle myself down again.'

He nodded. 'I'll keep you to that.'

In fact, since the day she had faced Ian with the news she was leaving him, she and Adam had made love less often than before. Marigold felt too confused and tense to relax properly and Adam was tired because he was extremely busy with his work. Most mornings, he told Marigold, he was up by six a.m. and travelling to a stately home forty miles away. The trustees of the estate had given him the job of restoring several pieces of important furniture before the house opened to the public in September.

'It's a big breakthrough for me, but a lot of work to handle. I've plenty of other stuff lined up, too.' Adam sighed. 'I'll have to wind up the selling end of my business. The shop's never attracted much attention, and more often than not, when a customer wants to come in, I'm not there, so I might as well close it down.'

'You could employ a part-time assistant.'

'No, it's not economically viable. Besides, I don't carry enough stock. I'll try and get private buyers for the few bits and pieces I've got left and then I'll turn the area back into living accommodation.' He glanced at her. 'It might come in useful.'

She nodded but said nothing. She knew they shared a friendship quite apart from their sexual attraction for each other, but there was still some way to go before either of them could give total commitment.

But, because he was so busy and to give herself something to do, most evenings Marigold would let herself into his house with the key he had given her and cook a meal for him. Afterwards, they would spend a few hours together and then she would return to Pat's home around midnight.

Every other day, she tried, without success, to contact Karen. She would dial her daughter's telephone number but when the familiar taped answer began to play, she replaced the receiver. She had left one message, that was enough. It was up to Karen now. Marigold was sure Ian had already told their daughter the bad news and she felt nervous and worried as to how Karen would react.

More leaflets began dropping through the letterbox giving

details of flats for rent. Marigold went to inspect them and was appalled at the disparity between the description and the reality. Uncertain of her future income, she had told the estate agents she couldn't afford a lot of money and the addresses she was given certainly reflected the comedown in her financial circumstances. Most of the flats were situated on the outskirts of the city, in roads that had seen better days. They were usually basement flats, so damp the wallpaper was peeling off the walls and, even worse, patches of fungus sprouted beneath sinks and in the bottom of cupboards. Marigold mentioned these things to the owners.

'Nothing a bit of decoration won't put right.' She was told.

One of her 'would-be' landlords, seeing her expression, took exception to her unspoken disapproval. 'This place is a palace to some you'll see, miss. Rooms for rent are in demand. Every year there's hundreds of students coming to York, all wanting accommodation. You'll be damned lucky to find a place just for yourself. Most people have to share.'

Tramping from one place to another, Marigold realised he had spoken the truth. She remembered the beautiful home she had walked away from and wondered if she had been mad – but deep down she knew she had not. If the worst came to the worst, she could move in with Adam for a little while. He would agree, she knew. And yet something told her it was not the right solution. Not yet.

However, her journeys through the damp, smelly, ill-equipped apartments of bedsit land made her aware of certain things. The first realisation was that she had led a privileged life. Never before had she had to worry about money. She had never tramped the streets looking for somewhere to live. She remembered the guarded expression that had appeared on Sheila Scott's face the first time they had met. Then, she had thought the woman unfriendly; now she knew why her visit had been unwelcome.

She saw herself as Sheila must have seen her – a stranger, a woman in expensive clothes, obviously living the good life, coming to lecture her on how to bring up her children. What cheek!

Well, they were now on a more equal footing which meant, perhaps, that their friendship could progress, for a friendship had been formed between them. Look how kind Sheila had been to her on her last visit. Acting on impulse, Marigold decided to go and see Sheila.

She glanced at her watch. Yes, Sheila should be at home now and maybe the boys would be there, too. She would like to see them. Since Sheila's husband had turned up unexpectedly, nothing had been arranged about her taking Jack and Billy for a few hours, as had been previously decided.

Marigold wondered whether Mike was still at home. For Sheila's sake, she hoped he was, but she also hoped he would be out when she called round. After the way she behaved the last time she called, the poor man must think she was having a breakdown.

'Well, what a surprise.' Sheila pulled open the door. 'Come on in. I've been thinking about you.'

'Is it a convenient time?'

'What? Oh, you mean, are we on our own? Yes, as it happens we are. For a change.'

Sheila looked so very tired Marigold dared to ask, 'Is everything all right?'

Sheila shrugged her shoulders. 'More or less. Mike's here and that's good, but not as good as I thought it would be.' She gestured to the easy chair. 'Sit down.'

'Thanks.' Marigold sat down and refused the cigarette Sheila offered her. She watched Sheila light up and tried a feeble joke. 'You haven't managed to crack the habit yet?'

Sheila didn't smile. 'No,' she said briefly. 'I'm smoking more than I did.'

There was a short tense silence. Sheila sat on the bed, puffed away for a couple of minutes and then, her thin form relaxing slightly, she asked, 'Come on, then. Don't keep me in suspense. Have you done it? Have you left your husband?'

Marigold nodded.

'You have?' Sheila's eyes opened wide. 'My God! I never thought you would, not when it came down to it.'

'Thanks for your faith in me.' Marigold felt hurt.

'Sorry, I didn't mean it like it came out. It's just that, well – you had a comfortable life. There was a lot to lose.'

With a weary gesture, Marigold rubbed her hand over her cheeks. 'Yes, I'm beginning to realise.' She managed a weak smile. 'I've been doing the rounds. Trying to find a flat to rent.'

A bleak look appeared on Sheila's face. 'Join the club. Still—' She dragged at her cigarette. 'You don't have two kids hanging around your neck and I suppose you've a bit of money put by.' She put up her hand. 'Not that I want to know, you understand.'

Marigold nodded. 'I know you don't, and you're right. I've told Ian I don't expect him to keep me but I do have savings and I suppose I can get some kind of accountancy work if I look for it. Not that I'm particularly enthusiastic at the thought, but I'll have to start earning my keep somehow.'

She sighed. 'I'm staying at a friend's house for the moment. Here—' She pulled an estate agent's property description sheet from her pocket and scribbled down Pat's telephone number. She handed it to Sheila. 'I might as well give you this. When I get somewhere permanent, I'll let you know the address.'

Sheila accepted the paper and asked, 'Are you beginning to regret walking out?'

'No.' Marigold said the word firmly. 'I did the right thing.'

For the first time, Sheila smiled. 'That's the spirit. What's the point of staying with a bloke who makes you miserable?' She pushed a stray lock of hair behind her ear. 'You'll be all right, Mari. You look good, you talk nice. You'll soon get a place to live and a job, and you're not really alone, are you?' She tapped the ash off the end of her cigarette. 'You've got this chap of yours. He's around to give you a cuddle when you get low.' She shrugged. 'You're lucky. Me and Mike, we're not doing much cuddling at the moment.'

'Oh?' Marigold looked at her inquiringly. 'You said he's still here. You wanted that, didn't you? What's wrong?'

'It's this bloody place.' Sheila frowned. 'I asked him to give up the travelling. I said I needed him here and he finally agreed, but he's not happy.' She waved her hand at their surroundings. 'Can you blame him? He says he can't stand being cooped up in one room. Well, tough luck!' Her face crumbled into a mask of despair. 'Why shouldn't he put up with it? Me and the kids have stuck it out for over a year.'

'Oh, Sheila.' Marigold got up and moved towards Sheila but was waved away.

'No, don't touch me.' Sheila gulped and pinched the end of her cigarette between her fingers. 'Sorry, Mari, but I can't stand sympathy at the moment. Do you understand?'

'Yes.' Biting her lip, Marigold went back to sit in the chair.

Sheila took a couple of deep breaths. Then she asked, 'Fancy a cuppa?'

Marigold nodded. 'Shall I make it?'

'No, you're the guest.' Sheila went to light the gas ring.

Marigold watched her. 'Will Mike be back soon? You see, I don't want to be in the way, although I'd like the see the boys—'

'He won't be in yet. We've had a row, see. He started on about he'd have more chance of finding a job if he went back on the road and I lost my temper and told him he was bloody crazy. I told him to grow up, face his responsibilities. I went too far, I know that now, but once I got started, I couldn't stop.' Sheila's face was pinched with worry. Her hands trembled as she put two mugs on the battered tin tray. 'I said lots of things – things I shouldn't have said – and now I'm frightened he'll take off again and this time, he might not come back.'

She glanced apologetically at Marigold. 'Sorry, I shouldn't be telling you all this.'

'Of course you should.' Marigold jumped up from the chair and went over to Sheila. This time she succeeded in comforting her. She slipped her arm around her shoulders and hugged her. 'You've listened to my troubles, Sheila, so what's so shameful about me listening to yours? Everyone needs a friend.'

Seeing the tears form in Sheila's eyes she held her for a moment longer and then released her. She was beginning to realise how difficult it was for Sheila to allow anyone to penetrate her shield of self-sufficiency. Quietly, she said, 'Where's Mike now?'

'Taken the kids to the park.'

'Were they . . .' Marigold paused, wondering whether she should voice her question.

Sheila anticipated it, anyway. 'Were they here during our row?' Her face twisted. 'Of course they were. And during all the other rows, too. Where else would they be?' She handed a mug of tea to Marigold. 'I know we shouldn't argue in front of them but . . .' She fell silent.

Marigold sighed. 'Lots of children witness worse things than their parents quarrelling.'

'I know that. And Billy's all right. Jack's the worry. He was so happy when his dad came back but now he's doing his silent act again. I can't get through to him.'

Sheila sipped at her tea and Marigold noticed that her hand was trembling.

'You don't think he'll get into trouble again, do you, Mari?'

'I doubt it. He's a sensitive boy and feels things very deeply but he's not a fool. He knows he was lucky over that drugs thing.'

'I hope you're right.' Sheila sighed, and then asked, unexpectedly, 'How did your daughter take the news, about your split with her father?'

'I don't know.' Seeing the surprise on Sheila's face, Marigold explained, 'Because of her job, Karen travels a lot. We often go quite long periods of time without contact. She was away somewhere when I told Ian I was going. I've left a message on her answerphone to ring me at Pat's house – that's where I'm staying – but I haven't heard from her yet.'

'But doesn't she ring you when she's away?'

Marigold shook her head. 'Not really. You see,' she sighed, 'we're not a very close family. I love my daughter and I think she loves me, but—' She shrugged. 'Karen has a busy life.'

Sheila made no comment but Marigold could see from her face that she disapproved, so she hurried on, 'I'm sure she's been told the situation. Ian will have found some way of contacting her. When she was growing up, the two of them were very close.'

Sheila pulled a face. 'Well, maybe I shouldn't say it, but your daughter sounds a bit self-centred to me; but then, young people are. I expect she'll be upset when she hears the news, but it won't spoil her life.' She looked at Marigold. 'Have I spoken out of turn?'

'No. I dare say you're right.'

They both jumped when children's voices sounded outside the door.

Marigold stood up. 'Good Lord, I didn't realise I'd been here so long.'

'Don't get fidgety, Mari.' There was an affectionate note in Sheila's voice and she actually smiled. 'And don't go scooting out as soon as Mike comes in. He'll think he has the plague or something.'

Seeing her expression, Marigold felt heartened. The bond between the two of them was strengthening and she also had the feeling that Sheila was still very much in love with her husband. She thought, They will come through this.

She nodded. 'OK. I'll stay for a little while. I'd like a word with the boys.'

The door banged open and Billy ran into the room closely followed by Jack and Mike.

'Oh, it's you.' Billy raced across to her and cannoned into her thighs. 'Have you come to take us out?'

'You've just been out.' Marigold ruffled his hair. She smiled at Jack and his father. 'Had a good time?'

They both nodded. Seeing them together, Marigold saw the resemblance between them. She had always thought that Jack was the image of his mother and so he was, but today he looked like his father. And then her heart lurched a little because she saw that the resemblance was in their expressions: both father and son looked haunted. There were marks of stress around their shadowed eyes and tension in the way they stood.

She bit back a sigh and said, lightly, 'Mike, I'm sorry if I behaved a bit strangely when I was here last. I was under a lot a pressure about something. I'm all right now. Sheila's helped me sort myself out.'

'Has she now?' Mike's expression remained strained. He nodded. 'Sheila's becoming an expert about knowing what people should do. I don't know why she's not a blooming social worker.'

Marigold noticed Jack's quick glance at his father's face.

She asked, 'How are you, Jack?'

'I'm all right.' He drew closer to his father.

Mike, feeling the movement, placed his hand on Jack's

shoulder. His next words to Marigold were more friendly. 'I gather you've been a good friend to my lads.'

'My pleasure, I assure you.' Marigold wondered if she was sounding patronising. She hurried on. 'I like children and my own daughter's grown up and away from home. Billy and Jack are good company.'

'Aye, they can be.' Mike stared down at the floor. 'Has Sheila made you a cuppa?'

'Yes, thank you.' Marigold wondered what to say next. It was all very well Sheila telling her to stay but how could she without embarrassing everyone? She and Mike were strangers to each other and with three adults and two children in the room, it was horrendously overcrowded. The one easy chair loomed large in her vision. Should we, she thought almost light-headedly, play musical chairs to see who gets to sit in it? She gave up.

'Well, I think it's time I was going.'

Billy tightened his grip on her legs and wailed. 'I want to come with you. I want to play with Paddy.'

A lump stuck in Marigold's throat. She bent to speak to the child. 'You can't, love, not today.'

'When can I?'

She looked at Sheila and then at Jack. 'I'm not sure. It's a bit difficult right now. Things have changed.' She saw Jack's eyes narrow and she couldn't bear it. She said to Sheila, 'Can I take them off for an hour, Sheila? Would you mind?'

Sheila looked towards her husband. 'Well . . .'

'I could take them to McDonald's. Please, I'd really like that. And then you wouldn't have to bother getting a meal for them.'

Sheila nodded. 'Have them back before six, will you?'

'I will. Thanks.'

Marigold nodded at Mike, grabbed Billy's hand and headed for the door. She prayed Jack would follow them. Halfway down the first flight of stairs, she heard Jack's footsteps behind her and she relaxed.

Beneath the garish strip-lighting of McDonalds, the three of them sat round a grey-mottled table on which had been placed two milk shakes, a beaker of coffee and two containers, each holding a cheeseburger in a bread bun, a small helping of chopped lettuce and a piece of sliced tomato. Billy's portion was half-consumed, Jack's was barely touched. Marigold sipped at her coffee, watched Billy eat and waited for Jack to speak.

Finally, he did. He asked, 'Has something happened to Paddy? Has he died?'

Marigold was shocked. 'Good Lord, no. What made you think he had?'

His set face relaxed. 'You said things had changed and I remembered you once told me that Paddy was getting old.'

'He's not as old as that.' Marigold managed to dredge up a smile. 'He's middle-aged in dog years but he'll be around for a long time yet.'

'So, we will be able to see him again?'

'Yes, but . . .' She dithered. 'Perhaps not for a little while.'

'Why not?'

She decided she must tell him the truth. Jack was ten years old but he was a damn sight more grown-up than some of the people she had met. She sneaked a look at Billy and thanked the fates, not for the first time, that Jack's brother appeared to put all his senses on hold when he was engaged in the process of eating.

She gazed at Jack and said, 'The truth is, I don't live at my home any more. I've moved out.'

He looked at her, coldly. 'Why?'

'Well, I—' She flushed. 'My husband and I are no longer

happy together. I think we'd do better living apart.'

'So you left Paddy behind, with your husband?'

'Yes.' His steady gaze disconcerted her. She fumbled to find the right words. 'Paddy's lived in that house all his life. He has a big garden to play in. I don't know where I'll end up living.'

Jack pushed his burger away. 'He must be very sad.'

'I know that.' She swallowed. 'I'm missing him but he'll be all right with Ian. My husband loves Paddy, too.'

'But Paddy's *your* dog.' Jack raised his voice. 'He doesn't know about your problems. He'll think you've just got sick of him.'

To her horror, Marigold thought she was going to cry. From the corner of her eye she could see that the young boy dressed in his pink-striped apron, standing behind the serving counter, was looking across at them. She turned her chair round in an attempt to secure some privacy.

'Jack,' she said. 'Please try to understand. I feel bad about Paddy, I really do, but I have my life to think about. There were good reasons for me to leave. I was very unhappy.'

'Who isn't?' Jack slammed his clenched fists on the top of the table and his eyes blazed. 'Grown-ups, I'm sick of the lot of you. You're all so selfish. You make a mess of everything you do and yet you tell us off about stupid things. You're all hypocrites.

'That police guy I had to see. He made a big thing about what I'd done but he only let me off because I helped him get some proper crooks. If I hadn't, I'd be in a remand home.'

'No, Jack. I don't think . . .'

'None of you think. You just do as you want and we have to go along with it.' He stared at her. 'I wish you could listen to yourselves. You talk about what's good for the children but you end up doing what's best for you and bugger everyone else. Kids and animals, you don't care about them. You don't care about Paddy – you left him behind just like Mum and Dad . . .'

315

He choked and stood up, knocking over his chair in his hurry to get away.

'Jack.' Marigold stretched out her hand to catch hold of his arm but he stepped back.

'I don't want to go out with you any more. I don't even understand why you ever started taking us out. But you can keep seeing him.' Jack threw a contemptuous glance at his younger brother, who was sitting wide eyed, staring at him, a rim of pink around his mouth.

'And you needn't worry about me. I'm not going to chuck myself in the river, if that's what you think.' He made a pitiable attempt at a sneer. 'I'm going for a walk and then I'm going home. So you needn't go telling tales to my mother. You don't have to worry her. Just drop Billy off and go away, will you. I'll manage OK. I always have.'

He strode away from her, out of the restaurant.

Marigold gasped and looked back at Billy. He frowned, gave her an inscrutable look and rammed another chip in his mouth. She glanced away, wishing she had his strong stomach. She felt sick, the more so because she recognised the partial truth in Jack's words.

'Will your son be coming back?'

'What?'

The boy from behind the counter had come up to their table. Marigold shook her head. 'No. I don't think so.'

'Then I can clear his food away?'

'Yes.'

The boy picked up the untouched container of food. 'Was there something wrong?'

'No. Not with the food.' Marigold put up her hand to her eyes.

The boy hesitated, then said, 'You don't want to get upset, missus. Kids say a lot of things they don't mean. My mum said

I was a terror when I was younger.'

She removed her hand and looked up at him. He looked all of fifteen. She found herself smiling at him. 'Thank you. That was very kind of you.'

He flushed. 'No problem.'

She watched him walk back to the counter. Broken marriages, parents on the dole, single mothers – no wonder modern children grew up fast.

She turned back to look at Billy.

He studied her expression and then asked, 'Can I have Jack's milk shake?'

Delivering Billy back home, Marigold asked if Jack had returned.

'Yes, he came in about ten minutes ago. He said he'd enjoyed his meal. He's out again now. Meeting a friend, he said. Why, did you want to tell him something?'

'No. It's not important.'

Sheila looked much more relaxed. The time alone with Mike had been good for her. Marigold found it impossible to puncture her more positive mood. She hugged Billy, said goodbye to Sheila and promised to keep in touch. But on the way back to Pat's house she kept reliving the scene with Jack.

God, she thought. Why is life so difficult?

She was unlocking the front door when she heard the telephone ringing. She hurried into the house and, going to the phone, she picked it up.

'Yes.'

It was Karen.

'Mother,' she said. 'Dad's told me what's happened. Have you any idea of the misery you've caused?'

Chapter Twenty-Four

After a thirty-minute conversation with her daughter, Marigold went to bed and bawled like a baby. Awaking next morning, after a bare three hours' sleep, she was overwhelmed by a mixture of feelings; predominantly of self-disgust and self-pity. However, she made herself get up and throughout the day she battled to make sense of her emotional disarray.

Karen had said that she couldn't understand how her mother could behave so badly. She said Marigold had turned into a cold selfish woman. She said her father, who had worked hard to provide a lovely home and a high standard of living for her, was completely devastated by her actions. And the way she had left him! It was so cruel.

When her daughter had drawn breath, Marigold had tried to explain that she had not meant to be cruel. She pointed out, delicately, that leaving had been her only option because, no matter how she tried to talk to Ian, he never listened.

Karen didn't listen, either. She had given an exasperated sigh before calling her mother hard and unfeeling.

Marigold had said they'd better postpone further conversation until they had both cooled down. Then she had rung off. Walking round the empty house and ironing things that didn't need ironing, like socks and tea towels, she began re-running the conversation over and over in her mind and she began to wonder if Karen was right.

Perhaps she had become unfeeling because, try as she might, she failed to visualise her husband as a devastated man. Annoyed? Furious? Embittered? Yes, she could imagine him being those things. But devastated? She shook her head.

But then she thought of Jack's outburst in McDonald's, and the remembrance caused her such pain, she knew that Karen had got it wrong. She wasn't unfeeling but she did feel guilty – because she cared more for a boy she had met recently than she did for her husband of twenty-seven years. And, in her book, that made her a very strange woman.

Her thoughts and emotions chasing round like a clockwork mouse gone mad, Marigold took the phone off the hook and shut herself in for another day and night.

The following morning, the front door bell rang. When Marigold opened the door, she saw Adam.

'Oh, hello.' She heard the flat, unenthusiastic tone in her voice but didn't worry about it. Adam was one of the pieces she was trying to fit into the mental jigsaw of her new life. He was an important piece, but right now, she didn't want to see him in the flesh.

He asked, 'Are you all right?'

His concern annoyed rather than charmed her.

She snapped, 'Of course I'm all right. Why shouldn't I be?'

'Well, you haven't been round . . .'

'We don't have a written contract, do we? I don't *have* to appear at your place at seven o'clock every night.'

His eyebrows rose. 'Perhaps I should go away again?'

'Perhaps you should.' She slammed the door.

A few seconds later, the bell rang again.

She opened the door.

He grinned. 'I'm not apologising. It's you that's in a filthy temper.'

'I'm not in a temper.'

'Oh, no?'

'Well, if I am, why don't you just go away and leave me alone?'

'I would, but I've a message for you. Anyway, you don't really want me to go away.'

'I do.'

'Then why were you waiting behind the door?'

'I wasn't.' She stared at him, then surprised herself by laughing. 'Yes, I was. How did you know?'

'You must have still been behind the door. You opened it so quickly.'

She conceded defeat. 'All right, mastermind. What's the message?'

'Danny and Helen are in York today, with their son. They rang me this morning and invited us to join them for lunch.'

'Oh.' Marigold hesitated. 'I don't think so, Adam. Not today.'

'Why not? You enjoyed our last meeting with them, didn't you?'

'Yes. You know I did, but—' Marigold shuffled her feet. 'I would feel a bit awkward now, seeing how the circumstances have altered.'

He studied her face and then looked upwards, admiring the flowers in the hanging basket suspended from the side of the house.

He said, 'You're having a rough patch, aren't you?'

'Yes, but I don't want to talk about it.'

He shrugged. 'OK.'

'You don't mind?'

He put out his hand to touch her then took it back. He said, 'I've been there too. Remember?'

She wanted to cry but didn't. She blinked back her tears and asked, 'Is Daniel here to do a poetry reading?'

'No. They've been staying with a friend who lives in the area.

They're coming into York to buy sports stuff and clothes for Alex, their son. The new school term starts next week, you know?'

'I didn't, actually. It's a long time since Karen was a schoolgirl.' The mention of her daughter upset her again. She drew a hard, deep breath.

'It might do you good to come out, mix with some company.' Adam went back to his study of the flowers. 'They'd like to see you and we needn't stay long.'

'How do you know they liked me?'

'They told me.' Adam smiled. 'They said I should hang on to you.'

'Yes, but that was before. Do they know what's happened?'

'They know you've split up with your husband. They haven't asked any questions.' This time, Adam did catch hold of her hand. 'Come to lunch, Marigold. Please.'

His hands were steady and warm. Marigold looked at him and nodded.

'All right. I will.'

The day was full of hazy sunshine and the streets were busy. The city centre was crowded with people with children in tow. The crowds were thickest near the major chain stores, where Marigold and Adam had to push their way through. The cafes they passed were also doing a booming trade.

'Danny and Helen are not the only people shopping for the start of school,' Adam commented.

Marigold thought she saw a fleeting expression of sadness on his face and she wondered if he was thinking about his daughter. Had he ever shopped for school clothing, she wondered?

In St Helen's Square, a street trader was pushing a new novelty toy. A small crowd surrounded him. Marigold stopped to see what he was selling.

On the floor around his feet were dozens of what looked like large, black, plastic spiders. They were attached to long pieces of coloured string. The man collected the ends of the string in his hands and gave a series of little tugs. Immediately, the toys came miraculously alive, jiggling and scattering in all directions.

The crowd, many of them children, shouted and backed away, then they laughed and clapped. Marigold found that she, too, was laughing. She turned to Adam. 'I think I'll buy one for Billy Scott.'

Adam nodded. He knew of Marigold's friendship with the Scott boys. He watched as she purchased a spider and then he said, 'Are you glad you came out with me?'

She gave him a quizzical glance. 'Do you mean when we first met or today?'

'Both.'

She tucked her arm through his. 'Yes, I'm glad I did.'

They threaded their way through the crowds of people then turned into a quieter street which led down to the river. Marigold noticed the leaves on the trees were acquiring a tinge of yellow and she heard them rustling in the light breeze. The end of summer's approaching, she thought. She wondered where she would be and what she would be doing a year from now.

She had advertised in a local newspaper, offering help and advice in the completion of income-tax returns. She had received no replies as yet. Susan Cambridge had offered her work before her breakup with Ian but Marigold wondered if the offer still stood. Susan was a great believer in the sanctity of marriage. One day she would go and see Susan, but not yet. Marigold didn't feel brave enough.

A huge bee bumbled into their path, distracting her from her thoughts. It banged against her bare arm and she flinched, and then laughed when it flew away and she saw it had left behind it a dusting of pollen. She raised her arm and blew the pollen away.

'He thought you were a large flower,' said Adam.

'Oh, yes?'

'Of course, you're wearing yellow.'

Adam watched the bee as it blundered its way through a patch of clover growing on the grass verge.

'Do you know?' he said. 'Scientists have proved that, aerodynamically, it is impossible for a bumble bee to fly?'

'Yes, I did know that.' She pulled a face. 'Typical of scientists.'

He took her hand. 'Now, now. You mustn't get bitter.'

'I know. I'm trying not to. It's just that I feel so confused. Every day I make less and less sense out of life.'

Adam squeezed her fingers. 'Perhaps that's the start of knowledge.' He grinned. 'After all, bumble bees don't think a great deal and they're doing OK.'

They had arranged to meet in the garden behind a well-patronised riverside pub. As they strolled into the garden, Daniel Crewe got up and came to greet them.

He asked, 'Don't mind eating outside, do you? It's such a lovely day and Alex here—' he gestured to the tall fair boy sitting at the table beside Helen. 'Alex is a bit too young to frequent the inside of pubs.'

'I'd much rather stay outside.' Marigold admired the rose bushes and flower beds and then looked towards the end of the garden, which ran down to the river. 'What a wonderful view.'

'Yes.'

They all watched as a river steamer, crowded with people, ploughed its way past. They admired the black and white paintwork, the fluttering flag and they waved to the passengers on board. Then, as the river calmed again, allowing the rays of the sun to paint patterns on the ebb and flow of the water, they sat down.

Marigold smiled at her friends and held out her hand to the young boy. 'Hello, Alex. I'm pleased to meet you.'

He shook her hand and smiled back. 'Me, too.'

Adam, the only one still standing, glanced at their table and asked, 'What are you drinking?'

Helen looked mischievous. 'Danny's drawn the short straw today. He's driving so he's on mineral water, but I'm on Pimms.' She laughed out loud when Adam pulled a face. 'I know, I know, but today I felt like a treat.'

'We've been rushed off our feet for the last three weeks and today—' She gestured to the collection of plastic bags at her feet. 'We've been shopping in a big way. Trailing round shops always makes me thirsty.'

'Pimms it is.' Adam transferred his gaze to Marigold. 'What would you like to drink, Marigold?'

She hesitated.

'Oh, be wicked, like me. Let's make it ladies' day, shall we?' Helen shot a teasing look at her husband. 'The men always have excuses for drinking whereas we, poor souls, let our hair down so rarely.'

'That's news to me.' Daniel Crewe snorted but the look he sent his wife was cheerful so Marigold nodded.

'Yes, please. I'll have the same as Helen.'

Adam found out what Alex wanted to drink and departed, promising to bring the menus back with him so they could decide on what to eat.

Marigold sat down opposite Alex and began to chat to him. He proved to be a sociable boy and easy to talk to. The drinks were brought out. She had never tasted Pimms before but she could see why Helen liked it. She started to relax.

After an excellent lunch and two more Pimms she was feeling good. She knew she was slightly tipsy but not enough to be out of control. When Adam and Daniel disappeared into the bar after the meal and Alex wandered off to see if there were fish in the river, she took the opportunity to tell Helen how much she appreciated their invitation to lunch.

'I'm so pleased I came. I almost didn't.' She paused, reflecting on her unfortunate choice of words. 'I wanted to see you all, of course I did, but I wasn't at my best this morning. I thought I would be poor company for you but instead, you have cheered me up.'

'Good.' Helen gave her a calm smile. 'Meeting other people makes you realise that life goes on, doesn't it?'

'Yes.' Marigold blushed. 'Adam's told you I've walked out on my husband?'

'Yes.'

Marigold waited for Helen to comment, or ask a question, but she said nothing more. She turned her head and looked over the river.

Marigold, although she felt grateful, couldn't leave it like that. She found she wanted desperately to know Helen's opinion of her action.

She continued, 'I'm glad he told you. I don't want to meet you under false pretences, and I want you to know that Adam was in no way connected with my decision. My marriage has been in trouble for a long time.'

'Yes, Adam did tell us that.' Helen turned her gaze back to Marigold. 'But I think you're deluding yourself, Mari.'

When Marigold's face clouded over, Helen covered her hand lightly with her own.

'I'm not being cruel, it's just that, in my experience, a woman will struggle along in a miserable marriage for years until someone comes along to whom she is attracted. Then the marriage becomes absolutely intolerable and she leaves. It's understandable.' Helen shrugged her slim shoulders.

'Adam's dear to us, but he's a grown man. We wouldn't dream

326

of prying into his private life.' A smile twitched at her lips. 'And Danny and I like what we've seen of you. I hope Adam told you that.'

'He did. You've both been very kind and understanding. I don't deserve it.'

'That's rubbish. Good grief, Mari, do you think you're the first woman who has left her husband and taken a lover?'

Marigold was surprised by the passion in Helen's voice. She looked at her and saw that a troubled expression had settled on her face.

Avoiding her eyes, Helen glanced towards the door leading to the bar and commented, 'Looks as though Adam and Danny are having a heart to heart. Maybe—' She hesitated. 'We should do the same.'

Making up her mind, she leaned towards Marigold and speaking rapidly, said, 'I'd like to tell you something, Mari.' She paused. 'I have another son. He's called John. He's twenty-one years old and his father was my first husband.'

'Oh, I didn't know. I . . .'

'No, don't talk. Just listen, please.' Helen squeezed Marigold's hand and then released it. 'Alex will be back in a few minutes.'

She sat back in her chair with a sigh. 'I did something much worse than you did, Mari. I left Charles, my first husband, when John was only nine years old.' She continued, rushing her words, 'I don't often talk about my life before I married Danny, but in your case, perhaps it might help.'

She paused for breath. 'I married Charles when I was eighteen. He was thirty and a successful solicitor. Our families knew each other and I'd had a crush on him since I was fifteen. Our marriage was happy – I thought. In hindsight, I now realise that our relationship was more like father and daughter than husband and wife. Charles made family decisions, he paid the bills, he listened to me indulgently and he bought me expensive presents.

'Around the age of twenty, I began to grow up and I realised that our marriage was not exactly perfect but, before I could really think about it, I became pregnant with John. When he was born, I realised what true love was.'

Helen smiled and spoke more slowly. 'John was the most marvellous baby, plump, pretty and placid. I threw myself into the role of mother and I managed to squash down the vague yearnings that had surfaced just before his birth. Well, we jogged along comfortably for eight years. I was halfway happy. I certainly never thought of changing my life. And then I met Danny.'

She drew in a deep breath. 'It was like being swept up in a tornado. I tried to run away from him. He promised to stay away, but it was impossible for both of us.' She shrugged. 'I needn't go through the rest of it, need I? Enough to say we made the usual promises and broke them. We suffered agonies when we were apart and a mixture of joy and guilt when we were together, and in the end, I packed my bags and left home.

'John was at boarding school. I couldn't uproot him and take him away from his father and his friends. Charles threatened that if I didn't return to him, I would never see John again, and for a long time, I didn't. When the divorce took place, Charles was given sole custody. It was fair, I suppose.'

Helen went quiet and Marigold asked, her voice low, 'But you see him now, surely? Now that he's grown-up.' She could see the shadows behind Helen's eyes and she felt her heart go out to her.

'Yes, I see him now. When he was sixteen years old, he told his father he wanted to get in touch with me, and Charles agreed. Although he was still bitter, the sharpness of my defection had faded somewhat.'

Helen seemed more relaxed now her story was told. She put

her elbows on the table and propped up her chin in her hands. 'John is much closer to his father than he is to me, and that's fair. But my son and I have become friends and I am hoping that when he falls in love himself, he will forgive me for my desertion.'

Helen turned her gaze on Marigold. 'So you see, I know very well the turmoil you are going through.'

'Yes.'

The fumes of the Pimms had long since departed. Marigold was stone cold sober again. She looked at Helen and marvelled at her courage in speaking so intimately towards her. Acting on impulse, she got up from her chair and, bending over her, she gave her a hug.

'Thank you,' she said.

Helen hugged her back and gave a shaky laugh. 'Ah, well. As I said earlier, us women have to stick together.'

There was a yell from the bottom of the garden. Alex, his white trainers covered in mud, vaulted over the low hedge and made his way towards them. His face was glowing. 'I saw some fish, Mum. Little brown ones. Do you think Dad will come down to see them? He'll know what they're called, I'm sure.'

'He probably will. I'll go and dig him out of the bar. Then, when you're done with the river, we'll have to start for home. It's getting late.'

As Helen stood up, Marigold said, quietly, 'Alex is a lovely boy.'

'Yes, he is.' Helen paused. 'But I can't help thinking of all the years I missed with John.'

She looked down at Marigold. 'The only philosophy I've gleaned at this time of my life is that we must accept with a full heart our blessings and learn to live with our sorrows without bitterness. And that's the end of my sermon.'

She put up her hand in a brief wave and went towards the bar.

Chapter Twenty-Five

After the departure of Danny and his family, Adam and Marigold stayed in the pub garden, talking and drinking coffee. It was late afternoon by then, but the sky was still blue and the sun warm. About five, Marigold looked at her watch and asked Adam if he wanted to return home and work for a couple of hours.

He shook his head. 'No way. I deserve a day off.'

'But I thought Mr Dundas was calling this evening to pick up his Edwardian chair?'

Marigold spoke apologetically. Adam had been working long hours for over a month and she knew he was tired but he had made excuses to Mr Dundas before and she knew the chair was still not finished.

'Oh, hell, I'd forgotten about Dundas.' Adam's forehead creased in thought then smoothed again. 'OK. I suppose it's time we went home, but I'm damned if I'm going to work when I get back. I'll ring Dundas and make some excuse. He can wait a little longer.'

Marigold didn't reply. She stared across the river.

The rays of the sun were falling across Adam's face. He squinted to see her expression more clearly, and asked, 'Why the prune face?'

She shrugged. 'You promised him, Adam.'

'I know I did,' he scowled. 'But it's hardly a life or death matter, is it? Anyway, I'm out of resin and I can't finish his chair until I make some more beaumontage.'

Looking for a way to defuse the possibility of an argument, Marigold asked, 'What exactly is beaumontage?'

'It's a mixture of beeswax and resin. You add shellac to it, or some other colouring that matches the type of wood you're working with, and use the stuff as a filler. In texture, it's a bit like sealing wax.'

'I see.' Marigold sighed. 'I do envy you. Adam. It must be so satisfying, restoring neglected and ill-treated furniture to its former glory. You're lucky to be able to earn your living doing something you enjoy.'

'Yes, I know. The only problem is that, in my line of work, there's either a feast or a famine. Up to a few months ago I was really struggling to make ends meet, now I'm struggling to keep up with the work I have.' Adam grinned. 'In fact, I was desperately short of cash the day we met. The only reason I was at the golf club was because I needed money.'

'Well, if you remember, I guessed you were no golfer.'

'You thought I was a groundsman.' Adam chuckled. 'In a way, I was. I'd spent two days laying a new green.' He looked thoughtful. 'It was a stroke of good fortune, us both being there on that particular day.'

He glanced at her sidewards, a questioning look.

Marigold allayed his fears by giving a huge smile. 'You've plenty of work now, so perhaps I've brought you luck?'

'Perhaps you have.' He nodded. 'Only I wish it didn't come in such large dollops.'

Marigold became serious. She leaned forward in her chair. 'You're spreading yourself too thinly, Adam. There's stuff at the house you need to work on, more work at your cottage and now you're travelling every day to Acre House. You can't keep on at this rate.'

'Oh, but I can. I've only Dundas's chair and chest of drawers at the house. The other bits and pieces are my own, so there's no pressure there. And the things at the cottage can wait for a little while. This contract with the owners of Acre House is a major breakthrough. I must make that my priority.'

Marigold sighed and ran her fingers through her hair. 'I worry about you working so hard and I certainly don't help, do I?'

He looked puzzled. 'I don't understand what you mean. What have you got to do with my work?'

'It's not so much your work, Adam, it's the house. You're only keeping it on because you think I'll end up moving into it.'

'Not true, Marigold.' Adam looked down at his hands. 'Why would I keep the house on? You've already made it plain that you have no intention of moving in with me.'

'But that's what I mean! You want to move out of York and go and live in your cottage. You've told me so. But you're keeping the house because you know Pat and Chris are due home soon and when they are, I'll have nowhere to live. You're going to suggest I move in there, don't deny it.'

'Well, it would be a sensible solution.' Adam concentrated on a snagged fingernail. 'You don't have to be stiff-necked about it. You can pay me a fair rent.' He looked at her and attempted a grin.

Once more, Marigold turned her gaze to the river. It was quiet now the pleasure steamers had gone. The water had turned light grey in colour. A couple of moor hens bobbed and ducked not far away from them.

She watched them and said, 'Chris and Pat will be coming home in two days' time.' She sighed. 'I have tried to find a flat, Adam, but none of those I've seen have been suitable.'

'I know.'

'But the thing is, I don't want anyone, even you, doing me favours.'

At his exclamation, she hurried on, digging her nails into the palms of her hand as she tried to explain. 'Please don't get upset. I know you're trying to help me. I know you care about me and I care about you.' She drew a deep breath. 'If I have to ask for help, then you would be the one I would turn to, but I won't ask. Not now and not ever, if I can help it. You see, I want to fend for myself. Can you understand?' She stared at him. 'People have always made my decisions for me and I'm sick of it.'

He shook his head. 'To be frank, I can't. Everyone needs someone, you know.' He saw her expression and shrugged. 'But I can see how strongly you feel about your independence so I guess I'll have to go along with your wishes.' He rubbed his chin. 'But if you can't find anywhere to live, you must tell me.'

When she didn't reply, he frowned.

'And let's set one of your misapprehensions straight. You being temporarily without a home has nothing to do with my hanging on to the house. The plain truth is, I can't get rid of the place. It's registered with an estate agent but not one person has been to view.' He sighed. 'Do you remember me telling you that it's not the kind of property to suit a run-of-the-mill buyer.'

Marigold blinked and the tension in her body eased. She said, 'I didn't know you'd actually put the house on the market.'

'You don't know everything.' His smile took the sting out of the words. He shifted in his chair and said quietly, 'This desire of yours, to live on your own and make decisions by yourself, does that mean other things are going to change? You're not considering living like a nun, are you?'

'Oh no.' Her mouth curved into a smile. 'I'm not giving up on things I've recently learned to enjoy.'

The conversation dwindled away and by mutual consent they decided it was time to go. Marigold said she wanted to leave because a cool breeze had begun to blow from the direction of the water and she felt cold. Adam said he wanted to go home because of her sexy voice and the look she had given him. They laughed and held hands as they left the garden. But even with the unspoken promise of lovemaking to anticipate, they still found themselves dawdling along the route home because it was the time of day when relaxation was the key word.

The bulk of shoppers having departed, the streets had sunk into a somnolent tranquillity. Away from the main thorough-fares, sparrows hopped along pavements searching for crumbs or remnants from Marks and Spencer's sandwiches eaten at lunch time. Buskers squatted as they put away their flutes and violins and counted the coins they had amassed.

Marigold and Adam crossed the road and headed for The Shambles and Adam's house. As they walked by a crumbling section of the old city wall, a bell-ringing practice began in a church close by. Immediately, a flock of starlings, roosting in a tree in the churchyard, flared into the blue sky like a shiny black rippling fan. They wheeled and turned in the air, chittering loudly, expressing their irritation at being disturbed.

Marigold stopped. She rested her hand against the ancient stone wall and lifted her head to watch the birds. She listened to the church bells and then she suddenly became conscious of the warmth of the stones. She took her hand away, spread her fingers wide and then pressed the palm of her hand against the rough-hewed surface of the wall. The warmth was still there. If anything, it seemed to intensify.

She told herself there was a logical explanation for the phenomenon. The day had been warm and sunny. The stones had retained the heat of the sun. But then, she thought, No, it's more than that. Why am I suddenly so optimistic, sure that things are going to work out? And why – she felt the stones almost vibrating beneath her hand – why do I feel as though I am experiencing a loving handshake from a dear friend?

'Come on, Marigold.' Adam was watching her, a puzzled look on his face. 'I'd like to get to Turnbull's before they close.'

Marigold blinked. What fanciful nonsense was she engaging in? Perhaps she had been in the sun too long. With a guilty feeling, she remembered the Pimms she had consumed. But as she hurried to catch up with Adam, she felt astonishingly light-hearted.

Making a detour from their usual route, Adam called in at a small shop off Little Stonegate to purchase items he needed for his work. Marigold waited outside. Since her relationship with Adam had deepened she had learned many things: one of which was that substances to do with furniture restoration usually smelled foul.

She glanced around and then crossed the road to look in the window of an art shop which sold pictures as well as artists' materials. She admired an impressionist painting on view in the centre of the window. It was all swirls of black, green and blue; striking, but not a painting, she thought, that she would like to live with.

A smaller painting to the left of the window then caught her eye. Marigold thought it must be a reproduction because she was certain she had seen the original in an art gallery somewhere. She studied the composition. By an open window, with the sun streaming in, stood a bunch of marigolds in a dark blue jug. She put her head on one side and admired it.

'Good, isn't it?' Adam had come to join her. His voice came from behind her shoulder. 'I noticed it a couple of days ago.'

She nodded. 'Yes, I really like it. I wonder how much it is?'

'We could ask.' Adam went to try the shop door but it was locked. 'Oh, they've gone home. Never mind. We'll come back tomorrow.'

She squeezed his arm. 'You're a nice man, Adam.'

'Am I?' He seemed bemused. 'Why am I?'

'You just are.'

How could she explain that his genuine enthusiasm to make her happy was balm to her wounded spirit.

He took her arm. 'Come on. We can get home this way.'

He took her round the corner into a small square which, a nameplate informed her, was called Back Swinegate.

'I don't believe I've been here before —' Marigold came to a sudden halt and then she laughed. 'No, I'm sure I haven't. I would have remembered him.'

'You mean, you haven't met Eadwig?'

'No. How do you know that's his name?'

Marigold walked across the square towards the head of a large bronze pig which was attached to the far wall. She stared into his comical face and put her hand under the stream of water gushing from his mouth and splashing into the bowl beneath him.

'There's a plaque. Can you see?'

'Where?' She looked. 'Oh, yes. Now I see it.' She read out, ' "Eadwig, the Swinegate pig." '

She looked at Adam. 'What a nice idea.'

'Yes. He brightens up this little square, doesn't he?' Adam studied the benevolent expression on the porker's face. 'I believe the Victorians put up lots of things like these, although I don't know what they called them. He's not exactly a fountain, is he?'

'He's lovely.' Marigold smiled and glanced through the window of a small restaurant which was to the left of Eadwig. She was surprised to see how busy it was.

All the tables seemed to be taken. She saw a waiter dashing about and the bobbing heads of the customers as they consumed baked potatoes and salads.

She watched the activity, felt Eadwig's icy water chilling her fingers and recalled the feeling of warmth she had experienced by the city wall. And then she gasped because, suddenly, she knew what she was going to do.

She pulled her hand away and gazed into space. Her mind flicked and whirled like lace bobbins in the hands of an expert. If I do this, she thought, if I do that, it could work! She turned her mind to calculations. The money she had saved. The money she must borrow.

'Marigold?'

She heard Adam's voice as if from a long distance.

'Marigold?'

She blinked her eyes.

'That's the second time you've blanked out on me. Are you feeling ill?'

'No, I'm fine.' She raised her wet hand and wiped her burning cheeks. 'But let's get home. I've had the most tremendous idea and I want to tell you about it.'

Adam, sitting in his rose-patterned chair, grasped the chair arms and stared at her. 'Let's get this right. You want to *buy* this house. You want to live in it and run it as a cafe?'

'Yes.' She nodded.

'But . . . How can you?'

'I've got some calculating to do but I think . . .'

He shook his head. 'How can you even think of it?'

'I know the front room's too tiny to be considered as the main . . .'

Adam jumped up from the chair and strode up and down the room.

'I'm sorry, but the whole thing's ridiculous. This house is totally unsuitable for what you're suggesting. There are too many stairs, the accommodation isn't right and anyway—' He stopped pacing to stare at her. 'How could you afford it?'

'Oh, I think I could manage.' Marigold, sitting on a chair near the window, put her chin in her hand. 'Of course, I don't know your asking price.'

'But you can't even afford a flat!'

'I didn't want to *buy* a flat, Adam. I said I couldn't see one suitable for me to rent. I do have some money, but what I have, I must put to work. If you do let me buy this house, I shall have to apply for a small mortgage.'

'And you think they would give you one? Will you tell them your plans?'

'Of course. They need to know I can earn my living.' She nodded. 'I think I could persuade them. You see, I know about money, Adam. I can submit plans for alterations and a projection of profit margins etcetera.'

She saw the scepticism on his face and frowned.

'I would make it work.' She clasped her hands together. 'You know I want a fresh start. I already love this house. I could be happy here and I know I could make a success of running a cafe. And you want to sell.'

'I do. But a cafe!' Adam shook his head. 'It's not possible.'

'Please, will you just listen to me?'

When he sighed, and nodded, Marigold told him her plans. 'Your present work room would be ideal for the main part of the cafe. It's huge, Adam. There'd be lots of room for the customers and the bay window's an attractive focal point. The cash desk could be behind the door and next to it I'd have a glass counter showing a display of the cakes, and so on. I'd make those, of course.' She paused. 'You know I make good cakes.'

'Yes, on a small scale. How would you cope with cooking for a crowd of people?'

She ignored him. 'We'd have to build a small extension for the washing-up area.' She gave him an impish grin. 'The top floor would remain unchanged, of course.'

He shook his head. 'You're crazy.'

'No, I'm not.' She threw him a defiant look and continued. 'The ground floor – your shop area – is too small to be of much use but I could put in a couple of tables and make it terribly attractive, to pull the customers. I thought copper bowls full of dried flowers and a special display of some kind in that wonderful fireplace.'

'You've forgotten the most important thing, Marigold.'

She stopped. 'What's that?'

'Where will you find the customers? We're not in a main street.' He ruffled his hair. 'For God's sake, we're at the end of an alley!'

'A snickelway,' she reproved him.

'It's the same thing.'

'It isn't.'

She jumped to her feet. 'York is a special place and the snickelways are special, too.' She stared at him, desperate for him to understand. 'These last weeks, as well you know, I've done a lot of walking. The first thing I realised was that The Shambles is *always* full of people, both tourists and local people, and they are all walking.' She paused. 'They have no option.'

'That doesn't mean . . .'

She frowned. 'Listen to me. Please.'

Adam sighed and flung himself back in his chair.

'I've been exploring the snickelways and I've noticed that most of them have painted signposts attached to their entrances. The signposts give information about the places of interest to be found down the various alleyways.'

Adam snorted. 'Those signposts give information on places of historical interest. The council won't advertise your cafe for you.'

'Perhaps not. But, as I was telling you, I've been down those snickelways and I've seen a seventeenth-century church I've

340

never seen before and a medieval dwelling house, and I seen lots and lots of people. The whole place is full of people like me, going around sightseeing.'

She paused. 'These people get tired and hungry. They want a sit-down and a cup of tea or coffee. You know how busy the cafes and restaurants are in the main streets. And I'll be there for them.' Marigold paused, then added, 'By the way, the signposts do give other information. The other day, I noticed a sign directing people to a Nearly New shop.'

'Did you?' Adam looked interested. 'I didn't know they allowed that.' He shook his head. 'Lowering the tone, don't you think?'

'Oh, you!' Marigold came and sat down on his knee.

He put his arm around her. 'I'm sorry. I don't enjoy being a killjoy, but I can't see your scheme working, Marigold.'

'But why?' She frowned. 'Didn't you see that restaurant in Swinegate. It was packed out.'

'Yes, but you said the operative word – that place is a *restaurant*. They serve evening meals. I went there once, had a good spaghetti carbonara, as a matter of fact. But if you'd looked closely you would have seen they had two waiters, and another man on the cash till. You can't afford to pay for three staff members, can you?'

'No. I will need some help, of course.' Marigold jumped up and went over to her handbag. She took from it a notebook and a pen.

Adam watched her. 'What are you doing now?'

'Thinking out a few things.'

He sighed and got up from the chair. 'I'm going upstairs.'

She looked up. 'Why?'

'I'm no use here, am I?' He shrugged his shoulders. 'I might as well go and finish Mr Dundas's chair.'

* * *

An hour and a half later, Adam heard a soft tap on his work-room door. The door opened and Marigold came into the room. She smiled at him and, a little grudgingly, he smiled back.

'What are you doing here? I thought you would have gone back to Pat's.'

'No,' Marigold came to stand by his side. 'Pat's house can look after itself.'

'Ah! So you want a bed for the night?' Adam put down the brush he was holding.

'Yes.' She put her hand on his arm. 'I'm sorry if my idea upset you, Adam.'

'You don't have to apologise, Marigold. I was the one who was throwing cold water on you.' He raised his hand and caressed her face. 'But I do worry about you.'

'I know, and that's nice.' She rubbed his hand with her cheek. 'But there's no need to worry. I know I sounded impulsive down there, but I shall check everything out before committing myself. I've spent too many years sorting out other people's financial messes not to be extra careful about my own business deals.'

'But your idea sounds so risky.'

'Yes, I know it does. And, no matter how careful I am, there *is* a risk. But I really want to do this, Adam. Will you let me buy your house?'

He put his arms around her.

'On one condition.'

'What is that?'

'That you come to bed with me, right now.'

She laughed. 'That's not a condition, that's a pleasure.'

Chapter Twenty-Six

Pat and Chris Harker arrived home at eleven thirty a.m. Marigold hugged them both, exclaimed over their tans and produced coffee and biscuits. They drank, talked about the holiday and laughed over the photographs. Chris and Pat were so radiant. Marigold couldn't remember being so happy when her own honeymoon had ended. Pat was even more delighted when Marigold gave her the postcard from Sam, which had dropped on the doormat two days earlier.

'He's in Paris now. Back home in three days.' Pat gave the postcard to Chris.

'Bang goes our peace and quiet.' But Chris grinned as he propped the card on the mantelpiece.

Marigold glanced at her watch. She showed Pat the well-stocked refrigerator, explained that delivery of the newspapers and the milk would start tomorrow and said she must leave them.

'Oh, don't go yet, Mari. You haven't told us *your* news. I want to know what's been happening.'

For the first time since entering the house, Pat looked serious. 'Have you seen Ian? Has he agreed to a divorce? And where are you living now?'

Marigold slipped on her jacket and gave her friend a brief smile. 'I'll answer all your questions but not now, love. I've an appointment with my bank manager and I mustn't be late. But I'll be in touch soon, I promise.'

Pat accompanied her to the door. 'At least leave me a phone number, so I can get in touch.'

Marigold picked up the message pad lying next to the telephone in the hall and scribbled down a number. She said, 'I'm staying at Adam's house in The Shambles.'

'Ah!'

At Pat's exclamation, Marigold coloured. 'Adam's very dear to me, as you know, but it's not as simple as you think. When I have the time, I'll tell you everything but I expect to be frantically busy for the next few days so don't worry if you can't get hold of me. I'll ring you when I can.'

Marigold opened the door and then paused. 'Keep your fingers crossed for me, Pat. What happens during the next couple of days could affect my whole future.'

'A lot has happened during our absence, hasn't it?' Pat touched Marigold's hand with the tips of her fingers. 'I can see changes in you.' She hesitated. 'Have you any regrets about leaving Ian?'

'No.' Marigold paused, then amended her statement. 'That's not strictly true. I've caused pain which I regret, but not enough for me to want to turn back the clock.' She glanced at her watch. 'And talking of clocks . . .'

'Yes.' Pat stepped back. 'Off you go. I'll be thinking of you.'

'Bless you.'

Marigold hurried down the path. By the gate, she waved. 'And thanks again for letting me stay.'

Pat waved back. 'You're welcome.'

Driving into the city centre Marigold did her best to concentrate on the forthcoming interview. She glanced at the green folder lying on the seat next to her and mentally checked through the points she hoped to raise during her interview with the bank manager. They were all positive.

One thing Marigold had learned whilst working in the tax department was that you must present an optimistic overall view. No matter how messy the case, you had to create confidence in the client that problems could be solved and, she reminded herself, most of them had been.

She had used the same method when drafting her proposal for her bank manager. But would Mr Paulson buy it? She chewed her lip. She would soon know.

From the corner of her eye she noticed an elderly lady dithering by the side of the road. She slowed the car and gestured for the woman to cross. She did so, giving Marigold a smile and a little wave as she passed by the car. Marigold drove on.

The incident reminded her of car trips with Ian. Her husband was an impatient driver and he had often berated her for stopping for pedestrians.

'Why don't they use a pedestrian crossing? You shouldn't encourage jaywalking. All you are doing is adding to the snarl-ups on the roads.'

Useless to point out to him that to walk to a pedestrian crossing, when you're old and arthritic, was akin to climbing a mountain.

Marigold sighed and drove on, wishing the incident hadn't happened because, ever since yesterday, she had been trying to banish thoughts of her husband from her mind.

She had been jittery after Karen had phoned again yesterday – so much so that her shortness of breath had returned – but the arrival home of Pat and Chris had calmed her. Now, she was breathing too quickly again and her hands were trembling. She swore beneath her breath and slowed the car.

The conversation between herself and her daughter had been

brief. Karen had said she was driving up to spend a couple of days at home and asked if Marigold would come to the house to see her and her father.

Marigold had said she would, and Karen had seemed surprised by her readiness to agree to her request.

'Dad says you've not been in touch.'

Marigold had explained that was not strictly true. She had contacted Ian to give him Pat's telephone number. He had put down the phone without speaking, and she had not spoken to him since.

'Whatever.' Karen had sounded sullen and resentful. 'You can't keep on ignoring each other. I've told Dad I'm coming home and I said I would ring you. He's taking a couple of days off so he'll be at the house. I should get there around one o'clock. Can you come soon after that?'

'Three o'clock would be better. I've an appointment at my bank and it's important I keep it.'

'Oh, well. I suppose we must fit in with your arrangements.' Karen had replaced the receiver.

Put it out of your mind.

Marigold was approaching the bank. She started looking out for a parking space. She slipped a mint into her mouth because her throat was dry. This meeting with Paulson was so important. She wasn't going to think about anything except her plan of action; the rest of her life depended on the showing she made.

Walking into the bank she wondered if she was becoming an unfeeling cow.

Walking out again, one hour later, she had dumped all her negative feelings. She felt one hundred per cent positive because Mr Paulson – the dear, astute, clever man – had agreed to back her with hard cash. He had listened to her, called for coffee, jotted down figures, uttered a few words of caution and made a telephone call. It was when he started talking about a built-in safeguard clause that she knew she had him. She was going to have a cafe!

Marigold beamed at passers-by as she left the bank. She went to her car. As she slid the key into the lock, it began to rain. She raised her face to the unexpected downpour and as she felt the cold droplets touch her skin she felt as though she was going through a baptism. She climbed behind the driving wheel feeling that her sins and failures in the past had been washed away and she was being allowed the luxury of a new, bright future.

She drove the car in the direction of her former home with a much happier feeling than she could have ever anticipated.

Karen's SKL Roadster was parked in the drive. Ian's car was nowhere to be seen. It must be in the garage, thought Marigold. She left her car in the roadway. As she walked up the path to the front door she heard Paddy barking. She smiled, anticipating seeing him again but worried whether she should walk straight into the house or ring the bell.

She was saved from making a choice when Karen opened the door. Her daughter must have been watching out for her. Karen opened her mouth to speak but before she could do so a black whirlwind pushed her to one side, rushed out and enveloped Marigold.

'Down, boy. Down.'

Marigold saw him coming. She saw the front door fly back and heard the clang as it connected with the radiator in the hall. She braced her body and put out her hand, trying to connect with Paddy's head, trying to calm him down. To no avail: he jumped at her, weaved round her, his tail bruising her legs as it banged against her. She gave up and knelt down on the gravel drive, careless of the effect on her sheer tights. She managed to put her arms around his neck and she hugged him, tears starting to her eyes.

'Yes, boy. Yes. I've missed you, too.'

He licked her hands, her cheeks, her ears, every bare bit of her he could reach and then he plumped down beside her, panting heavily. His tongue was lolling from his mouth and his eyes were bright.

'Well!' Karen stared at the pair of them. 'I'm never going to have a pet.'

Thank God for that, thought Marigold. But she didn't say anything.

'You'd better come in.'

Marigold and Paddy slunk into the house behind her trim figure.

Karen's hair was styled in a thick, sleek bob. She wore tight black pants and a flowing white shirt with a huge collar, over which was a green and black short waistcoat. She looked wonderful.

'Dad's in the sitting room.' Karen put her fingers through Paddy's collar. 'You're going in the garden.' She dragged the dog through into the kitchen. Marigold heard a door open and close and then a mournful howl. She bit her lip.

She had time to notice that the hallway looked immaculate. There was a bowl of roses on the hall table and no dust anywhere. Ian must have found a good cleaning lady. Marigold thought of Sheila Scott and she straightened up before going to face Ian.

He was sitting in a chair but he got up when she entered the room. Her first impression was that he, like the house, remained unchanged but then she thought he looked a little smaller somehow, a little greyer. It was nonsense, of course. His hair was still blond, although it was more closely cut to his head than she remembered and his figure was upright.

He said, courteously, as if to a stranger, 'Do sit down.'

She sat. So did he. They faced each other and there was silence.

Marigold cleared her throat. 'The house looks very nice.'

He frowned, offended. 'What did you expect?'

'Nothing. But I know how busy you are and . . .'

'I contacted an agency. A woman comes in three times a week. She cleans, does the laundry, gets in shopping. It works well.'

'I see.' She wondered what to say next. There was so much to discuss. But if they couldn't talk when they lived together, how could they talk now?

He coughed. 'Karen looks well.'

'Yes.'

'I was worried. I thought this business between us might have upset her.'

'I'm sure it did, but Karen is a very self-contained young woman. She has her own interesting life. She'll be all right.'

Ian's lips went invisible. 'Just the sort of remark I would have expected from you.'

She blinked. 'I'm sorry. I didn't mean . . .'

'To say hurtful things? You never do, do you? And yet you did – all the time. You never realised, of course; you were too busy concentrating on your own feelings. And then you walked out on me.'

She frowned. 'I didn't want to hurt you, Ian, but I couldn't stay. I knew things would never get better. We could never talk. Most of the time I didn't even know what you were thinking.'

'Oh, yes. We're back to the communication business, are we?' He snorted. 'You read pathetic articles in women's magazines about the need for communication in a marriage and you believed them. Real marriage isn't like that, Mari. It's about loyalty and commitment. Well, you haven't been very good at those, have you?'

'I tried, Ian.' Marigold fought to keep her voice even. 'I tried for over twenty years, but then I gave up trying. I decided I wanted some happiness in my life.'

'So you left me and went to live with another man. Does he make you happy?'

Marigold flinched. She had wondered whether Ian had heard about her relationship with Adam. Now she knew he had. She felt a great sadness for her husband. She knew how proud he was.

She asked, 'Who told you?'

Ian got up from his chair and went to look out of the window. 'Oh, there were lots of little hints and winks. Then a friend of mine in the science block came out with it.'

'I'm so sorry.' She bent her head. 'I wanted to tell you but it was impossible.'

'Nothing's impossible, Mari. At least, not for people like me. But you're not like me, are you? You're a self-indulgent woman who considers no one but herself.'

Marigold, bowing beneath the weight of her remorse, welcomed the spark of anger his words ignited in her. She raised her head and stared at her husband. 'I understand your bitterness, but there are always two sides to every story. I tried hard to make you understand how I was feeling. I wanted to save our marriage but you wouldn't listen to me. And I didn't leave you to go and live with Adam. I'd decided before I met him that . . .'

'Don't bother explaining.' Ian's face was tight. 'I might have known you'd use clichés to describe your infidelity. We're not characters in a magazine story, Mari. This is our marriage you've destroyed.

'Do you ever think about the other people you've affected? What about Karen? You think you're a good mother, but you seem strangely disinterested in your daughter's distress. And what will my mother and father think? I haven't found the courage to tell them yet.'

Marigold clenched her hands until her fingers hurt. 'Perhaps, if you'd had different parents our marriage might have been successful.'

As soon as the words were out, her mouth opened into an astonished 'O'. She jumped from her chair. 'I'm sorry. That was unforgivable. I think I'd better go.'

She hurried towards the door but before she was halfway across the room, Karen came in. She glanced at Marigold and then at her father.

'Oh, hell. What's going on?'

Ian turned back to the window without speaking. Marigold gulped a breath of air.

'I can't stay, Karen. It's too painful for both of us.'

Karen ran her hand over her silky cap of hair.

'But you've things to decide.'

'I know. But—' Marigold looked towards the silent figure of Ian. 'Perhaps we can communicate through our solicitors?'

'Dad?' Karen looked towards her father.

He nodded his head. 'It would be best.'

Karen's mouth began to quiver. 'Then, you're going to divorce?'

'It would seem that way.' Ian's gaze was set on the garden.

Before she went out of the room, Marigold paused and asked, humbly, 'May I collect some of my things? I took very little with me. I don't want jewellery, anything like that, but I need fresh clothes and . . .'

Ian turned round. The look in his eyes was strange, unreadable. He said, 'Take what you like.'

'Thank you.' She stared at him for a moment and then left the room.

Karen followed her out.

'This shouldn't have happened. Oh, why are you both so stubborn?' She twisted her hands together. 'I thought, if I got you two together, you'd figure things out. For God's sake, Mum, you've been married for years and years. You can't just walk away.'

Marigold turned and put her hands on her daughter's shoulders. 'You're not a child, Karen. You know marriages go wrong.'

'But not you and Dad.'

'We're not just Mum and Dad, we're people.' She sighed. 'And people change.' She patted Karen's shoulder and then turned to walk up the staircase. 'Do you want to come and talk to me, while I'm packing?'

Karen hesitated. 'No, I think I'll stay with Dad.'

'All right. But I'll see you before you go back to London?'

'Oh, yes. But where?' A frown creased Karen's smooth forehead. 'I don't want to meet your lover. I couldn't bear that.'

'Oh, Karen.' Marigold felt a wild desire to laugh. 'We must talk. I want you to know what's really happened, but . . .' Her words tripped over each other in her haste to communicate. 'I don't intend asking you to take sides. I would hate that. Let's meet outside the Merchant Adventurers' Hall tomorrow at one o'clock. We'll have lunch and I'll tell you what's been happening. Will you do that?'

'If Dad doesn't object.'

'Fair enough.' Marigold managed another smile before she went upstairs. In the bedroom she had shared so long with Ian, she took down a large suitcase from the top of the wardrobe and filled it with her belongings. It didn't take her long to pack away over twenty-five years of marriage. When she finished, she went to take a last look over the garden. She saw Paddy wandering restlessly round the lawn and she swallowed the lump in her throat.

She was humping the heavy case down the stairs when the door to the sitting room opened and Ian came out. Avoiding her eyes, he came to her and took the case from her hand.

She was about to protest but then she looked down and said, 'Thank you.'

He carried the case out to her car and stowed it in the boot.

She went to open the car door.

He hesitated. 'If you're short of funds, you must let me know.'

Again, tears almost destroyed her resolve. She replied, in a muffled voice, 'That's good of you, but you know I have savings.'

'Yes, but twenty-five years must count for something.' He cleared his throat. 'I suppose the solicitors will handle the financial side of things.'

'Yes.'

'Well, goodbye.' He turned away.

A low moaning sound came from behind the garden hedge.

Ian turned back to her. He glanced into her face and then looked away. 'If you want to see Paddy from time to time, take him for a walk or something, I have no objection.'

'Oh, Ian. Thank you.'

'Well, he could do with a bit more exercise than I can give him.' Ian shuffled his feet. 'Anyway, a dumb animal shouldn't have to suffer for our failures, should he? I would, though, ask that you come for him when you know that I am not at home.'

'Of course.'

They looked at each other and for the first time it struck Marigold that, although their marriage was over, perhaps something was left. Perhaps, when the pain was over, they might even become friends.

She inclined her head in farewell and got into the car. As she drove away, she didn't look back.

Chapter Twenty-Seven

The only place to park was in the car park by Clifford's Tower. Hoisting her suitcase from the boot of the car, Marigold wondered whether she could flag down a taxi. As The Shambles was a car-free area, she wouldn't be able to go all the way to Adam's house in a cab, but a ride would cut down on the walking distance and her suitcase was heavy.

She placed the case on the ground and was about to close the boot when she noticed a brown paper bag squashed into the corner of the luggage space. A peculiar claw-like thing protruded from the bag. Good God, she thought. What is it?

She reached in, poked the bag with a dubious finger and then grinned with relief. It was the rubber spider she had bought for Billy. She'd forgotten all about it. She took the toy from the bag and examined it. Being made of rubber it was undamaged, so she stuffed the spider in her pocket and then locked the car. She would take it round for him soon; she wanted to talk to Sheila about her ideas concerning the cafe.

No taxi came her way so she struggled along Piccadilly with her case. A little boy, racing between the knots of people on the pavements, almost cannoned into her but she side-stepped and he missed her. Marigold frowned and then smiled, realising that it was leaving time for the infant schools. It was easy to spot the new pupils. Clutching paint-daubed pieces of paper, a few children, mostly boys, raced along releasing pent-up energy. Others, more sedate, walked importantly beside their mothers, conscious of new school uniforms and bags and boxes decorated with Disney characters.

Just ahead of Marigold walked a young woman hand-in-hand with her small daughter. The child, dressed in a grey pleated school skirt, much too long for her, trotted along demurely, clutching a big crayoned-upon piece of paper.

Marigold noted her brand-new blue blouse and the regulation school hat perched on her shiny fair hair and thought not of Karen but of Adam's daughter. She realised how rarely Adam talked about his child. She had not yet seen a photograph of the girl. Why, she didn't even know her name. The realisation shocked Marigold. Adam knew all about her life. Why did she know so little about his?

She shifted her suitcase from one hand to another and felt sad. If she changed her mind, asked him to stay in the house, live with her, she knew he would agree. And she was tempted. It would be hard to live alone. But she knew it was not the answer. Perhaps one day they might become permanent partners, but not yet – not now.

Marigold gripped the handle of her suitcase and soldiered on. She was perspiring by the time she turned down Coffee Yard and followed the twists and turns of the path. Coming to the house at last, she put down her case, wiped her forehead and stared upwards at the bay window on the first floor. She felt she could almost see customers sitting behind the glass, chatting, drinking coffee and eating her cakes. She sighed. She couldn't wait to translate her dream into reality.

Unlocking the front door, she went into the house. She dumped her case at the foot of the stairs and then slipped into the front room. She listened to the soft ticking of the Edwardian clock on the mantelpiece and studied the creamy wallpaper flocked with the tiny orange and dark-blue flowers and she thought, I could turn this room into a very special place.

She said aloud, 'I must try and find crockery to match the flowers on the wallpaper.' She stared into space, visualising tables covered by round cream tablecloths with dark blue runners, a bud vase on each table containing a single bloom. Cool green ferns in the fireplace. Old-fashioned prints on the wall. Black and white line drawings, she decided. Maybe characters from Jane Austen's novels.

She laughed silently at her grand ideas but then thought, Why not?

She knew it would be the upstairs cafe that brought in the money. She hoped it would. She had ideas how that would be, too.

The decor would be bright and cheerful, the crockery and utensils plain and hard-wearing, dishwasher friendly. She would provide home-made cakes – all the old favourites – and muffins, scones, teacakes and plum bread. Everyone who tasted her plum bread went mad about it.

She might offer child-sized portions of scrambled egg and beans on toast. But no small children would be allowed in her downstairs tea room.

That's an idea! Her eyes widened. She would have plaques on the doors, specifying the difference. This room could be the Austen Room, ideal for people wishing a quiet chat with a friend or even a chance for a business man or woman to discuss their work. The upstairs cafe would be bright and bouncy. She'd have to think of a suitable name.

If Sheila agreed to come and work with her, she'd be perfect for upstairs. She was such a quick-moving, energetic woman and she was sharp, too. She would know how to deal with any boisterous customers. And for the downstairs room? Marigold put her head on one side. Perhaps a student, taking a year off before starting university. She remembered the girl busker she had talked to in Coppergate, the girl with the violin; someone like her would be ideal. And of course, she too would be in evidence. She didn't intend spending all her time baking.

Eyes shining, Marigold left the room, closing the door softly behind her. She picked up her suitcase and took it upstairs, placing it on the bed in the spare bedroom. Then she went for a shower. Half an hour later, dressed in jeans and a blue shirt, she came back downstairs determined to cook Adam a good meal. It may be the last proper meal for some time because, tomorrow, she would begin to put her plans into action. Her face sobered momentarily. And, of course, she was meeting Karen.

Adam was late home. He came in the back way, putting down a flat, paper-wrapped parcel by the door and sitting in a kitchen chair to take off his shoes and don his slippers.

'Something smells good.'

'Yes, it's sirloin steak.' Marigold was mixing together a green salad. She glanced at him. 'You look tired. Has it been a bad day?'

'Not really. Just busy.' He yawned.

Marigold nodded at the packet. 'Something interesting?'

'No. Something I need at work.'

Marigold lost interest and reached for the salad dressing. 'I don't want to be a bully, but can you go for your shower now? The meal will be ready soon.'

'Sure.' Adam picked up his shoes and walked towards the door. Reaching it, he asked, 'Aren't you going to tell me?'

She grinned. 'I was saving it until we ate.'

'At least tell me what the bank manager said.'

Marigold wiped her hands on her apron and looked at him solemnly. 'Looks as though you've sold your house, Mr Crewe.'

Adam stared. 'He agreed. He's actually given you the go ahead?'

Marigold pulled a comical face. 'Don't sound surprised.' She eyed him. 'You're pleased, aren't you?'

'Of course.' Adam walked over to her and kissed her. 'Congratulations, Marigold. You've proved me wrong and I'm delighted.'

'Thanks.' She clung to him for a moment and then gave him a little push. 'Go and have your shower. I'll dish up, open the wine and then we can start celebrating.'

Later that evening, with the dishes washed, a compact disc on the hi-fi and the second bottle of wine opened, the two of them curled up together on the sofa.

Adam reached for the wine and refilled both glasses. 'Not bad stuff this.' He squinted at the bottle.

'Nothing posh.' Marigold settled herself against his shoulder. 'I knew we had none in the house. I've been too busy to restock, but I had to have some for this evening so I grabbed a couple of bottles from a bin outside a wine shop on my way home. The chap in the shop said it was –' she quoted '– "an unpretentious member of the Cabernet Sauvignon family".' She chuckled. 'But it's not too bad, is it?' She took a sip and put her glass down. 'I nearly dropped one of the bottles on the pavement. I was carrying a packed suitcase at the time.'

'Yes.' He rolled a mouthful of wine around his mouth before swallowing. 'I spotted your case when I went upstairs. You should have left it in the car. I would have collected it for you.'

'Oh, no. I managed. I wanted to get at my clothes. I'm sick of wearing the same old things.'

'You always manage, don't you.' He looked at her thoughtfully and then smiled. 'You look nice tonight.'

'Thank you.'

With a friendly rather than amorous gesture, Adam slipped his hand inside the collar of her navy-blue silk shirt and caressed her throat with his thumb and forefinger. He said quietly, 'So you saw your husband at the house?'

She nodded.

'Feel like talking about it?'

'I don't know.' Marigold wriggled a little so he stopped touching her. She sat upright and looked down at her hands. 'It was difficult, obviously.' She paused. 'And sad, too.'

Adam sighed. 'I suppose you feel as though you've been through a wringer. Poor love. If you want to talk, I'll listen. You might feel better for letting it all out.'

A spark of irritation leapt into life inside Marigold. She moved a fraction away from him. 'Talk? Like you do, you mean?'

He looked bewildered. 'Sorry? I thought we were discussing your problems?'

'We were. We always do.'

Now it was Adam's turn to swing his legs to the floor and sit upright.

'What's the matter? What have I done?' A muted note of anger sounded in his voice. 'I love you. I was trying to be supportive. Don't you want that?'

'Sometimes.' Marigold bit her lip. 'I do appreciate your concern, Adam, but what about you? When are you going to open up to me?'

He looked at her with genuine bewilderment. 'What about?'

'Oh, for God's sake.' She raised her hands. 'What do you think? Your break-up with your wife.'

'But that happened years ago.'

'And you're still not over it.' Marigold saw him shake his head and her voice went higher. 'You never mention your past life. You never mention your wife, you rarely mention your daughter and yet I know you love her.'

Adam turned and stared at her and Marigold began to

perceive the struggle that was going on inside him from the expression in his eyes. She softened her voice and, laying her hand on his arm, said, 'If you want our relationship to have a future, Adam, I must know something of your past. Don't you see?'

'It was years ago,' he repeated. 'I'm over it now.'

She shook her head. 'I don't think so.'

He looked at her, then stared down at the carpet and began to speak, his voice unemotional. 'My ex-wife's name is Diana. She was, still is, slim, pretty, attractive. I fell in love with her when I was eighteen and married her when I was twenty-three. In between that time, Di had lots of boyfriends, but she married me.

'I wanted the best for her so I worked away a lot.' Adam gave a harsh sigh. 'In hindsight, that was a mistake. Still, I got her the things she wanted: a new bathroom suite, a better car. I built a patio on the back of the house for her. She loved sunbathing.'

He swallowed. 'We wanted a family but nothing happened. And then, just as we had given up hope, Sally was conceived. It was the best day of my life the day she was born. And then things began to go wrong. Di found she wasn't cut out to be a mother.'

Adam slouched his shoulders, an awkward, clumsy gesture. 'There were rows, more rows. She was never in when I got home. She'd dump Sally with anyone. I said it had to stop, that my daughter deserved a better mother. And then she told me.' Adam's glance towards Marigold was curiously shame-faced. 'She'd had lovers, lots of them. She'd been sleeping around for years. She said I must be a fool because I never realised.'

His voice cracked and Marigold moved to touch him but then drew back. Poison had to be let out. Dry-eyed, she watched him and listened.

'She said I was even more of a fool, doting on a child that

possibly wasn't my own. She might be, she said. She wasn't sure.'

Adam gave a shuddering sigh. 'I hit her then. I never thought I would hit a woman but I hit her so hard I broke her jaw.'

He sneaked a glance at Marigold and this time Marigold did move. She stretched out her hand and took hold of his.

Heartened by her response, he continued, 'I called the doctor and then I left. Thank God Sally was staying with Di's aunt that night.' He rubbed his hand over his face.

'Not much more to tell. I moved out of the family home. Di took out an injunction saying I was too dangerous to see her or my child. In time, she divorced me. The court awarded her custody. She was the mother and I had assaulted her. Perhaps I should have cross-petitioned, but I didn't. I was in a pretty bad way at the time.'

'Oh, my dear.' Marigold squeezed his hand.

He glanced at her. 'It's better now. Di's improved as a mother now that she's older.' He sighed. 'There aren't so many offers, I suppose.'

'And you get to see Sally now?'

'Yes. Over the last few years we've developed quite a relationship. I think the world of her.' Adam looked away. 'She doesn't look much like me but then, she has her mother's colouring. Perhaps she is my child . . .'

Adam's voice cracked and he began to cry.

'Oh, love.' Marigold threw her arms around him and pressed her cheek to his. 'It's all right. Really, it's all right.'

He accepted her embrace for a moment and then pushed her gently away. Avoiding her gaze, he pulled out a handkerchief and wiped his eyes. He even tried to smile. 'I'm sorry.'

'What for?'

'Being so weak.'

She wanted to shake him but instead she hugged him again.

'Will you stop trying to be a bloody hero. I don't want a hero. I want a man who thinks and feels things.' She shook her head. 'Why do men think it's so terrible to cry?'

He sniffed and blew his nose. 'Upbringing, I suppose. We worry that people will laugh at us.'

'I'm not laughing.' Marigold sat very close to him. 'I'm sorry you're upset but I'm glad you told me all this.' She took his hand and held it up to her cheek. 'You know, the main reason Ian and I split up was because of non-communication. We were living in our separate silences. That mustn't happen to us, Adam.'

'It won't.' Adam had put his handkerchief away and was rapidly regaining his self-control. He smiled at her. 'Some other time I'll tell you my life history but right now, I prefer to look forward rather than back. I'm looking forward to the future, Marigold, and I hope we can spend it together.'

'So do I,' she said softly.

'But for now—' He moved a little away from her. 'We're both terribly busy. You in particular. I remember how hectic it was when I moved in here and set up my business. I suppose the bank will require building plans, estimates, and so on?'

'Yes.' Marigold sighed.

'Perhaps I can help you with those. I have contacts in the building trade.'

'Oh, Adam. That would be great.'

'You'll have to check on planning permission.'

'I already have. I knew the bank would need written confirmation.' Marigold smiled. 'The papers should arrive in a couple of days.'

'I might have known.' Adam hesitated. 'And today, when you saw your husband, did you discuss a divorce?'

Marigold shook her head. 'Not in any specific way but Ian knows I have a solicitor and he's aware there's no chance of a reconciliation.'

'And then there's the problem of me.' Adam took her hands in his. 'What you were saying earlier, about me moving out.'

Marigold's heart missed a beat. 'Yes?'

'I'm going this weekend. I think it's right that we should put a bit of space between us.'

Her face paled. 'You make it sound final.'

'Good God, no.' He shook his head. 'Haven't you been listening to me?'

'Yes, but . . .'

'You're going to be frantically busy.' He smiled at her. 'I'm already frantically busy. So I am going to move into the cottage.'

'I see.'

'It's what you wanted, Marigold. If I'm not here, you'll be able to pursue your business plans without distractions. If I'm at the cottage, I'll save an hour and a half every day in travelling time.'

'It does make sense.' Marigold plaited nervous fingers together. 'And that's your reason for leaving? You're not getting sick of the whole ghastly mess?'

'You're the one who was against us living together,' he reminded her.

'I know I was.'

'Well, I've come to realise I agree with you.' Adam hesitated. 'I know I love you, Marigold, but I'm beginning to realise I don't know you all that well. In fact—' He grinned sheepishly. 'I realise my first impression of you was totally wrong.'

'Oh?' Her head came up.

'Yes. I thought you were vulnerable, a lady who needed looking after. I suppose that was one of the things that attracted me to you.' He paused. 'After Di, I fancied the idea of being a protector.'

'And so?' She look at him questioningly.

'Well, you're actually very strong.'

364

She cleared her throat. 'And that alters things.'

'In some ways, yes. But I still love you.' He laughed at her bewildered expression. 'Oh, for God's sake, let's leave off all this self-analysis. We've done enough for tonight. I've got something for you.'

He got up from the sofa and went into the kitchen. He came back holding the flat parcel.

'I lie, too. I lied about this being something for work. It's actually a present for you. I meant it to be a consolation if your deal fell through or a celebratory gift if you met with success.' He dropped the parcel on her knee. 'I'm glad it's the latter.'

Marigold weighed the parcel in her hands. 'What is it?'

'Open it and see.'

She slipped off the string and tore open the wrapping paper and then made a small sound of pleasure.

'Oh, Adam. Thank you.' She held up the canvas. 'It's the marigolds painting.'

'I knew you liked it. So did I.' Adam's face was bright now, his dark memories forgotten. 'You can have sole possession at the moment. Then—' He gave her a meaningful glance. 'If ever we do settle down together, I'll decide where to hang it. Is it a deal?'

'It's a deal.' Marigold jumped up, stood the painting on the sofa and stepped back to admire it. She looked across at Adam, her face lively with pleasure.

'And I know where I shall put it. It's going in the window of the front room, my Jane Austen Room.' She clasped her hands together. 'And I've had another idea. It's so logical.' She grinned across at him. 'I'll take marigolds as my motif. I'll call my cafe The Marigold Patch. I'll do the upstairs room in yellow and cream and I'll have little bowls of marigolds on the tables. I'll see if I can get a sign put up to advertise.'

'Like the Nearly New shop?' Adam grinned.

'Yes. Why not?' She smiled back.

He wrinkled his brow. 'Pity there aren't any marigolds in the back garden.'

'There will be, next summer.' Marigold went to him and threw her arms around his neck. 'I love you,' she said.

'I love you, too.' He grasped her hungrily. 'Let's go upstairs.'
She nodded.

Upstairs, in the high old-fashioned bed, they made love. The first time it was hot and urgent and soon over. Then they lay together, talked a little and touched a lot.

'I do love you,' she whispered.

'I know.' He brushed back her hair.

'And you don't think I'm mad, making all my weird plans?'

'No.' His voice was lazily quizzical. 'You can have all the marigolds in the world so long as I have the original.'

'You already have.' Her arms went round his neck, drawing him to her.

This time their lovemaking was leisurely. They touched and explored each other's body with tender solicitude and when the climax came they both became quite still, caught up in a moment that was almost mystical. Afterwards there was no need to talk. They lay side by side and through the open window they watched the stars.

Chapter Twenty-Eight

At five minutes to one, Marigold was standing outside the Merchant Adventurers' Hall. As she waited for Karen to arrive she was proud that her breathing was even and her stomach wasn't twisting in knots. She wasn't looking forward to explaining the breakdown of her marriage to her daughter but whichever way Karen reacted, she knew she would cope with it. Adam was right. She was becoming a strong woman.

Thoughts of Adam cheered her. Remembering their lovemaking, she actually smiled. Then she saw Karen cross over Fossgate and walk towards her and her expression became serious again.

Karen came up to her and asked, politely, 'Have I kept you waiting?'

'Only a couple of minutes.'

They exchanged glances and there was a short, hurtful silence.

This is my child, thought Marigold. She stared into Karen's delicately made-up face and searched for signs of the child she had loved and looked after but she saw nothing except a beautiful, expressionless mask.

She looked away and said, 'Let's go and find a place where we can have lunch and talk.'

But even that small thing proved impossible.

'It's worse than London,' complained Karen, after they had wandered around for quarter of an hour looking for a quiet cafe. 'Why can't they open a few more restaurants or something?'

In other circumstances, Marigold would have laughed. Instead, she sighed and admitted, 'I should never had suggested meeting you at this time. Still—' She brightened. 'I know a shop that sells very good sandwiches. It's only a couple of minutes walk away. Shall we buy something there and then go down to the river?'

Karen shrugged. 'I'm not bothered about food. I've got out of the habit of eating lunch. You get something, if you want.'

Marigold shook her head. 'No. I'm not hungry either.'

Lapsing into silence, the two women walked in the direction of the riverside gardens. They moved as if careful not to touch each other, both lost in their own thoughts. When they reached the river Marigold commented that the air was cooler. Karen nodded. They came to an unoccupied bench and by common consent, sat down.

The silence was becoming oppressive, almost competitive.

Marigold broke it by asking, 'Karen, please tell me how your father is. Is he coming to terms with all this?'

Karen's eyebrows pulled together and her reply was ungracious. 'Why ask me? You saw him yourself yesterday.'

'Yes, I know I did, but we didn't really talk.'

'What did you expect, a chatty conversation?' Karen scowled. 'Don't you realise what you've done to him?'

Marigold picked a piece of imaginary fluff from her skirt and asked, mildly, 'What have I done, Karen?'

'You've ruined his life.'

'Have I?' Marigold gazed across the river. 'I doubt it, you know. I've hurt him and I'm sorry about that, but – ruined his life?' She shook her head. 'I think not.'

'I can't understand you any more.' Karen stared at her mother in disbelief. 'How can you sit there and talk like that? What has happened to you to make you so cold and selfish?'

When Marigold looked away and didn't reply, Karen's smooth beautiful face crumpled into a childish expression and when she spoke again, her voice was shaking. 'Why are you doing this, Mum? You and Dad have been married so long. You were so settled. Why did you walk out? I'm sorry if you've been unhappy in some way but surely, you could have talked things through with Dad.'

'I did try, Karen.' Marigold's voice was quiet and her look, as she turned again to her daughter, was compassionate. 'But it was too late for us. We'd grown too far apart. And, as you said, we'd been married a long time.'

She sighed and absently brushed back a lock of hair that had strayed across her forehead. 'I'm not young any more. I woke up one morning and realised that my life had become so dull, so futile, that I couldn't bear it. I knew I had to make the break. It took a lot of guts to walk away from my marriage, Karen, but really, I had no choice. I realised that if I stayed with your father, both of us would end up bitter and unhappy.'

Karen was unconvinced. 'Dad doesn't see it that way.'

'No.' Marigold smiled suddenly and put her hand on her daughter's knee. 'Have you ever been in love, Karen? I mean, really in love?'

Caught unawares, Karen blushed. 'Well, there was Carl.'

'Ah, yes. Carl Paget.' Marigold frowned. 'That young man caused you a great deal of heartache, if I remember rightly?'

Karen nodded.

'But before that, at the beginning, can you remember how you felt?'

'Why yes.' Karen, momentarily forgetting about her father, looked shyly at Marigold. 'I felt that everything in the world was better because I was with Carl. Every single thing seemed fresh and new.' She blushed. 'Does that sound stupid?'

'No. It sounds exactly right.'

Marigold sat back. 'And what you've described – that's rather how I felt when I made the break from your father. That sounds terrible, doesn't it? Me feeling like that when I had walked out on Ian. But that's how it was. I *knew* I had done the right thing.'

Marigold stared anxiously at Karen. 'So you see, I'll never go back, Karen. Our marriage is over.'

'But don't you feel guilty?'

'Of course I do. It's possible to be sad and happy at the same time, you know. I feel sad about the hurt I've inflicted. I worry about you, I worry about your father – I even worry about Paddy – but it doesn't change my conviction that my decision was right and—' Marigold hesitated. 'I can't believe I've broken your father's heart, Karen. I truly believe that, when a little time has passed, he will function alone quite happily.

'Ian doesn't need people. His life is wrapped up in his work and he's doing so well now. His visit to Norway was a great success, you know. I expect he will travel abroad more and more. As to the house—' She smiled. 'He's already got that organised and, of course, he has you.'

Karen looked unconvinced. She fidgeted on the bench and then said, a little sulkily, 'So I'm supposed to take on responsibility for him.'

'Not at all.' Marigold's response was swift. 'I didn't say that. Everyone's responsible for their own life. Your father can take care of himself.'

'But you know what he's like.' Karen pouted. 'After dinner last night, we had a drink together and he was coming up with all kind of wild ideas. He suggested I might spend a lot more time at home.' She looked at Marigold, her eyes wide. 'I can't do that, Mum.'

'I know that and so does he. He knows you have your career to pursue. You know how proud he is of you. He wouldn't really want you to stay in York.' Marigold sighed. 'Your father's had his orderly life turned upside down. He's grasping at straws. He'll soon work out a new routine for himself.'

Karen considered her mother's words. 'Yes. I think you're right.' She looked at her mother curiously. 'You're a lot more definite about things than you used to be.'

'Not really. The difference is, I'm voicing my opinions now.'

Encouraged by the more friendly atmosphere developing between them, Marigold stretched and grinned at her daughter. 'Oh, Karen. I have such plans. I'm going into business, you see. I'm buying a property in The Shambles and I'm going to open a cafe. Remember how you used to enjoy my cakes?'

Karen's face registered shock. 'But, I assumed you'd go back to working for the Inspector of Taxes, or at least some kind of office work. You can't run a cafe. You don't know anything about it.'

Marigold laughed. 'I told you. I'm seeking new horizons.'

Struck by a new idea, Karen narrowed her eyes. 'Does a man own this cafe?'

Marigold stopped smiling. 'No. I told you. I'm going to open a new business.'

'But there is a man, isn't there? That's why you're so different.'

Marigold parried her daughter's question. 'Can't a woman change her life without there being a man involved?'

'Not usually.' Karen refused to take her gaze from her mother's face.

Marigold hesitated and then stared straight back at her. 'Yes, there is someone.'

Karen gasped and her eyes filled with tears. 'So it was all nonsense, what you were saying about wanting a new life. The truth is that you were sick of Dad and you found yourself a lover.'

'No. It's not as straightforward as that. Please, Karen, you must believe me.'

'Why should I? You've been lying to me.'

Karen was getting up from the bench and preparing to walk away.

She mustn't go. Marigold, nonplussed as to how to deal with the sudden development, resorted to sarcasm as a way of detaining her daughter. She said, 'Why, Karen, you're behaving like an early Victorian novelist. I thought you were a modern woman.'

Karen stopped and glared down at her. 'I can still be shocked.' She shook her head. 'I can't believe you're so calm.'

'And I can't believe you're so shocked.' Marigold's brow wrinkled. 'Why are you shocked? Because I'm sleeping with someone? Because I'm middle-aged? Because I'm your mother?'

'All of those things.' Karen's lips were tight with scorn. 'And because you betrayed your marriage vows.'

That hurt. Marigold's face paled and when she spoke again, her voice was quieter. 'Yes. That took a lot of living with.' She looked down at her hands after checking her daughter was not in a rush to leave.

'I'm not going to tell lies, Karen. I'm not saying that your father and I didn't sleep together any more. We did but—' Marigold strove for the right words. 'It didn't mean anything.'

She wondered whether to say more but decided to spare them both embarrassment. Instead, she said, 'Meeting Adam didn't make me leave your father. I had already decided to do that. But meeting Adam and feeling as we did about each other reinforced my certainty that my marriage was too dead to resurrect. And I was right. With Adam I now experience friendship, laughter,

closeness, all the things I never had with your father. Also—'
Marigold paused and said deliberately, 'I enjoy sex again.'

'I can't believe you're talking to me like this.' Karen sat
down, a look of shock on her face.

'Why? We're both adult women, aren't we?'

'Yes, but . . .'

'If we can't be honest with each other, Karen, we'll never be
able to be friends.' Marigold shrugged. 'I've slept with two men
in my life and I've loved them both. One was your father and the
other one's Adam. I don't feel I have to apologise to you for my
actions.'

She closed her mouth firmly and waited for Karen's reaction.

It was very quiet on the riverbank. They sat in silence as a
couple of boys appeared on the cycle path and rode past them,
fishing rods in their hands.

Marigold watched them until they were out of sight and then
she said, idly, 'When I was pregnant with you, I hoped for a boy.
Of course, when you arrived I thought you were the most perfect
baby in the world, but deep down, I still hoped I'd have a boy.
Of course, I didn't.' She looked at Karen. 'But, do you know,
now that you've grown up, I think I prefer having a daughter,
particularly if we can become friends.'

Karen turned her face towards her mother. She was pale.

Marigold noticed a spray of freckles across the bridge of her
daughter's nose that hadn't been visible since she was a young
child. Her heart contracting, she said, 'I do love you, Karen.'

'Oh, Mum.' Karen's face crumpled. 'I'm sorry.'

'Whatever for?' Marigold put her arm around her and hugged
her.

'Because I'm so selfish. I've known for a long time that you
were unhappy with Dad but I pushed it out of my mind. I wanted
everything at home to be nice and tidy. And then, when Dad
rang me, I was shocked. I came up to see him thinking how

sorry I was for him but when I arrived home, I realised I was sorry for myself. What I was really worried about was how the break-up would affect me.'

'That's understandable.' Marigold took a handkerchief from her pocket and gave it to Karen. 'We're all selfish at times.' She tried a smile. 'You must be following in my footsteps.'

'Don't say that.' Karen blew her nose. 'You've been a smashing mother.'

Colour ran into Marigold's face at the unexpected compliment. She hugged her daughter again but did not speak.

Then Karen asked, 'This man, Adam. What's he like?'

'Oh, he's nice looking without being handsome. He's about my age. He's middling tall and rather broad. He's not ashamed to show affection and he gives me lovely hugs.' Marigold's blush deepened. 'But you know what he looks like – you've already met him.'

'I have?' Karen looked at her blankly.

'Yes. At the golf club, remember?'

Karen was silent, thinking, then she gave a gasp of incredulity. 'The man on the terrace? The man you were talking to?'

'Yes. But I didn't meet him again until much later.' Marigold hurried to tell Karen about meeting Adam at the Arts Centre.

'It sounds as though he makes you happy.' Karen had recovered her composure. She looked at Marigold with interest. 'Later – after your divorce from Dad – will you marry him?'

'Maybe. I don't know.' Marigold picked up a pebble from the gravelled path and threw it into the river. 'I expect I will eventually, but first—' Her face brightened. 'There is so much I want to do.' She dusted her hands together and began to tell Karen her plans for the future.

Karen, listening and watching, realised she was seeing an entirely different woman. Her mother, for as long as she could remember, had always been calm and loving. The person sitting next to her now was still loving but also a vivid, attractive woman. No wonder someone had fallen in love with her.

She interrupted Marigold's flow of words to ask, 'I suppose I'll get to meet Adam eventually?'

'Would you like to, Karen?' Marigold's eyes glistened.

'Yes. But not yet, I think. When things settle down a bit with Dad. Anyway,' Karen sighed, 'I really should go back to London soon. I'll have to see how things go.'

'Yes, of course.'

Karen glanced at her watch. 'I'd better head for home.'

'Yes.' The animation left Marigold's face and figure. She looked uncertainly at Karen. 'I'm sorry you're having to deal with things at home.'

'Oh, it's not so bad. In fact—' Karen hesitated, unsure whether to speak or not. 'You know what you said about Dad?'

Marigold look rueful. 'I've said a lot of things. Maybe too many.'

'No, I think you're right when you said he'd soon recover.' Marigold paused. 'Last night, he was very quiet. After we'd had that drink I mentioned, he took Paddy for a walk and then he came home and wandered around for ages. He was just about driving me mad when he announced he was going into his study.

'Around midnight, I went to bed. I woke up at half past two and I saw the lights were still burning downstairs so I went to investigate. I thought . . .' She paused. 'Well, I didn't know what to think. Anyway, Dad was still in his study, working.' She stopped.

'And?' prompted Marigold.

'I went in to him and he was fine. That's what I wanted to tell you. In fact, when I spoke he looked up and I could tell he was surprised. He had completely forgotten I was in the house. He asked me why I'd come downstairs and I said it was time he was in bed.

'He actually smiled. Said he'd been working on a problem and had just solved it.' Karen gave her mother an apologetic smile. 'And somehow, I don't think the problem he was referring to was you, Mum.'

Marigold beamed. 'Oh, I'm so glad to hear that.' She jumped up and kissed her daughter's cheek. 'Thank you for telling me. I feel much better now.'

Karen shrugged. 'He was pretty miserable today.'

Marigold's smile faded. 'Ah, well. A day at a time.'

Soon after that, they parted. Karen went home and Marigold went to keep her appointment.

She spent some time with her solicitor and then she drove over to see the manager of a firm that dealt with the installation of catering equipment. She explained that her inquiry was only tentative as she still had to clear building plans. The manager was civil and helpful. She was impressed by him and left feeling sure she would use his services when the time came. In her mind, Marigold always used the word 'when'. She refused to contemplate the word 'if'.

With that in mind, she decided to call in to see Sheila. She was eager to tell of her plans for the future and she also wanted to give Billy his spider.

Only Sheila was home. She welcomed Marigold in and, as always, began brewing tea for them. She was unusually quiet and spent the time waiting for the kettle to boil with her back towards Marigold. Launching into her exciting news, Marigold didn't notice anything amiss.

Too excited to sit, she paced around the room, speaking of her plans for the cafe and her success with the bank manager.

Only once did she stop talking. On a wall shelf containing books, she spotted an exquisite carving of a fawn. The animal had been carved from bog oak, the black oak wood preserved for centuries in peat. Marigold had seen such work before but never a piece of such high quality. With an exclamation of pleasure, she picked it up. 'I've never seen this before.'

Sheila looked over her shoulder and then back at the kettle. 'Mike did it. It's his hobby.' Her voice was expressionless.

'But it's beautiful, Sheila. If he has any more like this, I'd love to buy one.'

When Sheila made no further comment, Marigold replaced the carving on the shelf hoping she hadn't offended her.

Accepting a mug of tea from her silent friend, she returned to her original subject, describing how she envisaged altering part of the house and how the cafe would be furnished. And then, like a magician producing a rabbit from a top hat, she mentioned her idea about Sheila running the upstairs cafe.

'I don't think so. I know nothing about waitressing.' Sheila, pale faced, buried her face in her mug.

Marigold paused, shocked by the lack of enthusiasm. 'But you'd be perfect, Sheila. And I was relying on you. We'd make such a good team. I understand about money matters and you've such a lot of common sense. It would work, I'm sure of it. Please don't turn the idea down without thinking about it.'

When no reply was forthcoming, Marigold drew breath and took her first proper look at her friend. Sheila had a peculiar frayed look. Marigold blinked and asked, her voice much quieter, 'What's happened, Sheila?'

'Nothing's happened.'

'Oh, come on.'

'Nothing's happened.' Sheila pressed a clenched fist against her forehead and attempted a smile. 'I've got a terrible headache. It's happened before, it will pass.'

'I'm sorry. I should have realised.' Marigold bit her lip. 'Have you taken anything. I might have some pills in my bag.' She began to rummage.

'I've taken some.' Sheila walked towards the bed. 'I think, if I lie down for a bit . . .'

'Yes, of course.' Marigold blundered to her feet. 'I'm sorry I disturbed you.' She walked to the door. 'You're sure you're all right? I can stay until Mike or the boys . . .'

'No, I'm better on my own.'

'Right then.' Marigold remembered Billy's gift. She put the bag containing the spider on top of the TV. 'This is a little toy I bought for Billy. I hope he likes it.'

'Yes.' Sheila was lying on the bed now. She turned her face towards the wall.

Marigold left the room and closed the door gently behind her.

Silently, on the bed, Sheila began to cry.

Chapter Twenty-Nine

Karen set off for London on Friday. She had stayed a week with her father. It was a longer visit than she had anticipated, or wanted. Twice she had mentioned leaving and twice her father had begged her to stay. Hearing the tremor in his voice and seeing the way he avoided looking her in the eyes upset Karen. She felt as though their roles had suddenly reversed: he was now the child and she the parent. And so, she had agreed to postpone her leavetaking. He had been extravagantly grateful, promising to cheer up, even take her out; but his promises were soon broken. After a matter of hours he retreated in his shell of isolation, shutting himself away in his study or going to work in the laboratory at the university.

His actions had frustrated and annoyed her. Why did he want her around if he couldn't be bothered to spend time with her? Bored, she wandered around the house and garden or went into York to shop. But the stores couldn't compare with the places she patronised in London so she was soon home again. In the quietness of the empty house she began to understand her mother's frustration. But, in spite of her dawning sympathy, she still felt anger – none of this mess was of her making. Why was she suffering the consequences?

She finally extracted herself from her situation by lying. When Ian came in one evening she told him she had received an important call from her agency. She must return to London immediately.

He had looked stricken. 'Oh, Karen. Must you go?'

'Yes,' she said firmly.

Now she was within an hour's drive of London. Above her, the sky had turned black and a few enormous drops of rain were spattering on her car windscreen. Karen cursed softly under her breath. If the threatened downpour arrived she would have to slow down, but not yet. She slightly increased her speed – a confident driver, she had faith in her car and in her own ability.

Five minutes later she had to switch on the wipers. As she did so, a Peugeot swooshed passed her, travelling too fast even for the motorway. Karen braked and swore under her breath. Stupid bastard. But her shrug was resigned. It was her car that did it. A young, attractive woman at the wheel of a sleek marvel like an SLK Roadster brought out the worst in some men – they couldn't bear the competition.

Her thoughts turned from men in general to one particular man and her brain buzzed with small worries. Although she had left her York telephone number with David, he hadn't rung her. But she had known that might happen – David had warned her that he had been called back to Paris and might be travelling for a few days, so that was OK.

The rain was heavy now, water washing across the road. She slowed down.

But David had also been sulky the last time they had seen each other. He'd managed to get tickets for a film premiere in the West End and his face had fallen when she had explained why she couldn't accompany him.

'It's on in two days' time,' he had protested. 'Surely your father can cope on his own for another two or three days?'

'David, my father's distraught. He needs me. I'm sorry, but I must go to York.'

A peevish expression had appeared on her lover's attractive face. Seeing it had disconcerted her – David had looked like a child whose favourite toy had been taken away from him. It didn't fit the image she had of him. She'd slipped her arms around his neck and coaxed him into smiling again, promising, 'We'll go wherever you want when I come back, my darling. There'll be plenty of other grand occasions we can attend.'

Karen had already realised David liked being seen at prestigious events. He had even admitted as much.

'It goes with the job, Karen. Just as you benefit from media cover, it does me good to be seen around at social events. I'm making my way in a highly media-motivated profession, you know.'

A disturbing thought had struck her. 'I hope that wasn't why you came up to speak to me on the film set?'

He laughed, softly. 'Don't be an idiot! I came over to get your autograph for my kid sister, remember? And one look into those gorgeous green-blue eyes of yours had me hooked.' He kissed her forehead. 'You could have been the tea lady, for all I cared. I would still have fallen for you.'

She had smiled and submerged her doubts in enjoyment of his expert lovemaking. And later, when she thought of his lack of sympathy for her family situation, she reminded herself that David was the product of a upper-class family.

In her experience, men who had been sent off to prep school early in life and then to a public school usually felt some affection for their parents but not the strong bonds of loyalty that held other families together.

Anyway . . . she would be seeing him soon.

She peered through the now grubby windscreen. She would be leaving the motorway shortly and negotiating her beautiful car through the hazardous rainswept streets of London. She put personal worries out of her mind.

The downpour stopped just before she arrived home. She let herself into the flat and wrinkled her nose. The place smelt musty; unloved. The first thing she did was open all the windows, before she watered her plants which were drooping in their pots as though they had pined for her. Then, with a peculiar feeling of reluctance, she approached her answerphone and pressed the play button. There were no messages. None at all.

Karen stared fixedly at her fingernails and told herself she had expected nothing else. She had spoken once to Claudia while staying with her father and David was obviously still away in Paris. But she couldn't help feeling a little hurt that no one else had missed her during her absence from the capital.

She thought about her last conversation with her mother, when she had called to see the house in The Shambles. Of course, most of the chatter had been about Marigold's plans for her future, but she had noticed how many other names had appeared in her mother's conversation. There was Pat, of course, whom her mother had known for ages, but she had also mentioned a woman called Sheila and her family, and another couple called Helen and Daniel. As well as finding herself a lover, her mother had acquired new friends.

Standing in the quietness of her sitting room, Karen realised how long it had been since she'd had a 'girlie' night out. When she had first come to London she had regularly met up with friends, usually other girls with modelling aspirations. They had gone out in a group and, although it had all been rather silly, they had enjoyed themselves. They had dressed up in cheap but flashy clothes, dined in small Chinese or Italian restaurants and gone to a pub for drinks or maybe, a reasonably priced nightclub. They had giggled and laughed and drank too much. It had been fun.

Whatever had happened to those girls?

Karen sighed and then jumped when the phone rang. She snatched at it. 'Hello.'

'Karen? Hi, it's Sarah.'

Disappointed, Karen frowned. 'Who?'

'Sarah. Sarah Fenton-Brown.'

'Oh!'

Karen was nonplussed. After initially meeting and talking to the tall, leggy girl with the fabulous looks, Karen had mentioned her to Claudia Steiner, telling her of Sarah's stunning potential and that the kid had signed with a mediocre agency. Claudia had done the rest: she had contacted Sarah, interviewed her and bought her contract from the original agency. And Sarah was proving a good buy – Karen had seen the layout proofs from her latest job. It was for a cigar ad and Sarah had been sprawled on a car rug in the briefest black-leather halter top and shorts blowing smoke rings. The heady combination of sleaze and class had worked a treat.

Karen had seen Sarah at the agency a couple of times but had never had the time for a proper conversation with her. So why was Sarah ringing her now?

Apparently understanding Karen's bewilderment, Sarah explained, 'I was talking to Claudia earlier in the week and she mentioned you'd had to drive to Yorkshire. Some kind of family trouble, she said – she didn't elaborate. Anyway, I thought I would give you a ring to say I hope things worked out.'

Karen smiled. 'That's good of you, thanks.' She gave a small sigh. 'There hasn't been a completely happy solution but it's better than it was.' She sat down on the carpet, cradling the phone against her face. 'As a matter of fact, I've just arrived back.'

'Oh, then I'm sorry I've bothered you. You must have things to do.'

'Not really.' Karen glanced around the silent flat. 'In fact, I was feeling a bit flat.'

She heard Sarah chuckle.

'I think I know what you mean. After I've been home to visit, I always feel like an orphan when I get back again. I'm the only girl out of a family of four and Mum and Dad spoil me rotten. I get breakfast in bed, the full works. They're sure I'm starving myself to death in London. They're lovely, really, but we've grown miles apart in a few short months. I'd go mad if I had to live with them permanently. Parents always want you to be like them, don't they?'

Karen thought of her conversation with her mother and was silent.

With a naivety that was charming, Sarah said, 'You've gone quiet. Sorry if I've put my foot in it.'

Karen burst out laughing. 'No, it's all right. In fact—' She paused. 'I'm glad you rang. I was feeling a bit lonely. I wonder . . .' She paused again. 'Are you busy this evening?'

'No.'

'Then perhaps we could meet for a chat? Nothing high key. You could come round here or we could meet in a wine bar. Where exactly do you live?'

Sarah told her.

'Oh, that's not so far away.' Karen thought for a moment. 'Do you know the Green Parrot Wine Bar in Kelsey Street?'

Sarah said that she did.

'Shall we meet there, then? That is, if you haven't anything better to do?'

'Sure, I'd like that. I was only going to wash my hair.' Sarah laughed. 'I'll see you in about an hour.'

When Karen walked into the Green Parrot Sarah was already there, lounging on a high stool, her elbows propped on the bar. Every man in the place under the age of fifty was staring at her. Karen could see why.

Wearing a short-sleeved lemon tee-shirt topped by a cashmere sweater slung around her shoulders, her long legs sheathed in lemon and blue silk trousers, Sarah looked like an androgynous version of a young Audrey Hepburn. When she turned and waved at Karen and her apple-sized breasts rolled a little beneath her tee-shirt, there was a collective sigh from the onlookers.

Karen couldn't help smiling. She felt no jealousy over Sarah's undoubtable effect on the wine bar's clientele. She knew her own slim but curvy figure and her blonde feminine looks served as a foil to Sarah's, enhancing both their appearances. She went up to Sarah and asked, 'What are you drinking?'

'Chablis. I bought a bottle. Was that all right?' Sarah picked up the bottle of wine near her elbow and showed it to Karen.

'Yes, that's fine.' Karen nodded to the man behind the bar and he handed her a wine glass.

Sarah gestured towards an empty booth. 'We'll go there, shall we? I think I can feel eyes boring into my back.'

'They're not interested in your back,' Karen laughed and followed the six-foot model to one of the booths. There was a soft exhaled sigh of collective breath and then a murmur of voices as the males in the bar picked up on their previous conversations.

Against a background of muted voices and soft music, Sarah stretched out her long legs beneath the table and looked at Karen. 'I'm glad you suggested meeting because I've been wanting to talk to you.'

'Have you? Why?'

'Well, we've seen each other at the agency but never alone.' Sarah paused. 'You see, I wanted to thank you.'

Karen wrinkled her brow. 'What for?'

'For mentioning me to Claudia Steiner.'

Karen flushed. 'Oh, that was nothing.'

'It bloody was!' Sarah twisted the stem of her wine glass. 'I was with a totally crap agency and you rescued me.'

'I saw your potential.' Karen shrugged. 'And I realised you were with the wrong people.' She sneaked an apologetic glance at Sarah. 'They should never have put you forward for the TV job.'

'I know.' Sarah gave a wide grin. 'Not exactly an English rose, am I?'

'No. And you want to thank your lucky stars you're not. There are dozens of English-rose types around but not many girls with your looks and body.'

'Thanks for the compliment.' Sarah raised her glass and gave Karen a mock toast. She drank. 'At least, I assume it was a compliment.'

'It was.' Karen studied her companion's face and said, 'I remember, when I first saw you, I thought I'd kill for those looks.'

'Really?' Sarah shook her head. 'How strange, because when I was a kid, I loathed everything about myself. Mum would stick me into a frilly frock and drag me off to parties where I always stood head and shoulders above everyone else, including the boys.' She grimaced. 'I was skinny, my hair was wispy and wouldn't curl and I inherited my nose from my paternal grandma who, by all accounts, was a female version of Rasputin.'

Karen laughed. 'Yes, but look how you've turned out! You're a walking advert for Hans Andersen's fairy story about the ugly ducking. You've turned into a swan.'

'Thank you for those kind words.' Sarah looked embarrassed. She changed the subject. 'But what about you?'

'What about me?'

'Well, it's all round the office that your TV debut is causing a few waves in important ponds.'

'Really!' Karen's eyes brightened. 'Nothing much had happened before I left London for Yorkshire. I've spoken to Claudia on the phone but she didn't say anything definite, only that a few possibilities had been sparked off.'

She looked eagerly at Sarah. 'Anything specific you can tell me?'

'God, no.' Sarah refilled their wine glasses. 'Claudia's far too circumspect to divulge hard facts to us mere models – but I'm positive things are looking good for you.' She raised her glass. 'Let's drink to our successful careers.'

They drank and laughed, talked and drank again. For comparative strangers, they felt amazingly comfortable with each other. They were also serious wine drinkers. At the end of their second bottle, Karen asked, with owlish intensity, whether Sarah was driving.

Sarah said, 'No. I came by cab.'

'So did I,' said Karen. 'So let's have another bottle.'

They watched the wine waiter uncork the wine of their choice and then, when he left them, they began to talk about boyfriends. Or rather, Sarah did. She had Karen helpless with gales of laughter as she described the men she had dated since coming to live in London.

Then she became more serious. 'I'm seeing Saul Clunny at the moment. Do you know him?'

'The name sounds familiar.'

'He's an angel – in the theatrical sense. He's backed a lot of West End shows. Filthy rich, of course.'

'Is that why you're going out with him?' Relaxed and hazy with wine, Karen had renounced the etiquette of asking noncontroversial questions.

'Not at all.' Sarah was unfazed by Karen's question. She shrugged elegant shoulders. 'Actually, I don't give a fuck about money.' She saw Karen's eyes flick and apologised.

'Sorry, I forget some people don't like the f-word. The county set use it all the time. Anyway—' She dismissed the subject of swearing and answered Karen's question. 'I go out with Saul because he's lovely. He's twenty-three years older than me, he's five inches shorter and he's got a paunch but he's the wittiest man I have ever met. He's kind and he's funny and when he's with me, he gives me his complete attention and that's rare nowadays, as I'm sure you know.'

'Too true.' Karen nodded owlishly and dredged up memories of her old boyfriends. She regaled Sarah with some of her funnier experiences with men, ending up with an exaggerated description of her television co-star Roddy Champion and his collection of Roman coins. The two men she didn't mention were Carl Padget and David.

When she had finished, the wine bar was almost empty and the barman was sending them meaningful looks. Karen yawned and stretched. 'I guess it's time we went home, Sarah.' She nodded towards the man behind the bar. 'Shall I ask that guy to phone the taxi company?'

'Yes, but not for a few minutes.' Sarah's face was flushed but there was a determined set to her mouth. She said, 'There's something I want to ask you, Karen.'

Alerted by the seriousness of her voice, Karen nodded. 'Fire away.'

Sarah fiddled with her empty wine glass. 'I hope you don't mind me asking, but are you going around with David Asher?'

'Why, yes.' Karen stared at her friend in astonishment. 'How do you know that?'

Sarah began a sigh which she immediately suppressed. 'I thought it was you,' she said. 'I spotted you leaving a restaurant with David. I only caught a glimpse of your backs but I knew David, of course, and I thought the woman was you.'

A sick feeling began to stir in Karen's stomach. She asked,

'What do you mean, you knew David?'

Sarah stared directly into Karen's eyes. 'I would know David anywhere. You see, I practically grew up with him. His mother and father have a house thirty miles away from my parents' home and, when we were young, David used to come over to play with my brothers. They all went to the same prep school.'

Karen smiled with relief. 'Oh, I see. I thought you were going to say you'd been seeing him too. Stupid of me, I suppose, but I know he goes to places where media people congregate and it would be perfectly possible for you to have . . .'

Sarah cut across Karen's nervous conversation. 'I guess I'm the one model he wouldn't go out with.'

Karen fell silent, frowning at her friend's remark. 'I don't see what you're driving at?'

Sarah leaned across the table and spoke rapidly but clearly. 'David's not bad – I'm not saying that – but he's not a man to fall in love with.'

'I'm not in love with him.' Karen's denial died on her lips as Sarah looked at her.

'Everyone falls for David. They can't help it. He's such a charmer. He can't help it, either.'

Sarah looked gloomy. 'But he's bad news if you're after a steady relationship. You see, he's like a kid with a box of chocolates. He has to taste every flavour. David's absolutely devoted to cultivating beautiful people who are in the news. Up-and-coming pop stars, writers, stage actresses, models—' Sarah gave Karen a significant look. 'The trouble is, after a few weeks with one, he starts looking around for the next conquest.'

Karen stared down at the table. 'But it wasn't like that with me. David had to come to the set to see the producer he works for. And, anyway, I'm not a famous model.' She raised her eyes and tried to outstare Sarah.

'Not yet.' Sarah nodded her head slowly. 'But the signs are

there for all to see. And David will have known that through his work.'

'Oh, this is ridiculous.' Karen pushed back her chair. 'If anyone made the running, it was me. I fancied him as soon as I laid eyes upon him. David only came over to me to get my autograph for his little sister. She wants to be a model when she grows up.'

A look of pity flickered across Sarah's face. She said, 'You really care for him, don't you?'

'Yes.' Karen's voice faltered. 'I do.'

In the short silence that followed her words, Sarah's long, pink-tipped fingernails drummed on the table. 'David's an only child,' she said. 'He hasn't got a little sister.'

Karen gasped. Her head spun.

Sarah got up and came round to her, putting her hand beneath Karen's elbow. 'Let's get out of here,' she said. 'We could both do with some fresh air.'

She walked with Karen towards the door, asking, over her shoulder, for the barman to ring for two taxis. She stopped to pull a handful of pound coins from her tiny clutch purse and threw them on to the counter.

'Thanks. We'll wait outside.'

The man nodded and collected up the coins, his face impassive.

'He thinks we're pissed,' remarked Sarah, as they stood outside the wine bar, beneath the smart green and white striped awning. 'I suppose we are.'

Despite her incipient sadness, Karen choked. 'I had you all wrong, Sarah.' She shook her head. 'I thought you were a quiet, nervous young woman.'

Sarah looked surprised. 'Who? Me?'

'Yes.' Karen shook her head and then clutched at it, groaning. Sarah's remarks about David were swimming around in her consciousness but they hadn't properly sunk in. When they did, Karen knew she would feel unhappy but for now, she had to concentrate on staying upright.

She said, thickly, 'At the interview, when we first met, you looked scared to death.'

Sarah snorted. 'I *was* scared to death. You have no idea how quickly my life changed. One minute I was grooming horses and eating cucumber sandwiches with my mother and her buck-teethed friends, and the next I was in a seedy little room in the east end of London having my half-naked body photographed by a peculiar photographer who looked like a cross between Mad Max and Vincent Price.'

Karen snorted. 'I've worked with him, too.' She leaned against the wall of the wine bar and screamed with laughter.

Sarah joined in. 'The Mad Max bit of him wasn't bad, was it?' She wiped her streaming eyes. 'Maybe he has a brother and we could go out as a foursome.'

They were giggling and clinging to each other when the taxis arrived.

Sarah flung open the door of the first cab and helped Karen get in. Then, her long figure doubled in two, she thrust her head into the cab and said, 'I've had a great night, Karen. Thank you.' Briefly, her hand enclosed Karen's. 'I'm sorry if I've punctured a romantic dream, but David isn't worth too many tears. He can be charming, I know, but he's a proper little shit when he doesn't get his own way. My brother chucked him in our pigsty a couple of times and he always deserved it.'

A brief smile, a squeeze of the hand, and she was gone.

Karen gave her address to the cab driver and, as he drove off, she glanced through the back window. The last thing she saw of Sarah was her amazingly long legs folding themselves into the parked taxi.

She sat back and dabbed away the tears on her cheeks. She

was sad. She was very sad. But then she thought of Sarah's last words and she remembered the way David had pouted when she had insisted on going home to see her parents.

She stared out at the near empty streets, at the rain puddles reflecting the street lamps, and thought she must ring Claudia tomorrow. If she was going to be a star, she wanted to know about it. And then, as the taxi approached her home, she had another idea.

She thought, When Mum's cafe is up and running I'll take Sarah to York for a weekend. I don't know what Dad will make of her but I bet she and Mum would get on like a house on fire.

Chapter Thirty

'Yes?'

Marigold was breathless when she picked up the telephone. She had been sitting on the floor in the bay-windowed room when she'd first heard it ringing and, initially, had decided to ignore it. She was busy. Surrounded by neat little piles of paper, she was trying to decide which job to tackle first. When the phone rang she was studying a plumber's estimate. But her caller was undoubtedly stubborn because the ringing went on and on, and finally Marigold stood up, brushed the dust from her trousers and rushed downstairs.

And now, the idiot on the other end of the line wasn't answering! 'Hello,' she said again.

As she waited impatiently for a response, she glanced around her. The living room was so crowded, she must find the time to do something about it. She had brought a few of her own bits and pieces from the house she now thought of as Ian's home, and they jostled for space with Adam's stuff. Adam was going to transfer more of his belongings to his cottage, he said, when he had time to spare.

Marigold looked at the rose-strewn sofa and chair and hoped he would leave them behind because, she thought, they belonged in this house – her house now. She smiled, relishing the thought, and marvelled at how much had been accomplished in a few short weeks.

The contracts had been signed and exchanged. She had paid the deposit and a few days ago, the arrangements for her new mortgage had been finalised. The planning permits had come through and next week the builders were coming in.

She was tired, mentally and physically, and she hadn't seen any of her friends for ages, but she was sublimely content.

'Mrs Goddard?'

At last, a voice. The person on the other end of the telephone was prepared to speak.

'Yes.' Marigold cradled the phone to her cheek.

'I have a message for Mrs Goddard.'

Marigold suppressed her feeling of irritation. Her caller seemed ill at ease, nervous rather than difficult.

She said, 'Yes, this is Mrs Goddard speaking. How may I help you?'

'Please, you must come at once.'

Her brow wrinkling, Marigold asked, 'Come where?'

'You must come at once to see your friend, Mrs Scott.'

Alarm bells began ringing in Marigold's head. She said, 'Why? What's happened to Sheila?'

'I am Mrs Aliraj. I live in the same house as Mrs Scott. She asked me to ring. I will go and tell her you are coming.'

The woman replaced the receiver and the line went dead.

Oh, God. What's happened now? Has one of the boys been hurt?

She looked down at her creased, dusty clothes. After Adam had moved out of the big upstairs room, she had scrubbed the floor twice but to little avail – the cumulative effect of his years of sanding down, scraping and polishing was not easily eliminated. The dust came from nowhere and she was covered in it. She looked decidedly scruffy, but had she time to change?

No. Better not. If Sheila wasn't able to phone for herself,

something was seriously wrong. Marigold found her purse and car keys and hurried to the door.

There was a hold-up in the traffic leading into the road where Sheila lived. Marigold, trapped between a red mini and a parcels van, fidgeted in her car and strained to see what was happening ahead of her. After several minutes fuming, she got out and walked forward to find out what she could. She saw that a traffic barrier had been erected just before the area of road where the bed and breakfast hotel was situated. A stern-faced, well-built policeman stood by.

Marigold, pushing aside a feeling of impending disaster, pasted a smile on her face and went up to speak to the police officer. 'Good day. Are you able to tell me why this road's blocked?'

In a chilly voice he told her that no access was available, 'at the moment.'

'Why? Has there been a road accident?'

She sneaked a look round his blue-clad bulk. There was none of the usual signs of a car crash: no skidmarks, no fragments of glass, no irate, red-faced drivers arguing. In fact, the area was remarkably quiet. There were a couple of beat-up cars parked in driveways but, as far as she could remember, they had been there for months.

Without warning, there was a cracking noise and a large roof slate came hurtling down from a height and smashed into smithereens on the road.

Marigold jumped.

The police officer coughed. 'You'd better return to your car, madam. This road will remain closed to traffic for some considerable time.' He gazed at her, an impassive look on his face. 'If you require help in re-routing your journey, a traffic policeman will be arriving in a few minutes. He will be able to help.'

'No, no. This road *is* my destination.' With a distracted gesture, Marigold ran her fingers through her hair. 'A Mrs Sheila Scott lives in there.' Marigold pointed to the bed and breakfast hotel. 'I've had a telephone message asking me to come and see her.'

'Mrs Scott?' The name had caught the police constable's attention. 'The woman with two young boys?'

'Yes.' Worry had made Marigold's throat dry. She swallowed. 'Has something happened to them?'

Instead of answering her, he asked his own question. 'You a friend of the family, then?'

'Yes, I am.'

He deliberated for a moment and then made up his mind. 'I'll let you go in. I daresay the mother could do with a bit of support.'

Then something had happened to one of the boys.

'Oh, thank you.' Marigold made a move to go round the barrier but the policeman barred the way.

'You'll have to pull your car out of the traffic first. The congestion's building up. I never knew so many people used this road as a cut-through.'

'Yes, I will.'

Thanking him again, Marigold hurried back to her car. She got in and, despite rude comments from the man in the van behind her, managed to edge her car backwards and pull out of the queue of traffic. She parked on a dilapidated piece of land fronting a block of four run-down flats. Cars were probably not allowed there but she had more important things to worry about.

She rushed back to the traffic barrier, nodded to the policeman as she hurried past and then crossed over to the hotel and ran up the flight of steps leading to the entrance.

Inside the building, in the lobby, a plump man wearing a navy three-piece suit was talking loudly to another policeman. He was red-faced and blustering, and Marigold guessed the man in the suit was the owner of the building.

The policeman waved him to silence and asked what Marigold was doing in the building. She told him the first policeman had given her permission to come in to see Mrs Scott. He nodded, waved her upstairs and turned back to the red-faced man, a look of resignation on his face.

Climbing the stairs was a strange experience for Marigold. She had been up them many times before but never had she felt such a strange atmosphere. She saw no one to speak to but the empty spaces seemed filled, charged with intense emotion. There was a feeling of voracious curiosity and excitement in the very air. On the landings, she heard whispers from slightly opened doors and twice she caught someone peeping out at her, but they shut the door quickly when they realised she had seen them.

When she came to the floor on which Sheila lived, a dark-skinned woman dressed in a blue sari stepped through her doorway. She had obviously been waiting for Marigold.

She smiled shyly and asked, 'Are you Mrs Goddard?'

'Yes. And you are . . .' Sheila couldn't remember the woman's name. She amended her query. 'You are the lady who phoned me?'

'Yes.' The woman's face took on a sad expression. 'You must go up there, please.' She nodded towards the next flight of stairs. 'Mrs Scott is up there.'

'Yes. Thank you.' With her heart beating uncomfortably fast, Marigold climbed the stairs.

She had arrived on the top floor of the hotel. Sheila was standing on the landing. There was a young policewoman with her. A metal loft ladder had been pulled down and the two women were staring upwards at the loft opening in the high ceiling. On the floor to the left of them lay a wooden kitchen chair, on its side, and a long pole with a hook on the end. Marigold thought she recognised the wooden chair as one belonging to Sheila.

'Sheila?'

She turned round. 'Oh, Mari. Thank you for coming. I didn't know who else to phone.' She rushed up to Marigold and caught hold of her hands. 'It's Jack. He's done it now.' She began to cry. 'I think he's gone crazy.'

Sheila's hands were shaking like those of an old woman with palsy. Marigold clasped them firmly. 'Where is he? What has he done?'

'He climbed up into the loft and now he's on the roof. If he falls . . .' Sheila's voice died on a sob.

'Are you a member of the family?' the policewoman asked. Her voice was friendly and calm but tension showed in the set of her jaw and in her stiff shoulders.

Marigold shook her head. 'No. I'm a friend, both to Sheila and her boys.' She looked around her. 'Where's Billy, Sheila?'

'At playschool. It was when I was out with him that Jack . . .' Sheila's voice faltered. She pressed her lips together, then said, 'Mrs Aliraj's going to pick him up for me.'

'And Mike?'

Sheila lowered her head. 'I don't know. He left us four weeks ago. Just before you called to see me, to tell me about your cafe.'

'Oh.' Marigold slipped her arm around Sheila's bowed shoulders and sadness welled up inside her. I should have been back to see them all, she thought. No matter how busy I was, I should have kept in touch. I knew they were having a tough time.

She glanced at the policewoman and asked, 'Can you tell me what's happening?'

The young woman hesitated.

'A man raised the alarm at eleven a.m. He rang the station and said something had smashed down just ahead of him as he was driving his car along this road. He got out to investigate and spotted someone on a roof throwing things down at the passing vehicles. The information was passed on to an investigating officer who came here. We found out Mrs Scott's son was the culprit. We Tannoyed a message to him, asking him to come down off the roof but he ignored us so we were forced to close off the road.'

'Jack's only ten years old.' Marigold glared at her informant. 'Are the police worrying about possible damage to cars, or about a disturbed, unhappy little boy endangering his life?'

'Both.' The policewoman sighed when she heard Marigold's sound of exasperation. 'We're doing our best, Mrs . . .?'

'Goddard.'

' . . . Mrs Goddard, but it's a tricky situation. The roof of this building is both steep and dangerous. Our main priority is for Jack's safety. But we can't do anything quickly.' She paused. 'We have a fire engine close by but we dare not use it yet. A policeman has tried to talk to Jack—' She gestured to the loft ladder. 'But the boy refuses to come anywhere near the window. I suppose he thinks we will make a grab for him, and he won't talk to us.' The woman glanced at Sheila. 'We're uncertain as to the state of his mind.'

Sheila gasped and Marigold patted her shoulder. She asked the policewoman, 'So what do you intend to do now?'

'We're trying to contact a teacher from his school – apparently he gets on well with him – and there's a police negotiator on the way.'

'A police negotiator? They're trained to deal with violent men, aren't they? Jack's a child, not an armed gunman holding hostages.'

The policewoman shrugged. 'What else can we do? He won't talk to me. He won't speak to his mother.'

She looked towards Sheila who had shrugged off Marigold's hand and was now pacing up and down the landing, seemingly locked in her own unhappy thoughts.

The policewoman lowered her voice. 'I gather Jack thinks the world of his father?'

'Yes, but that's no help. Sheila doesn't know where he is.'

Marigold stared upwards, into the darkness of the loft opening. 'We have to think of something to get him back inside.' She chewed at her lip. 'What's up there?'

'The usual. The loft is boarded up and empty. It's big – runs across the width of the house – but it's low. A grown-up can't stand upright in it.'

'And how did Jack get up there?'

'He must have found out where the pole was kept.' The policewoman nodded to the long pole lying on the floor. 'The loft ladder would be easy to pull down once he got the hook in the ring. There's one big skylight window in the loft which was locked. Jack smashed the glass and climbed out.'

'Can you see him, from the window?'

'Yes. I went into the loft with the policeman. When we looked for him we saw that he had crawled over to the chimney stack. He was sitting with his back to it. He was within talking distance but too far away for anyone to get a hold on him.'

The young woman shuddered. 'The roof's terribly steep and there's nothing for him to hold on to. I don't know how he managed to stand up and throw tiles down. He must have been in a terrible state, not caring whether he lived or died. I suppose the fact that he's wedged himself against the chimney pot is good. It means he is now aware of the danger he's in.'

Marigold made a decision. 'What if I offered to go up to the loft and talk to him. Would you let me?'

The police officer stared at her. 'It wouldn't be my decision. I would have to ask my superiors.'

Sheila stopped her pacing. 'What did you just say, Mari?'

'I've offered to climb into the loft and see if I can get Jack to talk to me. Then I might persuade him to let the fire officers come and get him down.'

Sheila shook her head. 'It's no good. He won't talk to anyone. He wouldn't even let the police take me up there. He said he didn't want to see me.'

'Yes, but you're his mother.' Marigold spoke soothingly. She could see from Sheila's appearance that she was close to a collapse. 'Since when did kids talk to their mothers?' She forced a smile. 'I thought, if I took things steady . . . talked to him about opening my cafe, asked him to help me by doing little painting jobs or something? Or I could talk about Paddy.'

Sheila listened to Marigold and then nodded. To the police-woman, she said, 'It might work. Jack always enjoyed seeing Marigold.'

Marigold thought about the last time she had seen Jack and felt slightly sick.

'Come on,' she said to the policewoman. 'You've nothing to lose.'

'But the police negotiator will be here soon.'

'Jack will respond more positively to me than to a policeman.' Marigold's gaze bore into the policewoman's face.

'Well . . . I can ask.' Looking dubious, the policewoman produced a mobile phone. 'I'll call them.'

She left Marigold and Sheila and went down the stairs to make her call from the landing below them.

'Oh, Mari.' Sheila's shoulders sagged and she leaned against the wall. 'Thank God you came. I don't know what I would have done without you.'

'I'll stay as long as you need me.' Marigold's voice was gentle. 'And maybe it won't be much longer. You heard what she said. Jack's sheltering by the chimney stack. That means he doesn't want to fall. We've just got to find a way of persuading him to come down. I'm sure we will. He's a sensible lad and he does love you.'

'Does he?' Sheila stared down at the floor. 'I'm not so sure.' She gave a harsh laugh. 'Not that I blame him. I've always been hard on him and since Mike left, I've been terrible. I deserve all this.' She wiped her hand across her face. 'I deserve this pain. I'm a lousy mother.'

Marigold shook her head. 'That's not true. You're only saying that because you're so upset. Good God, Sheila, you've had a rotten time of it. I dare say you've bawled Jack out from time to time, but you've kept your family together.'

'No.' Sheila raised her head and looked at Marigold. 'No, you haven't been there when things have been really bad. After Mike went, I was terrible to Jack. Billy escaped because he was so little, but I put Jack through it. It's no wonder he doesn't want to see me.'

She drew a quivering breath. 'Now I've lost Mike and I might lose Jack. If it wasn't for Billy . . .'

'Stop it, Sheila.' A dismayed Marigold tried to rouse Sheila from her misery. 'Talking like that is no good to anyone. Now, more than ever, you've got to be strong.' She glanced upwards, at the loft opening. 'If the police let me, I'm going up there and I'm going to get Jack to come back down. And when he's off that damned roof and with us again, I want him to see you smiling, do you hear?'

Sheila stared at her. 'But what if he's moved round to where he can't hear you?'

'Then I'll go out on the roof.'

'You'd do that?' Sheila shook her head. 'But it's so dangerous.'

'I don't care.' Marigold, surprised, realised she meant it. 'I'll do anything in my power to fetch him down safely.'

'But, Mari, you mustn't risk your own life. It's not as if Jack is your own flesh and blood.'

Tears stung the back of Marigold's eyes. She blinked. 'I wish he was, Sheila. Oh, how I wish he was.'

The policewoman was walking up the stairs. Marigold, nerves tensed, waited for her. 'What did they say?'

'You can try it. You can go into the loft and try talking to him through the window. If he's maintained his position by the chimney stack, he'll be able to hear you. He must be getting tired now and possibly cold, so he may listen to you. If he agrees, you can stay in the loft where he can see you but you'll have to contact us by mobile phone. Then we can ask the fire people to put up a ladder and bring him down that way. Oh, and I'll have to come up into the loft with you.'

'But that would be wrong. If Jack sees you, he won't cooperate with me. You said he wouldn't talk to the policeman.' Marigold smiled sweetly. 'Don't you think it would be much better if I went up there on my own? Besides, Mrs Scott got very agitated while you were downstairs. I think she needs your support.'

Marigold looked towards Sheila who nodded and clutched at the policewoman's arm. 'Please, stay with me.'

The policewoman looked undecided and then she nodded. 'All right. What you say makes sense. But you'll need this.' She handed Marigold her phone. 'Just press this button—' She indicated. 'And my boss will reply. He'll do anything you want to bring this business to a satisfactory conclusion.'

'Thank you.'

Marigold stuffed the phone into the deep pocket in her trousers. She looked up the metal staircase and, as she began to climb the steps, she thought how fortunate it was that she hadn't changed her clothes.

The loft area was as the policewoman had described: long,

low and dusty. Marigold sneezed as she edged her way towards the window on her hands and knees. Outside, she knew, the day was growing cooler but the loft area had retained heat from earlier hours and it was that which caused the perspiration gathering between her breasts and on her face. She moved to wipe her cheeks and a thousand dust motes danced before her eyes.

There were fragments of glass beneath the broken window. Again, Marigold blessed the fact she was wearing thick trousers. She edged forward and looked out.

The roof was frighteningly steep and the grey tiles gleamed in the setting sun. She looked round for Jack. Her heart ached at the sight of the thin form pressed against the chimney stack. She saw the profile of his white face; there was a grimy mark on his cheek where he had rubbed away tears. He was in a crouching position, his head back, his eyes staring at nothing.

As quietly as she could, she removed some fragments of glass from the wooden window frame and then put her head through. She said, softly, 'Jack.'

Stubbornly, he did not look. 'Go away,' he said.

'Jack.' She spoke louder. 'It's me, Marigold.'

Now his head did turn in her direction. He looked at her, shocked. 'What are you doing here?'

'Well—' She shrugged. 'You wouldn't talk to the policeman. I thought I'd give it a try.'

He turned his face away. 'I'm not talking to anyone. So you might as well go home.'

'Oh, no. Jack. I'm not going to do that. I've too much invested in you to give up on our friendship.'

She waited. He gave no indication of having heard her. Marigold silently debated her next move.

'Did you enjoy throwing down the roof tiles, Jack?'

Nothing.

'I don't suppose you wanted to hurt anyone. In fact,' she hastened to reassure him, 'I don't think you did, although you dented a few cars. I suppose you were so angry you wanted to do something outrageous. Well, you did. You've made your point. You're angry with everyone. But don't you think it's time you came down from that roof now, to actually tell someone what's upsetting you? Maybe, that way, some of what's wrong can be put right?'

Her heart leapt into her mouth because he started to move. He fitted his fingertips beneath the roof tiles he was sitting on and shuffled his body around so that his back was facing her.

She stared at his thin form and the sticking-up piece of hair on the crown of his head and felt despair. Why did she think she could help him when everyone else had failed? She had let him down, too.

When she spoke again, her voice was quiet with suppressed tears. 'I don't blame you for being angry with grown-ups, Jack. We've all let you down, haven't we? It's no wonder you don't trust us.'

She fell silent. He made no move but, looking at his back, she became sure he was listening to her. She dared to continue to speak to him. 'But what you've got to remember, Jack, is that grown-ups aren't much different from kids. They can't always control their lives, although it must seem that way to you. And like kids, they sometimes take out their sadness and their anger on other people, just like you did by throwing things down on the cars.'

Marigold paused and then said, quietly, 'I've been talking to your Mum. She's blaming herself for all this happening. She told me she was a lousy mother. She said she's behaved very badly towards you.' She thought she saw Jack hunch his shoulders but she might have been mistaken.

She spoke louder. 'I just feel it's pointless, you sitting out on the roof, and it's dangerous, too. You might fall. What a waste that would be, Jack.' She held out her hand, beseechingly. 'I've got a phone with me. Why not agree to let me contact the police? They could have a ladder up here in a matter of minutes. Then you could come down and we could talk things through.'

Jack turned his head and she saw his face. She saw the patches of dark shadow beneath his eyes and she saw he was crying.

'Oh, Jack,' she said. 'Please listen . . .'

'Shut up,' he shouted. 'Please, shut up. I'm sick of you. I'm sick of you pretending to be my friend and talking, always talking. You can't alter anything. It's a shit world and I'm not going to listen to anyone. You go on and on about talking things through but it doesn't do any good. I want you to go away and leave me alone.'

He paused, his mouth open. 'What are you doing?'

Marigold, her body halfway through the window, winced as a sliver of glass penetrated her trousers.

'I've stopped talking,' she said. 'I'm doing something. I'm coming over to sit next to you.'

Chapter Thirty-One

Inch by perilous inch, Marigold crawled her way towards Jack. As he had done, she used the tips of her fingers, hooking them around the over-lapping roof tiles to give her, if nothing else, an illusion of control. She kept her body as flat as possible to the roof and before every movement she tested the area around her with the toe of her sports shoe. When she reached the chimney against which Jack sheltered, she gave a huge gasp of relief.

'You'd better move to there.' His voice betraying no emotion, Jack pointed towards the side of the chimney stack.

Marigold groaned. 'Must I?'

'Yes. You can't stay where you are. The roof's too sloping. You'd have to brace your legs against the guttering to keep your balance and, if you do that, you might get cramp. If that happens, you'll probably fall off.'

Marigold glanced at the roof and seeing the sense of his words, inched her way to the place Jack had indicated. When she reached the relatively safer area, she dared to sit up, but she found she couldn't bear to look around her. She therefore fixed her gaze straight ahead and began to doubt the wisdom of her impetuous action.

There was silence for a few minutes. Marigold, using her eyes but not her head, glanced sidewards, towards Jack. He was watching her. He did not speak. Another five minutes went by. At least, she guessed it was five minutes. She dared not move to check her watch. She breathed deeply. How could she help Jack if she was paralysed with fear?

A few minutes later she began to feel pain at the top of her spine and in her neck. She sighed gustily.

Then Jack spoke to her. He asked a question. 'You're scared to death, aren't you?'

Marigold stared straight ahead. Jack's voice held a curious note of ambiguity. He sounded, she thought, as though he didn't know whether to despise or admire her.

'Yes.' Her voice was clipped. 'Aren't you?'

'Not really. You're safe enough, so long as you're careful.'

She didn't answer. She moved her eyes, glancing upwards towards the sky, where the blue was shifting away, leaving a pale, milky colour. She heard Jack's shoes scrabble on the tiles and wondered if he was coming to join her. She held her breath. He was not wearing trainers, she could tell from the noise he was making. She prayed the shoes he *was* wearing were not studded. What would she do if he fell? She heard more noises and forced herself to turn her head and look at him, and when she saw what he was doing the panic rose in her throat.

'Jack,' she said, her voice harsh. 'For God's sake, come away from the edge.'

'I'm all right.' Jack was on his hands and knees, peering over the edge of the guttering. 'There's a piece of drain pipe sticking up. I've got hold of it.'

She swallowed hard and watched his back as he bobbed up and down.

He stared downwards for a few moments and then turned his head towards her. 'There's lots of activity going on. Another police car's arrived and there's bluebottles everywhere. They're all looking up here.'

'Will you come away from there.' Marigold could feel the perspiration leaking out of her skin.

'If you like.' Crablike, Jack scuttled back to his place by the chimney stack. He looked across at her with a glimmer of a smile on his face. 'I guess it's because of you coming out. I bet they had heart attacks when they spotted you up here.'

'And I'm having one too. Can we go down now, Jack?' She stretched her neck and cautiously turned her head from side to side.

He ignored her question. He asked, 'Why are you doing that?'

'My neck hurts.'

He nodded. 'That's because you're not relaxed,' he said wisely.

'Oh, Jack.' Marigold felt an hysterical desire to laugh.

'Why did you come on the roof?'

Her wish to laugh disappeared immediately. Jack was talking to her. He was asking questions. She prayed she might come up with the right answers.

'You said I talked too much.' She paused. 'Maybe you're right. But if I do, it's only because I want to help you. But you said something else. You said I wasn't your friend. You got that wrong, Jack. I am your friend and that's why I'm here with you even though—' She forced her stiff lips to smile. 'I'm frightened to death.'

He turned his face away. 'I bet that's not true. The police asked you to come out here, didn't they? They want you to persuade me to come off the roof.' He looked away from her and began fiddling with something at the base of the chimney stack.

He's probably detaching another slate, thought Marigold, miserably. What the hell am I doing up here?

'The police didn't ask me anything. I asked them if I could go into the loft to try and talk to you. They told me to stay off the roof. I'm going to be in as much trouble as you when we finally go down.' She stared at him, willing him to react but he remained silent. She raised her voice. 'And of course I want you off this damned roof. I don't want to bash my brains out on the street below, neither do I want you to.'

He stopped scraping on the roof tiles to give her a thoughtful look. He asked, 'Have you been to see Paddy?'

'What?' She jerked her head backwards and then grabbed at the brickwork of the chimney as she felt her feet slide. 'What has Paddy got to do with this?'

'Nothing. I just wondered how he was.'

'Well, since you ask—' Marigold moistened her lips with her tongue. 'Paddy's fine. My husband and I have reached an agreement. Paddy will live with Ian but I can go and see him and take him for walks whenever I want.'

'That's good.' Jack nodded his head, gravely.

'Yes, it is.' Marigold, totally at sea with the strange conversation, lapsed into silence. She hadn't a clue what to say next.

It was up to Jack to make the next move. He said, quietly, 'You can go back into the house, you know. There's no point you staying out here when you're so scared.'

She shook her head. 'I won't go without you.'

Jack sighed and ran his hand over his hair. 'I won't jump. I'm not that stupid.' He paused. 'Although I know I was stupid to get into such a mess.' He shook his head.

'I'd like to know why you did it, Jack.' Marigold's voice was quiet.

He hesitated. 'I don't think I can explain. It sounds so . . .' He hesitated, then squared his shoulders and looked over at her. 'I think you were brave to come out here, so I guess I owe it to you to tell you what happened. The truth is, I got into a rage and then I went mad.' He bowed his head. 'The daft thing is, when I was coming home from school, I was feeling pretty good. I'd come top in my science exam and – oh, I can't explain. I expect you know that my dad's cleared off?' He brought up his head and stared at her.

'I didn't. When I came round today, your mother told me.'

'Well, I've been miserable.' He shifted uncomfortably. 'But today, for some reason, I felt better.' He sighed. 'When I turned the corner into the road, I saw the owner of this place pull up outside in a new car. He comes around about once a month.' Jack's lip curled. 'To pick up his money, I expect. He certainly doesn't come to see if the tenants are OK. Anyway, I stopped to look at his car. He'd got out and was locking it with one of those electronic bleepers. I was only looking. And then he turned and called me something.'

Jack drew a deep breath. 'There was no call for him to do that. I wasn't doing anything. And then he told me to keep my dirty paws off his property. And that's when it all started.' Jack hunched his shoulders and put his head down on his knees.

'I was really stupid. I know that now. I mean, heaps of worse things have happened to me but, somehow, I just couldn't help myself.'

He looked up at Marigold and she saw the tear tracks appear on his dirty face.

'It was like a kettle came to the boil in my head. I knew if I didn't get rid of the pressure I'd just flip, go really crazy. So I went up to the top floor and got into the loft.'

'You'd been there before?'

'Yes, but only to look around. But this time, I broke the window and climbed out on the roof. Even then, I didn't know why I was doing it. I just wanted to get away somewhere, be by myself. I stood up and looked round and I felt great. I wasn't afraid. I knew I wouldn't fall. I looked down and saw little people and little cars and it was as if I was the king. I could do whatever I wanted. It was wonderful until—' His voice sank into a whisper. 'I saw that fat git's car and then I felt different. I wanted to get back at him. I ripped up a couple of slates and threw them down. One hit his car, and then—' His glance at Marigold was shamefaced. 'I think I did go mad.' He rubbed his eyes with his knuckles. 'Do you think I'm turning into a psycho?'

'Of course not. You're just a young man who has had to cope with a lot of trouble.' Marigold's voice was steady, certain.

'But will the police think that? I've already been in trouble. They'll put me away for sure, after this.' Jack covered his face with his hands. 'It's not so much me, it's Mum. She's got enough to worry about.'

'Your mum will be fine, as soon as she knows you're safe on the ground again.'

'I don't know.' Jack's voice was muffled. 'I've been awful, lately. After Dad left, I gave her a hard time.'

'That's strange, because your mother told me something similar. But she said it was her who had given *you* the bad time.' Marigold wanted desperately to be beside Jack but she knew that was impossible, so she tried to put utter conviction into her voice. 'I've some idea of what you've all been going through, Jack. I know it's been bad but I still think things are going to get better.'

He shook his head. 'How can they? Dad's never going to get a job. We don't even know where he is. There's just Billy and me and Mum now and if they put me away there will only be Mum and Billy.' His voice cracked.

Watching him, Marigold forgot her fear of heights. She shuffled along on her knees until she could reach out and touch him with her hands. The position of the chimney stack made it impossible for them to sit side by side but she crouched down to the right of him and grabbed his right hand.

'Things will turn out all right,' she said fiercely. 'I swear it on my life.'

He glanced at her shamefaced, wiping his nose on the back of his free hand.

'You promise?'

'I promise.' Marigold released his hand, reached into the back pocket of her trousers and took out the mobile phone. 'I'm sick of being up here, Jack. Is it all right if they get us down?'

He nodded.

Within a matter of minutes the fire engine swung round the corner and stopped outside the hotel. Firemen in white helmets jumped off and scurried around, securing and manipulating various pieces of equipment.

Jack, on his feet again, reported to Marigold. 'They're putting up a ladder with a sort of cage thing on the end of it.'

'Are they?' she said, faintly. And thought, I don't even like lifts.

'They're good, aren't they?' Troubles temporarily forgotten, Jack watched in fascination as the cage, manoeuvred by the fireman inside, stopped elevating and moved closer to the roof of the building.

'Yes.' Marigold attempted a smile but failed dismally. She tried to move from her sitting position and realised her legs had ceased to function.

'You all right, lady?' The cage had now ceased moving. The fireman glanced at Jack and then looked over to where Marigold sat.

She nodded. 'I think so.'

The fireman studied her face. 'Maybe you should go down first?'

'No,' she croaked. 'I want you to take Jack.'

The man looked dubious.

'Please,' she said, forcing a smile. 'I'm all right. Jack's been up here hours longer than I have.'

'OK.' The fireman steadied the cage and beckoned to Jack. 'Come on, son.'

Marigold watched as Jack leaped nimbly into the waist-high metal contraption. He turned back and gave her an uncertain smile as the firemen operated a radio-controlled transmitter.

The fireman checked all was secured and then set some kind of mechanism working. Marigold didn't see what. He nodded at her. 'Sit tight, I'll be back before you know it.'

His timescale was obviously different to hers. It seemed an eternity before he reappeared. When he did, Marigold found she couldn't move. There was an embarrassing few minutes as he got on to the roof, coaxed her to move and then, all else failing, lifted her bodily into the metal cage. The descent wasn't much better. She kept her eyes shut until she felt the blessed moment when the cage bumped on to the ground.

The fireman – her saviour – lifted her out and she clung to him for a moment. She was dimly aware of a small crowd of people surrounding her and then she thought, Oh, God. What a sight I must look. She had been dusty when she arrived at the place, now she was positively filthy. She heard the fireman saying, 'This lady could do with a strong cup of tea,' and she wanted to kiss him.

Instead, she thanked him, stepped away and turned to face the people standing around her. The young policewoman was there, her face flushed and her eyes stormy. Marigold gave her an apologetic smile. There was a higher ranking policeman – Marigold knew by the stripes on his arm – there was a man in a dark suit who appeared to be in charge and – Oh, Lord! – there was a photographer. She ducked as he tried to take a picture of her.

'Move that man back,' barked the man in the dark suit. He took hold of Marigold's arm. 'Come with me, please.'

'I thought I was going to get a drink,' she protested.

'You'll get one at the police station.' He marched her towards a dark blue car and opened the back door. 'Get in.'

'But I want to go home. I need a bath.' Marigold was becoming more and more conscious of her dishevelled appearance. Then she realised she couldn't see Jack. She pulled free from the man and looked around.

'Where's Jack?'

'The boy, accompanied by his mother, has already been taken to the police station. You'll be able to see them there.'

'Oh, I see.' Marigold sighed and climbed into the back of the police car. As the man moved to close the door, she said, defiantly, 'I did get him down for you, you know.'

Everything became a bit of a blur at the police station. On arrival, Marigold was shown into a washroom where she was able to use the toilet and tidy up. Then she was interviewed by a polite, bald-headed man who arranged for a pot of tea to be delivered to his office. She didn't remember everything he said. She knew he expressed gratitude to her for persuading Jack to come down from the roof, but he also told her in no uncertain terms that she had been amazingly stupid to risk her own life and disobey police advice.

She nodded at appropriate intervals, drank two cups of tea and then asked if she could see Sheila and Jack.

The man frowned. He left the room, came back after five minutes and said she could see them shortly.

Another half hour passed as she waited. Eventually, a policewoman came for her and took her to another room on the second floor of the building. Inside, sitting by a table, were Sheila, Jack and a stranger – a man of about thirty years of age with curly hair and a thin, humorous face. The man stood up and introduced himself as William Meers, explaining that he worked for the Youth Justice Office.

'My job is to represent Jack's interests when dealing with the police and with the courts.' He sat down again, gesturing to Marigold to sit next to him.

She did so. 'You mean, you're on Jack's side?'

The man smiled. 'You could put it that way. But I'm not here to pat him on the head.'

He glanced at the boy. 'Jack knows how I feel about all the trouble he's caused. He damaged several cars with those slates. What if he had hit one of the drivers?'

Marigold shifted. 'It doesn't bear thinking about.' She hesitated. 'But there were extenuating circumstances, Mr Meers.'

The man sighed and rubbed his chin. 'There always are.'

He glanced across at Jack and his mother. 'Still, in this particular case, I'm hopeful we'll get a good result. You see, most of the juveniles I deal with have multiple problems. They are in constant trouble at school, often their parents have disowned them. No one cares for them and they have nowhere to go. When they're as young as Jack, then the courts have no option but to place them into care. But Jack's actually a lucky young man.'

He smiled at Sheila. 'He has a proper family, albeit with problems, and—' He switched his gaze to Marigold. 'A very good friend. Mrs Scott asked me to allow you to be present for part of this discussion. Normally, I would have refused, but as you've been so helpful . . .'

'She got me down from that roof.' A tide of red flooded Jack's grubby face. 'I'd have still been up there if it hadn't been for her.'

Marigold smiled at him, then looked at Mr Meers. 'Can you tell us what's likely to happen to Jack?'

'He's spoken to the police already. He was most cooperative. The interview was taped and I was there to represent his interests.

They'll let him go home soon, on my recommendation, but he'll be summoned to appear at a Youth Court in due course.'

Sheila spoke up. 'And then what?'

Mr Meers shrugged. 'Various options, depending on social service reports, et cetera. Jack could be lucky. He might get off with a caution. I would guess a conditional discharge.'

'Conditional on him keeping out of trouble in the future?'

'Yes.'

Marigold stared hard at Sheila. Acknowledging her look, Sheila spoke out. 'Mr Meers knows about the other business, Mari.'

'Yes. That was unfortunate.' William Meers paused. 'The lad told us, which was good – but it certainly caused a few waves. Fortunately, after a couple of phone calls, it was established that Jack was innocent of purchasing and selling of drugs. And when he found out what was going on and came to the police, his honesty led to a couple of nasty individuals being caught, so you have no need to worry about that episode.'

'Oh, thank God.'

Marigold smiled and then yawned so wide her jaw cracked. She blushed and apologised.

'That's all right. You must be exhausted, Mrs Goddard. That was a brave act of yours.' Mr Meers grinned. 'Particularly, as I gather from gossip circulating about the rescue, as you don't have a head for heights.' He glanced at Jack. 'You must be tired, too. I'll go and see if you can go home now. If they agree, I'll give you all a lift. Do you have a car, Mrs Goddard?'

'Yes, but it's parked by the hotel.' Marigold yawned again. 'I'd appreciate a lift home.'

'It will be my pleasure.'

The lights were on in the house, which meant that Adam was there. Marigold breathed a sigh of relief and leant against the bellpush, too tired to take her key from her pocket.

The door opened.

'For Christ's sake, Marigold. Where have you been? I was worried. I told you I was coming around eight o'clock and . . .' His words dried when he saw the state of her. 'Are you all right?'

Without waiting for her answer, Adam reached out and pulled her into the hallway. 'What's happened to you?' He paused and his face whitened. 'Have you been attacked?'

'No, no.' She rested her head on his shoulders and burst into tears. 'I've been sitting on a roof-top for hours and hours.'

He guided her through to the living room and sat her down on the sofa.

She gestured to her clothes. 'I'll make it filthy.'

'So what.' He sat down beside her and held her hand. 'What can I do, Marigold? Would you like a drink?'

She closed her eyes. 'I've had some tea.'

He snorted. 'I mean a *proper* drink. What about a brandy?'

'Well.' She opened her eyes and looked at him. 'Yes, I'd like that.'

'Right. Just stay there.'

Adam rushed off into the kitchen.

Marigold sighed and put a cushion behind her back. When Adam returned and handed her a glass, she managed to smile. 'Thanks.'

He nodded and took a gulp from his own glass. 'Can you tell me what happened?'

'I guess so.' Marigold put her glass down and bent over to take off her shoes. Adam pushed her back against the cushions and removed her shoes and socks for her. He sat at the opposite end of the sofa and, hoisting her legs across his lap, he began to massage her toes. 'Take your time,' he said, softly.

She felt like crying again. 'My feet smell,' she warned him.

He smiled at her. 'So what?'

She flopped back on the sofa and picked up her glass, taking a drink. 'Oh, this is bliss.' She closed her eyes.

Adam coughed. 'Before you nod off, I'd like to be told why you look as though you've been cleaning chimneys.'

She began to laugh and almost choked. She waited until she got her breath back and then she said, 'Well, chimneys do enter into the story.'

She told him what had happened.

When she finished he was silent. He looked at her gravely. 'Do you have to do these crazy things, Marigold? I know you care for this lad, but he's not your son.'

She squirmed a little. 'I know, but what else could I do?'

'You could have left it to the professionals. They would have got him down safely.'

'I suppose so, but I couldn't be sure. He was in a bad way, Adam. And he knew me, and, I hope, trusted me.'

Adam shook his head. 'What am I to do with you?'

'You could run me a bath.' Marigold stretched luxuriously. The brandy had worked wonders. She smiled at him. 'You mustn't worry about me. I'm perfectly all right, you see.'

'Thank God for that.' Adam stopped rubbing her feet. He stood up. 'Are you hungry?'

'I don't know.' Marigold considered. 'Yes, I think I am.'

'So am I. So, while you're having your bath, I'll go out and get us a takeaway. Chinese OK?'

'Ummm, yes.' Marigold stretched. 'What a treasure you are. I don't deserve you.'

'That's right.' Adam looked down at her, his face severe. 'Just remember that the next time you're prompted to do something heroic.'

Later that night, cuddled together on the sofa, they talked softly.

Marigold tried to explain to Adam her feelings for Jack, and for Sheila and Billy.

'I don't know why I feel so close to them, Adam, but I do. I think—' She paused. 'I met them when I was having a bad time and I knew they were, too. And Jack really gets to me because he tries so hard to be the man of the family while his father is away.'

Adam stroked her hair. 'Do you think his dad will come back?'

'Oh, I think so. He does love them all, I'm sure.'

He tweaked her nose. 'You're a romantic.'

'I hope so.' She snuggled up to him. 'And that's enough about me. What has your week been like?'

She felt his chest move as he chuckled.

'Not as hectic as yours, that's for sure. I've kept busy and I've also had two bits of good news.'

'Tell me?'

'Well, Di rang on Wednesday and asked me if I would take Sally for the whole of the Christmas holidays.'

Marigold twisted round and sat up. 'That's wonderful, Adam.'

'Yes.' Adam sounded reflective. 'I think that's the first time she's offered me a chance to see my daughter apart from the statutory visits.'

'Perhaps she's mellowing with age.'

'I doubt it.' He laughed but it was not a pleasant laugh. 'But age might have something to do with it. Sally's growing up fast. She's becoming an attractive young lady. Perhaps Di can't stand the competition.'

Marigold reached up and touched his cheek. 'That sounds bitter, Adam. Just be pleased you're going to see your daughter more often.'

He gave her a distant look and then his face relaxed. 'You're right.' He took her hand. 'I want you to meet Sally. I want so much that you and she become friends.'

'I want that, too.'

Marigold smiled at him but felt a stab of foreboding. She thought about her relationship with her own daughter and wondered why she was so much better with boys. Still, Karen had phoned on her return to London and had promised to visit soon and if Sally was anything like her father, she was bound to get on with the child.

She remembered Adam's words. 'And what's the second piece of good news?'

'Oh, that was business. The Trustees of Acre House have written to me. They say they are delighted with my renovation work and want to put me on a permanent contract to maintain the furniture in the house and work on any other pieces they acquire. They also intimated that they could find me other commissions, if I was interested.'

'Oh, Adam. That's wonderful.' Marigold threw her arms around his neck and kissed him.

'Yes, it's pretty good, isn't it?'

She pulled away and looked into his face. 'You don't sound terribly excited.'

He smiled at her and rubbed his forehead. 'Oh, I am. But, as always, success brings problems. I really will have to find someone to work with me now, but I don't know of anyone. And, if I do manage to find a good craftsman, he'll expect a good wage and I can't afford to pay too much. The Trust's not that well off. They give me a fair amount of money but it's not in the same league as if I was working in London, for example. And their work will be spasmodic so I don't want to lose my individual clients, who provide my bread and butter.'

Marigold nodded. 'Yes, I can see your problem.' She thought for a moment. 'I remember you telling me that some of the jobs you get, the customers could almost do themselves.'

Adam frowned. 'Yes, that's true. I do tell some of them that but they can't be bothered. And others, the ones with plenty of money, I don't tell.' He put his head on one side. 'What are you getting at, Marigold?'

A little spark of excitement began to glow inside Marigold. She said, slowly, 'You really need a good, all-round assistant, Adam. Someone who can drive, who's fit enough to lug furniture about and collect and deliver smaller items on his own. It would have to be someone reasonably intelligent and good with his hands. Good enough to learn how to do the jobs that don't need an expert's touch.'

'That's a pretty good summing-up.' Adam eyed her warily. 'What have you got in mind?'

'Just what I said. You need an assistant.'

'Yes.' He nodded. 'But where do I find one? It must be a man I can work with. I'm so used to working on my own.'

'You could still work on your own. But you could work without worry, knowing that the other chap was coping with the smaller jobs.'

'Do you know where I could find such a man?'

'Yes, I do.' Marigold paused, dramatically. 'I've met him and he's a nice chap. It's Mike Scott. Sheila's husband.'

Adam's face changed. 'Oh no, Marigold. Not even for you. I'm not taking on a no-hoper simply because you're trying to keep that family together.'

'He's not a no-hoper. The man can't help not being able to find a job. He's tried hard enough.'

'Well, in that case, I'm sorry for him, but I'm not giving him a job. Anyway, what makes you think you'll be able to get in touch with him? He's done a runner, you told me.'

'Yes, but he'll get in touch with Sheila soon, I know he will.' Marigold clenched her hands into fists. 'Mike loves his family.

He won't be able to stay away from them. He'll ring soon.'

'He can ring her as often as he likes, but I don't want him, Marigold. I need someone skilled with his hands. Didn't you tell me he used to work in a factory?'

'Yes, but he *is* skilled, Adam. I can show you evidence to prove it.' Marigold wished passionately she had the carved fawn with her. 'He does exquisite carvings in wood. Let me pick one up from Sheila tomorrow to show you. Please, let me do that.' She stared at him. 'If you don't like the carving, I'll never mention his name again.'

She waited, breath bated.

Adam pulled at his lip. 'You really thought it was good?'

She nodded.

'Well, in that case, I'll take a look at his work.'

'Oh, you lovely man.' Marigold flung her arms around his neck. 'You won't regret it.'

'I already am.' But he smiled and put his arms around her waist.

'I told you I was a treasure.'

'You are.'

She kissed him and then yawned. 'Can we go to bed now?'

He chuckled. 'I thought you'd never ask.'

Chapter Thirty-Two

It's no good chasing after happiness. If it comes at all, it creeps up on you when you're not looking.

Marigold thought those words one fine summer evening seven months after the opening of her cafe. She was alone at the time, sitting by a table in the Austen room and working on her accounts. The results of her labour pleased her. For the past three months her business had shown a steady profit.

Distracted from her columns of figures by a fluttering noise, she glanced up and saw that a butterfly, a Red Admiral, was in the room. It flew about erratically, investigating the fireplace tiles, bumping against the two blue and white pottery figures displayed on the mantelpiece – Marigold had a fancy the Regency couple resembled Elizabeth Bennet and Mr Darcy – and blundering into the marigolds painting by the window. Finally, it came to a quivering rest on the white muslin curtains framing the window.

Marigold put down her pen, stood up and walked over to rescue the butterfly. She slid her hand beneath the piece of muslin upon which the insect rested and, moving gently, rolled it on to her outstretched palm. It stayed there, motionless apart from a faint quivering of its wings. She stared down at it, admiring the richness of its colouring, which was enhanced by the rays of the sunshine flowing through the window, and she experienced the sensation of perfect happiness.

It lasted for perhaps a minute, or even less, and then the butterfly stretched its wings and Marigold, cupping her free hand over it, hurried from the room and into the back garden where she released it. She watched it fly away, awed by her experience and knowing she would never forget it.

Slowly, she returned to the Austen Room and her work; but she couldn't settle so she wandered around the room, rather like the butterfly had done, touching her collection of growing treasures.

She straightened the prints on the wall, although they didn't need straightening, and stood before her painting, admiring the glowing colours of the paint, the vibrant blue of the jug and the gold tones of the flowers.

Looking at the painting made her think of Tommy, the tramp, and she smiled. Now there was a man who might be able to explain her strange experience to her. Tommy, she had discovered, was a man of knowledge.

He had passed her on the street one day, about four months ago. She had nodded at him and smiled and, after a moment of hesitation, he had smiled back and then, surprising her, had spoken.

'Your cafe, how's it doing?'

His voice was creaky, as though from lack of use, but his accent was that of an educated man.

'Oh, quite well. I suppose.' She had paused, flustered by his knowledge of her life.

Soundlessly, he had laughed. The teeth he had left looked in good condition. 'Adam told me all about it. I walked that way about a week ago and took a look.'

'Did you?' Marigold felt a flicker of annoyance towards Adam. Tommy was an interesting character all right, but best kept at arm's length. If he took it in his head to hang around outside The Marigold Patch, it could spell disaster for her business.

She realised the tramp's light-grey eyes were studying her face and she blushed, uncomfortably aware he was reading her thoughts.

'It looked good. I liked that painting, the one in the window.'

She nodded, surprised at his talkativeness and, despite herself, intrigued. 'Yes. I was with Adam when we first saw it in a shop. It was the same day I decided to go into business for myself. So Adam bought it and I thought I would put it where people could see it, near the window.'

Tommy, as if coming to an important decision, dumped his black bin liner on the pavement and scrabbled in his jacket pocket.

'I do a bit of drawing and painting.' He produced a grimy exercise book which he handed to Marigold.

Conscious of being honoured, she took it gingerly and flicked through the pages. Then she gasped. Line drawings of animals, birds and flowers filled every bit of space. All were beautifully executed. She handed the book back to him.

'They're beautiful, Tommy. Tell me—' She hesitated. 'Did you study art, at a college?'

He thrust the book back in his pocket. 'I was an architect once.' He smiled his gappy smile. 'But I wasn't cut out for the life.' He picked up the bin liner and prepared to move on.

'Wait a minute.' Marigold spoke quickly, not giving herself time to consider the wisdom of her words. 'Can you paint as well as draw?'

He scratched his head. 'Used to. Not so much now, though.'

She explained. 'I've been thinking of getting a couple of small painted plaques, to put above the entrances of the snickelways leading to my cafe. I want something simple. Perhaps a bunch of marigolds and the name of the cafe. I'm hoping visitors will see the signs and be intrigued, so they come and check what they're referring to.'

She paused for breath. 'The authorities have agreed to the idea. They'll come and check to see if the plaques are in good taste and not intrusive but they say there should be no problems. Now that I've seen your drawings, I wondered whether you could paint them for me?'

Tommy considered her idea. 'I don't mind trying my hand.' He nodded. 'I'll do a couple and let you see them. If they suit, that's fine, if they don't—' He shrugged. 'It doesn't matter.'

'Oh, thank you.' Marigold pulled out her purse. 'Let me give you the money to buy the materials. How much do you need?'

For the first time since they started their conversation, Tommy looked uncomfortable. 'Not much. A fiver should cover it.'

'Nonsense. You need more than that.' Marigold offered him a twenty-pound note.

He backed away from her. 'No, that's too much.'

'Of course it isn't.' She held out the money. 'Please take it. You'll have to spend time on the painting. I must pay you for that.'

His eyes lit up with amusement at her comment but he accepted the money without further comment. He nodded goodbye and shuffled away.

One week later, someone knocked on Marigold's side door at half past ten at night. A little warily, she opened it.

Tommy stood on the doorstep. He carried a package roughly wrapped in old newspapers, which he thrust into her hands.

'There you are.' He turned to go.

'Wait a minute.' Marigold pulled off the newspaper and stepped out so that she could see the contents of the package beneath the lights of a nearby street lamp. She held up the plaques. They were perfect. On strips of smooth beechwood,

Tommy had stencilled in and then painted a loosely tied bunch of marigolds. Beneath the flowers, in flowing script, was the name, The Marigold Patch.

'I did three instead of two, so you can dump the one you like least.'

Marigold smoothed her fingers over the glowing flowers. 'I will not. They're all perfect. Thank you, Tommy. They're just what I wanted.'

He shrugged. 'I enjoyed doing them.' He turned away.

'Wait. Where are you going?'

'Why?'

'Why?' She wrinkled her brow. 'Because I must pay you for them.'

He shook his head. 'You already have. The money you gave me was enough.'

He began walking away. She ran after him.

'Tommy, the plaques are wonderful, but I can't accept them unless you allow me to pay you.'

'Throw them away then.'

She frowned. 'That's stupid. I won't throw them away. If you won't accept money is there something else you would like?'

He stood still and asked, 'Do you sell all the food in that cafe of yours?'

'Well, we budget carefully but . . .' She realised the drift of his question. 'No, we don't. We often have stuff left over.'

'Is that so?' He glanced at her. 'Pity to throw food away.'

'Why, yes, it is.' She hesitated. 'Perhaps you could find a use for it, Tommy?'

'I dare say I could.'

'Well, then.' She scratched her chin. 'Suppose you call round every few days, say on Tuesdays and Fridays? I could bag up the surplus food and have it ready for you.'

He grinned. 'That's a fine idea. Thank you.' He started down the road again and then stopped, turned his head and said, 'I'll come late, around nine o'clock at night. I reckon that would suit both of us. And if you're out or you don't want to see me, just leave the bag outside the door.'

He gave her an amused look and went on his way and the arrangement was now well established.

At first, Marigold had worried about their agreement. Tommy was a colourful character but he was also a tramp with unpredictable habits. Suppose he came round when he was drunk or argumentative? She mentioned her worries to Adam who laughed at her.

'I've known Tommy ever since I came to York and he's the most gentle man I've met. You'll have no trouble with him.'

And four months after the deal had been struck, she knew that Adam had been right. Tommy was a gentle man who happened to be a tramp and during their brief, doorstep chats she had come to like and respect him. He was, she realised, an educated man. He had read about alternative religions, folklore and poetry. Now she thought that Tommy might be the only man in the world who would understand her experience of perfect happiness.

She was still staring at her painting when Sheila tapped on the door and came hurrying in.

'That girl has to go, Mari.'

Marigold blinked. 'What girl?'

'That girl that comes in Wednesdays, Thursdays and Fridays. Sonia something, or Sashia, something like that.'

'By go, you mean fired. Why should I do that?'

'Because she's a lazy little cow. I'm always chasing after her and all she does is give me a lot of lip. She smokes in the staff toilet and today I caught her stubbing out a fag in the kitchen.'

'Oh dear, that is bad.'

'Exactly. What if a food inspector had been there?'

Sheila stood very straight and folded her hands over her stomach. She was now Marigold's chief of staff and she relished the post. She chivvied delivery men, cleaners, waitresses and Marigold herself. In appearance, she was still small and thin but she had certainly grown in confidence.

So much so that Marigold occasionally had to give her a gentle reminder that she was the owner of the establishment. This was one of those times.

She shook her head. 'I agree with you about the smoking thing, Sheila, but I think it would be a little harsh to sack the girl. Also, we have to remember she's very pretty and popular with our regular customers. Perhaps you should give her a stern warning that the next time we catch her smoking she will have to leave. And impress upon her that you expect her to work as hard as the other girls.'

Sheila sniffed. 'Warnings don't work with her.'

'Nevertheless, that's my decision.' Marigold studied Sheila's flushed face. 'Has it been a bad day?'

'No.'

'Well then, what is it? Are *you* feeling the need for a smoke?'

'Me!' Sheila's voice shook with indignation. 'I *never* smoke on the premises, you know that.'

'Yes, I do, and I admire your self-control, but I do think your anger towards Sonia might be due to your own frustration.' Marigold made a decision. 'Have you finished for the day?'

'Just about. I was going to check the stores cupboard but I suppose it can wait until tomorrow.'

'Right. Well, why don't you get one of the girls to make us a pot of coffee and then come and sit in the garden with me for ten minutes and drink it. You can have a cigarette there.'

'I thought you were working on the accounts?'

'I was, but they can wait, too. Come on, Sheila.' A coaxing

note entered Marigold's voice. 'It seems ages since we had a chat.'

Sheila began to smile.

After locking away her books, Marigold went through into the back garden and sat down. As she waited for Sheila to join her, she admired the view. Every spare minute she could snatch from her business, she spent working out here. She had dug out all the rubbish, pruned the original plants and shrubs and added more, deliberately mixing colours and flowers of different heights to create a cottage-garden look. And now she was beginning to reap the reward of all her labours. The garden was becoming a riot of colour.

The grey stone wall, which she had covered with all kinds of containers, looked particularly good. Old bicycle baskets held yellow trailing nasturtiums and ancient chimney pots overflowed with gypsophila and godetia. She looked at them with pride and pleasure and had a particular smile for a patch of flowers growing close by the wall. She had told Adam she would grow marigolds, and she had.

Sheila came out to join her carrying a tray which she deposited on a white wrought-iron table. Marigold moved up on her bench to let her friend sit down.

Sheila handed her a cup of coffee, took one herself and sat down.

'I'm not making you late for anything, am I?' Marigold glanced at her watch.

'No. I'm all right for half an hour.' Sheila produced a packet of cigarettes from the pocket of her overall, lit one and sat back with a sigh of pleasure.

'Has Mike given up trying to reform you?'

'For the moment.' Sheila narrowed her eyes against the smoke. 'I've said the day we move into our own house again is the day I give up smoking for ever.' She paused. 'I mean it, too.'

Marigold lowered her eyes. 'I hope it won't be too long.'

Sheila smiled at her. 'Mike and I are going to see another flat this evening. From the advertisement in the paper, it sounds really nice.'

'I'll keep my fingers crossed for you.'

Marigold knew that the flat presently occupied by the Scotts was far too small and cramped but she also knew it was one hundred times better for them than the bed and breakfast place had been.

She asked, 'Are the boys going with you?'

'No, they didn't want to. A neighbour's looking after Billy for us and Jack's having tea with a school friend and staying there to play until Mike picks him up.' Sheila drank more coffee. Looking down into the cup, she asked, 'You haven't seen him for a while, have you?'

'No, but I've been busy and so has he.' Marigold smiled at Sheila. 'You mustn't feel guilty because Jack's not seeing me so much. I'm actually very pleased.' She shrugged her shoulders. 'It means he's forgetting the bad things and becoming a normal boy again. Of course, having his dad back makes a tremendous difference.'

'Yes.' Sheila nodded. 'And we have to thank you for that, too.'

'Not at all. Adam needed an assistant. Mike was perfect for the job.'

Sheila nodded. 'He does seem to be getting on well, and now something else has . . .' She broke off and gave Sheila a sheepish look. 'Jack hasn't forgotten you, Mari. In fact, he was going to come and see you at the weekend, if that was convenient, but now he can't because he's helping Mike.'

'Are they doing something exciting?'

'Not exciting exactly.' Sheila squirmed on her seat. 'They're going over to Stockton to see Mr Crewe and Alex.'

'Mr Crewe and Alex?' Marigold stared. 'Do you mean Daniel Crewe?'

'Yes.'

'I didn't realise you even knew them?'

'I don't really but Mike and Jack do.' Sheila puffed energetically at her cigarette. 'Mike's been to the school where Mr Crewe works to do a bit of maintenance work. Apparently the caretaker there is getting a bit too old for the heavy work.' She glanced at Marigold. 'I'm sure I told you.'

Marigold shook her head. 'You didn't. I had no idea you had any connection with Danny.'

Sheila coloured. 'Oh, well. Maybe I forgot.' She paused, hung her head and then mumbled, 'Actually, Mike thought I'd better not mention it. He thought Adam might not like the idea of him working for his brother.'

Marigold frowned. 'Adam won't mind, so long as it isn't in his time.'

'Oh, no. Mike has only worked for Danny Crewe on a couple of Sundays. He wouldn't cheat on Adam, he owes him too much.'

'But how and when did they meet each other?'

'Mr Crewe has called in a couple of times at the cottage to see Adam. He met Mike there. They got talking.' Sheila glanced at Marigold. 'You know what Daniel Crewe is like. Mike said he'd never met such a chatty bloke. Anyway, Mike mentioned that he could turn his hand to anything and Mr Crewe asked if he could handle some weekend work.

'Mike went to work at the school on two Sundays, that's all, but he took Jack with him and Jack met Alex.' Sheila smiled. 'The two kids hit it off immediately, so much so that Alex said he'd like to see Jack again. His dad said he would bring him through to York when he came this way and he did.'

Sheila paused dramatically. 'They called unexpectedly at the flat. I was there with Jack and Billy. I was a bit upset at first. I mean . . . the flat!' She shrugged. 'But it didn't seem to bother Mr Crewe and Alex. Anyway, Alex spotted some of Mike's carvings. He thought they were terrific so I gave him one – I knew Mike wouldn't mind.' She thought for a moment. 'It was a carving of a badger, I think.'

Marigold listened, spellbound.

'Alex stayed with us until his dad had finished his business in York and then they went home. But apparently, Alex showed the carving to his school-friends and now they all want one. They want to give them as presents to their parents.' Sheila laughed. 'Daniel Crewe realised what had happened and contacted Mike. There's a school fête this Sunday and he suggested Mike set up a little stall and sell his carvings there. Mr Crewe thinks he'll do very well.'

'I think so too.' Marigold grinned. 'I hope he sells out and has to make some more. He is very talented, Sheila. I was amazed when I first saw that fawn, remember?'

'Yes.' Sheila was still a little uneasy. She asked, 'Do you think Adam will mind?'

'No. But I think he ought to know what's been happening. Shall I tell him?'

'Would you?' Sheila stubbed out the tab end of the cigarette and stood up. 'We'd both be grateful to you. Mike didn't want to keep Adam in the dark about his work for his brother but he felt awkward bringing it up. He nearly didn't go to the school but, as you know, we need all the money we can get.'

'Yes, I know that and so does Adam. I'm sure there'll be no problem.'

'Thanks.' Sheila picked up the tray. 'I'll have to go now.'

'Yes.' Marigold stood up too. 'Perhaps you'd mention to the boys that I'm having Paddy here next week. Ian's going to Italy for five days. If they want to come round to see him they would be very welcome.'

'Oh, they'll want to come, I'm sure.' Sheila lingered. 'How is your husband?'

'Much the same.' Marigold sighed. 'Wrapped up in his work, as usual.'

'Well, he always was, wasn't he?'

'Yes, but I hoped he might change. Another couple of months and our divorce will be finalised. He'll be completely alone then.'

'He sees your daughter, doesn't he?'

'Only occasionally.' Marigold tried to smile. 'She's in America at the moment, living the high life.'

'Well, she must be happy with her life.'

'I think so. It's hard to tell with Karen. One minute she's bubbling with happiness, the next minute she's in the depths of despair. I rang her at the weekend and she was totally miserable. She and her boyfriend had broken up.'

Sheila gave Marigold a keen look. 'You can't do anything about it, you know. Ian's living the life he chooses to live and he must be successful because he's always flying off somewhere. As for Karen—' She sighed. 'I know I'm the last one to talk. How can you stop worrying about your kids? But it's so pointless. Whatever you do or say, they'll do things their way, so you might as well let them get on with it.'

'I know.' Marigold shrugged. 'But thanks for reminding me.' She looked up at Sheila. 'You'd better get off.'

Sheila turned towards the house. 'Yes, I must. See you tomorrow.' She waved goodbye.

Marigold thought she ought to go inside too, but then she looked at her garden and decided to allow herself ten more minutes.

*   *   *

Adam came round at eight thirty. He rang the doorbell instead of using his key.

Marigold opened the door and stared at him. 'You look posh. Have you been on a shopping spree?'

Adam fingered the lapel of his new jacket and grinned. 'Casually smart is the expression, I think. When you said you felt like a proper night out, I decided it was time to use my credit card. I looked in my wardrobe and realised most of my clothes were falling to pieces.'

He shook his head. 'You and I have been working much too hard, Marigold. I think it's time we realised that.'

'Perhaps you're right.'

He took a proper look at her and stepped back. 'Thank God I did make an effort. You look wonderful.'

'Ah, you approve, do you?' Marigold swirled round in the tiny hallway. She was wearing a cream beaded evening sweater and a long, slim black skirt. The past months of hectic activity had slimmed her figure and she looked lean and elegant.

'Absolutely.' He followed her down the hallway into the sitting room.

'Now I realise why Karen is such a successful model.'

Marigold hooted with derision. 'Karen looks nothing like me, and she works out regularly to keep her figure trim. My new shape has evolved through hours of slave labour over hot ovens and bashing pastry around. I don't look very poised then, I can tell you.'

'Is that so.' A crease appeared between Adam's eyebrows. 'You're not regretting anything, are you?'

'Oh, no.' She smiled widely. 'I still love my work. Anyway, it's becoming easier. I've taken a woman on to help me with the baking. She follows my basic recipes and I do the fancy bits. I still make the plum bread, though. It's very popular in the cafe.'

She picked up a fine gold bracelet from the mantelpiece and

fastened it on to her wrist. 'Do you know, my plum bread got a mention on the local radio a few days ago.'

'Really?'

'Yes. One of the presenters brought a producer in for a working lunch. They went into the Austen room and when they left the producer was raving about the decor and my plum bread, so the presenter gave me a plug over the radio.'

She turned towards a drinks tray set out by the sofa. 'Want a drink before we leave?'

'Why not?' Adam looked at the contents of the tray and opted for a dry white wine.

Marigold filled two glasses. 'What has your week been like?'

'Hectic.' Adam sat down with a sigh. He patted the sofa and Marigold sat beside him.

'I got back from Lincoln yesterday to find Mike had worked miracles. He'd shifted rubbish from the barn, stripped and polished a chest of drawers, renovated a mirror for a client who has been complaining about how long we've had it and delivered a set of chairs to another customer who lives in Settle. I don't think that guy stops to eat.' He drank some wine. 'I'm so glad I took your advice about him.'

She smiled. 'I'm thankful I was proved right. However . . .' She told him about the contact with Danny.

For a moment, he looked grim and then he sighed. 'I wish he had told me but I suppose I understand why he didn't. I feel more cross with Danny. You think he would have realised his action might have caused trouble.'

Marigold put her hand on his arm. 'You know Danny. He acts without considering the consequences.'

'Yes, you're right. Let's forget it.' Adam drained his glass. 'Shall we go?'

'Yes. Where are we going?'

'A new place, French. I've heard good reports about it. It's

438

not far from the Masonic Hall. Would you like to walk, or shall I ring for a taxi?'

'Let's walk. It's a lovely evening.'

The whole evening was lovely. The food was good, the wine sparkling, and because she hadn't seen Adam for a week, his company was even more dear to Marigold than usual.

They talked a lot.

Marigold told him Susan Cambridge had called in at the cafe. 'Her husband has been in often. I think it was he who jogged Susan into coming. She was a bit severe with me at first.' Marigold sighed. 'She doesn't believe in divorce.'

'You didn't let that worry you, did you?'

'Just a little. I respect her right to her convictions. Still—' Marigold shrugged her shoulders. 'She did say I'd done a good job with the cafe. Perhaps that was a sign she was prepared to come and visit me again.'

Adam talked of his trip to Lincoln and his daughter. 'Sally's looking forward to spending some time with us in the summer holidays.'

He then told her about a carved wedding chest, sixteenth-century, he had acquired cheap at a sale. 'Hardly any damage, Marigold. It would look great in the cottage.'

He paused. 'I did think I might give it to you, as a wedding present.'

'Oh, Adam.' She leaned across the table and rested her fingers upon his clenched hand. 'I would love it, darling. But remember, my divorce isn't finalised yet.'

With his other hand, he twisted the stem of his wine glass. 'And when it is finalised?'

'I love you,' she said, softly. 'And I *will* marry you, but not yet, Adam.'

He looked away from her. 'Can I rely on that?'

'Oh, God. Yes.'

The passion in her voice reassured him. He looked back at her and smiled. 'Then I'll start work on restoring the chest?'

She nodded. 'Yes. You do that.'

They walked home, silently and hand in hand, beneath a huge white moon.

In the house, Adam pulled her to him and kissed her. 'I couldn't bear to lose you, Marigold.'

She stroked his hair. 'You won't, darling. You won't.'

He cleared his throat. 'Shall we go to bed?'

'Yes. You go up. I'll be there in five minutes.' She smiled at him.

After he left her, she waited a moment and then, unlocking the French windows, she went out into the walled garden. She stared up at the moon. Worries over Ian and her daughter came into her mind but she dismissed them. Everyone was responsible for their own lives. It was arrogant to assume you could solve their problems for them.

She shut her eyes and heard the silence. There was no hoot from a night owl, no rustling in the trees and bushes. She remembered a phrase she had read, a phrase which had appealed to her without her really understanding it.

'The stillness between two waves of the sea.'

Now, she thought, I understand. It means a special time, a quiet time when nothing seems to happen and yet a great deal happens that cannot be put into words. A growing time. She smiled, remembering her experience with the butterfly that morning. And then she went back into the house and up the stairs to where Adam was waiting for her.

A selection of bestsellers from Headline